A MIDSUMMER
MADNESS

GUY FRANKS

A MIDSUMMER MADNESS

iUniverse books may be ordered through booksellers or by contacting:

iUniverse
1663 Liberty Drive
Bloomington, IN 47403
www.iuniverse.com
1-800-Authors (1-800-288-4677)

Because of the dynamic nature of the Internet, any web addresses or links contained in this book may have changed since publication and may no longer be valid. The views expressed in this work are solely those of the author and do not necessarily reflect the views of the publisher, and the publisher hereby disclaims any responsibility for them.

Any people depicted in stock imagery provided by Getty Images are models, and such images are being used for illustrative purposes only.
Certain stock imagery © Getty Images.

ISBN: 978-1-5320-4691-9 (sc)
ISBN: 978-1-5320-4692-6 (e)

Library of Congress Control Number: 2018905033

Print information available on the last page.

iUniverse rev. date: 05/08/2018

For Mom, who shares her birthday with the Bard.

A summer's day will seem an hour but short,
Being wasted in such time-beguiling sport.
Shakespeare

The playing field is baseball's equivalent of a stage.
Roger Kahn

1
CHAPTER

What's in a name?
Romeo and Juliet

Shakespeare Louis Glover was born in San Francisco on April 23, 1939 and the church bells rang. They rang because it was a Sunday, but his mother, laboring in childbirth, imagined that they were proclaiming the birth of her first child. In her mind, they were an omen and one of many meaningful signs that attended his birth and naming. After all, it was the same day that Ted Williams hit his first home run, going four for five as a rookie against the Athletics.

It was also the anniversary of William Shakespeare's birth, who was born April 23rd, 1564. The fact that Shakespeare Louis Glover was born on the exact same day as the Bard was no small coincidence, but the fact that so many elements—courting, conceiving, gestating, laboring—all had to line up to make it so bent one to the belief that *there is a special providence in the fall of a sparrow.*

To fully appreciate how "Shake" Glover (as he came to be called) was christened Shakespeare Louis Glover, and why that name out of all the sensible names available to parents in 1939 was chosen above the rest, one really needs to understand a little about John and Mary Glover.

John and Mary were married in August of '38 at Saints Peter and Paul Church in North Beach. A little less than nine months later Shake was born, yet no eyebrows were raised about the cart before the horse and years later Mary would joke, somewhat cryptically, that Shake got a good lead and stole home while no one was looking. The two first met at St. Francis Memorial Hospital where Mary worked as a nurse. John had come to visit his father, who was suffering from kidney stones, and was immediately smitten by the red-haired, green-eyed evening nurse named Mary Bunner. On his second night there, when she entered the room to check on her patient, John boldly announced,

O, she doth teach the torches to burn bright!

Which Mary smiled at, recognizing it as a line from *Romeo and Juliet* without having to be told. Forward men were nothing new to pretty Nurse Bunner. Working women in the thirties did not run off to the HR Commissar, citing chapter and verse of the sexual harassment policy, but instead learned to parry such advancements. Clever women like Mary, who was also known to be "sharp-tongued," could cut such mashers to the quick by belittling their anatomies or by comparing them to a clod of dirt. But at these words, Mary neither parried nor compared John to a clod of dirt, and instead merely smiled.

Mary Bunner grew up in Daly City where the stiff ocean breezes and thick morning fog ingrain themselves into your DNA. She graduated from high school and later worked a part-time job at night while she attended nursing school during the day. Life at the "Top of the Hill" in Daly City was a mixed blessing; their house was small, even for three kids, and her lower middle class upbringing had its ups and downs. Her dad was a house-painter, often unemployed, but he introduced her to her one great passion (until John came along) and that one passion was baseball. On his days off, he would grab his young daughter and hop the trolley to Recreation Park at 14th and Valencia Streets and watch the San Francisco Seals play professional baseball.

Mary fell in love with baseball the way, it could be said, Juliet fell for her Romeo—at first sight, deeply and completely. She loved everything about it: the shouts of beer vendors, the smell of fresh cut grass, Jujyfruits and lemon-lime sodas, the crack of the bat, the roar of the crowd at a well-turned double play, the boos, the catcalls, and especially the ball-players themselves. She knew every player's name and stats and would on occasion remind a player warming up in the on-deck circle to "keep his elbow up" or "look first-pitch fastball" and it was usually good advice. The Pacific Coast League in those days ran long seasons, sometimes over two hundred games, and Mary never missed a game either in the stands, on the radio, or in the morning's sport's section. She had a particular fondness for middle infielders, especially ones with soft hands and quick feet who could hit for average like Frank Crosetti, Al Wright, and Nanny Fernandez. She was a regular at Recreation Park and even Lefty O'Doul, their longtime manager, would smile and wave to her in the stands. When she became a nurse, she purposely took the evening shift at the hospital so she could attend day games, and it was because of this devotion to her beloved Seals that she met her future husband.

John Glover grew up in Russian Hill, the second son of upper middle-class parents, in a family of scholars and educators. Like his parents, aunts and uncles, he was expected to become an academic and did not disappoint, ending up as an Assistant Professor in the English Department at Cal Berkeley. At age thirty, when he first met Mary, he was teaching a course on Shakespeare and had his own office in Wheeler Hall.

The subject of his lectures was no coincidence, and if Mary's passion was baseball, John's passion was William Shakespeare.

He pursued his passion the way, it could be said, Romeo pursued his Juliet—exuberantly and nearly to the point where *virtue itself turns vice*. It shouldn't be surprising that a young boy growing up in a house full of academics would know his Shakespeare. The Bard, along with Tennyson, Keats, and other great poets, was often quoted around the dinner table, but at age six John felt that passing fancy morph into something more when the family went to see the play *A Midsummer Night's Dream*. Seeing and hearing a play acted for the first time turned on a light switch and soon John was staging his own plays in the living room and pestering his parents on the meaning and correct pronunciation of words like "horning" and a "coxcomb."

But John was not quite the dutiful son he appeared to be. His consuming passion for Shakespeare was just one thing that troubled his parents, along with a bohemian streak that frankly baffled them. He wore a white fedora and yacht shoes to work, and he avoided dating the girls his family navigated him towards—staid, academic types—and instead found himself ineluctably attracted to street-smart, sharp-tongued dishes. And it was this same bohemian streak and his penchant for Betty Davis-types that caused him to speak so boldly to Mary.

John pursued—writing numerous love sonnets—and Mary let him, and their first date was the movie *Lost Horizon* at the Roxie. From there love blossomed and they were engaged six months later. And as for their fixations—one for baseball and one for Shakespeare—it never became an issue: John was not a big baseball fan (his game was tennis) and Mary could barely sit through *Richard II* without nodding off, but they made no demands on the other to share their passion. Instead, they appreciated each other's endowments the way one might appreciate another's musical talent without having an ear for it themselves. No better evidence of this broad-mindedness could be seen than the exchanging of their wedding vows when John spoke of "hitting one out of the park" and Mary quoted Juliet's boundless bounty. They were married for forty-two years and it could be said that they grew together

> Like to a double cherry, seeming parted
> But yet an union in partition,
> Two lovely berries moulded on one stem.

There was much debate about names leading up to Shake's birth. They had settled on William for a boy's first name until John realized there was an increasing chance the birth date might fall on April 23, the date he and many Shakespearian scholars believed to be the Bard's true birthday. In early April he announced that if, indeed, his son happened to be born on the Bard's birthday "William" would simply not do and his first name would have to be "Shakespeare" to appropriately honor the portentous event. Mary smiled, called him a "silly ninny" but agreed. Being the one with common sense, she knew that any boy with the first name "Shakespeare" would choose to be called by his middle name, and it was up to her to find a good solid middle name. That it had to be a favorite ball-player went without saying, but as a Catholic she knew it had to be a saint's name, so a challenge confronted her.

Her sister suggested Louis, which also happened to be a favorite uncle's name, but Mary resisted at first. There were only two Lou's who had played for the Seals—Lou McEvoy and Lou Koupal—and they were both over-the-hill pitchers and she'd be damned if she'd name her son after an over-the-hill pitcher. But her sister reminded her of 1927 and everything fell neatly into place for Mary. In 1927 the great players of their day—Babe Ruth and Lou Gehrig—had come barn-storming into Recreation Park and Mary had begged and pleaded and redeemed every soda bottle she could get her hands on to get herself and her dad a ticket. And her dad—through connections she had no idea he had—took the young teenager down on the field after the game and introduced her to Lou Gehrig. The big man had smiled at her, shaken her small hand, patted her on the head, and called her "kid." It was one of the greatest days of her life.

So Louis it was and Lou it would be. Lou Glover even sounded like a second baseman. Lou Glover, starting second baseman for the New York Yankees. Any lingering reservations over the name were forever dispelled once her sister pointed out that Shakespeare Louis Glover's initials were "SLG" which also stood for "Slugging Percentage." She told John and there was no argument from him given the fact that Shake-speare Lou-is Glo-ver scanned nicely at three trochaic feet.

In 1939, expectant fathers paced nervously in the waiting room. There was no Lamaze, screaming recriminations or clenched hand-holding. Instead the nurse came in, called your name and gave you the good news. Upon hearing he had a healthy son, John hurried to the maternity ward anticipating his wife's first two questions: "Shakespeare Louis Glover?" (which was more a confirmation than a question) and "Did the Seals win?" He answered yes to both. With that he kissed his wife, held his new-born son, and couldn't help but rejoice and say,

> *Why then, the world's my oyster,*
> *Which I with sword will open.*

To review the box score, Shakespeare Louis Glover, born on the Bard's birthday and the same day Ted Williams hit his first home run, was named after the greatest poet/playwright in history and after one of the greatest ball-players of all time. Even "Glover," which Professor Glover loved to point out to his students, was Middle English for a maker of gloves and, yes, the Bard's father had been a glover. On top of that, the Bard's father and mother's names had been John and Mary. Many years later, a close friend of Shake's—Dark Lucy, who fashioned herself a witch—revealed more signs to him: Based on his birthdate, his Life Path Number was four. Lou Gehrig was four. Shake as a player wore number four (for most of his career) and played second base which is the four in a 4-6-3 double play. Scouting reports on Shake during his career always noted his speed on the base paths and his willingness to "get dirty." According to Dark Lucy this was predestined given his Chinese astrological signs were Rabbit and Earth.

If you remain a skeptic and don't believe that *there is a special providence in the fall of a sparrow* at least you have to admit, confronted as you are by these irrefutable facts, what Hamlet in similar circumstances pointed out to his battery mate Horatio—simply that *there are more things in heaven and earth than are dreamt of in your philosophy.* The Bard would have seen it as clearly as a fat pitch down the middle of the plate and roped it for a stand-up triple. He would have seen the stars at work, laws of attraction and manifestation afoot, and all the auspicious signs attending his namesake's birth would have inspired him to say,

> *There is a tide in the affairs of men,*
> *Which taken at the flood, leads onto fortune*

Shakespeare Louis Glover rode on this tide, to a kind of fortune and father's pride.

2
CHAPTER

Baseball has been good to me since I quit trying to play it.
Whitey Herzog

Shake Glover became a Bard-loving professional baseball player and later a Bard-quoting minor league manager. His success at the first endeavor was less than spectacular while the second—as the manager of the Double-A New Britain Kingsmen in the Eastern League—was where he found his calling. It was there that the seemingly disparate passions at work within him, one the olive oil of elegant poetry and the other the balsamic vinegar of dirt and grass, blended together to make a heavenly vinaigrette.

But it wasn't as though those two passions had warred within him while he was growing up. On the contrary, they had always seemed complementary to him in the same way his parents seemed to complement one another. He did not intellectualize it; he simply felt it. The music of Shakespeare's metered verse, his cutting wit, his insight into the human soul, paired nicely with the perfect distances of baseball, with its theatrics and homespun wisdom. When Shake listened to Leo Durocher he heard Prospero. When Coriolanus offers his services to his enemy Aufidius it reminded him of Jackie Robinson getting traded to the Giants. But this kinship and all its merry parallels did not become a harmony of purpose, a symbiotic whole, until Shake found coaching.

How he got there is worth noting.

When Shake was four his parents bought a house in Daly City. He was already being called "Shake" by this time despite the efforts of his mom to stick him with "Lou." Family legend varied on its origin, his sister claiming it was because he used to shake presents under the Christmas tree to figure out what was inside, while his droll Uncle Lou said it was merely a common beheading—Shake lopped off the body of speare. Either way "Shake" seemed to fit the active and somewhat precocious boy.

If his mom and dad each harbored a secret dream of turning their first born son into the next Lou Gehrig or into a famous playwright, respectively, it was never openly admitted by the other or allowed to become a skirmish of wills. When it came to their passion, neither was a fisher of men, but each shared their enthusiasms with their son—as they did with all their kids—and only proselytized if one of them showed true desire. At six, Shake was playing catch and taking grounders. At eight, he saw the movie *Henry V* (the one with Olivier) and, carried away by its marshal spirit, promptly went home and read the play so he could re-enact the St. Crispin's Day speech in the living room ("*We few, we happy few, we band of brothers!*"). This twin desire was constantly nourished: If he wasn't being peppered with grounders by his uncles he was being peppered with couplets by his dad in a game he called "come-backers."

The game "comebackers" tested Shakes' knowledge of the Bard and his works. At any given time, but usually at the evening dinner table, his dad would throw out a quote and Shake would have to come back with the play, the speaker and, if he could, the Act and scene. He enjoyed this as much as he did sitting next to his mom at a Seal's game helping her keep score ("that was a single and an error on the left fielder, E7, and an unearned run"). "Comebackers" kept him on his toes and made for lively dinner conversation. Only once, when he was ten, did it lead to any kind of trouble with his mom. She was setting down plates of chicken and dumplings:

Dad
Here it comes...
Why, there they are, both baked in this pie,
Where of their mother daintily hath fed,
Eating the flesh that she herself hath bred.

Sister
Ooh, that's a hard one.

Shake
Titus Andronicus. Act five, the last scene, I think.

Dad
Very good.

Mom
What does it mean, the 'eating the flesh' and all that?

Shake
There's this evil Queen and Titus kills her kids then cooks them up and feeds them to her in a pie.

Mom
I see. There will be no more talk of eating people at the dinner table.

Dad
Yes, dear.

Despite the scolding, the game continued and grew more sophisticated over the years.

Shake attended Jefferson High School where he starred in baseball and ended up getting a scholarship offer to Pepperdine. Even though Pepperdine was a well-known baseball factory, Shake was a bit disappointed that he did not receive similar offers from schools with better English Lit Departments. He had warned big league scouts not to try and sign him since he planned to play baseball in college and get a degree, but the lack of scholarship offers had made him second guess that decision.

This is when his dad had stepped in. By this time, John was a tenured professor at Cal. After calling in a few favors, his son got a call from George Wolfman, Cal's baseball coach, who offered Shake a scholarship, which Shake happily accepted. Cal had a solid baseball program and one of the most prestigious English Lit programs in the country. It was a match made in heaven. When Shake thanked his dad, he received only two words of advice: "Beat Stanford."

he played four years under Wolfman at second base, wearing number four, and in his junior and senior years, he led the AAWU in fielding percentage. He hit for average, didn't make errors, and when graduation rolled around in June of '61, Shake collected his Bachelor of Arts degree in English Literature and signed a major league contract with the San Francisco Giants.

But before we follow Shake into the minor leagues, a little must be said about his love life, since it colors the rest of our story. Young men who are captivated by *Romeo and Juliet* are suckers for love and Shake was no exception. But a transformation took place that shook his foundation. Shake went from a youth believing that love is *the star of every wandering bark* to a jaded young man who became convinced that

> *Love is merely a madness and, I tell you,*
> *Deserves as well a dark house and a whip as*
> *madmen do*

Shake was a virgin until age eighteen when he was readily seduced by a neighbor of twenty-six. This in itself did not turn him against love. She was an attractive woman and "experienced" and he was horny and more than happy to learn from her. In a way, it was sort of like having Ted Williams as your personal hitting coach. But he went off to college and she quickly replaced him with one of his buddies, and he was left a little wiser for the wear. He didn't think he'd been in love, or maybe he had been (he wasn't sure), but he was left with a bittersweet feeling plus two other legacies: one, a budding belief that women were *cunning past man's thought*, and two, a perennial attraction to older women.

Cupid's deathblow came a few years later when Shake fell madly in love with Mimi. She was a grad student two years older than him and their love was deep and fulfilling… for a time. They were practically living together without appearing so (this was 1960), and both talked of marriage and having a family. She loved baseball and came to all his games, wearing a floppy sun hat and keeping score, and afterwards they often double-dated with his good friend Pauly and his girlfriend. Herein lay the canker in the rose. Pauly, a childhood friend of Shake's, broke up with his girlfriend but still hung out with the two lovers. He was heartbroken and they felt sorry for him, but after a while Shake became convinced that Pauly and Mimi were secretly in love with one another.

Lovers and madmen have such seething brains, and in Shake's seething brain the truth glared back at him—in the way they looked at each other, touched hands when they spoke, and giggled at their private jokes. He confronted them and they called him crazy, but when he saw her crying in Pauly's arms on a bench in Sproul Plaza, he called her a whore and ended it. A couple months later, right before he was due to leave for spring training and feeling a bit remorseful, he had called her up but her roommate said she had quit school and moved away. That had sealed the deal for him as far as love was concerned.

Shake left for spring training, got assigned to their Class-A Springfield team, and played professional baseball for the next twelve years. Over that span, he was called up, sent down, optioned, outrighted, put on waivers and picked up again in a recurring theme that would have discouraged most others. But unlike women, his passion for baseball was unconditional; he loved it and the fact that it didn't return the feeling never disheartened him. Whether it was Class-A or Triple-A, he was playing baseball. He was still lacing them up, stealing bases and handling tricky hops. In his minor league career, he accrued a 287 batting average, a 322 OBP, and was always in the league's top five in fielding percentage wherever he played.

Five times he was called up to the big leagues. Three of those times didn't count for much. They were September call-ups where he got to pinch run or play second base late in blow-out games, but he never hit and was lost in the crowded dugout with all the other call-ups. He had two extended stays in his third and fourth years as a pro. In both those stints, Shake got to field and bat. He didn't set the world on fire but he didn't embarrass himself either and made two lasting memories by breaking up a Bob Gibson no-hitter with a swinging bunt and by getting a clutch, two-out hit late in the season to beat the Dodgers. But it wasn't enough to get him to stick and he was soon thereafter labeled "NP" (No Prospect).

Most ballplayers who toil in the minor leagues live in perpetual hope that they are just an injury away from the big leagues. Shake never held any such illusions. By his sixth year he realized he wasn't going to be a big leaguer, but he was making money doing what he loved and was having fun doing it, so he stayed with it—stayed with the bus rides and cramped clubhouses and cheap motels—and over time became an "organizational ballplayer." He had traits that were appreciated: he was a leader in the clubhouse, ingratiating, well-liked, but also hard-headed when he needed to be. He was also intelligent and baseball smart—someone who could quote the Bard but also appreciate the beauty of a bloop and a blast. The organization recognized these talents and kept him on so he could display good work habits and mentor rising stars, and all the while grooming Shake to become a minor league manager.

He went straight from ballplayer to assistant coach in '74 and in a couple years, at age thirty-seven, he was given the manager's job in Single-A where he distinguished himself as a skipper who could both win and develop talent. It was there that he cemented his reputation as something more than just a baseball coach. In a close game, an umpire blew a call at third base and Shake flew out of the dugout to air his grievance. The ump ignored him and turned his back to Shake. When he did, something snapped and Shake, drawing from his extensive mental library, leaped in front of the umpire and called him "*a whoreson, beetle-headed, flap-eared knave.*" Everybody heard it—the fans, the players, the other umps—and laughter rippled through the small stadium. The umpire wasn't sure what it all meant but he knew it wasn't good and tossed Shake from the game. But a minor league legend was born and after that fans and players and even umps came to expect his poetic outbursts. Shake didn't disappoint.

In '79 he became manager of the organization's Class-AA ball club. As hoped, his success carried over and he continued to win and produce talent. If the big club thought him a bit eccentric with his odd language and seventeenth century slang, they let it go and considered it part of Shake's winning formula. He got results. Prospects who came out of his program into Triple-A and onto the big club knew how to play baseball "the right way." They shaded lefties to pull, went the other way on an outside pitch, bunted down the third base line, and did one and a hundred little things that showed they knew the game. And if, on occasion, they called someone a "jackanape," or answered "anon" when their manager called them, it was all considered a sign of their proper training and was given the stamp of approval.

With coaching, Shake found his calling and the Bard and baseball found a harmony of purpose. Both came together into that savory vinaigrette of transcendent poetry blended with sublime action upon a diamond. The Bard might have wondered at it—was it fate or freewill that brought his namesake to this point? His parents certainly had their own view of it: The Bard or Lou—they had taken an oath, to get neither but a little of both.

3
CHAPTER

This way, my lord, for this way lies the game.
Henry VI Part 3

W e lay our scene in New Britain, at Beehive Stadium, right off Route 9 amidst the rolling hills and wooded green of Connecticut. It's the year of our Lord nineteen hundred and eighty-six and it's opening day in the Double-A Eastern League between the New Britain Kingsmen and Vermont Reds. A good house is expected.

***

Manager Shake Glover of the New Britain Kingsmen sat at his desk going over his opening day's line-up. He liked it. From top to bottom, he liked it. There was speed at the top, thunder in the middle, and grinders at the bottom. The pitching match-up felt good as well. Though he never took anything for granted, you had to like your chances with their big lefthander on mound—Steve Basset, 16 and 6 last year, leading the league in strikeouts—against their guy Platko who was thirty-four and coming back from Tommy John surgery. Yeah, he thought, we

16

could do worse. And coming from a guy who was wary of jinxes, that was saying a lot.

He took a sip from his thermal coffee mug—the same one he'd been sipping on since four this morning—and leaned back in his squeaky chair. He lifted his cap and ran his palm over his thinning hair and gazed up at the ceiling with his hazel eyes. At forty-six going on forty-seven, Shake was still in pretty good shape. He weighed one-eighty-six, six pounds over his playing weight, and he had a bit of a boiler, but at 5'11" with broad shoulders and a jump in his step he still looked like he could turn a double play if he had to. His trimmed beard, like his hair, was auburn (a gift from his red-headed mother), with no hints of gray yet, and if it was said he looked like anybody famous it was probably the guy who played Rambo's colonel in the movie *First Blood* (Richard Crenna). But that guy had all his hair. Shake's hair had not so much thinned as it had receded, leaving him with a high forehead which he covered up most of the time with his ball cap.

His gaze left the ceiling and settled back on his line-up card. Yeah, he thought, not bad—and for a tiny, infinitesimal moment he indulged a feeling of satisfaction. It was spring, opening day, and there was not another place in the world he'd rather be. Normally he'd squelch such a feeling and give it an intentional pass but today, at this moment, he felt like pitching to it despite the danger. Part of it was fed by the calm before the storm. Game days were always hectic but opening days were especially so. On top of running his team, there were city dignitaries to meet, owners and league officers to schmooze, heightened clubhouse commotion, ceremonies, touchy weather, and finally a game to manage. Any minute his office door would open to a problem, but for an exquisite moment he looked at his line-up card—the symbol of his goodwill towards men—and let a smile crease his lips.

Shake can be forgiven the smile. The New Britain Kingsmen were an excellent team with top prospects. They had finished first last year and the year before that and *Baseball America* picked them to finish first again this year. Going into his eighth year as manager, Shake had been named "Manager of the Year" in the Eastern League four of those eight years and nobody would be surprised if he won it again this year. They were not a bunch of sad sacks being led by a foul-mouthed, tobacco-chewing reprobate nor (like some Disney fantasy) a ragtag team of misfits led by an outcast who, despite the mighty odds against them, find a way to win the big one. Nope, the Kingsmen were well-coached and full of talent and did one thing consistently—win.

There was a quick knock and the door opened. His assistant coach Rick Burton stuck his head in and said, "Forty minute delay, but we're good to go."

Shake nodded. He already knew about the rain delay. They had cancelled batting practice because of rain, but it was supposed to clear out and be a nice day. "Ask Prince to come in here. Thanks," he replied.

Hank Prince was a late add to the roster, coming down from Triple-A just two days ago, and Shake had not had a chance to really talk to him at length. The kid was leading off and starting in centerfield. Normally Shake would wait until after the game for such a talk but the rain delay gave him a window to dig into his new problem child. Hank signed a fat contract out of high school and in two years was playing for the big club, but after a year of missed curfews, missed signs, and lackadaisical play he was sent down to Triple-A to shape up. Now he had been sent down to Double-A. This kid was a "can't miss," a rising star who had stopped rising, and when a rising star stopped rising it was considered a coaching problem. Shake was expected to turn the kid around.

It was a ten second walk from the player's lockers to his office and after a few minutes of waiting Shake got up out of his chair. Hank appeared just then and he sat back down. "Hank, have a seat," he said.

The angular youth nodded without smiling and eased into the chair across from Shake. He was just twenty-two and his smooth, coffee-colored cheeks didn't look like they needed to be shaved very often. At 6'2" he wasn't particularly tall but his raw-boned physique, long arms, and chin-up look of defiance (born of the inner city) made him seem taller than he really was. His afro was shaped into a kind of flat-top like Ricky Henderson and Shake made a mental note of that.

"Heard you found an apartment... in the City Center," said Shake.

"Yeah."

Shake waited for a little more but when he didn't get it he added, "Not the best neighborhood."

"Why? Cause it's black?"

"Don't know about that," replied Shake, not taking the bait. "It's got a high crime rate. Drug and gang problems."

"Dunno 'bout all that. Seems fine. Like where I grew up."

"Fair enough... I got you leading off. I know they had you batting sixth or seventh last year but I like you at the top of the order. Okay with that?"

"Sure."

"With your eye and your speed—and you got some pop—you're a natural born lead-off hitter and table-setter. When you get on look for the green light. I like putting the pressure on. You could easily have forty stolen bases this year."

"Or more."

"Or more," repeated Shake with a grin. That was his cue and he looked into Hank's eyes. "You're capable of more. But right now you're in the dog house. I didn't put you there but you're in the dog house and you need to show me you want out. Three years ago you were the youngest rookie in the majors. The next Ricky Henderson. Now you're in Double-A and going the wrong way. I don't know what the deal is—you're too young, the money went to your head, too much pressure—don't know and don't care. You need to show me you *want* to play. I already know you *can* play. But I want to see that other thing. That fire. Are you ready to do that?"

Shake half expected an answer filled with excuses and finger-pointing but what he got back was a pleasant surprise.

"I know, man... I know, coach. I'm gonna turn it round. I want outta that dog house. I'm here to turn it 'round. You can believe it."

"Good to hear," said Shake. He waited a moment and added, *"Be not afraid of greatness."*

"Is that some of that Shakespeare shit I've been hearing 'bout?" asked Hank, smiling for the first time.

"Well, not exactly 'shit' but yeah. The actual quote goes something like this:

> *Be not afraid of greatness. Some are born great;*
> *some achieve greatness,*
> *and some have greatness thrust upon them.*

"Cool, bro. Love it," replied Hank, bouncing his head to show his approval.

"I'll have you quoting *Hamlet* back in the big leagues," said Shake. They talked for another couple minutes until Shake was satisfied that the young man was sincere about turning things around and not conning him. He let Hank go and followed him out the door where he found the owner Rex Lyon in the hallway. The old man stood next to a much younger man in levis and a sport coat, who Shake recognized as Orson Kent. He was the son of one of the big club's owners and had been sent down to the farm system to learn the business.

"Rex," greeted Shake.

"Glover," replied Rex with a nod. The old man called everyone by their last name. It was a quirk of his.

"Hot links on the grill?

"Yea, and all the lumber's nailed down."

Shake smiled at the private joke. He didn't expect Orson to get it—he'd fill him in later—but it referred to four years ago when the ball club was in Bristol. Back then, Rex wanted to move the club ten miles over to New Britain where a newer and bigger stadium beckoned, but he was locked into a lease and the landowner—a tightwad named Allen—wouldn't let him go even though the park was sub-par and they weren't drawing. But Rex Lyon, owner and CEO of Lyon Bolt Manufactory, a multi-million dollar business he built up from scratch, was not a man to be deterred. He knew that Allen owned the land but he—Rex Lyon—owned the stadium that sat on the land, every nail and two by four. And given the stadium was built in the thirties, that was a lot of nails and two by fours.

Rex concocted a plan and enlisted a number of co-conspirators including Shake. First he created the New Britain Professional Baseball Inc, made himself president, and signed up shareholders (of which Shake was one) with the promise of fortune once they moved into the bigger stadium. Next, in the dead of winter 1983, after Allen the snowbird had left for his winter home in Florida, Rex hired contractors to dismantle the park. Even Shake helped out. Muffled by the snow, they removed every board and plank, loaded it on trucks, and left nothing but the plumbing. When Allen returned he went ballistic and filed an injunction. Rex filed a counter injunction, and after legal threats and haggling back and forth, Allen admitted defeat and the New Britain Kingsmen opened their '83 season in their new stadium.

One other thing made that story memorable: it was how the Kingsmen got their name. In Bristol, the team had been called the "Chrysanthemums," better known as the "Bristol Mums" and Shake hated that name. As a condition of becoming a shareholder (and co-conspirator), Shake demanded the name change. Rex Lyon wanted the "New Britain Bolts" for obvious reasons but Shake played hardball and said he wouldn't go along with the whole scheme unless Rex and the board agreed to the "Kingsmen." Not wanting a rift with Shake, whom he recognized as a talented manager, Rex finally relented and the board unanimously approved the "Kingsmen." And all ended well: Rex got his new stadium and kept his franchise, the big club was happy with the new venue, and Shake got his name change and shares in the New Britain Professional Baseball Inc. The shares hadn't made him a fortune yet but that didn't matter to Shake. The old man had pulled it off and he admired him for it.

"This is Kent—Orson Kent," said Rex pointing to the young man next to him. "Horace Kent's kid. Here to learn the ropes. Kent, this is Coach Glover."

Orson stepped forward and shook hands with Shake. They both exchanged knowing smiles (they'd been introduced by Rex two days ago). Just then one of the parking attendants rushed in and stopped in front of Rex.

"I'm out of breath," said the parking attendant bending over. He raised a finger to give himself a moment.

"How can you be out of breath when you have the breath to tell me you're out of breath?" asked Rex. "What's wrong?"

The story came out between huffs and puffs that part of the parking lot was flooded by last night's rain and they were running out of parking space.

"Get some brushes and squeegees out there!" yelled Rex. "Come with me," he added in a voice that was resigned to the incompetence of other men. The two left to solve the parking problem. Shake noticed that Orson was startled by Rex's roar (Shake, on the other hand, was long used to it). He nodded to Orson to follow him into his office.

Shake offered him the same chair Hank had been sitting in. Orson opened his sport coat, hiked it up, then sat down genteelly and crossed his legs. Shake knew both of Orson's parents and it was obvious to him that the young man took after his mother. He had the same doe-like eyes and turned-up nose, and the fact that his dark hair was perfectly coiffed, with tailored bangs to fit his oval face, made the similarity with his mother even more striking.

"He forgot he already introduced us," said Orson after he settled into his chair.

"Yeah, he's got a lot on his mind. Opening day and all."

Orson leaned forward and lowered his voice. "I think it might be more than that," he said. "I mean I drove over here with him and he got lost—lost driving to his own ballpark."

Shake chuckled and shrugged his shoulders. "Well, yeah, the guy's, what, eighty-two? Hope I can still find my way to the ballpark at eighty-two." He looked at Orson's skeptical face and saw he hadn't made a dent. "Rex is a throw-back. He's his own GM. He sells tickets, counts receipts, replaces toilet paper, sells advertising, spreads the tarp. He knows the name of every season ticket holder in the stands. Once in a while he forgets stuff but I wouldn't worry about it."

He could see that Orson wasn't convinced. Hell, he knew Rex was getting forgetful. Everyone knew that. But he wasn't about to let anyone make more out of it than that.

"Why doesn't he get a GM?" asked Orson.

"He was supposed to. When he turned eighty, he was going to make his youngest daughter Corey the GM but they had a falling out. So, for now, I'd say you're the GM... And I'd take it as a personal favor if you'd look out for the old guy."

"'Course," replied Orson. He reached out and turned the statue that sat on Shake's desk. "Who made the hat?"

The thing in question was a foot high statue of William Shakespeare. The Bard, dressed in fitted hose, jerkin and cape, stood in a thoughtful pose with a book under one arm and other hand stroking his beard. On top of his normally bald head sat a miniature New Britain (NB) baseball cap.

"I think Speed made it but he won't admit it."

"Speed? The clubbie?"

Just then there was a knock at the door and Orson jumped up to let the groundskeeper in. He was with his assistant, and they were both in boots and covered in mud. His name was Doug (which Shake always imagined was spelled "Dug").

"Seen Mr. Lyon?" asked Doug. "He told us to report to him."

"He's out in the parking lot," said Shake. "How's the field looking?"

Doug straightened to attention and his assistant Barry followed suit. "Excellent. Most admiral," he replied proudly. "We just got down putting absorbine on the mound. You're prima facie. The rest of the field's in star-studded shape. We just need to make our repository to Mr. Lyon."

"Good work, men," said Shake as he glanced at Orson, who was holding back a laugh. "As you say, most admirable. You'll find him in the parking lot." Both groundskeepers nodded and shuffled out the door leaving a trail of mud. Once gone, Orson snorted a laugh in disbelief. "Don't say it—just get used to it," Shake said with another shrug. He nodded to the Bard's statue on his desk. "As the man once said, *'They have been at a great feast of languages, and stolen the scraps.'*"

It was nearly time to take the field so Shake parted ways with Orson and headed into the locker room. He had heard the noise earlier but now it got louder as he walked in: dueling boom boxes. There was Country and Hard Rock mixed in with Latin Salsa vying against what he guessed was Hip Hop. He had a rule against boom boxes (only one at a time was allowed in his clubhouse) and in past years he had tried different tactics to solve the problem but with mixed results. He had a better idea for this year: a compilation CD. He would have Speed burn a compilation CD with all their music on it and it could play on one boom box. Problem solved.

Rick Burton saw him and yelled at the room to "pipe down!" Everyone left off what they were doing—playing cards, taping up, shooting the bull, reading *Baseball America*—and shifted their attention to their manager. The boom boxes went off. Shake nodded at Rick, who besides being his assistant coach was also his bench coach. Gathering up next to Rick were his pitching coach Larry Benedict, hitting and first base coach Teddy Larkin, third base and assistant hitting coach Bob Kalecki, and their trainer Mike Faust (who, along with four players, made five Mikes in the clubhouse). Lurking behind them in a three piece suit was the big club's Director of Player Development, who was here for opening day.

Shake surveyed the faces of his twenty-five-man roster. Young and not so young, white, black and Hispanic, from small towns and big cities, they made up a microcosm of America. Like everywhere else in America, the blacks hung out together as did the Hispanics (or "Dominicans" as they were all called no matter what country they hailed from), while the whites tended to congregate by background. There was also a pecking order: at the top were the high draft picks—the top prospects—while next came the lower draft picks followed by the faded stars looking for a last hurrah. Elsewhere in the mix were the holder-ons, the guys who were kept on to provide a good example for the others (like he'd once been). It was a good mix; a good chemistry. Some managers dismissed chemistry as over-rated but he was a great believer in it.

One thing he saw on all their faces was a combination of eagerness and hope. The opening day face. It was there every year at this time, like blossoms on a cherry tree, and it always brought the same quote to Shake's mind:

> *True hope is swift, and flies with swallow's wings:*
> *Kings it makes gods, and meaner creatures kings.*

Manager Shake Glover gave his team a short pep talk and they cheered their approval. "On the field in five!" he yelled and turned around and almost ran into Speed. "Whoa, watch it, Speed," said Shake as he danced aside. Clubhouse manager, equipment manager, and gofer par excellence, Speed was like a sprite who was anywhere and everywhere. He did the laundry, supplied the seeds and bubble gum and chewing tobacco, sewed uniforms, and provided the post-game spread making sure everyone got their favorite beverage. He slept on a cot in the laundry room and lived and breathed for the New Britain Kingsmen. There was also not a thing that went on in the clubhouse that he didn't know about.

"That reminds me," said Shake, putting his hand on Speed's shoulder, "I need you to make a compilation CD with everyone's music mixed on it. Make a few."

Speed
Make a what?

Shake
A compilation CD, with everyone's music on it.

Speed
A copulation seedy?

Shake
Com-pil-la-tion

Speed
That's what you said—cop-u-la-tion. How can I make you a copulation anything, even a seedy one? You have to do your own copulating.

Shake
That's not what I said… I don't have time for this. It's opening day.

Speed
Good. You need an opening for copulation.

Shake
True enough.

Speed

Do you want me to wait for the opening or force an opening before I do your seedy copulation?

Shake
Criminy, Speed. Wait for it then. Meanwhile, be gone before I put my nine and half up your butt.

Speed
You're talking about your shoe, right?

Shake
Ha! Go!

Speed sauntered off with a shit-eating grin on his face. "Why don't you get rid of that fool?" asked Rick Burton, who had listened to the exchange.

"Find me a better clubbie in the Eastern League and I'll fire him tomorrow," replied Shake. "Anyhow, Lyon loves him." He pulled the line-up card out of his back pocket, waved it at Rick, and said, "Let's go to work."

They headed for the double doors that led out to the field. Shake glanced up at the motivational saying above the doors. The big club had wanted him to put up the standard fare, stuff like "Practice winning every day" or "Winning is a habit, Success is a choice" but being who he was he opted for *It is not in the stars to hold our destiny but in ourselves.* It was from *Julius Caesar* and hit the mark as far as he was concerned.

They walked through the short tunnel and into the sunlight. After twenty-four years in professional baseball and thousands of games, Shake always got the same jolt when he walked out onto the field. The manicured infield, the vast green outfield, the looming stands, and the advertisements that plastered the outfield fences (giving it almost a tie-dyed look)—all of it gave him a pleasant jolt in the same way other people, walking into church, got that same happy jolt.

It was a sunny day with a few clouds left over from the morning's rain. He left Rick and walked out towards third base. The chalk lines were in, the mound looked good, and there were no puddles to be found. He turned around and scanned the stands. They were filling up quickly. Across the diamond, the Reds were filing into their dugout. Suddenly the bright sunshine dimmed as a cloud passed across the sun. The deep, sonorous voice of the PA Announcer sounded over the stadium speakers:

> *The uncertain glory of an April day,*
> *Which now shows all the beauty of the sun*
> *And by and by a cloud takes all away!*

Shake smiled and saluted up to the press box.

In short order the players were introduced to the sold-out crowd, speeches made, and "The Star-Spangled Banner" sung. Their twenty-three year old ace lefthander got ready to lead his team out onto the field and Shake took *his* spot at the end of the railing next to the bat rack. He would stand there for most of the game taking it in, rubbing his chin, giving signs, yelling encouragement, and thinking three steps ahead of everyone else. "O Fortuna" (the theme song from the movie *Excalibur*) started up and the Kingsmen took the field.

"*Shake!*" he heard someone whisper loudly. He glanced around but didn't see anyone trying to get his attention. After a moment he heard it again. "*Shake!*" This time he noticed Orson Kent crouched over at the opening of the tunnel summoning him with his finger. What the hell was Orson doing, thought Shake as he walked over to him.

"What is it?"

"Mr. Lyon, he's lost."

"Then go find him."

"No, he's right there," replied Orson, pointing into the tunnel. Shake strained his eyes and looked into the dark tunnel where he saw a figure standing motionless. "He's lost. He doesn't recognize me," added Orson with a worried look.

Shake quickly put two and two together and sent Orson up to his seat. He'd take care of this. He found Rex Lyon looking down at a blank piece of paper in his hand, and Shake came up to him and gently touched his arm to get his attention. Rex glanced up at Shake with a confused and slightly frightened look on his face.

"Rex, it's Glover," said Shake calmly. "It's game time." He stared into the old man's eyes waiting for the light of recognition to come on but it didn't. Shake took the piece of paper out of Rex's hands, folded it up, and looked thoughtfully at the finished product. The old man loved baseball trivia—arcane, off-the-wall baseball trivia—and he often played it with Shake when they found a moment together. That gave Shake an idea.

"Alvin Dark… 'They'll put a man on the moon before he hits a homerun,'" said Shake with a grin. He waited for the comebacker. Another moment passed. "O Fortuna" was winding up and he could hear his left-hander's warm-up pitches popping the catcher's glove. Rex suddenly looked up as though he was tracking a lazy fly ball. He caught it.

"Gaylord Perry," he answered with a smile, the light of recognition returning to his eyes. "And when did he hit it?"

"One hour after Apollo 11 landed on the moon."

The old man sniffed a short laugh. "Right," he said.

"Let's go," urged Shake. "Game time." He watched as Rex glanced out the tunnel at the bright sunshine then back at him with a nod of understanding. "*This way, my lord,*" added Shake, "*for this way lies the game.*" Rex followed him out of the tunnel and Shake stopped to watch the old man climb the steps that led into the stands before taking *his* spot again next to the bat rack. He was in time for the first pitch. It was a strike, ninety-six on the gun, and they went on to win seven to one.

4

CHAPTER

Their sweep was in jeopardy. After taking games one and two against the Reds, the Kingsmen were behind 6-4 going into the bottom of the seventh inning. Mental errors had cost them and Shake was none too happy about it.

Leading 4-2 going into the inning, their pitcher Chuck Davis walked the number eight hitter to open the inning. Walks were like avoidable accidents and they drove Shake crazy, especially when it was against a career .245 hitter who has already struck out twice against you. The next hitter, the Reds pitcher, did exactly what everyone in the park knew he would do—bunt. In these situations, the organization taught their infielders to aggressively crash the corners, with the shortstop and second baseman rotating to second and first respectively. Shake was a great believer in the play. Done right, there was a high probability of gunning down the lead runner at second and about a twenty-five percent chance of turning a double play if the hitter wasn't too fast. This probability diminished if they sent the runner on the pitch.

On the 1-0 pitch, the Reds sent the runner and their pitcher laid a bunt down the third base line. The walk aside, this was mental error number one. When the runner broke, yells of "He's going!" rang out, but the Kingsmen third baseman Mike Goff, who heard the yells and had to know the runner was going, fielded the bunt and forced a throw to second. Not in time—and the throw back to first base was too late. That put runners on first and second with no outs.

Next came mental error number two. The Reds lead-off hitter lined a 2-1 pitch into the left center field gap that Hank Prince cut off nicely. The play there is to concede the run and hit the cut-off man, keeping the other runners at first and second, but Prince decided to show off his arm and throw home. The throw was off-line and late and both runners moved up to second and third. It was 4-3 with no outs.

Davis got the Reds number two hitter to pop up and there was one down, but their next hitter got lucky and hit a bleeder down the third base line that Goff, who was playing back at double-play depth, was not able to get to in time. That made bases drunk with the Reds clean-up hitter and big bopper coming to the plate. Shake knew this guy to be a first-pitch fastball hitter; the scouting report said he was a first-pitch fastball hitter; hell, everyone knew he was a first-pitch fastball hitter. Mental error number three: Davis shook off the curve and went fastball, outside corner, but he caught too much plate and the result was a bases clearing triple. Shake looked over at his pitching coach as if to say "Are we the only ones who read the scouting report?" Larry Benedict nodded and asked Shake whether he wanted him to go out and talk to Davis.

These options played out in Shake's mind:
1. Pitch to the next guy and play the infield in.
2. Pitch around him, see if he chases, then go for the strike out.
3. Pitch around him, walk him, and set up the double play.

Shake knew these hitters, knew their stats and had read the scouting reports, but stats didn't tell you everything. The next batter, the Reds number five hitter, was a big RBI guy, a free-swinging Dominican who might just chase, but anything close could be disastrous. It was a righty-righty match-up but his pitcher was having control problems. The Reds number six hitter was streaky—hot and then not—and had grounded out to second last time up. That was a righty-lefty match-up, and going against percentages he made up his mind and gave Larry his instructions.

The pitching coach jogged out to the mound and gave everyone the plan: Davis was to pitch around their clean-up hitter ("nothing close") and go hard after the next batter. Everyone was to play back for the double play. Benedict jogged back to the dugout.

"How's he feel?" asked Shake.

"He's fine," answered Benedict. After a pause he added, "Estrella wanted to pitch to him."

Jose Estrella was their catcher, a top prospect, and a Dominican. "I'm sure he did," said Rick Burton cryptically. Shake eyed him. He knew all about Rick's crazy theory—call it a conspiracy theory—that Dominican batters hit better when they got into the box next to a Dominican catcher. Rick couldn't prove it with stats but he was sure it was true. *I have drunk and seen the spider,* mused Shake as he turned his attention back to the field.

The unintentional-intentional walk went off without a hitch and the Reds number six hitter stepped into the box with a man on first and third. He lined the first pitch deep and foul then took the next pitch for a ball. On a 1-1 count he hit a sharp grounder up the middle that looked like a base hit, but the Kingsmen's second baseman Dane Hamilton made a back-handed grab, stepped on second, and threw a pea to first for the double play. It was a thing of beauty.

"Looked like you on that one," said Rick, who had played with Shake in the minors.

Shake smiled at that and yelled "Nice turn!" to his second baseman as he came into the dugout.

"Louie Louie" by The Kingsmen blared out over the loud speakers. At all home games in the bottom of the seventh, the PA announcer put on "Louie Louie" and the crowd sang and danced. Ushers roamed the stands looking for the best dancers, who were rewarded with a coupon to Round Table Pizza. The grinding tune fed the shift in momentum.

As chance would have it, the man who had just given them that defensive gem—Dane Hamilton—led off the inning and got a single. He eventually came around to score and they went into the eighth down by one. Davis struggled in the top of the inning but gutted it out to stay down by one. In the bottom of the inning, Estrella hit a monster home run to tie things up going into the ninth. Shake brought in his reliever, who set the Reds down one-two-three in the ninth, and they came back in to hit. The top of their order was due up. The planets were aligned and Shake wanted to end this thing in the ninth, especially since it was get-away day and they had a bus to catch in the morning.

Hank Prince strode to the plate and Shake went through the scenarios. If Hank got on base he could:

1. Straight-steal
2. Bunt him over
3. Hit and run
4. Steal on the first pitch and bunt him over to third.

He liked the last scenario the best. On a 2-2 pitch, Hank blooped one down the third base line that was a sure hit but he tried to stretch it into a double and was thrown out at second. Some managers would chalk that up to aggressiveness but not Shake. *Tis one thing to be tempted, another thing to fall.* It was another mental mistake: Hank had run through Coach Larkin's stop sign at first, and despite having the whole play in front of him when he made his turn, he had failed to see the inevitable. Troubling. Shake tried to make eye contact with Hank as he came back into the dugout but Hank avoided it.

The next hitter, shortstop Gary Hoffman, was hit by a pitch. It was now one on with one out and Shake wasn't going to eat up another out with a bunt. He'd let his number three hitter Mike Goff hit away. The Reds pitcher, rattled by the hit batsman, walked Goff on four pitches. That brought the Reds manager out who called in a new reliever. The starting pitcher walked slowly off the field to the tune "Hit the Road, Jack" and taunts from the fans behind the Reds dugout. The right-handed reliever warmed up and got ready to face the Kingsmen clean-up hitter Travis Burks.

On the first pitch he saw, Burks scorched a grounder past the third baseman. Game over. The players leaped out of the dugout to pound Burks on the back while Shake and the other coaches skipped gingerly onto the field to get into the handshake line. The loud speakers blared out "Smokin" by Boston.

Back in his office, Shake fielded questions from the local press. The local press consisted of the *New Britain Herald*, the *City Journal*, WDRC AM 1360 (who broadcast the games), and a journalism student from Central Connecticut State University. They crowded into his office while Orson Kent stood in the doorway listening in. The interview was almost over.

"You got Pittsfield coming up," said the *Herald* reporter. "Another opening day. How do you like the match-up?"

The Pittsfield Cubs were the Chicago affiliate, a big league club Shake had played briefly for in the 70's before they released him. He didn't have fond memories of the Cubs and enjoyed beating them whenever he got a chance, but he kept all that to himself. "Lookin' forward to it," answered Shake. "Opening days in another ballpark are always tough, but we got Andy going and we're hitting the ball pretty good right now, so I like our chances." The reporter turned off his recorder and Shake looked around the room. "Is that it?" he asked.

"One more," said the journalism student. He had introduced himself as Balt Porter. The young man was smooth shaven with thick brown hair and wore Clark Kent glasses. Shake signaled okay, and Balt asked his question in his soft-spoken voice: "In the seventh you pitched around Segura to get to Bailey, so instead of going with the righty match-up you went with the lefty match-up. How come?"

"A hunch," replied Shake. "Bailey had grounded out his last time up and we needed a double play. I got lucky."

There were a couple "we-know-better" chuckles from the veteran reporters as they got up to leave. "Okay, guys," said Shake with finality, "See you later." As the reporters filed out, Orson stared keenly at Balt as the young reporter passed him by in the doorway. Shake caught the exchange and asked Orson, "You know him?"

"Huh… Oh, no." Orson seemed in a bit of a daze but came out of it quickly. "So why did you pitch around Segura and go after Baily?" he asked Shake. "Really? The numbers were against it."

Shake could feel another sabermetrics spiel coming on. Orson was a big disciple of sabermetrics which used empirical analysis of baseball statistics to predict tendencies and performance. Davey Johnson used it with the Mets but Shake was not a big believer in it. Orson was a graduate of UConn with a Sports Management Degree (whatever the hell that was) and like any young grad he loved showing off his knowledge, but before he could get going Shake decided to enlighten the lad.

"Baseball statistics are like a girl in a bikini," he said. "They show a lot, but not everything. I've watched Bailey the last couple years and he's a streaky hitter. When his front side's down during his swing, he drives the ball but when it's not he hits a lot of grounders, especially against righties like Davis who have a two-seamer that rides in on lefties. When Bailey's on I probably pitch to Segura there but he's not at the moment and all the stats in the world ain't going to tell you his front side's late in his swing. You got to pay attention."

"Hmm," replied Orson. "Bailey almost got a hit though. Hamilton made a nice play."

"He sure did." Rex Lyon appeared in the doorway, saving Shake from having to explain the obvious any further.

"Nice game, Glover," said Rex.

"Thanks, Rex," answered Shake. He quickly looked the old man up and down. Rex wore the same old suit and tie combination, with the tie loosened and top button undone, which always gave him a distinguished yet hands-on appearance. He sported close-cropped white hair, and under his bushy white eyebrows a pair of piercing blue eyes held steady on their target. Rex always reminded Shake of one of those whaling captains that one saw pictures of in the maritime museums.

After his quick assessment, Shake concluded that the old man was back on his game. Rex appeared quick and alert. He'd given a nice speech to the Booster's club before the game today, and had even helped roll out the tarp after their rain-shortened game yesterday.

"Five-hundred and sixty-five feet."

Shake raised an eyebrow at Rex's blurb. He noticed Orson was glancing at him as though to say "Here we go again" but the kid didn't get it. The old man was giving him the distance of the longest homerun in baseball history.

"Mickey Mantle," shot back Shake. "Griffith Stadium... '53."

"Right or left-handed?"

Shake thought for a moment (Mantle had been a switch-hitter). "Shit, Rex, you got me... Left-handed?"

"Uh uh. Right-handed, off lefty Chuck Stobbs."

"Damn, you got me. You're the man."

"And don't you forget it." Rex rapped his wedding ring on the door jamb (he was a widower). "Got things to do and so do you. I'll see you when you get back."

Shake did have things to do. He needed to finish his post-game summary and fax it off to the big club then shoot on over to The Mermaid Tavern, their local watering hole, for the real post-game analysis with his coaches. He chatted a minute longer with Orson then let him go so he could start his paperwork. He first went over to his filing cabinet where a cassette player sat next to a small stack of cassettes. Shake grew up in the rock and roll era of the fifties and sixties but his taste in music ran more toward Sinatra and Dinah Washington. He liked some contemporary stuff like the Police and Billy Joel, and he took out a cassette for The Little River Band, popped it into the slot, and hit play.

Shake finished up his game report which included a rundown on his pitchers. The big club was interested in all their prospects but especially their pitching prospects. In his report he noted that Davis had started out strong, topping out at ninety-one and hitting his spots, but in the seventh had tired and started missing location. In the eighth, his four-seam was down to eighty-nine but his two-seam and slider were still effective. Overall line: eight innings pitched, six strikeouts, four walks, and five earned runs. Not bad for his first start.

Shake replied "Yeah" to a knock on the door and Rick popped his head in.

"Meet you over there," he said.

"Yeah, almost done," replied Shake. Rick closed the door and Shake finished up his game report and faxed it to the big club using the rickety fax machine in his office. He changed into street clothes and headed out into the locker room. All the players were gone except for Dane Hamilton.

Dane sat alone at his locker. He was almost six feet tall with hazel eyes and dark blonde hair that was cut short. His close-cropped hair and a slightly receding hairline hair accentuated his forehead and made him look—at least to Shake's eyes—like a cloistered monk. The fact that Dane's eyes always seemed to be lost in thought and his brow knit in perpetual worry added to his monkish look. But his body was anything but monkish; it was a middle infielder's body. He was strong in the shoulders, light on his feet, with cupped hands and a slight stoop that any baseball scout would have recognized immediately as a second baseman's body.

Shake walked over to him. Dane's hair was wet and combed back and he straddled the bench in front of his locker, head down, reading a book. The kid's a bit of an odd duck, thought Shake. In spring training he'd seen Dane playing chess in the clubhouse. Not many players went in for chess; it was usually cards or Strat-O-Matic Baseball or a board game like Risk that could go on for days—but rarely chess. His story was also an odd one, too: he was drafted out of college (Cornell, no less), played a year in the minors where he showed great promise, then had up and quit and gone back to college to get his Master's degree. Now at age twenty-six he was back in baseball.

"What you reading?" asked Shake as he came up to him.

Dane dog-eared the page and closed the thin paperback. "Camus," he said looking up.

Shake looked down at the cover. He was familiar with the book. "Kind of heady stuff for April baseball," he said.

"I've read it before." He tossed the book into his open locker as though he was disgusted with it.

"Words, words, words."

"Cornel, right? What was your major?"

"Philosophy"

"Jeez. And I thought I was a stranger in a strange land... I feel for you. I was drafted out of college in '61—Cal-Berkeley. Most kids back then were out of high school or maybe had a year or two of JC, and most of the coaches were suspicious of college grads. Intimidated might be a better word. It's a little better now-days. But Ivy Leaguers are still a rarity, like an honest man in congress."

"*To be honest,* quoted Dane, *as the world goes, is to be one man picked out of ten thousand.*"

"Ahh," laughed Shake. "You know your *Hamlet,* I see."

"Here and there," replied Dane with a smile. "My mom loves Shakespeare."

"My dad did, too." Shake liked this kid. They probably had a lot in common and he'd have to sit down with him some day and have a real talk, but right now he had places to go. They talked a few moments longer before Shake turned to leave. "That was a nice play in the seventh," he added, glancing back. "Probably saved the game."

"I was expecting it. Thanks. See you tomorrow."

The kid's a thinker, concluded Shake as he walked away. Thinking could be good in baseball and it could be bad. Thinking through situations was good thing; it aided reaction and execution. Thinking about the absurdity of existence in the batter's box was a bad thing.

Shake walked out to the poorly lit parking lot and saw a figure standing by a car. As he got closer, he recognized the figure immediately as Corey Lyon, Rex's daughter. She'd been a fixture at the park ever since he'd become manager. Her father doted on her, and she followed him around happily running errands for him and learning the business. She knew more about the business of baseball than most men and everyone expected her to take over for Rex once he retired, but they had a falling out after she married a punk rock musician. Now she was banished from the park, banished from his house, banished from his life. In Shake's mind she was a sweetheart and nothing would ever change that and the whole situation saddened him.

"Hey, little girl!" said Shake with a big grin.

She bounded towards him—"Shake!"—and gave him a big hug. She'd always been skinny but he could feel her ribs as he hugged her. Her short blonde hair was spiked on the top and she had the same piercing blue eyes as her father. The hair was a "punk thing," figured Shake, and it contrasted oddly with her pretty face which had both mature and empathetic features to it.

"What you doing out here in the shadows?"

"Yeah, well, you know. I waited for my dad to leave. I was hoping to talk to you, see how he's doing. My sister doesn't tell me much. I was here for opening day hiding out with the bleacher bums. I saw you help my dad into the stands. What was that all about? That was a smart move in the seventh, walking Segura. Bailey's pounding the ball into the ground right now. Looks like Estrella bulked up over the winter… So how's my dad doing?"

Shake chuckled. She had a frenetic speaking style and she could throw a lot at you in a short amount of time, kind of like a relief pitcher warning up in the bullpen with the bases loaded. "He's fine," replied Shake. "Same old Rex—everyone's favorite S-O-B. He misses you but won't admit it."

"Really? How do you know? He called me last week and asked me if I had anything to say to him. I told him I loved him and he says, 'Is that it, do you have anything else to tell me?' I said 'no, nothing' and he says, 'nothing comes of nothing' and hung up on me. I've heard some things, too, like he's forgetting things, almost like he has Alzheimer's. What have you seen?"

He respected Corey, found her to be highly intelligent, and so he told her the truth—what he'd seen recently, the forgetfulness, the episode in the tunnel—all of it. They talked for over twenty minutes in the darkened parking lot and she asked a bunch of questions that he tried his best to answer. She told him Rex was having tax problems and had signed his company and estate over to her older sister for protection (that's the first he'd heard of that). She handed Shake a slip of paper with her phone number on it "for emergencies." He told her to come over to his place any time if she wanted to talk and, before parting, they hugged again and he told her she was getting skinny and needed to eat. She promised she would and disappeared into the night.

Shake drove downtown to The Mermaid Tavern and joined his coaches and Orson at a table in the back. They were already on their second pitcher of beer. He wasn't in the mood for beer so he went up to the bar and ordered a drink. Don the bartender knew him by name and knew just how much Bacardi dark rum and diet Pepsi to pour into a tall glass. While Don mixed his drink, Shake looked around the bar. The place was half full but there were no ball-players. They knew it was the coaches' hang-out and usually avoided it. They had their own hang-outs. He glanced around for Lucy—"Dark Lucy" was her nickname—the owner of The Mermaid, but she was not around.

"She's upstairs," said Don as he placed the drink in front of Shake.

Shake nodded and took his drink (he didn't need to pay, he kept a running tab) and walked back to his table. He sat down and jumped into the conversation which, at the moment, was about the true age of Dominican ball-players—in this case Manny Ortiz, who was one of their outfielders. Manny said he was twenty-four but Rick Burton claimed he was thirty while Bob Kalecki was sure he was twenty-six. Teddy Larkin said they were both wrong—he got it straight from Mike Faust the trainer. Faust taped Manny's ankles before every game and ankles never lied. He was twenty-eight.

In many ways, these post-game get-togethers were the best part of being a manager. Shake loved them, loved the repartee, the camaraderie, the bullshit. At this table, on any night, one could hear pearls of wisdom, tall tales and hilarious stories. The post-mortem on the game-just-played always contained keen insights which only men who have dedicated their lives to a profession can provide. It was like listening to seasoned playwrights talk about the theatre. The wit was dry, the one-liners fast and furious, and the jokes tended to be bawdy if not downright lewd and crude (especially as the beer-buzz increased). For Shake, maybe it wasn't the best part of managing but is was certainly the most fun.

Orson had been invited into the inner sanctum and Shake kept his eye on him. The young man appeared to appreciate the compliment and listened quietly, occasionally asking a question or adding a stat if it was relevant, but mostly he sat and listened with a smile. Certain gestures and turns of a phrase caused Shake to wonder if he was gay, but since he didn't care to find out one way or the other he left it as a passing thought.

"How you boys doing?" asked the cocktail waitress. Her name tag said Bernice but everybody called her Bernie. She and

Larry Benedict had dated at one time but it had gone bad, and now every time they confronted each other (which was usually when she came over to refill their orders) a lively banter ensued which bordered on trash talk. The others at ringside enjoyed it and waited for the bell to start the next round of boxing.

Bernie
Shake, another? And I should have said 'men', 'how you men doing'. There's only one boy at this table.

Larry
I'm surprised you noticed. This young man here is Orson Kent, UConn grad and owner's son. He comes from money, which makes him young and rich. Just your combination. Come to think of it, you better watch out, Orson. She'll sink her teeth into you.

Bernie
First off, the only boy here is you. Mentally about twelve years old I'd say. Second off, Orson, it's a pleasure to meet you, but don't listen to him—he's a pervert and clinically insane. And don't talk to me about sinking teeth into people, I still have the mark on my ass where you bit me.

Teddy
You bit her ass?

Larry
She's fantasizing again. But I did kiss her ass once.

Shake
It that a metaphor?

Larry
No, really. It was dark and I thought it was her face.

Bernie
The only thing you ever mistook in the dark was a pencil for your penis.

Larry
God, there you go again, hitting below the belt. Why do women always go for the crotch? They're like pit bulls that way. That's why I'll never get married. I don't want to spend the rest of my life walking around the house with a cup on.

Bernie
The fact that you'll never marry only brings joy to the women of the world. I can't imagine being married to you. It'd be like hell and Bellevue and Captain Kangaroo all rolled into one.

Larry
Don't imagine 'cause it'll never happen. I'm a committed bachelor, like Shake here. The only way you'd get us to marry is by stringing us up by our toes. Even then I'd rather live without toes than wear a wedding ring.

Bernie
I'd least then you'd be good for something. We could sell your toes for lobster bait.

Larry
They use herring for lobster bait.

Bernie
Exactly. You're one big red herring.

Larry
I'm sure that means something but I'm not sure what, so why don't you, like an actual cock-tail waitress, go fetch us

another pitcher of beer and stop talking to us about lobsters and kangaroos.

Bernie

You always want to shut it down when you're losing... Ah, ah, don't say it, don't say it. I'll get your beer. Shake, the same? Okay, except for *him*, don't go away.

Larry

Turn around and show us your best feature. Bye, bye.

Bernie spun around and put her hand behind her back and flipped Larry off as she walked away.

"One of these days she's going to pour a pitcher of beer over your head," laughed Teddy.

"That'd be more refreshing than all the crap that comes out of her mouth," replied Larry.

They had a good laugh at that and more. The topic changed to relief pitching, and over the next hour ranged from baseball to Mike Tyson to the growing ban on smoking. Rick and Teddy, who were both married, left around 1:00 along with Orson. Bob was divorced but living with a gal and hung in there until 1:30. Shake and Larry kept at it until Don yelled "Last call!" just before 2:00. Shake got up and stretched. He'd only had three drinks and felt fine. They had a bus to catch at eight in the morning. He looked around for Lucy but she was not in the bar. She'd come down an hour before and said hi to them, stood next to him and tickled his ear, then went back upstairs to "work on my taxes." He was tempted for a moment to go upstairs and knock on her door but he thought better of it. They had a bus to catch at eight in the morning.

Shake walked out onto the sidewalk and breathed in the cool, clean Connecticut night air. Three loud Harley Davidson motorcycles passed by and he did a double take at one of the passengers.

"You see that?" he asked as Larry came up behind him.

"See what?"

"The guy on the back of the bike. It looked like Prince."

"Hank Prince? You sure?"

Shake thought about it. He didn't want it to be Hank. "No," he said.

"Seeing as it's way past curfew and he's on a motorcycle—a direct violation of his contract—let's hope not. He's not that stupid."

Shake rubbed his chin in thought and then said goodnight to Larry. He hoped so, too. He was too beat to think it a warning; they had a bus to catch in the morning.

5
CHAPTER

This great stage of fools
King Lear

After a six game road trip, the New Britain Kingsmen stood at 7 and 2 and atop the Eastern League. In Pittsfield they lost opening day, got rained-out on Saturday, and swept a double header on Sunday. In Nashua they took two out of three from the Pirates and might have swept them if Hank Prince hadn't been picked off third in the ninth inning of the second game. 7 and 2 was nothing to sneeze at but Shake knew that ending up first in the regular season didn't amount to much. There were eight teams in the Eastern League and four of them made the play-offs. In a three out of five play-off format any team could get hot and win the league.

Their archrivals the New Haven Admirals were due in town Friday for a three game series, but today was Thursday, an off-day, which wasn't really an off-day because players and coaches were obligated to attend the yearly Lyon picnic. It was tradition and happened the middle of every April at the Lyon Estate in Avon, Connecticut. Everyone in the organization was expected to attend along with their wives or girlfriends. The press and local dignitaries were invited and all together over a hundred people attended the shindig. Shake enjoyed it. So did most of the players. There was great food, lots of booze, and a live band that went until midnight.

The tables were laid out under large canopies across the vast, rolling lawn that surrounded the castle-like estate. On years it rained, the party was moved indoors to the great hall, but it was sunny today and the mansion looked as though it was locked up. Shake found that a bit strange until he remembered what Corey had told him about Rex's tax problems. He wasn't sure if there was a connection there or not. The food and booze were as good as ever, the fanfare the same, but there was one other odd thing: the pool was drained. Every year it was full and open for business and kids and grown-ups could swim in it all day. He asked one of the bartenders what was with the pool and got the reply, "Mrs. Cornwall had it drained."

Mrs. Cornwall was Rae Cornwall, Rex's oldest daughter. He had two daughters and no sons. Rae was from a previous marriage that ended in divorce and Corey was from his second marriage. Between the two there was no comparison. Shake found Corey to be a sweetheart while he found Rae to be—well, Larry called her a "certified bitch on wheels"—and maybe that wasn't too far off. She and her husband Ed lived in the mansion with Rex. And now, according to Corey, the house was in her name. So was his company. Shake knew that since last year, Ed Cornwall pretty much ran Lyon Bolt Manufactory, which three months ago announced a big lay-off. This all reeked of money problems and Shake suddenly felt very sorry for Rex. *Timon of Athens* came to his mind:

> *For bounty, that makes gods, does still mar men.*
> *My dearest lord, bless'd, to be most accursed,*
> *Rich, only to be wretched, thy great fortunes*
> *Are made thy chief afflictions.*

"Lost in thought?" asked Rick.

Shake stood by the drained pool, drink in hand, looking up at the locked mansion. "Huh?... Yeah," he replied. "She drained the pool."

"I heard. Linda and the kids are bummed. Also heard Rex and her got into a big row over it and she threatened to cancel the picnic. She hates 'em."

"Always knew that," commented Shake. They strolled back towards the bandstand. Rick Burton was Shake's best friend. They had met in the minor leagues and hit it off even though they were opposites in many ways. Shake was an infielder, Rick an outfielder; Shake was a committed bachelor, Rick a dedicated family man; and Rick, despite Shake's efforts, preferred Louis L'Amour to the saintly Bard. Plus the taller Rick had a full head of hair that Shake secretly envied. But despite these differences, Shake saw in Rick a keen baseball mind that was matched with a kind heart and a guardian's soul. Shake knew that Rick had his back, and there was no better thing you could say about a friend than that.

"I was talking to Orson the other day," said Rick. "He's dialed in to ownership and all that finance stuff, and he says she wants to sell the team."

"What?" exclaimed Shake. He stopped and looked around. "Why? The team's making money. We've got the best attendance in the league."

"She can make more by selling it. Orson says there's a renaissance going on in minor league baseball and the price tag for ball clubs has gone sky high, even Single-A. He's says they could get a million for the Kingsmen, easy. The big thing now is consortiums backed by movie stars like Bill Murray. It's a trendy investment.

"Yeah, I've heard all that, but I don't see Rex selling. It's still his ball club... Plus I'm a shareholder," he added with a whimsical smile (cause he knew better).

"*Right,*" said Rick, smiling back. "If they want to sell, they'll sell. You won't get out of the way of that beanball."

"I still don't see Rex selling."

"You're probably right. The old man loves it too much. She'll have to wait until he steps aside or kicks the bucket."

Shake dreaded the thought.

Orson had a problem. He was bewitched and bewildered. He couldn't lie to himself about it any longer—he was infatuated. Crushes could be a problem if the other person didn't feel the same way, but his problem was bigger than that. The object of his infatuation was another man.

He had dated girls in high school and college—normal stuff—but when it came to sex there was something missing. He'd gone to bed with three women and each time he was left feeling as though something key was missing. It was more a letdown—like stroking a fourteen foot putt for par only to have it come up an inch short from the cup. And they had felt it too because each time, after having sex, they had let the relationship fizzle out on its own. It was a bedeviling concern. Was he gay? How did a person know if they were gay or not? Was it like being born left-handed versus right handed, and even if you were left-handed and your dad tried to make you right-handed were you still, in the end, left-handed? He'd been attracted to men before, usually athletes who exemplified the male form (like Michael Jordan), but he chalked it up to a Greek-like admiration. But now it was more than that, he was sure of it. What he felt for Balt Porter was love.

He first saw the journalism student in the clubhouse and he was immediately smitten by him. Balt had delicate features for a man, along with thick brown hair, and though he wasn't an athlete, he carried himself like one with a certain gracefulness. Orson had to admit that Balt was even a little effeminate which confused him even more. But that really wasn't the problem. The real problem was twofold: if he was gay, he would have to confront that truth. He knew gay people—some of them even lived openly about it—but being gay was not a thing that would go over well with his father or family. Not at all. The second problem was more immediate and sat across the table from him. How did he get Balt to love him back?

Orson had introduced himself to Balt a couple weeks ago and shaken his hand, which turned out to be soft like a writer's hand. He now saw Balt sitting with the media people—albeit aloof, head down studying his notebook—and Orson came over and re-introduced himself. He had an ice-breaker. He was a recent grad and Balt was a junior at CCSU, so he quickly started in on the "college experience." As they talked, he noticed Balt was fidgety and slightly distracted as though he had somewhere else to go.

"Late for an appointment?" he finally asked Balt.

"No... Well, yes," replied Balt in his soft-spoken voice. "I do have to leave soon."

"Balt, what's that, short for Balthazar, right?"

"Right, and you're named after who... Orson Bean?"

"No. Orson Welles. My dad's good friends with him."

"Really?"

"Yeah, he's also good friends with Arnold Palmer but luckily he didn't name me Arnie."

"Arnold Palmer?"

"Yeah, the golfer."

"I know who Arnold Palmer is. Ninety-two tournament wins. He said 'What other people may find in poetry or art museums, I find in the flight of a good drive.' I love that quote."

"You play golf?"

"Occasionally... When I have time."

"We should get together for a round. They got a good one there off Hartford Road. Stanley Golf Course."

"Maybe... I'll have to get back to you on that. Got a busy schedule right now."

"Sure. Understood."

There was a moment of awkward silence and Orson's mind raced to quickly fill the gap. But Balt filled it for him: "Orson for Orson Welles... Could be worse. You could be named Shakespeare."

They both laughed at that and Orson's heart skipped a beat when he heard Balt's beautiful laugh. He boldly stared into Balt's brown eyes which were obscured by those godawful black-rimmed glasses. Orson wanted to reach over and gently take those glasses off him but he restrained himself and just kept staring. Suddenly Balt looked away and Orson caught (what? could it be?) a slight reddening in his cheeks. The man was blushing.

What did that mean, wondered Orson. If he was a woman and blushed like that Orson would have thought there was a connection between the two of them, but who knows. Maybe Balt was embarrassed by his staring. How did someone find these things out? It wasn't like being in a foreign country; you couldn't go around asking everyone you met if they spoke English until you found someone who did. This was dangerous territory. Subtlety was required. One had to rely on minimal cues. Was the blush a minimal cue? He wasn't sure.

"I got to get going," said Balt gathering up his notebook.

Orson was crestfallen. He was obviously wrong about the blush. "Oh... Okay," he replied lamely.

"But I was thinking," added Balt as he stood up, "I'd like to get some insight into ownership and the financial side. Maybe you'd grant me an interview?

Hope burst anew in Orson's chest. "I'd love it," he said. "Anytime. We can talk about ownership, the big club, money, whatever. Maybe over dinner. I think you'd gain a lot of insight." He caught himself. He was talking too fast so he slowed down. "Anyhow... Let me know... Give me a call."

"That'd be fine," said Balt. "How do I reach you?"

"I'm at the ballpark, of course. But if you want to set something up ahead of time just give me a call... Here." Orson fumbled for a pen and wrote his number down on a paper napkin. "I have an apartment in New Britski. There's my number." He handed the napkin over. Instead of shoving it in his pants pocket, Balt folded it neatly and put it in his shirt pocket.

"Appreciate it."

No problem. See you then." And Orson watched as Balt walked away. He had baggy pants and walked with exaggerated long strides which only endeared him more to Orson.

"Yeah," thought Orson with a wry smile. "I've got a big problem."

Three pitchers sat together at a table shooting the bull. They were kicking back. Empty beer bottles cluttered the table in front of them and they talked baseball, gossiped, and commented on the local fare. The local fare consisted of young, single, attractive women who always seemed to flock to these events looking (if the truth be told) for handsome pro ball-players who might someday become millionaires. Chuck Davis was married and his wife was on the dance floor with Phil Cappadona's girlfriend. Phil was a relief pitcher, a submariner with a nasty fastball. The third pitcher was the Kingsmens' second starter Luis Santiago. Luis came with a date but she had left in a huff after he hit on another woman in front of her.

"See Basset's girlfriend?" asked Phil. "Knockout."

"Looks like a model," agreed Chuck.

Star pitcher Steve Basset sat next to his beautiful girlfriend a few tables over. There was camaraderie in the minors but like any institution that thrived on internal competition there were also rivalries and envy. And Steve Basset, a handsome stud with a gorgeous girlfriend, who also happened to be a hot prospect that everyone agreed was ticketed for the big leagues, was a natural target for such emotions. That's not to say that any of the Kingsmen pitchers wished him ill-will. On the contrary, they'd be the first to cheer and pat him on the back at his promotion to the bigs. But did each one harbor a secret desire to be Steve Basset with the live arm and big contract and beautiful girlfriend? Of course they did, and some more than others.

"They're engaged," added Luis with a sip of his beer. Luis Santiago, or "Tiago" as some of the players called him, had been first starter in the rotation last year until Basset came on board. Now he was number two. Luis grew up in Rancho Cucamonga where he attended Catholic schools and excelled in sports. His grandparents had emigrated from Mexico but the family did not consider themselves Mexican but rather Spanish. His father in particular had drilled into his son's head that they, the Santiagos, were descended from a noble Spanish line and not tainted with Indian blood. It was no surprise that Luis had inherited from his father a rather Ricardo Montalban-like haughtiness to go along with his handsome features.

"I saw the rock. When they get engaged?" asked Chuck.

"Spring training," replied Luis. "They didn't want to tell anyone until he got assigned. Her name's Gwen Cymbel. She was Miss Clemson a couple years ago and works as an intern for some law firm in Hartford."

"No shit," said Phil. "How do you know all that?"

"I went over and introduced myself."

"Where was Basset?'

"At the bar.

Chuck and Phil looked at one another. Luis was known as the team's Casanova. He was a playboy who sported a new girlfriend every week. Even at away games, in nightclubs, he could pick out a girl, go up and talk to her, and within minutes be out the door on the way to her place. They'd seen him do it.

"You didn't hit on her?" asked Chuck incredulously.

"No, not really. I could have."

"Bullshit," said Phil. "I mean, I've seen you work, man. You're an artist. But she's out of your league, dude. Seriously."

"Bet me."

"Bet you? What? Bet you won't hit on her? I'd never make that bet."

"No, I bet you I can have her."

"You're kidding."

"Nope. Bet you a hundred bucks."

"Bet you a hundred bucks that you can steal her away from Basset?"

"Didn't say 'steal.' I said I could have her. Go to bed with her. One hundred bucks."

"Tiago," interjected Chuck, half-laughing, "it ain't gonna happen and I ain't makin' that bet."

"I'm talking to Phil. One hundred buck says I get her in bed before the all-star break."

Phil was no longer taking this as a joke and studied the label on his beer bottle weighing his chances. Evidently he thought them pretty good because he smiled back at Luis.

"You're not taking this guy serious, are you?" said Chuck to Phil.

"Maybe."

"Shit, Phil, come off it. What's a bet like that gonna prove? It'll just cause problems. Someone's gonna get punched in the nose... Count me out."

"You're out. We just need you to witness the bet."

Chuck looked to his wife on the dance floor, trying to ignore them. "Whatever," he said indifferently.

"Okay," said Phil as he turned to Luis. "How you going to prove it?"

"What do you want?"

"How about the rock on her finger?"

"That'd be tough. How about the locket she's wearing. It's gold with two hearts intertwined. Basset gave it to her."

They all looked across the rows of tables to see the locket around her neck. Even Chuck glanced over to see it. Steve Basset, sitting next to his beautiful fiancé, noticed them looking over and waved with a friendly smile. They smiled back.

"Deal," replied Phil. "One hundred bucks says you won't fuck her before the all-star break, and if you do you have to hand me that locket as proof. Chuck, you're my witness."

"Sure," replied Chuck, failing in his attempt to stay out of it.

"Then it's a bet."

"It's a bet," agreed Luis, raising his beer bottle. The two clicked their beer bottles together to seal the wager.

Dane Hamilton sat by himself rubbing his chin in thought and listening to his transistor radio. He carried it around with him the way some people carried a pack of cigarettes, and he listened to it regularly, even when he was shagging flies during batting practice. His preference was news-talk radio. At the moment he was listening to a news report covering the U.S. raid on Libya. Two days before, fighter jets had bombed army installations and Gaddafi's home but reports indicated that Gaddafi had gotten out in time. Too bad, he thought. That would have been one less nutcase in the world. News talk radio was filled with pundits from the left and right giving their reaction and assessment. Dane found their comments to be predictable: the left condemned it as a naked act of aggression while the right praised it as an act of self-defense. Which was true, he wondered.

One of the pundits complained about the "U.S. acting like the world's policeman." So what, he thought. He had no illusions about mankind. The world needed a cop. Mankind did not particularly delight Dane but he did not set himself above the fray. He ranked himself with the barbarous multitudes. Again, what was true he wondered—the human race that showed great charity and produced beautiful works of art or the human race that showed great cruelty and perpetrated acts of terrorism and genocide on itself? Evidently both were true. But one had to admit it, the attack was a bold act and he rather admired it.

Loud voices caught his attention and he pulled out his earplug to listen. Off to his left, three people were arguing amongst themselves. They were far enough away from the main crowd not be seen or heard but Dane could clearly see and hear them. One of them he recognized as the owner Rex Lyon, while the woman arguing with him he guessed to be his daughter. Another man appeared to be trying to mediate the dispute. The argument was over the band. She wanted the band shut down and sent home. Rex demanded they keep playing—it was his party, not hers, and she had no right to give orders. This went on for another minute until the woman ordered the other man to "send the band home!" The man put his head down and headed towards the bandstand. With that, she turned her back on her father and walked briskly back up to the house with Rex, all red-faced, blustering obscenities close behind.

Even in the best of families, thought Dane, smiling to himself. His family was messed up with the best of them. For ten years he had sat witness to his parents' loveless marriage. Then one day he had come home from school to find his dad dead in the garage from carbon monoxide poisoning. From then on his family had been just he and his mom.

Mentally he stepped out of the batter's box and cleared his head. He turned off his radio and let his mind percolate. A term he had heard earlier—"create an edge"—popped into his head. It came from Greg Rosecrans. Greg was a back-up infielder in his fifth year in the minors and he was looking for a way to turn his career around. Greg had been feeling him out over the last week, dropping hints, and earlier today had let slip the word "Deca." Deca was short for Deca-Durabolin, a steroid.

Greg did not come right out and tell him he was going to take Deca. Instead he worked around it, passing on the rumor that their catcher Jose Estrella was taking Deca. The truth was in the results, he claimed. Last year Estrella looked like them and now he looked like Lou Ferrigno in catcher's gear. Two weeks into the season and Jose already had five homeruns. He had ten all of last year. He had created an edge, Greg said, and maybe it was time for him to create an edge, and what did Dane think about it. Should he or shouldn't he?

Dane didn't give him an answer. That bothered Dane because he knew the answer. It was cheating and it messed up your body, maybe permanently. He also knew the defense for it: it wasn't a banned substance and it worked, increasing arm strength if you were a pitcher and bat speed if you were a hitter. It gave you an edge and with so much at stake, players needed an edge, whether it was nicotine, amphetamines (whites) or something else. Plus everyone was doing it. Dane turned off his radio and walked back towards the crowd. Yes, he thought wryly, that was man's great savior. No matter what people did to "create an edge"—take drugs, steal or blow up people—they could always say "everyone was doing it."

Shakespeare Glover was holding court. As had become tradition, every year towards the end of the Lyon's Picnic, as the lights dimmed and the families shuffled on home, Shake would attract a crowd of players and coaches under one of the canopies to listen to him expound on baseball, life and the Bard. Usually it was after midnight once the band quit, but this year, for whatever reason, the band had quit early and so Shake's gabfest had gathered early. Shake sat talking, nursing a beer, while players and coaches, some in chairs, some sitting cross-legged on the grass, huddled close to hear every word.

It usually started with a question.

"What's a harder jump," asked a player. "Single-A to Double-A, double to triple, or triple to the show?"

"Single-A to Double-A is the toughest jump in the minors," replied Shake. "A lot of guys spend their whole career in A ball, or leave and end up in an independent league. It's a gladiator pit and only the strongest make it out. Triple-A is a turnstile; there's always guys coming and going. The only thing worse than playing in Triple-A is...?" He glanced at Rick Burton.

"Not playing in Triple-A," replied Rick on cue.

"Exactly. Double-A is a sea of tranquility by comparison. Rosters stay pretty stable throughout the year, and here you get time to hone your craft. The quality of play is high and you play in front of good crowds, plus the buses are air-conditioned. But getting here's the trick. If you're a pitcher, you gotta have a good off-speed pitch to go with your fastball, and if you're a hitter, you gotta be able to hit ninety-four *and* the off-speed stuff. And once you're here you can just as easily jump to the bigs as you can from Triple-A. Look at Canseco."

"Not many make it to the majors," said a player.

"I read somewhere it's about four percent" said another.

"I think it's higher than that,' replied Shake. "It depends on how you calculate it—ten days in the majors, ten years, or just one day. Even if it's one day you can still say you made it. If you play long enough in the minors like Kalecki here you can get a "good guy promotion." Nearly twenty years in the minors and they call you up in September and give you some at bats as a way of saying thank you. Can't beat that—to stand out on a big league diamond with a major league uni on and your family in the stands. Nothing beats that. Meanwhile you're playing professional baseball. And where would you rather be? Selling cars? Eating nachos on the couch? There's no place I'd rather be. I love coaching Double-A and they pay me to do it."

"As long as you win."

"It's a balancing act. Yeah, they expect you to win—you wanna win—but my real job here is to produce talent. The farm system is like a big company's R&D department. Like Bell Labs. The big club pumps a lot of money into their R&D department and my job—all our job—is to develop talent and get you ready for the big leagues. But if you expect to stick around you also gotta win. That's just talking straight."

"Is it better nowadays to get signed out of high school or college?"

"Depends on your situation. If your family needs the money and they offer you a big contract out of high school—hell, yes, take the money and run. But if you got the resources, my advice is to go to college. Look at Bonds and Clark: right out of college and into the bigs. Granted, not everyone is Will Clark, but I guarantee you everyone here was a hotshot in high school. Am I right?"

"Except for Santiago."

"Yeah, he was too busy getting laid."

"Everyone should be good at something," laughed Shake. "But here's my point: being a hot shot in high school, winning a state championship, getting named all-league—most of us can lay claim to that. But coming out of college, maybe being named All-American—that's something different. A good college program like Arizona or Texas gives you an advantage. The level of play is at least as good as Single-A and it gives you a head start. But that's just my opinion. In the end it comes down to talent and hard work."

A waiter came by and with noticeable embarrassment announced that the picnic was over. "Mrs. Cornwall wants the Kingsmen to go home." They ignored him and he went away.

"Where'd the Kingsmen come from?"

"I heard you named 'em."

"I did," confirmed Shake. "It's from Elizabethan England. Shakespeare's time. Acting companies back then needed a license to perform, and if you wanted to succeed you had to have noble patronage. Shakespeare's patron was the Queen herself and actually, back then, they were called the 'Queen's Men' but I didn't think you'd be too happy playing for the Queen's Men. After she died they became the 'King's Men' under King James, so I went with that. And it has nothing to do with all that King Arthur stuff they got going on at the ballpark. That's all Rex's idea—the jousting knights, Galahad the mascot, Round Table Pizza.

"The Kingsmen were talented performers. When they weren't performing on the London stage they were traveling the countryside, going from town to town plying their trade. Just like you guys. One week you're in Pittsfield, another in Nashua and another in Waterbury... Some of you have heard me talk about this before. The ballfield is like a stage where everyone plays a part. You have an audience. You have heroes and villains. A game of baseball is identical to a Shakespearean play, like *A Midsummer Night's Dream*. It has a beginning, middle and end and is filled with surprises and twists of fate. It can be a *comedy of errors* or a tragedy like *Julius Caesar* where you get a knife in the back in the bottom of the ninth. Comedy or tragedy, it's one or the other, unless you're playing an old rival like the New Haven Admirals. Then it's more like *Henry the Sixth* and the War of the Roses."

"Did they have baseball back then?"

"They had cricket, which is a close cousin. I'm sure Willy was a fan. I can see him sitting in the sun eating capers and drinking sack while taking in a game. And he knew his baseball even though it hadn't been invented yet. That was his genius. How else can you explain the line from *Macbeth:*

I'll catch it ere it come to ground.

There was laughter from the huddled masses. Shake smiled and looked down the spout of his bottled beer. There was still some left so he finished it off with a long swig and then finished off his lesson with something he always added at these gatherings: "Count your blessings. Be grateful you're playing pro ball in New Britain—in New Britski, The Hardware City, home of the coat hanger—and not some Podunk town in Single-A. You get good crowds here and ownership takes care of things. Rick and I have been on teams where the owner refused to call a game in a monsoon because he didn't want to lose the gate, where we worried about umpires showing up on time and there were gunshots in the parking lot. So look around, gentlemen, and count your blessings."

In a large living room with a vaulted ceiling, Rex Lyon stared down his daughter. They had been going at it for an hour and it showed no signs of letting up.

Rae
If you don't like it move out.

Rex
It's my house. I built it!

Rae
My name's on the title or have you forgotten that, too.

Rex
That gives you no right—

Rae
It gives me every right! It's my house now and I'm sick of these events and these people eating our food and tearing up our lawn. It's a big waste and I'll not have it. This is the last *baseball* picnic at my home.

Rex
Fifteen years! For fifteen years I've had this picnic. It's tradition!

Rae
Screw tradition! That's all you got anymore—tradition! You got no money and no more sense but, hey, you got tradition.

Rex
You've got a tongue like your mother. A snake's tongue! I've raised a thankless daughter. Get away from me!

Rae
Don't bring my mother into this. This house should have been hers but you cheated her out of it. Now it's mine and you can

move out for all I care. Go move in with your precious Corey. Oh, wait, you can't. You kicked her out of your life. Perfect! There's a father for you!

Rex
You'll see!... God help me... I'll get you back for this... The whole world will see, I'll do such things... I don't know what... but I'll do such things... terrible things...

Rex collapsed on the floor and his daughter turned her back muttering, "You'll do nothing" and walked away. Just then her husband rushed into the room (he had heard the yelling), saw Rex on the floor, and came to his aid. He called an ambulance and Rex was rushed to the hospital where he was diagnosed with a coronary artery spasm, treated, and let go the next day. He went home but shunned his harsh daughter, staying upstairs away from the bother.

6
CHAPTER

Hank pulled up to the curb in front of Quick's Cocktail Lounge and walked around back through the ally. It was almost one o'clock and he had to report to the ballpark in a couple hours. He needed a blunt. A couple tokes before the game calmed him down and made him play better. His connection did business out of Quick's and sometimes slept in the back room.

He guessed right. Papi's motorcycle, a purple-chromed Harley Davidson, sat parked next to the back door. Hank rapped on the door. He heard rumblings and swearing behind the door and the doorknob twisted, shook, twisted again, and flew open with a kick. Papi Stallworth lurched out the door. At 6'-2", three hundred and twenty pounds, he was wide in both directions, almost spherical, with a pronounced gut on him like one of those offensive linemen you see in the NFL. His black head was shaved but he wore a thick black beard that was sprinkled with snowflakes of white hair.

Papi squinted up at the sun and looked away, cleared his throat with a mighty hawking noise, and rested his bleary eyes on Hank. "Wat up?" he said

Hank grinned and shook his head at his friend. He got a kick out of Papi. Easily in his fifties, the old jelly-belly with his purple hog was a wannabe gangster who dealt in dank, drank, and cookies (marijuana, codeine, and crack cocaine). He did not deal brown (heroin) because, he claimed, it was "tore-down shit" that put you in with too many "crazy-ass niggas." Papi hooked Hank up with his smoke but also quickly took him under his wing. The big man knew his baseball, knew who Hank was, and made him his homie and together they kept up a line of friendly trash talk that the others around them couldn't match.

Papi's belt was loose and he fumbled to pull his pants up fully so he could tuck in his flowing shirt. He was obviously suffering from a hangover.

Papi
Wat time's it?

Hank
Why you care wat time's it? Yo wasted, man. King Cobra's bit u-again. Can't even keep yo pants up. Wat u-do, find some chickenhead last night to polish ur-knob? Wat-ju care 'bout time, nigga, less it's time for a ho or score some white or chug down one of them gawd-awful malt-lickers of 'urs that taste like moto-oil? Ur an ol' G-n, man. Wat-ju care wat time's it?

Papi
Now u-talkin, dawg. Playas like us do our biz-ness at night, unda the moon an' stars, not the sun. Wat we care 'bout time. So wat up, Sweetness? Though I doin think I'll call-u 'Sweetness.' You got none.

Hank
None?

Papi
No, not ev'n nuff to sweetin' a bowl a' Wheaties.

Hank
Not ev'n if my pitchurs ona box a' Wheaties.

Papi
When that day come, we'll call ya king. *King Hank*. Hammer'd Hank, King a' Smoke. An' when that day come, Sweetness, yo'll make me a rich man. Yo'll hook me up wid-yo big time bros an' make me a for-chune sellin' 'em butta an' chewies. Then lady luck be on my side. I be-on toppa the world.

Hank
If'n you was on toppa the world you'd crush it like a grape. Naw loosin dat belt fo' you busta gut. Wen's the last time ya saw ur shoes?

Papi
Wat I need-ta see my shoes fo? They can take care of dem-selves. They loafers... Hell-be-gone I gotta hang-over. Feelin' lowdown. Wat-ju want anyhow, Sweetness?

Hank
Blunt.

Papi
Ta blunt yo senses, ha dawg. Got scratch? No, nev'a a penny to yo name, ha nigga. You'a big bonus baby but nev'a got a dead prezdent to yo name. Yo lucky u-know me an' I like-u, cause I keep coverin' yo ass. U-got credit wid Quick's, credit wid Busta, credit with me. Yo a credit to yo race.

(Papi rummages behind a box, pulls out a half full bottle of King Cobra, and takes a long drink.)

Hank

Yo the one wid bills all o'vr town, bubba. You owe ev'rybody, foo, even-yor skanky-ass ho's.

Papi

True enuf, nigga. I like-ta keep my money to myself where's safe. But as fo my skanky-ass ho's, I don' see-u sayin no-ta pussy. Did'en-u bus-a-nut on that buttahead LaShundra the otha' night? Sho-u did and-u paid her in full, am I right? So keep it real, homie. As fo me, I ne'vr pay fo it. They's grateful fo my biz-ness. Don't laugh, nigga. They's grateful fo a real man… Sheet, I'm hungry. Let's git sumthin to eat. How 'bout Denny's? Moon o'vr my hammies. Wat-u say, dawg?

Hank

Already ate. Cum-on, Fats Domino, I gotta go. Gotta game t'day. If I stood 'round all day watchin u-eat an' drink I'd grow old an' die.

Papi

Eatin' an' drinkin' is wat I do best—an' fuckin'. Can't fo-get dat. Eatin', drinkin', fuckin' an hangin' out with my homeboys. Wat-u got 'gainst that, Sweetness? If-yo 'gainst eatin', drinkin', fuckin' an' hangin' out with yo homies then-u 'gainst the whole world. Even the jakes eat, drink an' whore—which re-mines me. There wassa off-duty pope in Quick's las-nite. Knew 'bout-ju.

Hank

'Bout wat?

Papi

'Bout you. But wat's worse than a black cop? Nuthin—can't think a' wat's worse with this hangover but I'll cum-up with sump-in. Anyhow, he knows who-u are and says yo-hangin' with the wrong people, gettin' a bad rep. He know'ed 'bout-u hangin' 'round Quick's with Fo-Five an' Busta. I said he's right—they's bad people and I'd do my best ta-look out fo-u. I'm 'ficially lookin' out fo-yo ass, Sweetness. I'm yo personal cop.

Hank

Gawd help us. You a cop? You'd let ev'ryone go. It'd be chaos.

Papi

Nah, nah, nah. Jus' the ho's an' dope-dealers 'cause they's fillin' a nccd. But if you thieve—steal a' man's prop'ty—then boom I'd hang yo ass. Do a drive-by—boom—hang yo ass. Beat up yo baby mama—boom—hang yo ass. I'd be one mutha-fuckin, badass hangman. Then I'd do mo hangin'—hangin' with my homies like you to keep you outta trouble.

Hank

That's like havin' the devil look out fo-me. *'And lead us not into temptation, but deliver us from the evil one.'*

Papi

There now, u-got a wick'd talent for quotin' scrip-ture on my ass. Shame on you. You could co'rupt a saint. I use-ta-be innecent befo-u came along. Now I'm a sinner who's lost his way. But I'm gonna change all that. I've seen the light. I'm not gonna let sum sweet-talkin' bonus baby lead me inta damnation. I seen the light.

Hank

De-only light you've ev'r seen is the Bic in front of yo blunt. Speakin' a-which.

Papi

Tru-nuff, Sweetness. I'm gonna hook you up, jus-a-sec. But say, dawg, I gotta big score lined up fo' t'night. Some Yalies are in town an' they're lookin fo-sum buku buddha and I got 'em covered. I'm talkin' Yalies, homie. *Yalies!* With their Cosby haircuts and fat wallets. Ya-gotta come with me, homes. We'll have a good laugh.

Hank
Yo trippin', man. An' that wassa quick conversion from sinnerman to seein' the light an' back to sinnerman again.

Papi
It's my callin'. It's no sin to follow ur-callin'. Here's yo blunt, ur-highness. Jus' the way you like it.

(Enter Busta)

Busta
Wassup?

Hank
Yo, Busta. Wassup?

Busta
Hey, Sweetness. Wat's with ol' man Stallworth here. Hungova' huh? Wat up, Chief? Looks like u-sold yo soul las' night fo King Cobra an' a piece'a ass.

Hank
That's wat I told 'em. He gave da devil his due.

Papi
Keep the devil outta this. He's got e'nuff problems. We got'sa big score t'night. Tell 'em, Busta. Tell him to come with. He wone listen ta-me.

Busta
Mutha-fuckin' Yalies.

Papi
Tha's right. An' I'm thinkin' 'bout goin' gangsta on their asses. Scare 'em shitless. Take all their money and keep the buddha. It'll be dope, bro. Garren-teed killa' hoot. Tell 'em. Tell 'em to come with.

Busta
Come with.

Hank
Yo both trippin' No way. I ain't no dealer.

Papi
Show us some balls, Sweetness. Show us yor-a Prince... Wat? Hold on a sec.

Busta
Ansa' yo page, Chief. Let me talk to 'em.

Papi finally found the beeping pager in his coat pocket and read the number. He tied off the white bandana around his head that he normally wore when riding or doing business. It was white because white was a neutral color and he didn't want to incite any gangbangers to take a shot at him. He was fully dressed now in baggy pants that were bloused above gold high-tops, with a flowing shirt open at his neck to show off his bling, and a navy pea coat with a worn-out Chief Petty Officer insignia on the left sleeve. Among the many things he claimed to have been was a Chief Petty Officer in the U.S. Navy. Hank didn't believe it at first but others attested to it and passed on the many rumors that he'd been court-martialed for dealing dope, or had left for the good of the service after nailing the C.O.'s wife and bragging about it, or had deserted, gone AWOL, after receiving his orders to deploy overseas (and was still on the run). Only one of those was true. Nevertheless, that's why some called him

"Chief" which seemed to fit his blustering demeanor. All in all, his bark was worse than his bite.

After Papi disappeared back into the bar to find a phone, Busta took Hank into his confidence. They all planned to prank Chief Stallworth at the drug deal that night. First they were going to hide his Harley, then after the deal went down with the Yale students, they were going to jump him and take his money. "Jump him" meant jump out disguised in hoodies, brandish toy guns, and watch the fat man drop the money and run. It would take him awhile to find his Harley, enough time for them to get back to Quick's, and then they'd wait for him to show up and tell his story which promised to be hilarious.

Hank laughed just thinking about the story Papi would make up. He was only worried about one thing—Fo-Five. He knew that the old man never packed—maybe a knife but never a gun—but he knew Fo-Five packed for sure, that he wasn't quite right in the head, and that Fo-Five was going to be with Papi at the drug deal. Busta assured him that Fo-Five was in on the prank and planned to run off when they jumped out in their disguises. It was all good. Hank thought about it. It was down by the river at midnight so there was no conflict with his game. He couldn't pass up the fun. Soon enough he'd have to pass on the fun and get serious, but not yet. He was in.

"Where's my mutha-fuckin hawg!" hissed Papi. It was dark and Papi turned to the figure next to him. "I park'd it right here! Fo-Five, right here, right."

Fo-Five shrugged his shoulders. "I don' 'member. It's too dark."

"Son of 'a mutha-fuckin' bitch. Right here. It was right here!"

"Maybe fatha' down."

The big man stood silent for a moment and looked up at the stars. "Maybe," he said. "Com-on!"

Hank and Busta hid behind bushes nearby trying to stifle their laughter. So far everything had gone off without a hitch.

Busta had told Papi that he couldn't talk Hank into coming with. Busta also couldn't make it because he had to go bail his brother out of jail. That just left Papi and Fo-Five to do the deal. They followed Papi and Fo-Five in Busta's car and parked it up by the main road and snuck down towards the river in their black hooded sweatshirts. They came upon Papi's Harley and rolled it down the gravel road and hid it behind a dumpster next to a park station then ran back and hid behind some bushes. The deal was for fifty dubs of marijuana, which meant Papi would be carrying $1000 in cash.

Papi and Fo-Five approached them in the darkness and Hank took his toy gun out of his sweater pocket. It was a black BB gun that looked real enough. Busta took hold of his gun and they both jumped out of the bushes.

"Freeze, mutha-fuckas!" yelled Busta.

As planned, Fo-Five yelped and ran off into the darkness causing Papi to curse after him: "Wat the hell! Git back here, nigga! Coward!"

"Shut the fuck up, fatso! Give us the scratch now or-yo a dead man!"

Papi backed up and reached into his pea coat. They knew he didn't pack so Hank and Busta expected him to pull out the dough. Instead he pulled out a knife.

"Come get-it, sucka," said Papi, waving his knife.

"This is fo' real, ol' man!" shouted Busta as he turned his gun sideways and pointed it at Papi's chest. "I'll pop a cap in yo' fat ass. Now! Or I keel yo ass!"

The big man, who looked like a large goblin in the darkness, wavered slightly but held his ground. At that, Busta raised his piece and fired it into the sky. The loaded forty-five roared out in the night and Hank hit the ground. Papi threw down his knife, a purse of money, and ran towards the river. Busta tucked his gun away and grabbed the knife and purse.

"Com-on, Sweetness. Let's git outta here," he said grabbing Hank's arm.

"Wha the fuck!" cried Hank jumping up. "You said fake guns!" But he didn't wait for an answer as they were off running towards the car. Thoughts raced through Hank's head: He couldn't be caught. A shooting. A drug deal. He couldn't be caught. He'd lose everything.

He ran harder, cursing himself for his stupidity. They reached the car and jumped in where Fo-Five was waiting for them.

"Tha' was purfec', man. Purfec'," chirped Fo-Five. "Git the cash?"

"Got it all."

"Wha the fuck, Busta," said Hank. "You said fake guns."

"Chill out, Sweetness," replied Busta, putting the car in gear.

"The po-leece will be all ov'r this."

"Nah, stop worrin'. I know'd he wasn' gonna budge less'en I motivaded 'em. So I motivaded 'em."

"The po-leece will be all ov'r this."

"Ya said that. Chill out, Sweetness. It's all good."

"Yeah," added Fo-Five. "Chill out, nigga."

Hank looked at both them. They were smiling and their teeth gleamed white inside the darkness of the car. He sat back and rolled down the window to listen for sirens. There were none. They obeyed all traffic laws on the drive back, and by the time they rolled into Quick's parking lot Hank was feeling better.

They went around back and smoked a jay while they waited for Papi to show. Over a half hour later they heard his Harley coming up the street and Fo-Five hid behind some boxes. Another friend of theirs—LaRon, who was also in on the prank-- stood in the back doorway of the bar. Papi got off, flipped down his kickstand with a flourish, and eyed the three of them.

"The clap on o' cowards!" he bellowed. As his curse hung in the air, he demanded a drink and ordered La-Ron to get him one—a King Cobra, and ice cold. When La-Ron didn't jump, Papi turned his wrath on him yelling, "Don-jus stand there grinning like Unca' Reemus. Git me a drink, cuzz. Now!" La-Ron grudgingly disappeared back into the bar and Papi, satisfied that his orders were being carried out, repeated his curse on all the cowards of the world, adding, in a mock plea, that they put him in a rocking chair and leave him to die because there was no honesty left in the world.

"Wat up, Chief?" asked Hank innocently. "You look like a tub of melted butta. Wha' happened? How'd the deal go?"

Papi gathered up his immense girth, along with his outrage and victimhood, and vented his self-righteous frustration. He'd been "ganked"—ganked in his own hood. The world was a "mutha-fuckin' fuck'd up place" and he was the only honest man left in it. He stopped his rant briefly to accept a King Cobra from La-Ron, and took a swig before continuing. "Jus' let me grow old and die," he declared in his wounded pride, repeating his curse on the world and on all the cowards in it.

"Yo'all got jumped? Where's the money?" asked Hank.

"Gone, bro. Gone with the wind," he replied sorrowfully.

Busta wanted to know how many had jumped him and Papi told them "eight or mo' an' packin heat," but as the tale progressed the number grew from eight to ten or more. He'd gone after all of them with his knife, maybe killed a couple (he wasn't sure, he couldn't see in the dark), and had them on the run before they started shooting. "You must'a heard the shots?" he asked, showing them a hole in his coat as proof he'd been shot at. But the robbers had finally overcome him with sheer numbers and taken his knife and money.

"Yo lucky to be alive," said Hank, catching the eyes of those standing around Papi.

Papi agreed whole-heartedly and figured that the only reason they hadn't killed him—instead they had knocked him down and kicked him around like a laundry basket—was because they knew who he was "an' didn't want gangbangers comin' afta' them fo' revenge an' shit." His reputation had saved him.

"I never knew u-was such a badass, Chief," declared Hank. Both Busta and La-Ron agreed, stifling a laugh, and added that it was lucky for those fools that Papi hadn't been "packin' cause there would'a been a bloodbath." But where was Fo-Five, they all wanted to know.

At that question, Papi's pious outrage returned in full force. Fo-Five? That "jive-ass nigga" had lit out as soon as they got jumped. If he ever saw Fo-Five again he was "gonnna stomp his slip'ry Bendic' Arnald-ass into the ground." And with that threat he added his curse on all cowards of the world.

Busta wanted to know if Papi would tell that to Fo-Five's face. "Dat an' mo'," replied Papi, standing up to his full height. Busta was skeptical and kept it up, but each time Papi vowed he'd get justice out of Fo-Five. Finally Fo-Five, who didn't like being called a coward even if it was a game, popped out from behind the boxes.

"Callin' me a coward?" Fo-Five demanded to know.

"Where u-been, nigga? Hidin' in the alley?" shot back Papi.

"Callin me a coward?" repeated Fo-Five in a cold voice.

Hank could see the dead look in Fo-Five's eyes (the bro wasn't right in the head), and he put his hand on Fo-Five's shoulder and told him to "chill out." Fo-Five shrugged the hand off and continued to stare down Papi. But Papi knew better than anyone how to handle Fo-Five. He shrugged at Fo-Five's question and said, "Me? No. I ain't callin you no coward. Gawd strike me dead if I'm callin' you a coward. I jus wish I could run as-fast-as you."

Everyone laughed and Hank took the cue to step into the middle of the group and sum things up. "So let me recap this here," he said playfully. Papi had done his deal, got jumped by ten or was it twelve hoods, fought them all with his knife and maybe killed a couple, but got taken down and "ganked" of his knife and money. They'd left him alive only because they feared revenge from Papi's gang. Did he have that right?

"You'd make'a good weatha'man," agreed Papi.

Hank laughed out loud and called Papi "a lyin' sack of shit." That lie was as fat as Papi's ass, he announced, and with that he pulled Papi's knife out of his pocket and handed it to the dumbfounded fat man. "Here. I think you fo-got this!"

"Where'd you find that?" demanded Papi, but as he looked about at the other laughing faces he quickly began to catch on.

"Where-u left it," answered Hank, who was having his fun now. Here was the *real* story: The twelve hoods? That had been he and Busta. And what had Papi done? He'd lit out like a big fat scardy cat. "I didn't think yo fat-ass could run that fast. Surpris'd u-didn' jump in the river," laughed Hank.

Papi maintained his dignity and simply answered, "If-u haven't notic'd, I have a pro-pensity for sinkin'."

"Ha! So take-a deep breath, homie," said Hank. "Take-a chug a King Cobra an' come up with anotha' story an' it betta be good."

Papi appeared unfazed. The big man took a long drink of his King Cobra and laughed his own laugh. "I don't know wat you'all laughin' at. I'm a mutha-fuckin comedian an' I make others inta mutha-fuckin' comedians," he deadpanned. So, they wanted the straight dope? Sure, he'd tell them what happened. *He knew it had been them all along.*

He waited for the jeers to die down before he continued. Yeah, he knew it had been them all along. How could he not make out Sweetness and Busta in their hoodies, even in the dark? Of course he could, but he wasn't going to hurt the bonus baby, so he'd just played along and let them do their thing and made it look good. It was "the Gawd's honess truth." But what about the money, he wanted to know. Did Hank have it? Yes he did.

Papi

Ah, yo the man, Sweetness. I could kiss yo cheek for dat. Yo a Prince among Princes. Here, give-me five. Oh, wat a night. They should make-a movie outta it.

Hank
An' call it 'Runnin Away'.

Papi
Ah, no mo' a dat, Sweetness. Let's light up-a fat one an' have-a drink, an' one mo' time, bro, take it to the brink.

7
CHAPTER

The Kingsmen had dropped the first game in the three game set against the New Haven Admirals and Manager Shake Glover was annoyed by it. It was not that it was a loss—losses were a part of baseball—but it was how they lost. The score was 13 to 3, a blowout for sure, but it didn't turn into a blow-out until the top of the eighth. That was the first thing that irked him. The fact that it was against their rivals the Admirals and his personal adversary Bennie Jonson, who called a double steal in the top of the ninth with a ten run lead, also irked him. And the fact Hank Prince committed two critical errors in the eighth also added to his irksome mood.

The game was tied going into the eighth when their pitcher Luis Santiago, who had pitched well over seven innings, gave up two walks. Shake pulled him for a reliever who promptly walked the next hitter to load the bases. The following hitter popped up for one out, but the next Admiral hit a long fly ball to the warning track in center. Hank sprinted back and squared up for the catch but, almost as though he were showing off, tried a basket catch a la Willie Mays and dropped the ball. Two runs scored. Shake noticed a group of black fans in the bleachers, and one who was exceedingly fat with a white bandana, playfully dogging Hank after the error. The next hitter sent a rising liner to right center that was more right than center and clearly Manny Ortiz's ball, but for some reason Hank came streaking across at the last second, clipping kneecaps with Manny, and they both went down as the ball rolled to the wall for an inside-the-park homerun and 8-3 lead. The game pretty much unraveled from there.

It was a new day, and as Shake watched batting practice he kept his eye on Hank. Whether he was hitting, waiting to hit, or shagging flies, Shake studied his body language and demeanor. The kid was a growing concern. The day before he had arrived late to the clubhouse wearing sunglasses (a dead give-away) and had seemed a step slow all night. He didn't have evidence that Hank was breaking curfew and carousing all night. Not yet anyway. But that kind of stuff eventually revealed itself just like a leaky roof. He was under strict orders from the big club to play the kid every day so benching him was not an option. Fines were an option but it was too early in the season for that. So for now he watched and waited, giving the benefit of the doubt, and resisting the gnawing concern that:

> *The hope and expectation of thy time*
> *Is ruined, and the soul of every man*
> *Prophetically doth forethink thy fall.*

Shake walked back into the clubhouse and into the trainer's room. Usually the trainer's room was a zoo, especially deeper into the season, but Shake found the trainer Mike Faust by himself.

"Hey, Mike."

"Hey, Shake. What's up?"

"Has Prince been in here to see you?"

"Prince? No... well he came in yesterday to get a couple aspirins. I think he had a hangover."

"Nothing else? No pulled muscle or bad ankle?" he asked, but before getting an answer from Faust he added: "How'd he look when he came in for the aspirin? I mean, other than a hangover, how'd he look to you."

"Hungover," deadpanned Faust. "Not sure what you're looking for." He cleared his throat and looked away before adding, "Other than the hangover he looked fine."

Mike Faust was hired late last season as the trainer and Shake was still learning to read him. He wasn't sure he liked him or not, which didn't mean anything one way or another as long as Faust was good at his job, but he had a habit of clearing his throat and looking away whenever Shake asked him a probing question. He'd read somewhere that those were signs of lying. A couple times last year he had asked Faust about the severity of a player's injury only to get the clearing-of-the-throat with the look-away before getting a guarded answer. It was like he was hiding something. Maybe players were paying him off to lie, but Shake laughed at the thought. That sounded like one of Burton's conspiracy theories.

"Well, not sure either. If anything pops up on your radar let me know," said Shake. Faust assured him he would and Shake walked out the door and immediately ran into Speed. The clubbie held out three CD cassettes.

Shake
Yeah.

Speed
I got your seedy copulations.

Shake
All right. Thanks. Think they'll like it?"

Speed
Though I didn't get the clap from the copulations, I'm sure they'll clap for the copulations.

Shake
So you practiced safe sex?

Speed
There's nothing safe about sex.

Shake
How so?

Speed
It's all banging and screwing. And from there it gets even worse.

Shake
I hate to ask. Why's it get worse?

Speed
They get knocked up.

Shake
So they do. What's on the CDs?

Speed
We got a little Van Halen mixed in with Prince and Michael Jackson, some Willie Nelson for the rednecks, some Public Enemy and Run-D.M.C. for the brothers, Grupo Niche for the Dominicans, plus some other stuff they gave me. I even added in your Chairman of the Bored.

Shake
That's Chairman of the Board, smartass. Get thee to a punnery... I don't think they'll appreciate Sinatra on there. You're kidding, right?

Speed

Always and never. I did top it off with Klymaxx.

Shake

That's always a good way to top it off.

Speed

No. Stay with me. I'm talking about the song 'I Miss You' by Klymaxx.

Shake

I get it. Thanks, Speed. Go try 'em out.

Speed

I got a riddle for you first.

Shake

A riddle? Will this take long?

Speed

What does the Prince and Bob Marley have in common?

Shake

Prince the singer? No? Another Prince? What does he have in common with Bob Marely? Beats me.

Speed

Ganja, man.

And with that Speed was off, leaving Shake to piece together the clues. The guy reminded Shake of Radar O'Reilly from *MASH*. It wasn't so much they looked alike but that Speed always seemed to know what was going on in camp before anyone else. Prince—Bob Marley—Ganjaman. From experience, he knew it probably meant something but Speed had to play his games. He rolled it around in his head as he walked back to his office. Burton thought Speed was a fool but Shake knew better.

> *This fellow is wise enough to play the fool,*
> *And to do that well, craves a kind of wit.*

Game time rolled around and Shake stood in his dugout and watched his players. Some stretched, others laced up their shoes, while a few checked their bats, stuck chewing tobacco into their mouths or filled up their back pockets with seeds.

Shake took the line-up card out to home plate. Three umpires and Bennie Jonson awaited him. The night before, in the blow-out game, Jonson had called for a double steal with a ten run lead. It worked, leaving first base open, and Shake had quickly filled the vacancy by having his pitcher plunk the next batter. That emptied the benches and resulted in both teams getting a warning from the home plate umpire.

"Good even and twenty, gentlemen," said Shake merrily. "How fares thee, Bennie?"

"Is the warning still in effect for tonight's game," asked Bennie, ignoring Shake's greeting.

"Why should it be," replied Shake. "It's a new game, a new world."

"A fool may talk, but a wise man speaks."

"The more pity that fools may not speak wisely what wise men do foolishly," quoted Shake.

One of the umpires chuckled at this and Bennie reddened. "Is the warning still in effect?" he repeated. "I just want to know." He was rather stout with a rocky face that included a thick nose and curly brown hair.

"No," replied the head umpire Rob Goodfellow. "I would have told you, but if I see another beanball there will be warnings issued."

"That'll be too late. You saw what happened last night."

"Yeah, you saw what happened last night," added Shake. "Pitch gets away, accidently hits your guy and you lead the charge outta the dugout."

"You drink what you brew."

Shake quickly glanced at each umpire, and with a glint in his eye said, *"Why, sirs, for my part I say the gentleman had drunk himself out of his five senses."*

"And I'll knock you senseless," said Bennie taking a step towards Shake.

"These words will cost ten thousand lives this day."

Goodfellow raised his hand for silence and looked up into the sky as if to say *"Lord, what fools these mortals be."*

"Ok, enough," he scolded. "We're still in April and you're already going at it. You'll be worn out by September. Now give me your line-up cards and let's get this game started before I run you both just on principle."

On that note, line-up cards were exchanged and the meeting was adjourned. As Bennie walked away, Shake called after him. "Hey Bennie, good luck." Bennie grinned and winked back at him.

Everybody in the Eastern League knew the history between these two managers. They'd been teammates together in Triple-A—Jonson at short, Glover at second—and had led the league in double plays two years in a row. They hung out together, drank together, competed in everything, and were the best of buds during the season. Somewhere along the line there was a falling out, though the reason was unclear and even Rick Burton couldn't get the straight scoop out of Shake. It definitely wasn't over a woman as Shake had made a vow many years before never to let a woman get between friends. More likely the competitive nature of their friendship had burned out the ball bearings until there was nothing left but metal on metal.

And so they became rivals on the field and eventually across the diamond from each other. It was not a vicious rivalry, not even heated really, but it was deep-seated in the same way the rivalry between two politicians—one from the left, the other from the right—was deep-seated. They spoke well of the other in the press, each extolling the virtues of the other's managerial skills, and even on occasion had a beer together in The Mermaid, but when game time came they were Ali versus Frasier. Neither liked losing but they especially hated losing to each other.

Shake walked back to the dugout and watched three pregnant women throw out the first pitch. It was "Bellies and Baseball Night" and all pregnant women got in free and had their pick of exotic food (like anchovies and ice cream) at the "Cravings" booth. The players had fun with it and yelled out: "Don't break your water!" and "You know they found a cure for that!" and "You throw like it's a girl!" The pitches were thrown, the three women escorted off the field, and the P.A. announcer fired up "O Fortuna."

"Ladies and Gentlemen, the 1984 and 85 Eastern League Champs, here come your New Britain Kingsmen!"

Chuck Davis finished his warm-up pitches, the throw went down to second, and the Admirals lead-off man Hank Percy strode to the plate. Shake liked this kid. In many ways he was the mirror image of their own Hank. Both were five-tool players and centerfielders batting lead-off, but this Hank played with more fire and was even a bit of a hot-head. Hank Prince had yet to show that fire, and Shake caught himself wishing, with a little guilt, that their Hank was his Hank.

Percy beat out an infield hit, stole second and moved over to third on a ground-out to second. The next Admirals hitter lifted a medium fly ball to right and Percy tagged up and scored easily. At the end of the first half inning it was 1-0.

The Admirals pitcher was a new-comer that no one knew much about. Shake had read the scouting report but it was mostly based on spring training and had gaps in it. He had a good fastball and slider but there was no mention of other secondary pitches. They'd have to feel him out.

Shake watched Prince stroll to the batter's box and dig in. His routine (and everybody had a routine) was to stand outside the batter's box, swing three times, then straddle the outside line of the box while he twisted a hole in the dirt with his back toe. With the hole dug, he stepped fully into the box, rolled his head around, and then raised his bat up before settling it down on his back shoulder.

Hank was ready and popped up the first pitch to the shortstop. He touched first and veered off towards the dugout with his head down.

"What kind of stuff's he got?" asked Coach Burton. Hank ignored the question and sat down while a number of players nearby sniffed a laugh.

It stayed 1-0 until the bottom of the fifth when Estrella hit a two run homer. In the sixth, the Admirals got two on with no outs but Hamilton and Hoffman turned a nice 4-6-3 double play. With a man on third and two outs, Davis struck out the designated "beer batter" to the delight of the crowd. Before every home game, the P.A. Announcer revealed the "beer batter." It was a player on the other team, usually the seventh or eighth hitter, who triggered a half-off beer sale whenever he struck out. On strike three a louder than normal cheer would go up as a crowd of people, mostly men, jumped out of their seats and rushed to the nearest beer stand.

In the bottom of the eighth with one out and the score still 2-1, Prince lined a single to right. That brought Hoffman up who usually put the ball in play. Paranoid of the steal, the Admirals left-hander threw numerous times over to first to keep Prince close. On the fourth throw over, the crowd began to boo loudly. When the count got to two and one, Shake signaled for a hit and run. Prince did not break on the pitch but it didn't matter. The first baseman was holding Prince on, leaving a big hole on the right side, and Hoffman grounded the pitch through for a hit. Prince raced to third.

The next hitter Goff chopped a slow grounder to second. Prince broke for the plate. The Admirals second baseman was playing back for the double play but got caught between charging the slow grounder or waiting on it. The hesitation cost him as he was able to get the force at second but not the back end as Goff beat the throw to first. Prince scored and it was 3-1.

Shake liked 3-1. He had his ace reliever Cappadona warmed up in the bullpen for the top of the ninth. 3 to 1 felt warm, and when Burks hit a two run homer to make it 5-1 he felt even warmer.

Estrella settled into the box with two outs and none on. The first pitch buzzed the tower, a fastball high and in, and Estrella hit the ground. He popped back up and glared at the pitcher while both benches came up to the rail and screamed at one another.

"What the hell's that!" yelled Burton. "That's bush league, Bennie!"

"Never seen a fastball up and in before!" Bennie yelled back. "Gimme a break!"

"I'll give you a break! Bring it on!"

"You're talkin big. Anytime you like, Burton!"

"Hey, enough!" shouted the home plate umpire. Goodfellow took off his mask to better make his point. "The next idiot to make a sound is gone! Hear me? Gone! Now shut-up and play ball!"

"*With thy brawls thou hast disturbed our sport,*" quoted the P.A. Announcer as the song "We Are The World" started playing over the stadium speakers. Many of the fans who had been shouting angrily at the Admirals immediately recognized the song, laughed, and started singing along.

"That ape's in bad need of a facial," said Burton.

"You wouldn't be the first to break that nose," replied Shake.

'Hey, check out Percy," said Benedict.

Shake and the others looked out at Hank Percy. The Admirals centerfielder had run in to the dirt of the infield with his glove off ready for action. He looked around for any takers. Goodfellow noticed him and walked out in front of the plate and regarded him, with a tilt of the head, as one might regard a small delinquent on the playground. Bennie yelled at his centerfielder to get back into position. Percy backpedaled, pointing angrily at the Kingsmen dugout before reluctantly returning to centerfield.

"Hothead," commented Benedict.

"Didn't he get suspended last year for charging the mound against the Reds," asked Burton.

"Yep," replied Shake. "One game. Then he did it again a week later and got a three game suspension. *'He wears his wit in his belly, and his guts in his head.'*"

The next pitch to Estrella was outside and on a 2-0 pitch he flied deep to centerfield. Percy raced back to the warning track and made the catch, pumping his fist as he did so. That ended the inning but Cappadona set the Admirals down one-two-three in the ninth to seal the win.

Shake walked up the stairs at The Mermaid and tapped quickly five times on the door. Lucy let him in without a word, kissed him on the cheek, and handed him a pewter goblet of his favorite red wine. He took a sip and watched her walk over to her small bar. She wore a see-through black negligee that revealed a black thong and a batwing bikini bra. In the muted light, which was highlighted by ultraviolet lamps, her bare legs and arms had an almost translucent, lavender hue to them.

Not many fifty-year old women could pull that look off but she did and Shake admired her form. She was neither petite nor delicate but what he considered to be handsome. She was a handsome woman. He imagined what Sigourney Weaver would look like at fifty, only shorter and slightly broader in the beam, and that was Lucy. Shake followed her over to the bar where he turned her around and gave her a lusty kiss. She returned the kiss.

"*You are most hot and furious when you win,*" she said, quoting Shakespeare's *Coriolanus.*

Some men get turned on when women talk dirty to them but in Shake's case it was the Bard. If he was already in the mood, like now, a well-turned couplet or clever quote from the Bard put him over the edge. It was the struck match to his fuse; the spark to his powder keg. He hungrily kissed her neck and came up to her ear where he whispered, "*Let witchcraft join with beauty, lust with both.*"

"Lead on and do what thou darest," she whispered back, playfully biting his ear. They moved together towards the bedroom, almost stumbling a couple times, and within minutes were entangled in *the deed of darkness.*

We'll leave them there in private to enjoy their fun.

Afterwards, Lucy sat cross-legged on the bed with a pewter plate on her lap that contained cannabis. She was naked and Shake was in his boxers lying next to her watching her perform her little ritual. Everything she did, from cleaning herself to dressing to making breakfast in the morning, had a ritual to it that Shake found strangely calming. He figured it was all tied to her Wiccan thing. Lucy fashioned herself as Wiccan and called it "the Old Religion" which, she claimed, traced its origins back to the Stone Age. Her beliefs seemed genuine and she certainly dressed the part. In the evening she wore medieval dresses that were usually black and purple with long sleeves and a collared v-neck. This look was accented by her dark hair (now tinseled with silver) and dark eyes that led to her nickname "Dark Lucy." On top of that was the jewelry—rings, pendants, bracelets, ear rings, along with occasional choker and circlet—that all contained images of either a pentagram, crescent moon, or horns. In the daylight, though, her place was bathed in sunshine and she dressed in whites and blues and looked almost like a different person.

Larry Benedict introduced him to Lucy. Larry was dating the cocktail waitress Bernice at the time. She was Lucy Jourdain, proprietor of The Mermaid Tavern, and Shake found her eccentricities to be an entertaining diversion. They talked, and she seemed interested in him, and the more they talked the more Shake realized she had a gift for poetry and ritual. In short order their relationship became sexual, mostly due to her boldness, and they had enjoyed a free and easy carnal-fest ever since. She explained Wicca to him and even gave him a book to read but his Catholic sensibility, even tarnished as it was, found the whole thing to be no more than pagan witchcraft. But it was amusing and he didn't judge her for it. What he appreciated most about her, besides the fact that she was older, a handsome beauty, and sexually uninhibited, was the fact that she had no expectations of him. Their relationship was without one-upmanship or recriminations and could end tomorrow without any hurt feelings. It was almost like managing a perfect game.

As is the case with women, what Lucy saw in Shake was a little more nuanced and dwelled in her subconscious caldron of passions and desires. He was a man and she liked men, but he also had a poetic side. The beast and the poet—she had been married to men like that, had affairs with men like that, and that duality was rooted in her psyche like the tree of good and evil. It's what attracted her to Wicca with its Moon Goddess and Great Horned God. But there was something more to Shake than that. How else could she explain three years with him in an almost monogamous relationship? He was a leader of men. That was one thing. He possessed *grace and rude will* and understood that love and hate inhabit each human heart. That was a second thing. What she couldn't put her finger on was the third thing though she felt it nevertheless.

The third thing she couldn't put her finger on was something Keats called Negative Capability. It was the capacity to hold two contradictory ideas in your mind without trying to reconcile them, and it was a capacity possessed by all great artists. If Negative Capability had ever been explained to Dark Lucy she would have said "yes, that's it." Shake was familiar with the concept because he had studied Keats in college, but he would never have recognized the capacity in himself any more than an ace reliever would ever have recognized his unique ability to slow his heart down, yogi-like, in times of great stress.

Lucy finished her little sacrament and lit the rolled joint. She took a good hit and handed the joint to Shake. He was not a big toker, or even a big drinker for that matter, but on occasion he partook and it was usually with Lucy. He took a hit and handed it back to her as a thought came to him.

"Where do you get that stuff?" he asked.

"It's local," she replied as she exhaled another hit. She offered it again to Shake but he declined. "I get it from a guy over at Quick's Cocktail Lounge... the seedy part of town... He's the local connection."

"What's he look like?"

She laughed softly. "He's a big black guy... almost rotund... He's got this bushy beard and wears a white bandana... Looks like Blackbeard the Pirate... Rides a Harley. He's quite a character."

"Huh," said Shake as he rolled onto his back and looked up at the ceiling. It was decorated with stars and a crescent moon that glowed in the black light. He suddenly got Speed's riddle. "Ganjaman" was really "ganja, man," Bob Marley's smoke, and "Prince" was Hank. Shit, he thought, so that was it, but he wasn't going to worry about it now. For now he had Dark Lucy next to him; a cup he would fill once more to the brim.

8
CHAPTER

If you're going to be lucky you've got to think lucky.
Luke Appling

Sunday was a day game and the rubber match against the Admirals. Rain was expected—heavy rain—and everyone including Shake expected the game to get called before the end of the fifth. But sometimes luck or the baseball gods have a different outcome in mind.

Game time was 1:05 and the storm was forecasted to hit around 2:00 and rain steady and hard for the rest of the day. It was Little League Day, which made the crowd bigger than expected given the weather forecast. The Little Leaguers were paraded onto the field before the game to the delight of their parents then unceremoniously hustled off by the umpires who wanted to start the game early. Despite their efforts, first pitch was at 1:03.

After three quick innings it was scoreless and Shake stepped out of the dugout and looked north. On the outskirts of the city a black ceiling of rain clouds creeped ominously towards the ballpark. He figured they had about twenty minutes if they were lucky. Andy Ellsworth pitched a scoreless top of the fourth and the Kingsmen came into hit with the black ceiling nearly upon them.

The lights came on as Gary Hoffman settled into the batter's box. On a 3-1 pitch he lined a single to left. Calculating time and distance the way a NASCAR driver calculates speed and position before making his move, Shake figured his window of opportunity and went for it. Goff was due up followed by Burks, and Burks was hot right now. He gave Goff the bunt sign and Hoffman broke for second on the pitch. As luck would have it, Goff missed the pitch and the catcher air-mailed the throw to second into centerfield. Hoffman popped up and easily took third.

Shake was curious to see what Jonson would do next—play this like a normal fifth inning or play it like the ninth given the impending storm. The Admirals decided to play the infield back and pitch to Goff. Shake smiled to himself but quickly started worrying again once Goff tapped back to the pitcher, freezing the runner at third, and they walked Burks to set up the double play. That brought up Estrella the catcher, who didn't particularly run very fast. But Jonson's gambit back-fired when Estrella hit a long sac fly to center to score Hoffman. That made it 1-0 with two outs.

As their first baseman Matt Horn strode to the plate, Shake took another look out at the approaching storm. The black ceiling, which was now a black wall, was into the parking lot but oddly enough seemed to hesitate there like a monster that had decided to catch its breath before creeping up any further. Just maybe, thought Shake. Just maybe. On a whim he took a bat out of the bat rack and stepped out of the dugout where he raised the bat like a large wand and pointed it at the storm. He traced a figure eight in the air, performing his incantation, and replaced the bat back in the rack.

"I hate to say it," said Burton, smiling at Shake's antics, "but we could use a quick out here."

Shake was thinking the same thing but didn't reply. The Admirals pitching coach came out to the mound and after a minute and a half was still there. "Come on, Blue!" yelled Shake to the home plate umpire. "This ain't *War and Peace*!"

The umpire went out and broke up the confab but the pitching coach walked back to the Admirals dugout about as slow as a man could walk. This time it was Benedict: "Move it, Callahan! Pretend it's chicken dinner and move that fat ass!"

Everyone waited as Callahan eased himself into the dugout. Jonson was stalling for time, hoping that the rain would wipe out New Britain's one run lead. Shake knew what was next. After the first pitch—high and outside that Horn swung at for a strike—the Admirals catcher took his mask off and walked slowly out to the mound.

"Shit, here we go," sighed Burton. Other players on the Kingsmen bench yelled out at the catcher—"Get his number and call him later" and "Really? Really? Why don't you just crawl on all fours"—but this time the umpire was on it and followed the catcher out to the mound to quickly break it up. The pitcher shook off ten signs before delivering a pitch in the dirt that Horn swung at for strike two. The Admirals catcher took his mask off again and walked out to the pitcher's mound. A funked-up version of "Your Cheatin' Heart," sung by James Brown, started up over the P.A. system.

"They're stalling for time!" cried Burton. Of course everyone knew that, but now the crowd was into it and started booing the catcher. The ump swiftly broke it up. The pitcher stared into his catcher and shook off one sign after another. The catcher called time and took off his mask but the umpire said something in his ear that caused him to glance over at Jonson, put his mask on, and squat back down.

"This ain't no gameshow!" yelled Jonson. "There's no buzzer. He's gotta a right to talk to his catcher!" The home plate umpire ignored him and signaled the pitcher to make his pitch.

Shake chuckled to himself and thought about Bennie's predicament. If it was him, he would have picked this moment to bring in a relief pitcher to stall for time but Bennie had no one warming up in the bullpen. Too bad. He watched as the next pitch finally came in, this time right over the plate, and Horn swung and missed for strike three. The crowd cheered.

"Tally ho, go, go, go!" shouted Shake at his bench as his players leaped up and ran out to their positions. He looked back out at the storm. Still, inexplicably, it sat motionless above the bleachers, perched like Godzilla ready to strike. He fully expected the Admirals hitters to crawl to the batter's box, take a lot of pitches, step out on every pitch to re-adjust their batting gloves and play rope-a-dope until the rains came.

But the home plate ump would have none of it. He hustled the first hitter into the batter's box and when the hitter attempted to step out again on a 1-1 pitch, he gave the pitcher the signal to throw causing the hitter to jump back into the box. It was a called strike two. There were howls of indignation from the Admirals bench. "I love this guy," said Burton, echoing Shake's very sentiments about the umpire.

On a full count, the hitter took strike three for the first out. The next batter took two strikes but swung at the next pitch, fouling it off his foot. He hopped out of the box in obvious pain. Catcalls came from the Kingsmen bench ("Toe jam!" Call a toe truck!") as he limped around, trying to shake it off. He glanced into his dugout and suddenly went down on one knee. Jonson and the trainer came out to look at him as boos rained down from the stands. "Kearny is down on one knee," commented the P.A. Announcer, "and here comes the Admirals manager and trainer... Pay no attention to that man behind the curtain." And on that note "The Great Pretender" by the Platters played over the loudspeakers.

Shake watched as the next five minutes played out in a comic pantomime. The umpire wasn't buying any of it which lead, inevitably, to an argument and Jonson getting tossed from the game. As Bennie exited the field he looked up at the storm and gestured angrily at it as if to say "Whaddya got against me?"

The batter limped back into the box, milking it for all it was worth, and watched the next pitch sail over for strike three. The next hitter didn't wait around and popped the first pitch sky-high in the infield. As the ball landed into Hamilton's glove for the third out the heaven's opened up and the deluge began. The crowd cheered as they scrambled for the exits. The umpires quickly convened and halted the game. Doug the groundskeeper and his assistant Barry appeared in rain gear, and with the help of some of the players began rolling out the tarp. The P.A. Announcer cleared his throat and said:

> *The quality of mercy is not strained,*
> *It droppeth as gentle rain from heaven*

Shake laughed and waved up to the announcer's booth as the song "Love, Reign o'er Me" by The Who blasted out over the loudspeakers. He knew that the rain delay was only a formality. In an hour they'd call it, and with five innings on the books it was an official game and a win for the Kingsmen.

Shake sat in his office with Burton and Kalecki shooting the bull and waiting on official word from the umps. Doug and Barry came by in their muddy boots to give them a situational report.

"What's the word?" asked Burton.

"Doesn't look good," answered Doug. "Raining cats and hogs. The tarp's been appealed but the rest of the field is getting drenched, plus it's wet. The umps are gonna call it, I'm sorely certain."

"Cats and hogs, huh?" said Kalecki with a wink at Shake.

"Buckets," added Doug.

"Buckets," agreed Barry.

Shake had never heard Barry speak before. "Wow, sounds like a whopper," he said. "Looks like you got your work cut out for you tomorrow getting the field ready. But couldn't be in better hands. You guys do great work. Thanks."

"Your pleasure," replied Doug with a grin, nudging his partner. "Condiments are always welcome. Hopefully tonight we'll get good drainature and tomorrow we'll put the absorbine down and rake away the potty spots. We got big squeegees if need be and we can sqounge the outfield grass to get the standup water. We'll have her ready for you, boss, come rain or shine but hopefully shine."

"I'm sure you will. Thanks for the report."

Doug and Barry nodded in appreciation and tramped off down the hall. Shake gave Burton and Kalecki a "such-is-life" shrug and they shrugged back. "I just hope they sqounge out those hogs," added Burton.

Ten minutes later word came that the game was called at four and a half innings. Kingsmen one, Admirals nothing. Speed appeared at the door with a note in his hand.

Shake
What you got?

Speed
A note.

Shake
What kind of note?

Speed
What kind would you like? C sharp or a D flat? If you're a person of note I can give it to you a cappella.

Shake
Just give me the straight do-re-mi.

Speed
Suit yourself
(Hands him the note.)

Burton
What's it say?

Shake
It's from Bennie… It says 'Lucky bastard'… Here, take this back to him.

(He writes on the back and hands it to Speed.)

Speed
'It takes one to know one'. Hmph, what's that mean, you're both bastards? Brotherly bastards? The Battered Bastards of Bastogne? In your case—let's see, you both played for the Birmingham A's, right—'The Battling Bastards of Birmingham'.

Burton
Clever. Don't you have laundry to do?

Speed
I do and my first load is your dirty mind.

Burton
Good luck with that.

Speed
I'll need extra strength Cheer.

Burton
Out!

Speed

Fare thee well, gentlemen. I'll deliver your D flat to Bennie and the Jets... Yo, Junior, find the Ultra Cheer.

Shake stood up and playfully drummed his chest. He was feeling good about the universe. (*One touch of nature makes the whole world kin.*) "Let's get the troops going on their indoor drills or let them go to the gym," he said. His post-game report to the big club was going to be a short one and he wasn't sure how he was going to explain the benevolence of the baseball gods. "Meet you over at The Mermaid at, what, five? First pitcher's on me."

"Works for me."

"Sounds good."

"Which reminds me," Shake added, looking at Burton. "Did you talk to Hamilton about listening to his radio in the dugout?"

"Yeah. Didn't know Ivy Leaguers could be such knuckleheads."

"What's he listening to? Mozart?"

"No, talk radio I think. Anyhow, I told him to cut it out."

Shake nodded and sat back down at this desk to start on his game report. His coaches left to motivate the troops. Pitchers with off days would toss underneath the stands; those who wanted could hit off a tee and take instruction from Larkin or Kalecki; the rest would head to the local gym to run through their customized work-outs. It was their job, even on rainy days.

The local press popped in to get a few quotes. Orson was with them. Shake had noticed that young Kent was taking a keen interest in the fledgling career of the journalist student—what was his name? Balt. Anyhow, Shake gave them their quotes and finally finished up around four-thirty and headed out to the parking lot under his umbrella. He stopped when he noticed a bunch of people gathered around one of the refreshment stands that sat underneath the bleachers. Curious, he walked closer and saw Rex who beckoned him over. Rex had opened up one of the taps and was giving out free beer to his employees.

Rex handed him a freshly poured cup of beer as he walked up. He raised it in thanks and looked around at the others. They consisted of concessionaires, parking lot attendants, ticket-takers, and general gofers, all of them young, underpaid, but happy with their job and even happier to be getting free beer from the boss.

"Here's to the rain," toasted Shake.

"To the rain," they all echoed back cheerfully. Shake took a sip and looked at Rex. The old man looked downright chipper. But it was unusual for him to open the beer tap like this. He did it once or twice in a season and never this early in the year. He must be feeling lonely, concluded Shake, and as that thought settled in he noticed that everyone was looking at him in anticipation. Of course, a quote. It was expected, like Chardonnay samples from a winemaker.

> *I would I were in an alehouse in London!*
> *I would give all my fame for a pot of ale, and*
> *safety.*

They laughed and cheered his quote and Shake smiled in return and looked back to Rex. "What's the occasion?" he asked.

"None. Felt like it," he replied, then thought about it some more. "Didn't feel like going home. Plus it's nice and cozy down here."

Shake had to admit it was nice and cozy under the bleachers and out of the rain. Up above them the rain pelted the aluminum benches and made it sound like heavy applause. "And the beer makes it even cozier," he said with a smile. He paused a moment before deciding to jump into it. "I saw Corey the other day."

Rex's brow darkened and he walked a few steps off. Shake followed him.

"She looked good—a little skinny—but she looked good. She asked how you were doing."

Rex stared down into his beer without responding. Shake wondered if he should push it. The old man was touchy at times, even volatile, and one had to tread lightly. Baseball trivia worked to break through or sometimes a common cause. In this case he'd try Ronald Reagan.

"I told her you were still everyone's favorite S.O.B." He noticed Rex crack a grin at that so he pressed his advantage. "But what do I know about daughters, right? God spare me from daughters. Look at Reagan. What's his daughter's name, the one who took her mother's name—Patti Davis. She just published another book trashing her dad. Makes him out to be a terrible dad. You'd think he'd disown her but, no, he still loves her and she's still welcome in the house. But it must be tough on him."

"Yeah, must be."

"Maybe it's Nancy. Maybe she keeps it all together."

"Maybe... Moms are good for that," said Rex, his voice trailing off. And with that, he poured his beer onto the ground and shifted suddenly into boss mode. "That's it. Drink up, let's go," he barked at his young employees. "We got work to do. We got a game tomorrow."

The employees jumped up as though jolted by an electric shock. Some downed what was left of their beer while others followed their boss's lead and poured it out, many of them glancing accusingly at Shake at the sudden turn of events. Shake felt momentarily like a villain—one minute they were all enjoying a fresh brewski under the stands, nice and cozy, and then he comes along and it's back to work.

"I know what you're trying to do," said Rex locking eyes with Shake. "I get it. But it's best to stay out of my private affairs. We all have our problems. Don't we? I have problems with my daughters and you're pushing fifty with no wife and no kids. We all have our fatal flaws. Don't we, Glover? So don't try to fix mine and I won't try to fix yours."

Shake wilted a bit under the millionaire's hot stare and staccato delivery. The old man had mastered his technique and knew how to effectively put an underling in his place. But this wasn't the first time that Shake had been dressed down by some bigwig owner and he quickly regained his composure. "*Do, kill thy physician, and the fee bestow upon thy foul disease.*" he replied evenly. "Thanks for the beer."

On his drive over to The Mermaid Tavern, Shake replayed his talk with Rex in his head. It was unfortunate. Usually the round-a-bout way worked with Rex but not this time. With the rain-shortened win he'd been feeling rather pleased with himself but this whole Rex encounter put a damper on it. It was like going 3 for 3 only to strike out in the ninth with the winning run on base. And what was with this whole "fatal flaw" thing? Yeah, he was pushing fifty. No wife. No kids. That was not a fatal flaw; that was a conscious choice. Where'd Rex get off calling his life choices a fatal flaw? But the more he thought about it the damper his mood got.

His mood lightened once he stepped into The Mermaid. Burton, Benedict, Larkin and Kalecki were sitting at the back table. A small cheer went up from the Kingsmen fans who hung out in the tavern. Don the bartender waved at him and Lucy, who stood next to the till counting out twenties, smiled at him. Shake immediately forgot about the whole Rex thing. It was like coming home and stepping off the bus after a long grueling road trip.

When he came up to the table, Larry and Bernie were already going at it.

Larry
Shake, thank god you're here. Save me from this harpy. She's trying to tell me that we're bachelors—you and me—because no decent woman will have us.

Bernie
I didn't say Shake—I said just you.

Larry
'Just me'. Hmm, you still got a thing for me, don't you?

Bernie
You're like the clap. Easy to catch and hard to get rid of.

Larry
You'd know about that better than me. But why suffer; they have pills for that.

Bernie:
What? Valium, Zoloft, Prozac? I've tried them all and you're still here. And my point was this—Shake, don't listen to him—my point was this: you're still a bachelor because no woman in her right mind would have you.

Larry
Then thank god for right-mindedness. Hallelujah for it. Ever seen a bull with a ring through its nose? That's a wedding ring. Not for me. No, no, sweetheart, not for me. That's your dream.

Bernie
You got it wrong, Mr. Benedict. I've got the same opinion of marriage you do. I'd rather hear a dog bark than hear a man say he loves me.

Larry
Well, if a man *did* say he loved you, he'd be barking up the wrong tree. But, hey, stay that way. If you did get married you'd just end up scratching his face.

Bernie
In your case it'd improve your looks.

Larry
Listen to you. If I had a car as fast as your mouth I'd win the Indy 500.

Claiming victory, Bernie laughed and walked off. Shake settled into his chair and poured himself a glass of beer. Larry watched his adversary walk away with a sly grin on his face. Rick leaned back and chuckled while Bob took his hat off, rubbed his head, and looked at the three of them.

"Never seen anything like that," said Bob. Obviously he'd been waiting to get something off his chest. "Have you?" he asked them. "That storm just sat there like it was waiting on us. Weird. And if Goff doesn't miss that bunt we probably end up zero-zero."

"Yeah," replied Teddy. "He gets the bunt down and it's one out with a man on second. They walk Burks to set up a double play and probably get out of the inning."

"Don't forget Estrella's blast to center," added Rick. "Hoffman tags and goes to third, Burks with his speed takes second. Now you have two outs but two men in scoring position. Who knows what happens then."

"Estrella doesn't hit that ball to the track," said Shake. "You can't say that."

"Oh, here we go again," laughed Rick. He was referring to the ongoing debate he and Shake had about chance and fate in baseball. Shake called it the "Ron White Fallacy" which referred to a player and a game they had managed together back in Bristol. In that game, their player was called out on an attempted steal of second even though it was obvious to everyone he was safe. The next hitter Ron White singled to right. It was Rick's argument that if the runner had been called safe, White, who was destined to get a hit, would have singled him home to win the game. Shake disagreed. If the runner had been called safe at second, everything would have changed—strategy, pitch selection, positioning—and that would have made White's single less probable.

"I'm just saying," countered Shake. "Everything changes and nothing stands still. Jose doesn't get the same exact pitch there with a man on first and second and maybe he hits it out or grounds out or misses it. 'You can't step twice into the same river.'"

"Is that Shakespeare?"

"No, some old Greek guy named Heraclitus."

"But that was weird, right," insisted Bob. "How does that storm just sit there and wait until we complete an official game?"

"The baseball gods," said Rick.

Each man nodded solemnly. They each knew about the baseball gods and fervently believed in them in the same way test pilots believed in gremlins. They explained the unexplainable. And they had learned at an early age, even back in little league, how to appeal to those baseball gods. Outsiders called it superstition but any ballplayer worth his OBP knew better. You didn't step on the foul line because the baseball gods didn't appreciate perfectly-drawn fouls lines stepped on. You didn't mention a no-hitter because the baseball gods were just waiting for some nitwit to mention it so they could thwart it. Out of spite. It was the reason why, during a hot streak, you sat in the same place, ate the same food, and wore the same underwear. It was the reason why Wade Boggs ate chicken and Richie Ashburn slept with his bat. It was to appease the baseball gods.

Rick's statement about the baseball gods had attracted Lucy's attention and she came over and sat down with them. She didn't normally sit down with Shake and his pals, or with any of her patrons for that matter, unless it was for something that caught her fancy. The baseball gods caught her fancy. She knew about them because Shake, a little stoned one time, somberly told her about them. He cited game six of last year's World Series as proof of their existence. Denkinger blows a call at first and the Cardinals unravel, losing a game and a series they should have won. Lucy didn't need convincing since she lived in a world where unseen forces were constantly manifesting themselves. He also told her about curses, and she had looked into the matter herself to confirm that there were three active curses in baseball: Boston, Chicago and San Diego. The Red Sox and Cubs knew they were cursed. The Padres didn't.

"What's this about the baseball gods," she asked, settling down next to Shake. She wore a white and lavender dress with a v-neck that showed off the ornate pentagram that hung from her neck.

Shake explained what had happened during the game, highlighting the strange behavior of the storm. When he was done, she rested her hands on the table and smiled knowingly at the five of them.

"It makes perfect sense," she said. "There's a lot going on today and you just need to be attuned to it. For one"—and here she patted Shake's hand—"Taurus is ascending. It's also the Waxing Half Moon which is a time when energies are most conducive to action. It's a good time for magic, for things outside you, which is why that storm stayed back."

"Good magic for us, bad magic for Bennie," laughed Bob.

"There's someone you could put a curse on," said Larry. "Have you ever put a curse on someone?"

Lucy stared at Larry, considering his question. She finally answered: "Yes, when I was younger… My last one was on Richard Nixon… But no more. It's negative energy."

"Well anyhow, here's to the baseball gods," said Bob hoisting his glass.

"One word of advice," warned Lucy, her eyes taking them in one by one. "Don't talk too much about them… lest you want their attention."

Each in his thoughts sipped slow and took heed, at Lucy's warning and her witches' creed.

9
CHAPTER

But for my sport and profit
Othello

Monday started a three game set against the Waterbury Indians. Game time was 7:05pm. Leading up to first pitch were the typical rhythms and movement of an awakening ballpark. The parking lot opened at 3:30 and the ticket windows at 5:00. Galahad the mascot usually wandered into the stands around 6:45 and started doing his shtick and taking pictures with kids. The umpires and managers met at home plate at 6:55 and the National Anthem played at 7:00. Unless of course it rained, then all bets were off. It was Rex's job to call the game ("bang it") on account of rain before the umpires and managers met. After that it was the umps' call.

Wrapped around this timeframe was Shake's schedule. For night games, he was usually up by 8:00 in the morning and put on his gym clothes. After pouring his morning jo and grabbing a bran muffin, he jumped in his car to drive over to Gold's Gym for a work-out. Shake spent a half hour on weights then finished with a strenuous forty-five minute work-out on the treadmill where he read the sporting section of the *Herald* and scoured over the box scores. After a shower and shave, he changed into street clothes and usually ran errands—the store, the bank— before ending up in his office at Beehive Stadium around noon where he finished up paperwork then suited up at 1:30. He met with the players and personnel he needed to meet with, often times talking to the Director of Player Development on the phone, then headed out to batting practice at 4:15.

Batting and infield practice were routines that ran like clockwork and Shake watched and listened. Occasionally he offered a tidbit of advice but for the most part he let his coaching staff run the show. Monday was no different. The field had dried out nicely over the day and the groundskeepers had done a great job in getting the field ready for tonight's game. Shake walked around like a home inspector looking for puddles or soft spots but didn't find any. A loud whack of the bat caught his attention and he watched a ball sail high over the left field fence. Estrella was in the batting cage, and hitting coaches Larkin and Kalecki stood nearby admiring his swing. Shake walked over to them.

"Three hours a day," he heard Bob say.

"I heard it was six hours a day, seven days a week," replied Teddy.

"What's that?" asked Shake.

"Jose's work-out regimen in the off-season," answered Teddy. "I heard it was six hours a day."

"That's a lot a time in the gym," said Shake. "But it sure paid off." They all watched as Estrella crushed another pitch over the centerfield wall.

"He may end up in Phoenix before the all-star break."

"I talked to Lefebvre the other day. They're already carrying three catchers but he's definitely got their attention." Shake's voice trailed off as he watched another soaring drive.

"Hey, Larry!" yelled Kalecki out to Benedict who was throwing batting practice. "Give him a breaking ball!"

Larry raised the ball in his pitching hand to acknowledge Kalecki and threw Jose a lollipop curve. Jose tattooed it high over the left field wall and up into the bleachers. Players around the cage playfully oohed and aahed. "Check that bat," said one. "The ball's juiced," said another.

"Something's juiced and it ain't the ball," whispered Greg Rosecrans into Dane's ear. They were in the second group waiting to hit and stood off from the rest.

"What makes you so sure?" asked Dane, keeping his voice down. "He's got all those supplements in his locker. It could be protein shakes and hard work."

"That's just for show."

"What makes you so sure?"

"He told me."

"He told you he was taking Deca?"

"In so many words... There's a least five other guys on it."

"Bullshit. Who?"

"I can't say but trust me."

"Where they get it?"

Greg leaned in closer to Dane's ear. "I'll tell you but you can't tell anyone else."

"I'm not going to tell anyone."

"Promise."

"Promise."

Greg looked around to make sure no one was within earshot then leaned back into Dane's ear. "Faust," he whispered.

"The trainer. Bullshit?"

"I'm tellin' you."

Yeah, you're telling me, thought Dane. He shook his head in mild disgust (because that's all he could muster) and watched as Estrella walked out of the batting cage. The guy was ripped. He had all the tell-tale signs of Deca use—at least what Dane had read up on—including dramatic muscle growth, bulging veins and acne across his chest and back. If it wasn't Deca then something else rotten was going on. But why was he surprised about that. Man was a piece of work and capable of just about anything. He wasn't buying the "five other guys" or the whole

Faust connection. That sounded like someone trying to talk themselves into a thing and Greg was definitely working hard at talking himself into taking Deca. He was just tired of Greg trying to make him his co-conspirator. He could come straight out and tell him it was a bad idea but what good would it do? Greg was past that point—there was nothing either good or bad with him that thinking couldn't make it so.

Their group was coming up to hit and Dane flipped his bat onto his shoulder and rested it there. He'd made a decision. "Stop talking to me about it, dude," he said to Greg. "Do what you want but keep me out of it."

"Okay, I just thought you'd find it interesting."

Dane ignored him and stepped into the batting cage. Shake had told him that the big club wanted to see him get some time in at the two spot in the batting order. See how he handled the bat with men on base. He meant to work on his bunting and on taking pitches to the right side. That was first on his agenda. Everything else was background noise.

During batting practice the pitchers stood around in the outfield shagging flies. They were usually in groups of two or three and one of those groups consisted of Chuck Davis, Phil Cappadona and Luis Santiago. Phil and Luis were talking together when Chuck, catching a fly ball in front of them, sauntered over and joined them.

"Is the bet still on," he asked hoping the answer was "no."

"No one's backing out," said Phil.

"It's only April, amigos," replied Luis with a confident smile. "I have till the All-Star break. I need time to work. An artist needs time."

"I see you and Basset are becoming fast friends."

"That we are."

"You forgot he's a born-again Christian, which means his girlfriend is too and probably a virgin."

"Oh, she is," assured Luis. "So is he. They don't plan on having sex until they're married."

"Is that why you joined his prayer group? He'll see right through you"

"You think so? I'm a Catholic, born and raised. Baptized, confirmed, the whole nine yards. He's got no clue." Luis took out the crucifix he wore around his neck and showed it to them to emphasize his point.

"Perfect," sighed Chuck. "You're gonna piss off Basset and piss off God all in one shot."

"Not so. God doesn't care if I take Gwen's virginity. It's not like they're married. God doesn't care if I get her first or Basset. It's all the same to Him. And what's the big thing about virginity, anyhow. You can't say it's a good thing or else you'd be insulting your mother. It goes against nature. It's completely unnatural to preserve virginity; if we did it'd be the end of mankind. Virginity is a murderer. Plus I never met a virgin who couldn't wait to be a non-virgin. The whole virgin thing is out of fashion and they know it. They can't wait to get in fashion."

"I see you've made a study of it."

"What's your plan? You got a plan, right?"

"Of course I've got a plan, but I'm not going to tell you two. You'll try and sabotage it. But I got a plan. A flawless plan. For one thing, she comes to all his weekend home games, whether he pitches or not. She sits right up there."

"What good's that do you?"

"When I chart pitches on my off day I'll have her all to myself."

"Since when do you chart pitches on your off day."

"Never too late to start."

Both Chuck and Phil laughed. Luis was notorious for paying off rookie pitchers to chart pitches for him on his off-day. Now his plan was to chart his own pitches and work his magic on Gwen. It had a certain flair to it.

They stopped talking and tracked the flight of a fly ball that was heading straight for them. None of them moved or raised their glove. Suddenly Steve Basset streaked in front of them and caught the ball before it hit one of them.

"Hey, wake up, you guys!" he yelled back at them with a friendly grin.

In Shake's office, with the door closed, Balt Porter was interviewing Orson Kent. Orson had set it up with Balt beforehand and gotten permission from Shake to use his office during batting practice. Here they could be alone. They were fifteen minutes into the interview and Balt had asked a lot of questions about the financial side of baseball. Orson answered each one carefully and professionally, though he couldn't help admiring the part in Balt's thick brown hair. It was on the right side instead of the left.

"Your father is majority owner but there are other owners," prefaced Balt, "but here Rex Lyon is the single owner. Is that common in the minors?"

"Not so much anymore," Orson answered. "Consortiums are the growing model for minor league ownership. Even here there's New Britain Professional Baseball Incorporated. Rex is president but there are shareholders." Orson went on to explain that even though NBPB Inc. had shareholders they weren't really co-owners and Rex still ran the show financially.

"I heard a rumor that the Lyons were looking to sell the club."

Even though Orson wanted to impress Balt in the worse way with his knowledge about baseball operations, a warning light went off in his head. He needed to be careful here. "That's just a rumor," he said. "I work with Rex on a daily basis and he's never mentioned any such thing. As an affiliate, he'd have to tell my dad if he was shopping the club and my dad's said nothing about it."

"No truth to the rumor then?"

"None that I know of."

Balt reached for his can of cherry cola and took a drink. Orson watched in delight as Balt's Adam's apple slid up and down. He wanted desperately to change the subject, to get onto a topic that would lower Balt's guard, but so far he'd been unsuccessful. Balt set his soda can down but kept his hand on it, and Orson admired his short and beautifully manicured fingernails.

"You get manicures?" he asked nonchalantly. "Some of my frat brothers got manicures and swore by them, but I never got one."

"Oh, yeah I do. My sister turned me on to them."

"How about a pedicure? I got one once on a dare and kind'a liked it. It was from a guy—in the shop—not a gal but a guy. That was a little weird but it felt great. Sensuous is the word, or is it sensual, I can never remember."

"Sensuous, I think. Sensual has a more erotic connotation."

"Then it was sensual, for sure. The way he worked my foot was definitely erotic—least it felt erotic.

Balt laughed lightly. "I'll have to try one," he said

"But from a man," Orson added quickly. "I think that made all the difference... Bigger hands—that's the key."

"Bigger hands," repeated Balt laughing again. Orson hoped he'd follow his lead, maybe even get the jest of it, but Balt to his disappointment changed the subject.

"What's Lyon clear in a year? He's got the best attendance in the league, so it's got to be above average. What, a couple million?"

Orson was growing impatient with this interview. He had hoped for an opening, a chance to make his intentions known, to find out if Balt leaned the same way, to tell Balt he loved him and have him say it back, but every time he rattled the door knob he found it locked.

"Is it a million?"

"No, not that much," he answered blandly. "You can ask Rex for sure but I'm not sure he'd tell you. It's less than a mil. Minor league owners aren't in it for the money—or at least to become rich. There are better ways to get rich. Most get into it because they love baseball."

"You love baseball?"

"I love one thing... I love it enough to..." But Orson, so close to saying it, stepped back from the cliff, afraid of being wrong, afraid of the consequences of being wrong.

"Enough to what?"

"Nothing," he said in a deflated voice. "Nothing."

Balt studied him for a moment with those soft brown eyes. Orson even imagined for a moment that he caught a wave of warmth pass over those brown eyes. But like everything else he wasn't sure. It was maddening.

Balt asked him a few more questions then wrapped it up and thanked him for his time. It was an opportunity squandered, thought Orson disgusted with himself. As he watched Balt turn off his recorder and put his stuff away he noticed a button on Balt's satchel that said "LPGA." He beat back his self-disgust and tried again.

"You cover the LPGA?"

"I did. I covered the Open last year in Springfield for my college paper."

"If I remember right, you play golf. Weren't we going to get up a game?"

Last time he'd asked him about playing a round of golf, Balt had put him off, and he half-expected the same now. But this time something wondrous happened.

"I'd like that very much," replied Balt with a slight blush.

During infield practice, Kalecki hit fungoes to the outfield as the players practiced throwing and hitting the cut-off man. Hank Prince worked through the drill flawlessly despite being stoned off a blunt he had smoked earlier in the day. Weed relaxed him and made him feel like he played better, though the high usually wore off after his first at bat. The drill ended and Hank jogged towards the dugout but saw Coach Glover waiting for him by the foul line. His paranoia level jumped slightly.

Coach called him over and he veered off and jogged up to him. "Yeah, Coach," he said, tucking his glove under his arm. He wore sunglasses and kept his cap pulled down low.

"You okay?" asked Shake.

His paranoia level jumped higher. "Whaddya mean?" he asked innocently. Being stoned kept his voice calm.

"Just wondering. Everything okay with you, your family? Your mom okay?"

"Yeah, good. Why ya askin'?"

"Eh, I don't know. You seem off, like something's wrong... Sure everything's okay?

"Yeah, Coach. It's all good." He looked at his coach through his sunglasses and wondered what this was all about. Did he give something away during drills that made his coach suspicious? He waited a moment, hoping their talk was done.

"Take off your sunglasses," said Shake.

Hank's paranoia level went into high alert but he calmly removed his glasses and looked at his coach.

"You stoned?"

"What? Nah, that's crazy talk. Why ya askin' me that?"

"I know you've been hanging out at Quick's with some lowlifes getting high. You've been breaking curfew and coming late to the park. If it keeps up I'm going to fine you and then start benching you."

"I doin' know where ya heard all that. Someone's punkin' me."

"I know what I know, so keep it straight. You can't keep hanging out with those people. You're destined for something else—for greatness—and it's right there in front of your face. You can't be draggin' yourself down with those lowlifes. Wake-up. You were heir-apparent to Leonard on the big club. Now he's fighting injuries and you could be up there playing centerfield, but instead you're down here getting stoned and partying."

"I ain't stoned, man. I doin' know where you're gettin' all that. I mean, I've been down ta Quick's and all but I doin' hang out or nuthin'. And I ain't gettin' stoned. You'll see. I promise ya right now that I'll make the all-star team and get called up in September. It's guaranteed."

"Good to hear… Look, I'm not naïve. I know guys drink and get high on occasions but you can't make a habit out of it. If you do, everybody knows it, and you don't want that kind of rep. Balance in all things."

"Yes, sir. Trust me, ya don't need ta worry. You'll see."

"All right, Hank. Go on, go get dressed."

Hank nodded and started to jog off, his paranoia beginning to evaporate like released steam. He felt like he'd dodged a bullet but knew he'd have to play it smarter from now on.

"One more thing," said Shake. Hank stopped and looked back at him. "If you miss another sign I'll fine you."

"Yes, sir."

Shake walked back into the clubhouse. The players were changing into their orange and black home uniforms and one boom box (one!) was playing a mix of their favorite music. Shake hovered about, one moment with the trainer, another with a player at his locker, another in his office shooting the bull with whomever happened to stick their head in.

In the hallway he ran into Rex, who greeted him with a "Hey, Glover" and a smile. Yesterday was forgotten, which didn't surprise Shake. When he turned into a squall he raged and blustered but soon after turned pleasant once again.

The middle of humanity thou never knewest,
but the extremity of both ends.

"Ray Chapman," said Rex, initiating the game.

"The only player to die from a beanball," replied Shake. "Who was the pitcher?"

"Carl Mays, a spitballer. He's the reason they outlawed the spitball."

"Should be in the hall of fame."

"He's got the numbers," agreed Rex, but his voice trailed off as he walked past Shake and headed for the concession stands.

Shake shrugged it off and went back to the scouting report he held in his hand. He had yellow-highlighted key sentences and words and reviewed them as he walked back to his office. There he re-filled his thermal mug with fresh coffee and walked out to the dugout, thinking about the game.

Every game was a Rubik's cube of its own, a unique puzzle that had to be solved. Shake stood in his spot in the dugout and worked the cube. He immersed himself in the game like a chess master studying the pieces on the board, looking for the right set of moves that would give him an edge. Sometimes the right move was to do nothing and let the situation play itself out, other times a small thing like a visit to the mound made all the difference, and sometimes a big thing like making a pitching change at the right moment was the difference between winning and losing. And the job never ended. After the game came meetings, the post-game report, then off to The Mermaid for more analysis. And at no time, from coffee in the morning to slipping off to sleep at night, did Shake stop thinking about the game—about match-ups, tendencies, what he did right or what he did wrong, or an idea he had to help turn-around a struggling ballplayer. Whether in morning still or the evening mob, the business of baseball was a full time job.

10
CHAPTER

Love is the most important thing in the world,
but baseball is pretty good, too.

Yogi Berra

Thursday was the beginning of a long, ten day road trip that opened with a four-game series in New Haven and ended with a three-game series in Glens Falls. So Wednesday wasn't really the get-away-game since the bus to New Haven, which was only thirty-three miles away, didn't leave until noon on Thursday. For young twenty-year-old ball-players and even a few forty-year-old coaches, that was an invitation to party it up after Wednesday's night game.

Wednesday was also April 23 and Shake's birthday. His mom called him on his phone in his office and they talked for about fifteen minutes. She wished him a happy birthday, told him she loved him, and wanted to know which players he was excited about this year. Jose Estrella was really crushing the ball, he told her, and Steve Basset was targeted for the bigs but he really liked a kid named Dane Hamilton who was a second baseman with soft hands, a quick bat and good baseball smarts. "Sounds like you," she said.

His father had passed away in 1980 and his mom lived alone in the house in Daly City where he had grown up. He didn't worry about her too much since his two sisters lived nearby, visited often, and kept her busy taking care of grandkids. She had season tickets to the Giants and was a permanent fixture in her seat behind the Giants' dugout on the first base side at Candlestick Park where she kept score and stayed for the last out even on cold and windy night games. Besides his two sisters, he also had two brothers. His youngest brother had also played baseball in the minors and was now a college coach.

His other brother Gilbert surprised him by popping into his office right before batting practice. They hugged and Gil wished him "a happy forty-seventh" and he sat down and they talked for a while. Every family has a black sheep and Gilbert was the black sheep of the Glover family—not that he was a jailbird or a lowlife. It was just a case of squandered talents. Everyone in the family agreed that Gil would have made a sterling professor of English Lit at any college in the U.S., but Gil had decided to focus his energies on get-rich-quick schemes. And there had been many over the years. Shake invested in a couple early on but had learned his lesson and stayed out of them now. He half-expected Gil to hit him up for money after Gil told him he has headed for New York to meet with people about setting up a video game company. Video games were "the wave of the future" he told Shake and he was sure that this investment in a start-up would pay off big. To his credit, he didn't ask Shake for money and they hugged each other goodbye, promising to get together for dinner once Gil's business in New York was done.

Right before going out onto the field his players sang "Happy Birthday" to him and then went out and won him a close one 3-2. It was a quick game, only two hours and ten minutes, and Shake was done with his post-game report by 10:00. He didn't feel like The Mermaid Tavern tonight or a bunch of company on his birthday so he asked Rick if he wanted to go out and get a drink. "Sure thing," said Burton.

They hit a couple spots before ending up in Sliders where a West Coast game between the Giants and the Dodgers was on the TV. Shake ordered rum and cokes and kept them coming. Rick got the sign early on that Shake was in a serious drinking mood, so he nursed a beer knowing he would have to drive them both home at the end of the night. He'd never seen Shake really drunk, as in falling-down drunk, but he'd seen him well-oiled on occasion—never mean or sloppy but rather loose and talkative. He and Shake were close friends but Shake rarely talked about his personal life. On these occasions, when the rum and cokes began to pile up, Shake opened the vault on his personal life like someone taking out an old classic movie (one they only shared with special guests) and popping it into the VCR. But before that happened—and a sure-fire signal that Shake was headed in that direction—he started quoting the Bard. He always quoted Shakespeare at least once a day, but when he was rum-happy the flood-gates opened.

Fernando Valenzuela was pitching for the Dodgers and had a 4-1 lead going into the bottom of the fifth. *"Make you ready your stiff bats,"* quoted Shake as they watched the Giants come to bat. Valenzuela got through the inning as the last Giants batter flailed away at a pitch in the dirt. *"How poor are they that have no patience,"* said Shake and ordered another drink. In the bottom of the seventh, the Giants got a rally going, and when a hit drove in a run Shake yelled, *"A hit, a very palpable hit!"* There was laughter around the bar. Except for one guy.

"What the hell you sayin'?" he croaked loudly. The guy sat three stools down and looked pretty drunk.

Shake and Rick ignored him and watched as the Giants rally fizzled out at one run. After seven innings it was Dodgers 6, Giants 4.

"Do you wish you could'a played longer in the majors?" asked Shake.

"Sure, don't you?

'Yeah, if I could'a had a career like Joe Morgan."

"What's Joe doing these days?"

"He's getting into broadcasting."

"Really? You know, I think I heard that."

"He'll do well. He's good at anything he puts his mind to."

They talked about ex-ball-players becoming broadcasters and gave their opinion on who were the best and who were the worst. They agreed that neither one of them would have made a good announcer, though Rick insisted that Shake would have gone over well with all his Shakespeare quotes. Next time they looked up at the TV, Valenzuela was getting the last out of a complete game to win 6-4.

"Roger can't be too happy with that," said Rick referring to the Giants manager.

Shake nodded his head thoughtfully and quoted *Macbeth*:

> Let us seek out some desolate shade, and there
> Weep our sad bosoms empty.

"Cut it with the faggot talk!" croaked the drunk guy three stools down. "You're hurtin' my ears." Some Kingsmen fans who were standing near shushed him and told him who Shake was. "I don't care if he's George Steinbrenner! Shut him up!"

Rick leaned forward and looked down at the drunk. "Hey, friend, we're not botherin' you," he said nicely. "Let us buy you a drink."

"Buy *him* a drink and shut him up," came the belligerent response.

Shake stood up and stared down at the drunk. Rick expected to see fire in his eyes but instead there was a playful glint. Shake raised an eyebrow and quoted *Cymbeline*:

> I beseech you, sir,
> Harm not yourself with your vexation;
> I am senseless of your wrath.

There was laughter and some clapping from the patrons around the bar but the drunk was having none of it. He nearly slipped off his stool but quickly righted himself and walked towards Shake. Rick swiftly got between them.

"I told you to shut that faggot talk up!" yelled the drunk.

Rick noticed the bartender signal to the bouncer standing by the door. Rick held the flat of his hand against the drunk's chest while Shake stood behind him. Suddenly Shake raised his fist up next to his ear. *By this hand, I will supplant some of your teeth,*" he said to the drunk lightheartedly.

That triggered the drunk to push into Rick's hand, but before he could start anything the bouncer whisked him away. "Get him outta here," ordered the bartender. The drunk yelled back at Shake as the burly bouncer hustled him towards the door. Shake stepped away from the bar and with a flourish of his hand said, "Begone lout, thou unmannered dog, thou knave and jackanape. Hie thee home to bed, varlet. You're past saving, you bull's pizzle, you soused gurnet. Begone!"

The patrons erupted into cheers and applause at this spectacle and Shake doffed his cap and bowed. He came back to his stool and sat down with a chuckle as Rick laughed and slapped him on the back. The bartender handed him a fresh drink. "On the house," he said.

"Thank you, kind sir," replied Shake. "You're a noble tapster."

Shake took a sip of his drink as he settled back in. Two college-age men came over and asked him to autograph the bill of their Kingsmen caps. Shake asked them their age and whether they played ball and they talked a bit before going back to their table. He was quiet for a spell as he worked his swizzle stick.

"How's Linda and the kids?" he asked Rick.

"Good," replied Rick. "I called Linda a bit ago and Ricky threw a one-hitter today and Gordy was four for four."

"How about my princess?" asked Shake referring to Rick's daughter.

"She's got a dance recital May eleventh at 6:00. We got a day game. She said Uncle Shake better be there."

"Wouldn't miss it." The Burtons were like a second family to him and in many ways the bond between Rick and Linda—the closeness, the comfortableness—reminded him of his mom and dad. It was one in a million. He'd known Linda for years, back in Triple-A when she and Rick were first dating, and she was a woman he could imagine himself being married to. His relationship with Linda was an amusing one: she treated him almost like a wayward husband at times—playfully haranguing him, giving him advice and looking out for him—but never left any doubt that Rick and only Rick was the love of her life.

"Know what Rex said to me the other day," he added after a moment of thoughtful silence. "He said I had a fatal flaw—that I was pushing fifty with no wife and no kids and that was my fatal flaw."

"He's a senile old man. What's he know? His whole family hates him… Anyhow, you're not the marrying kind. You can be happy and not married, believe me. Just look at Wilt Chamberlain."

"I wonder how many kids he's got that he doesn't know about?" said Shake. "But who says I'm not the marrying kind? I can still get married."

"To who? Lucy?"

"No… But I could still get married and have kids, I'm only forty-seven. Bing Crosby did it."

"Bing, huh? I don't see it. You're married to baseball. Baseball is the love of your life." Rick paused for a moment and watched Shake stir his drink. His buddy had the birthday blues, he concluded. "You know," he added, "I used to think it was women you didn't trust but that wasn't it. Then I thought it was marriage—the institution of marriage—but that wasn't it. Linda says it's love—you don't trust love—and I think that's it."

"Base hit, up the middle."

"Okay, that's it then. So what you got against love?"

And so Shake told him:

There lies within the very flame of love
A kind of wick or snuff that will abate it.

Rick thought of a way to respond to that with the only Shakespeare he knew, though he wasn't sure he could remember it exactly right. "Isn't that the same guy who said: *'Love is not love which alters when it alteration finds, or bends with the remover. O no! it's an ever-fixed mark that looks on storms and is never broken.'*"

Shake did not correct his friend's mistakes and instead countered with:

The oath of a lover is no stronger than the word
of a tapster; they are both the confirmer of false
reckonings

"Well," replied Rick, throwing up his hands, "that's all the Shakespeare I know, so I give up... But if I remember right, didn't you almost get married in college. Obviously you loved her?"

"I did. Mimi... We almost got married... But I got it in my head she was cheating on me with my best friend so I broke it off."

"Was she?"

"No. I saw him at my high school reunion. My ten year high school reunion. He said they had nothing going on, that it was all in my head. And he had no reason to lie to me after ten years."

"Whatever happened to her?"

"I tried to maybe patch things up but she'd taken off. Her roommate told me she moved back East. A few years later I ran into a mutual college friend of ours and she told me Mimi died."

"Jeez. Sorry to hear that."

Shake pushed his drink away and sighed deeply. "Maybe cause of me," he said softly. "I broke her heart... We said we'd be together always... She said she'd love me till the day she died—said that with all her heart and soul, and then she took off... But maybe I..." but Shake broke off, his voice cracking as he fought with his emotions.

Seeing Shake like this bothered Rick. He'd seen Shake cry before, seen him choke up on the last day of the season, seen him get misty-eyed when he accepted "Manager of the Year" award, even seen him downright weep when his father died, but he'd never seen him get like this over a woman. Never. It was unprecedented, like seeing an umpire change his call. It bothered him and he didn't want to see his good friend go down this road any farther.

"Come on, Shake," he said cheerfully, patting him on the shoulder. "Let's get outta here, it's late. You'll stay at the house. Linda's expecting you."

Without a word, Shake got up and they left the bar and Rick drove them home to his house. Linda was waiting up for them. She gave Rick a kiss when he came in and was ready to playfully start in on Shake for keeping her husband out late when she suddenly thought better of it. Something in his eyes told her not to. Instead she kissed him on the cheek and said, "Hey, sweetie. Happy birthday. You're in the den. The bed's all made up for you."

"Okay, thanks you two," he said with a lopsided smile. As he walked into the den he could hear Linda peppering her husband with vital tidbits: her husband's stuff was already packed for the road trip, he'd better get his butt out of bed in the morning to say goodbye to his kids, the dog jumped the fence but they found him two blocks over, he had a message from his dad but it was nothing urgent, and she loved him and it was time for bed.

Shake sat down on the edge of the bed and took off his shoes. He unbuttoned his shirt but sat there without taking it off. He saw Linda's slippered feet coming towards him.

"You okay, big guy," she asked him tenderly. She lifted up his chin with her finger. "What's going on in that blotto'ed brain of yours?"

He closed one eye and looking up at her said:

> *Some unborn sorrow ripe in fortune's womb*
> *Is coming towards me and my inward soul*
> *With nothing trembles.*

"No, it's not," she said as she helped him off with his shirt. "You're drunk and feeling sorry for yourself. Now take off that dirty cap—here, let me have it—and lay down. In the morning you'll feel better." She laid him back and deftly unbuckled his belt and pulled his pants off without disrupting his boxers. "You've got a big road trip coming up and better things to worry about," she said as she put the blanket over him and tucked him in. 'Now get some sleep, sweetie" she added, kissing him on the forehead. He smiled his lopsided smile and watched her slippers leave the room. He turned over and was asleep in less than a minute.

At noon the next day he boarded the bus with the remnants of a hangover and took his seat up front next to Rick. The windows on the bus were tinted, giving the insides a cool, shady feel to it, but Shake kept his sunglasses on and worked to focus his thoughts. His birthday was over and with it doubt; there was work and baseball to think about.

11
CHAPTER

On Saturday, April 26, two things of import occurred: the Kingsmen played a day game against the Admirals in New Haven, and in Chernobyl the Soviet's nuclear reactor exploded releasing radioactive fallout into the atmosphere. In Dane Hamilton's mind the two were not comparable. One was inconsequential—a baseball game—which in his mind should have been cancelled, and the other was an accident of catastrophic magnitude that threatened the earth with death, decay, and genetic mutations.

The Kingsmen had taken the first two games, and with a win today could take the series, but Dane's mind was not on any of that. With his transistor radio he tried to keep up-to-date on the reports coming out of Soviet Russia. That was difficult during batting and infield practice where his undivided attention was required. He'd already been warned about listening to his transistor during the game but today, frankly, he didn't care. The reactor fire was releasing plumes of radioactive isotopes that would cover Western Europe and eventually make its way to the East Coast bringing with it thyroid cancer, leukemia and birth defects. He kept the transistor radio in the inside pocket of his warm-up jacket and ran the earpiece up under his collar. As he waited for his at-bats, he'd throw on his jacket, plug in his ear piece, and keep abreast of the approaching Armageddon.

So far the President had not declared a state of national emergency. No doubt, thought Dane, they were still assessing the scale of the catastrophe and would issue a declaration in a couple days along with evacuation orders. Would it be in time and would people listen? Scenes from the movie *The Day After* played out in Dane's head. Burdened with these thoughts, Dane went 0 for 4 and committed two errors at second. The second error cost them the game.

"Shake wants to see you in his office," said Coach Burton.

Dane sat at his locker slowly dressing and listening to his radio. He looked up distractedly at Coach Burton and nodded.

"And get rid of that goddam radio," added Burton.

Dane took his earpiece out and nodded again to Coach Burton. Obviously he was in hot water but once he talked to Shake, about what was going on, there would be understanding. He didn't expect that understanding to come from Burton or any of the other coaches. All they knew was baseball. And he didn't expect understanding—even comprehension—to come from his fellow players. They were too interested in calculating their stats, playing grab-ass, or figuring out where they were going to go out night-clubbing in New Haven. But Coach Glover—Shake— was different. From what he'd seen so far, Shake was broader-minded. He had an awareness of the precarious absurdity of human existence. Dane was sure of it. He was also sure that Shake not only comprehended the disaster that had just befallen mankind but would certainly understand and probably share Dane's consuming dread.

Dane quickly finished dressing and walked through the oblivious clubhouse and knocked on Shake's office door.

"Yeah," was the answer. Dane pushed the door open and stepped in. "Dane, take a seat," said his no-nonsense manager.

Dane could see that Shake was upset with him but it would only be for a moment. Once this man fully appreciated the irrefutable facts of the matter he would calm down and empathize with him.

"I don't know where your head was today," said Shake, "but it wasn't in the game. And if I catch you listening to your radio in the dugout again I'll confiscate it. Just like fourth grade. It'll go in the drawer at Beehive along with all the other crap I've confiscated over the years including knives and dildos. Understood?"

Dane nodded and was about to respond when Shake cut him off.

"Cause if I catch you with that radio again I'm gonna take the cord and strangle you with it until your eyes bug out and you lie dead on the dugout floor. I might go to prison but I'll happily do my time knowing I did the right thing. Am I clear?"

Dane wasn't sure how much of this was kidding, but he nodded and was about to respond when Shake cut him off again.

"You're paid to do a job and that job includes your rapt attention. You don't get commercial breaks. When you're in the dugout your rapt attention should be on the game, on the opposing pitcher—on what he's throwing and in what count—on your last at bat and your next at bat, on what your coaches are talking about and on a hundred other baseball things. Not news-talk radio. If you pulled that crap at NASA you'd be fired. If you pulled it in Beirut you'd be dead... So where was your head today?"

Dane waited a moment until he was sure Shake really wanted him to answer. "My head was where everyone else's head should be today," he answered excitedly (now was his chance to get it out). "I'm sure you know what's going on in the world right now as we speak. A nuclear plant in Russia just exploded and radioactive fallout is poisoning Europe and heading our way. Millions will die. Millions. How does that reality stack up to a game of baseball? What we should be thinking about right now is not game situation or the price of a beer but our lives. Our very lives are at stake. Why aren't we evacuating or finding shelter? This is where our rapt attention should be. How can we—"

Shake cut him off here. "That's why you booted a double play ball in the eighth—because of Chernobyl?" asked Shake. "You're anxiety over what's going on four thousand miles away caused you to go O for four and cost us the game in the eighth—while the rest of us kept our heads in the game and played hard? That makes you, what, George Shultz and the rest of us schmucks?

"I didn't say that."

"Sounds that way to me… Look, son, I know you're concerned about Chernobyl. We all are. But I haven't heard anything about millions dying. No one's reporting that or saying that, so I don't know where you're getting numbers like that. My advice is to calm down and wait until they sort it out."

"You know the Soviets are lying. What the world knows about this—which is bad enough—I guarantee you is ten times worse. They know it and maybe even our intelligence agencies know it, but they're not going to say anything for fear of causing panic."

"So now it's a conspiracy theory. You're not one of those conspiracy nuts who think the moon landing was staged or that fluoridated water is a plot to control our minds?

"You can make fun all you want," retorted Dane, his voice rising. "But look at the facts. That's all I ask. Look at the facts and draw logical conclusions. The world's in trouble."

"Of course it is. It was in trouble yesterday and it'll be in trouble tomorrow. Learn to live with it. You've got to keep your perspective—keep your balance… '*Give me the man that is not passion's slave, and I will wear him in my heart's core.*'"

This was not going the way Dane hoped it would go. His manager was not the enlightened soul he thought he was. It was like trusting your shortstop to be at the bag for the throw only to find him still standing at short ignoring you. And that made him angry, and when he got angry he made it his aim to belittle his opponent the way the "Against" competitor would on his Cornel Debate Team.

"I know you like to quote the Bard," he replied. "You're famous for it. But sometimes your quotes are taken out of context and don't mean what you think they mean—but they sound good so everyone goes along with it. Take that quote. I know it's *Hamlet*, but how you meant it is not how Shakespeare meant it in the play. If I remember right, Hamlet is going to put on a play wherein he'll catch the conscience of the King, and he lectures the actors not to go overboard or be too tame in their play-acting. It has nothing at all to do with holding strong opinions."

"Very good," said Shake with a smile. "Now we can talk *Hamlet*. I'm all ears... Granted, on occasion I throw a quote out there because it sounds good, but sometimes the sound of words are more important than the meaning of words. But in this case... no, I think I nailed it. Hamlet admires men who keep their cool. And that's what I'm telling you—keep your cool."

"Cool is for James Dean. Dead and gone. I don't want to be *'a man whose blood is very snow-broth, one who never feels the wanton stings and motions of the sense.'*"

Shake chuckled. *Measure for Measure*, huh? You're on a roll, kid. Didn't you tell me your mom loves Shakespeare? She taught you well. For me it was my dad. We used to play a game called "comebackers" where he'd throw out a line or two and I'd have to give him the play, the act, and the scene, if I could. I got pretty good at it. We'll have to play it one of these days. Maybe over a beer. But baseball first. There's probably three or four guys on this club who have the talent right now to get called up and you're one of them. The big club wants to see you in the two hole. There's a reason for that. They see a place for you and they want to groom you for it. Work hard at it and keep your glove going and you'll find yourself basking in the California sunshine come September. Are you with me?"

Dane knew he was being played—like a flute—and he hated being played but there wasn't much he could do about it. The man could be disarming. No doubt about it. He had a way about him.

"Yes, sir," he said, surrendering the high ground he once held.

"Good. Meanwhile, if you're a conspiracy nut or just plain mad, deal with it. Personally, you just think too much. Turn it off like the knob on your radio. Once you're on the field, you need to know the difference between a hawk and a handsaw."

Dane nodded and failed at suppressing a smile. He still liked Shake. The guy knew a lot. He didn't know everything, but he knew a lot.

"All right, then," said Shake. "If our faces don't melt off tomorrow, I expect one hundred percent out of you. Now go catch up with your buddies." Dane got up to leave but Shake added, "Does your mom like baseball?"

"Loves it."

"Shakespeare *and* baseball. Hmm, a woman after my own heart. Bring her by sometime so I can meet her."

"Will do."

Dane had almost forgotten his dinner date with Delia McGivers. Not that he would have minded forgetting their date; he really didn't want to have dinner with her anyhow. But she was his girlfriend, or his ex-girlfriend, and that made things more difficult. He thought about that as he drove over to the restaurant: was she his girlfriend or his ex-girlfriend? He had formally broken up with her a year ago but she ignored it and still acted like they were a couple. Why'd he let her get away with it? It was like taking someone out on a double-switch only to have them refuse to leave the field. There were rules against that. Yet she still called him and sent him letters and they still, on occasion, had sex. It was complicated.

Delia sat across from him in the restaurant wearing a blue dress. She looked good in blue. It complimented her big blue eyes that carried a sumptuous sadness to them. Her long blonde hair was folded neatly over the front of her right shoulder, while on the strap of her left shoulder she wore a pink and white corsage. Dane didn't give her the corsage. Whenever they went out she wore a corsage like it was some kind of badge or something. Not that it didn't look nice.

As soon as they sat down at their table, Dane started in on the Chernobyl disaster and Delia sat and politely listened to him. He knew her to be a damned polite listener and it was one of the things he disliked about her. She sat there and watched him with her blue eyes and politely listened to him like some five-hundred-dollar-an-hour psychotherapist. Occasionally she would nod or ask him to clarify a point, but she never stopped watching him with those big, sad blue eyes.

Dane stopped his dissertation when the waiter came over to take their drink order.

"A glass of chardonnay," said Delia. The waiter took their orders without writing it down and said he'd be right back. "That's not what they're saying on the news now," she said, turning her undivided attention back to Dane. "The worst of the fallout's contained to the Ukraine. In Western Europe maybe Finland and Sweden will get some of it, but by the time it gets to the East Coast it will be negligible."

"And you believe that?"

"Why shouldn't I?"

"Because governments lie. They're made up of people and people lie."

"Do you lie?"

Dane paused because he saw it starting again and he didn't want it to. Whenever they got together it was always the same thing. It always went the same way: it started with small talk and then she would strike, trying to get a rise out of him, and when she finally did get a rise out of him she'd get emotional, make some grand gesture, and he would have to calm her down and they'd end up having sex. It was like a punishment from Zeus where he was made to perform the same task over and over again until the end of time.

"Course," he replied easily. "Everybody lies and I'm everybody. Have you decided what you want?" he added, picking up the menu.

"You're not everybody," she said and left it at that as she picked up her menu. The waiter came with their drinks and took their dinner order. Dane hoped to avoid rolling the rock up the hill again but it wasn't to be.

"Have you ever lied to me?" she asked.

"Sure."

"When? When you said you loved me?"

"I never loved you."

"That's a lie."

He rubbed his chin in thought. She awaited his response. They met at Cornel and they started dating and it got hot and heavy and it stayed that way until he didn't see any further point in it. Yes, he told her he loved her, but love was the lie. All part of the Big Lie. So was it a lie if you told someone to go to hell even though nobody believed in such a place anymore? He didn't think so. But she awaited his response.

"I used to love you," he said.

"And I believed you."

"You shouldn't have believed me. Since all people lie and you know they lie, you shouldn't have believed me."

"But *I did* believe you because *you did* love me. What changed?"

"Let's not have this discussion again. Please. We've had it a dozen times before."

"What changed?"

Dane downed the rest of his beer and looked for the waiter to order another one. He wasn't anywhere to be found. He looked back at Delia. Sometimes you had to be cruel to be kind.

"You want marriage and kids and I don't."

"I never said I wanted to get married. When did I say that? I never said I wanted kids."

"You said we'd be together forever, so what's the difference. Besides, it's in your DNA. Your parents, your sisters—it's all about family and kids—and you're just the same."

"What's wrong with family and kids?"

"Don't want 'em."

"But why?"

"Christ, Delia, you know the answer to that question. The world is filled with liars and cheaters and worse—people who kill for pleasure, who get off on hurting children. It's a horrible place and I'm weary of it. Why would you want to bring another liar into the world? Why would you want to breed more killers? You'd be better off dedicating your life to charity work."

"I don't like it when you talk that way."

"Sorry." He finally flagged down the waiter and ordered another beer. He needed one.

"You know, both my dad and brother say I should break up with you. My dad doesn't trust you and my brother says you just stick around for the sex."

"You should listen to them."

Delia stared at him with her blue eyes. In the last thirty seconds they had gotten big and moist. Here we go, thought Dane. Here we go again. She reached into her purse (for a handkerchief, he thought) and pulled out a wad of paper. She handed them across the table and said, "Here."

"What's this?"

"The letters and poems you've written me."

"They're yours. I wrote them for you. Keep 'em."

"I don't want them. Here, take 'em."

Her hand remained outstretched over the table holding his letters, frozen there as though she were holding a small dagger meant for his heart. There it was—the beau geste. Wonderfully melodramatic. That was just like her. Just like a woman. He shrugged his shoulders and took the letters.

His beer came and then dinner and they ate quietly for a while until the small talk started up again. He told her about the game, without varnish, and related his whole conversation with Shake. She even laughed in spots.

"So you think they'll call you up in September?" she asked.

"Maybe, as long as I don't break a leg or think too much."

"How will you manage that—not thinking too much?"

"Easy. I'll think about screwing."

"Oh, you're sharp tonight. Someone ought to take the edge off."

"Yeah, someone. Want desert?"

"I'm looking at it."

And there it was. The rock was almost to the top, just a few more pushes before it rolled down again. He went to her place where he made her purr, and afterwards left the letters with her.

12
CHAPTER

April showers brought May homerun powers and by early June the Kingsmen sat atop the Eastern League by four games. Estrella kept hitting them, Goff and Burks got theirs, Horn had seven and even Dane Hamilton, now in the two hole, had four dingers. It was an embarrassment of riches or a juiced ball, one of the two.

Which brings us to the middle innings of our story. The middle innings is when the game within the game begins; it is when hitters begin to figure out pitchers, when signs are stolen, and when managers start to get serious about their upcoming chess moves. If this were a Shakespeare play, it would be the pivotal third act. Act III is when Romeo kills Mercutio, when Hamlet catches the conscience of the King, and when lovers are tricked, friends turn against friends and confusion reigns.

***

During infield practice Shake scanned the sky. It was cloudy but not expected to rain. He sniffed the evening air and felt it. Something wasn't right. He walked closer to the stands and sniffed again. Like a sea captain who knows his ship inside and out, Shake felt something wasn't right even though there was no visible sign of it. Then it hit him—there was no barbecue smell. By 5:00, at every home game, Shake could smell the aroma of barbecuing hot dogs and hamburgers wafting out from underneath the grandstands. It was past 5:00 and it was missing. That was odd, thought Shake. Usually Rex was all over that, barking orders at the Concessions Manager, checking each refreshment stand for readiness, even firing up the grill and flipping burgers if he had to. Fans were beginning to file in and not one of them held a hot dog in their hand.

Out of curiosity he walked into the stands then down again to the concession level where he found Orson Kent and the Concessions Manager huddled next to a padlocked cabinet.

"You wouldn't happen to have the key for this, would you?" asked Orson as Shake walked up.

"Nope," he replied. "Rex does. Don't you have a set?" he asked the Concessions Manager. The young man nodded no, which didn't surprise Shake. Rex paid him minimum wage and treated him like crap. It was a high turn-over job.

"No one changed out the propane tanks last night," explained Orson, looking a bit flustered. "They're empty and the new ones are locked inside and Rex's not here."

"Not here. Really? Then hacksaw it off," Shake said to the Concessions Manager. The young man just stood there with a "Huh?" expression on his face. "Go find Speed. I'm sure he's got a hacksaw, then come back here and cut that lock off and get things going." The young man nodded and walked off on his mission. "What do you mean Rex is not here?" he asked Orson.

"As in 'not here'," replied Orson. "He's probably at home but he's not answering his page. I picked him up yesterday and gave him a ride home last night—it's a long story, I'll tell you more later—but he went into this big tirade about his ungrateful daughter and how I better hope I don't have kids 'cause they'll just turn against me. I remembered what you told me about his younger daughter, so I told him maybe he should call her up and mend fences. Then he really went off, calling me a 'spoiled rich kid' and that the world was full of 'spoiled rich kids' and to stay out of his business and get out of his sight. So there you have it. I guess I'm going to have to wear a disguise if I want to keep working around here."

Shake shrugged his shoulders. Rex wasn't his problem. "He'll show up," he said as he headed back to the field. But he thought better of it and turned back to Orson. "Do me a favor. If he doesn't show, try calling him or go over there and find out what's going on."

"I will."

Shake walked back onto the field and watched the last of infield practice. He also kept a close eye on Prince running through his drills in the outfield. Would the kid come over to talk to him, he wondered. Shake had already posted the line-up for tonight's game and Hank was not starting. Instead he was going with Joe Svoboda, who was a fourth outfielder he used for spot starts and pinch hitting. He'd explained the situation to the big club and they agreed—bench Prince. After their talk in late April, Hank had put on a show and for a month had shown himself to be the best player in the Eastern League. In one game he had stolen four bases and scored six times. The kid was a marvel. But over the last couple weeks Hank had gone from spectacular to mediocre, showing up late again, missing signs, and generally playing like he was bored with baseball. So he was benched—without notice—and Shake was curious if he cared enough to come to him for an explanation.

The Kingsmen beat the Glens Falls Tigers 4-2. Ellsworth pitched a solid game and Hoffman and Hamilton turned three double plays. In the eighth, with the score tied 2-2 and runners at first and second with one out, everyone in the park figured Shake would pinch-hit Prince for Svoboda. But he didn't. He glanced down the bench at Hank, saw he was anticipating the call, then ignored him and told Svoboda to "Go get 'em." Svoboda was a fan favorite. He was of Polish descent and New Britain had a large Polish community. Whenever he walked up to the plate, the P.A. Announcer would play the "Mazurka" and the fans would go crazy. It was fun to watch. Svoboda rewarded his fans with a double off the wall that scored two runs.

There were other positive things going into his post-game report. Besides the three double plays, Dane Hamilton had got a big hit in the third to put them up 2-0. He was a natural in the two hole, moving the runner along, executing the hit and run, bunting when needed and even showing some power on occasion. Shake was sure he'd make the All-Star team. There were no more transistor radios or rants about nuclear fallout. Given the fact that it was now June and no one had keeled over from radioactivity no doubt had a calming effect on the young man. But that last part wasn't going in his report.

Shake expected Hank to pop into his office for a heart to heart but it never happened. Fine, thought Shake. He'd be on the bench again tomorrow. Shake finished up his paperwork, dressed into his street clothes, and looked around for Orson before he left the park. He found him in Rex's office going over gate receipts.

"No Rex, huh?" said Shake.

"No," replied Orson, looking up and losing count. "I tried calling but no answer. I'm about to drive over there."

"Why don't you wait until tomorrow morning?"

"Can't, got something going on. Plus I'm a little worried. Has he ever missed a game?"

"Never."

"So I'm heading over there as soon as I'm done."

"All right. Probably a good idea. If you find out anything weird give me a call or come by. I'll be at the Mermaid."

"Gotcha. Thanks."

At The Mermaid Tavern, he had a beer, talked baseball with his coaches, and ended up sitting alone at the bar with Lucy. Larry Benedict was still there but he sat by himself at a table—but not really by himself as Bernie stood over him arguing with him as usual. Shake and Lucy watched the two go at it. It almost looked like Larry and Bernie were enjoying themselves.

"Think they still got the hots for one another?" wondered Shake out loud.

"Maybe," replied Lucy. "He did a number on her a few years ago."

"That's her story."

"Is there a different story? He told her he loved her, wanted to marry her, even took her to see his parents. Then dumped her."

"He's a sworn bachelor."

"You think so."

"I know so."

"You don't know as much as you think you know, Coach." Here Lucy—Dark Lucy—pointed one of her black fingernails at him and said, "How about this? We'll play a little game in the name of love. You tell Larry that you overheard Bernie tell me she still loves him, and I'll tell Bernie I overheard Larry tell you he still loves her. See what happens."

Shake chuckled. The little plot tickled his fancy. *"Some Cupid kills with arrows, some with traps,"* he quoted. "I'm in, but what do you think will happen?

"They'll either take it for a lie or lower their guard and let the truth shine through."

"Maybe. But no casting spells to make them fall in love," he joked.

"I can't make anybody love anybody. That should be obvious?" Lucy slid gracefully off her bar stool and said "I'll be right back," and went upstairs.

She returned in twenty minutes, hiked up her dress, and slid back onto her bar stool where she crossed her legs. He smiled at her and she smiled back. She smelled of weed but also of musk and rose oil. Don the bartender came over and she ordered a soda water with lime and asked Shake if he wanted a fresh beer. He'd been nursing the same beer for almost an hour and it was still half full. He was good, he told her. She waited for her drink and then leaned into Shake. She put her arm around him and started talking dirty in his ear. He answered yes to all her questions and waited for the cue to go upstairs. She slid her arm off his back and took his chin between her thumb and finger.

"We make a good pair, don't you think?" she asked.

"Sure we do."

"*Sure we do,*" she repeated, dropping her hand down to his leg where she ran her black fingernails along his quadricep. He could tell she was stoned and maybe a little more than usual.

"What's on your mind, witchy-woman?"

"You know... But I was thinking... There's a big festival coming up. Lithia. The summer solstice... It's Saturday the twenty-first. There's a ritual at sunrise and I'd like you to come... I'd really like you to come."

"You always like it when I cum."

"Listen," she said slapping him playfully on the thigh, but her eyes were unusually serious. And so Shake listened—something about the Sabbat and the Sun God and the Fire Festival of Lithia—and she finished and looked at him awaiting his answer.

"What time you say it was?"

"Sunrise, so it won't interfere with your game. It's no more than an hour or two, and it's a powerful time for couples."

Shake suddenly had an image of himself standing in the morning fog in the middle of the coven with a ritual robe on. "Sunrise," he said apathetically. "I'm still sleeping at sunrise."

"Please. As a personal favor to me."

He studied her for a moment. She was oddly serious about all this and he didn't know quite what to make of it. Some of her Wicca stuff was fun but this sounded like a big deal. She wasn't trying to recruit him was she? He was more likely to go to sea on a merchant ship than become a Wiccan. But her plea was something new—the whole personal favor thing—and he didn't know what to make of it. It made him stop and think and he rubbed his chin. Another image of himself dancing with her witch buddies around a bonfire popped into his head.

"I'll have to think about it," he said. Right after he said it he noticed a change of hue in her face.

"You do that," she replied curtly. She turned back to her soda water with lime and called Don over to talk some business. When they were done, she rubbed her forehead and said, "I've got a splitting headache. I'll see you tomorrow night, right?"

"Yeah, probably."

She nodded slowly, kissed him on the cheek and went upstairs.

Shake watched her walk upstairs and rubbed his chin again in thought. He'd gotten up for sex, was all ratcheted-up for it, and now he had to push the reset button. It was like hitting a blast to left field and thinking it's a homerun only to see it die on the warning track for an out. What was that all about, he wondered. *Who is't can read a woman?* She seemed almost angry with him. If so, that was a new dynamic, but he was sure she'd get over it. There were no obligations between them and he liked it that way. He was a free agent having a good run of it with one ball club. If she was angry about something she'd get over it and tomorrow they'd be back to normal.

Orson pulled into the horseshoe driveway of the Lyon estate. He went up the steps and used the lion's head knocker to rap on the door. A middle-aged man in a cardigan sweater opened the door.

Orson
Hi, may I talk to Mr. Lyon?

Servant
It's a little late. Who are you?

Orson

Orson Kent. I work with Mr. Lyon at Beehive Stadium.

Servant

You're one of those baseball people?

Orson

Yes, I am, and I'm looking for Mr. Lyon. He didn't show up for the game tonight and I've paged and called him but no answer. I just want to make sure he's all right. Is he home?

Servant

It's really too late for this, and I have strict orders from Mrs. Cornwall not to let baseball people into this house.

Orson

'Baseball people', huh? Look, I just want to know if Rex is okay.

Servant

Mr. Lyon is none of your business. Not at this hour. Come back tomorrow.

Orson

Okay, Mr. Belvedere. Go get Rex or go tell someone I'm here. I'm not leaving till you do.

Servant

Get your foot out of the door. Don't make me call the police.

Orson

The police! Go ahead, you big fat jerk!

Servant

You have no call to insult me! Get your foot out of the door before I call the police.

Orson
I'll get you to call somebody! I'll wrap that stupid sweater around your neck!

Servant
What! Hoa! Stop!... Help! Help!

(They scuffle in the doorway and Rae and Ed Cornwall enter.)

Rae
What the hell? Stop this instant! Who the hell are you? Ed, call the police.

Ed
Everyone calm down. Let go of his sweater... Now what's your name?

Orson
Orson Kent. I work for the Kingsmen.

Ed
You're Horace Kent's kid, right? Pleased to meet you. I just talked to your dad a few days ago. Here, everyone, calm down. I'm Ed Cornwall and this is my wife Rae. Orson, right? Orson, come into the den and sit down with us.

Orson
No, thank you, sir. I was just looking for Mr. Lyon. He didn't show up for the game today, which is unheard of, and folks want to know if he's okay.

Rae
My father doesn't live here anymore. He moved out.

Orson
But I thought he owned this house?

Rae
You thought wrong. He was a guest in *my house* and now he's not.

Orson
Where can I find him?

Rae
Your guess is as good as mine. Try the Travel Lodge out on the inter-state... But what was the meaning of you accosting poor Chester here?

Orson
Chester! That figures. Cause I don't like his face.

Rae
Maybe you don't like mine either?

Ed
Now, dear, he didn't...

Orson
Well, to tell the truth I've seen better faces on a horse's ass.

Rae
Out! Get out! You baseball people are all alike. Chester, if he's not gone in five seconds, call the police.

Orson
No need. I'm leaving, Ma'am. Thanks for your hospitality.

The next morning Orson had a golf date with Balt. Tee time was 7:30. He was still a little flustered from last night and had yet to track down Rex, but he pushed that all from his mind once Balt walked onto the first tee carrying his bag.

They were paired up with two other guys to make a foursome. The two were big guys—they looked like old frat buddies to Orson—and probably played football together in college. Now in their late thirties, they were company men fighting the battle of the bulge. Golf was probably the only exercise they got nowadays.

They flipped coins for starter and Balt won. He took his driver out of his bag and accidently walked up to the woman's line.

"Hey, Alice, you're back here with the men," joked one of them as he nudged his buddy with a laugh.

"Oops. Shit. I'm still asleep," said Balt hoarsely. "I tied one on last night."

"Tell me about it," replied the other frat brother.

Balt hit his drive down the center of the fairway but not too far.

"Very dainty," quipped one of the frat brothers as he stepped up to the tee. His buddy chuckled. Orson glanced over at Balt and rolled his eyes as if to say, "We've got eighteen holes to play with these knuckleheads." The frat brother's drive traveled significantly farther than Balt's but hooked left into the rough.

Orson hit a nice drive down the middle of the fairway. The second frat brother drove one past Orson but hooked it like his buddy. The Baked Potato Pi Brothers were both in the rough.

"Two peas in a pod," said Orson with a smirk as they walked off the tee.

The same pattern developed over the next five holes: the frat brothers continued to have fun with Balt's drives while Orson took a verbal shot at the two whenever he had a chance. But once on the green (and to Orson's delight), Balt proved himself to be an excellent putter, and somewhere around the sixth hole the quips stopped. After the last hole, they shook hands all around and headed for the clubhouse.

Orson grabbed a table for two, asked Balt what he wanted to drink, then went over to the bar and ordered a Heineken for himself and Bloody Mary for Balt. He opened a tab with the thought of having a few drinks with Balt. They sat down together and talked about the round and made fun of the frat brothers, and when Balt finished up his Bloody Mary, Orson started up to get him another one.

"I got to go," said Balt, pushing back his chair.

"Just one more?" entreated Orson.

"No, got to go, but I owe you a drink. I'll make it up to you next time."

Orson liked the sound of that. "Well, hey," he said standing up with him. "Let me pay the tab and I'll meet you out in the parking lot."

"Sure," replied Balt as he headed out to get his bag. Orson paid off his tab and walked past the frat brothers on his way.

"Taking off?" asked one of them. "Sit down and have a drink with us."

"Love to, guys, but gotta run. Game day."

"That's right. Good luck."

"Say goodbye to your buddy for us," said the other one. "You know he's as queer as a three dollar bill."

"Wouldn't know about that," replied Orson as he walked away. He was going to give them two free passes to a Kingsmen game but kept them in his pocket instead.

As he retrieved his bag he thought about that crack—"He's as queer as a three dollar bill"—and wondered why, if it was that obvious to the Baked Potato Pi Brothers, why it wasn't that obvious to him? He wanted it to be true and had wrestled with the question for months. The answer meant everything to him, and if it was clearly apparent to two strangers what the answer was then it should be good enough for him. In his worried mind, the clouds suddenly cleared and the sun came out. That was it. Let the truth be told.

He came up to Balt as he was loading his golf bag into his trunk. Orson noticed a bumper sticker that said "ERA YES" and another one for the Boston Red Sox. Balt closed the trunk and smiled at him and held out his hand. Orson took it eagerly.

"That was fun," said Balt. "Let's do it again."

"Yeah."

"See you at Beehive later today."

"Yeah.

They had walked, rather awkwardly, around the car to the driver's door with their hands still clasped. Orson was going to use it to pull Balt into him but he hesitated for a moment, looked around, and let go of Balt's hand as three golfers with bags in tow walked past them. Balt opened his car door and it was now between them. Orson looked longingly at Balt and gracefully shrugged his shoulders. Suddenly Balt leaned over the door and kissed him quickly on the lips. With a blush in his cheeks, Balt jumped in his car, closed the door, and sped off without looking at him.

In his yearning heart, Orson leapt for joy, from shock and awe left by his golden boy.

13
CHAPTER

Why, this is very midsummer madness.
Twelfth Night

Saturday, June 21st rolled around and the Albany-Colonie Yankees were in town. The Kingsmen were riding an eight game winning streak. At the park it was Black & Decker Day and some lucky fans stood a chance of winning a cordless drill, a 12 inch chain saw, and the most coveted gift of all—a 208cc gas-powered snow blower. It was also the Summer Solstice and the Fire Festival of Lithia but not many folks were aware of the Lithia part of that. Shake was aware of it because Dark Lucy had invited him to the sunrise ritual. He never gave her a straight answer about going or not, but Lucy hadn't brought it up again so he was off the hook.

All-Star votes were in and Shake asked Rick to gather up the team before batting practice so he could announce their names. The Dominicans were in the trainer's room perfecting their English by watching reruns of *All in the Family*, Steve Basset was in the laundry room leading his small prayer group, and Hank Prince was on time for once and at his locker without sunglasses on. When Shake looked around the locker room, everyone was present and accounted for.

The Kingsmen led the league in all-stars with seven. Shake read off the names that included four pitchers (Basset, Santiago, Ellsworth and Cappadona) and three position players (Burks, Estrella, and Hamilton). Conspicuously absent from the list was centerfielder Hank Prince. His counterpart on the Admirals—Hank Percy—had been voted in ahead of him. Shake congratulated the all-stars—he himself would manage the East Team—and the players clapped and quickly slipped into good-natured ribbing.

A locker door slammed shut loudly. It was Hank. Next he opened it, threw clothes in and slammed it shut again. Players around him stepped back to avoid flying objects. Hank grabbed his bat and glove and stormed out of the locker room but stopped at the water cooler, took aim with his bat, and smashed the plastic jug, sending water flying in all directions. With that he stomped out the tunnel and onto the field.

"Something you said?" quipped Larry.

"I guess that got his attention," added Rick.

"Guess so," agreed Shake. He looked at the cracked water jug and the wet floor. "Watch it on your way out," he deadpanned to his team. "Wet floor."

Shake walked back to his office and thought about Hank. Nearly three months into the season and he had worked at getting the young man's attention—at getting some fire in his belly—with talks, fines and even benching, but nothing seemed to stick. Now the All-Star voters had done what he couldn't: they had gotten Hank's attention. But would it stick, he wondered. He hoped so.

He heard loud yelling (now what?) and walked back out where he found Rex shouting at the top of his voice. Speed stood nearby holding towels.

Rex

Who in the goddam hell broke my water cooler! Who, goddam it! They're gonna pay for it by god—and clean up this mess! Which one of you did this?

Shake

Calm down, Rex. It was one of my players. We'll take care of it.

Rex

The hell you will, Glover! I wanna know who did this. I want them suspended!

Shake

I'll take care of it. Stop your shouting. We'll get it cleaned up. Speed's got towels.

Speed

Crying towels for some.

Rex

I want the vandal suspended! It's vandalism!

Speed

The pump don't work 'cause the vandals took the handle.

Shake

Quiet!... I'll talk to the player, Rex. I'll take care of it.

Rex

I want him suspended, Glover, not talked to! If you don't suspend him, I'll call Horace and he'll suspend him!

Speed

You'll need a pair of suspenders for that.

Shake

You're not getting anyone suspended. Stop pushing me, Rex. I'm trying to stay calm here but you're pushing me. You're not calling anyone. It's my job to discipline players—not yours. Your job is the stadium, my job is the ball club, so stay out of my business.

Rex

Then do your job! Suspend him now or I'll have you fired!

Speed

Fired and brimstone.

Shake

You've lost it! You're outta your mind!

Rex

I'm warning you! Don't fuck with me!

Speed

Face to face or back to back?

Shake

Speed! ... You really want to go down this road with me! Over a water cooler! Huh, Lyon? You got zero clout with the front office. Zero! The only thing you're gonna do right now is shut your mouth and get out of my clubhouse.

Rex

I'll have you fired!

Shake

Outta my clubhouse! Now! If not, I'll pick you up and throw you out myself!

Speed
Make it a knuckleball.

Rex
He threatened me! You all heard it!

Rick
We haven't heard anything. Just your big mouth.

Shake
I'm done with you. Outta my clubhouse... Out!

Rex
How dare you. I'll have you fired.

Speed
You better go, sir, before he throws you for a strike.
(Rex exits.)

Shake took his cap off and ran his hand back and forth across his hair then shook his head in wonder as if to say "Can you believe it." The players who witnessed the altercation looked either shocked or amused. They'd been treated to two sideshows in less than fifteen minutes.

Speed threw towels down and began cleaning up the mess and Shake stepped around him and walked out to the field. He was flustered and mentally needed to step out of the box and clear his head. Rex acted like a madman. Shake felt sorry for him—for his financial and family problems, his memory loss, his exile from the homestead. It was all sad, but enough was enough. The old man was now completely off his rocker and the best course was to stay out of his way. Rex was like a great wheel rolling downhill. If you tried to hold on you were apt to break your neck.

Shake walked onto the field and looked up at the sky. The cloudless blue sky went on forever. It felt about seventy-two degrees and there was a slight breeze. A great day for baseball, he told himself, but it wasn't convincing. Something like foreboding swam underneath his thoughts and it wouldn't go away. Twice this morning, before the first pitch even, the dark side of the force had manifested itself (yeah, he was a *Star Wars* fan). What else was coming, he wondered. It was best to keep a heads up.

Mischief, thou art afoot.
Take thou what course thou wilt.

The game with the Yankees kicked off at 1:00 without a hitch. There were one and a half innings in the book before the weirdness began.

The stands were packed and the Kingsmen were tied 2-2 in the bottom of the second. There were two on and two out and the count stood at 2-2 on Ortiz, whose number was twenty-two.

"Deuces are wild," noted Rick.

(At that moment, up in Fenway with two outs and a count of 1-2 on Don Baylor, strike three got past the catcher on a wild pitch. Romero scored, Buckner went to second and Baylor was safe at first. The next batter Dwight Evans would hit a three run homer. In Tallinn, Estonia, at that moment, Heike Drechsler leaped and set the women's long jump record at 7.45 meters. It was her second jump. Back at Beehive Stadium, Ortiz swung hard at a 2-2 pitch and missed. His bat flew out of his hands and nearly hit Kalecki in the head who was coaching third.)

In the top of the third Benedict started barking at the home plate umpire. Todd Clinton was behind home plate and Shake considered him the worse ump in the Eastern League. In the field he was bad enough, but behind the plate he was a crime against humanity. He had a floating strike zone that was confusing to both hitters and pitchers, and a strike on the outside corner early in count wasn't necessarily a strike later in the count. It drove Shake mad. He and Clinton had had their run-ins before. Twice last year, Clinton ejected Shake—once for arguing balls and strikes and another time for a brutal out-call at third base. In Shake's opinion, the guy was strictly bush league.

At ball four, Steve Basset snapped the throw back from Estrella and walked off the mound to cool down.

"Hey, Blue, hammer that plate down!" yelled Benedict. "It's moving around!"

"Mix in some consistency once in a while!" added Shake

Benedict kept it going: "Did your glass eye fog up? If he's pitching too fast we can ask him to slow it down for you!"

Clinton took his mask off and stared into the Kingsmen dugout.

"Can you see that far?" shouted Burton, getting into the act.

"Yeah, we're on the third base side, not the first base side!"

Clinton took three steps towards their dugout and yelled, "Enough from you! One more word and your outta here!"

Benedict coughed "Bullshit!" into his fist but the umpire missed it or ignored it and walked back behind the plate. "Let's get a batter up here!" he shouted before putting his mask back on.

Shake and company kept their cool for the rest of the half inning—at least until Hoffman and Hamilton turned a nifty double play to end the inning. The call at first was close but correct.

"Hey, Avery!" yelled Shake at the first base ump. "Nice call. You might want to think about giving lessons." Avery pretended to ignore the compliment but Shake saw him crack a smile.

In the bottom of the third, Prince singled and promptly stole second. That brought up Hamilton. On a 1-1 pitch, Dane bent out of the way of an inside pitch only to have it called a strike. Now Kalecki got into it. "You better swing," he cried out from the coach's box. "You're standing in the strike zone!" Dane ended up grounding out to first, and Goff lifted a high fly ball to left to end the inning.

As the Kingsmen ran out to take the field, the P.A. system started playing the theme from *Love Story*. That was a cue that some guy in the park was about to propose to his girlfriend. Shake noticed that his infielders had stopped throwing the ball around and were watching the proposal up behind the dugout. His coaches and all the bench players stood up and looked over the roof of the dugout to check it out. Shake ignored it all.

What he missed was this: a guy in jeans and a t-shirt, with his Kingsmen cap turned backwards, was on one knee in front of his girlfriend, holding a small black box up to her. The entire crowd awaited her reaction, only it wasn't what they expected. She was shocked—shocked as though a searchlight had just been thrown on her—and she quickly became upset. Cornered, she looked around. Next she blushed deeply, shook her head no, and ran for the exit. There were yelps and groans from the crowd as the embarrassed young man stood back up. His buddy on the other side of him started laughing uproariously and the young man turned around and punched him in the face. A fight broke out.

"What's going on?" asked Shake as he heard the odd crowd noise and noted the reaction of his players on the field.

Rick lowered himself back down. "Unbelievable," he laughed. "She said no and ran off, and his buddy started laughing so he punched him. Now we have a fight."

Shake went up the dugout steps to take a look. Sure enough it was a fight and security people were rushing to break it up.

"It's getting weird out here," said Rick as they came back down into the dugout.

Shake took his spot and mumbled to himself, "*There is something in the wind, that we cannot get in.*"

Luis Santiago was up in the stands in his civvies charting pitches. Or pretending to. He waited until Basset's girlfriend Gwen Cymbel got up from her seat and then followed her. She went into the Women's restroom and Luis waited for her and pretended to run into her when she came out.

"Whoa," he said in mock surprise as he flung his arms around her. "Oh, hi, Gwen. Sorry about that."

"Luis, hi. What you doing down here?"

"Charting pitches. I came down to use the restroom." He still held her in his protective embrace. They were face to face. "You okay," he asked.

"I'm fine." She smiled and looked at both his arms. "You can let me go now," she added. "I won't fall. I promise."

"Oh, sure. Sorry about that," he said... "I could get used to that," he slipped in under his breath but loud enough for her to hear. She ignored the comment so he quickly shifted gears. "Steve's looking good out there. The ump's kind of a jerk, but you just have to work through it."

"Yeah, he's getting a little frustrated. But like you say—he's got to work through it."

"What you looking for?"

"Huh? Oh, a soda, but the lines are too long."

"We'll take care of that," he said with a wink. He grabbed her hand and quickly led her over to the concession stand. "What do you want?"

"Diet Coke."

Luis stuck his head in the side door and got the concessionaires attention. They knew him immediately and happily took his order. In thirty seconds he had a medium Diet Coke and handed it to Gwen with a flourish.

"Impressive," she said.

"My pleasure." He saw that the Diet Coke bought him some time and she was willing to stay a minute and make small talk.

"How's Cathy?" she asked.

"Who? Oh, Cathy. She's fine, I guess," he replied with some confusion. But he quickly sorted it out: Cathy had been his date when he had gone out to dinner a couple weeks ago with Steve and Gwen. The double-date was part of his plan to ingratiate himself with the two of them while all the time working his magic on Gwen. He was sure it was working. As for Cathy-- she was a local and one of the many women he dated over the season. "She's not my girlfriend," he clarified. "Just a date."

"She seemed nice," added Gwen, sipping her soda through a straw.

"Yeah. I don't have a girlfriend. I'm still looking for the right gal. You wouldn't happen to have a twin sister?... No? Too bad. Hey, have you seen my new car yet? It's right over here—you can see it through the fence." He grabbed her hand again and led her away from the concession stands.

"You bought a new car?" she said cheerfully. "Let's see it."

He held on tight to her hand and walked her away from the lines of people and over to a chain link fence where he pointed out to the parking lot. "See, over there. The red Corvette. Two hundred and thirty horsepower. Convertible. Totally awesome, right?"

"Wow, looks fast."

Luis liked to think he knew women, and one thing all chicks dug—even devout Christian chicks like Gwen—were fast cars. "Yeah, I just picked it up Thursday. Cost a fortune but had to have it... Now where's Steve's car? Over there, right? The beat-up looking Nissan. Really? Come on, Gwen, you need to get him to upgrade his ride. Make him get a Camaro or maybe a Trans Am. Something with balls. Oops, I mean something with a little oomph." (He pumped his fist out to make his point.) "You know what I mean?"

"Right now we're saving our money for the wedding," she said innocently. "Maybe after we settle down."

"The vette's got leather seats," he added quickly, ignoring her remark about settling down. Her hand had gone limp—the signal to him to let go—but he still held on tightly. There was less than three weeks before the All-Star break and his bet was on the line. This was his opportunity to make his move and no one was better at making *The Move* than him. "You need to check it out. Go for a ride. I'll put the top down. How about after the game?"

"Steve and I are going out to dinner."

"Perfect. Later then. I'll pick you up at your motel."

"No, that's too late for me."

"It's never too late," he insisted. She frowned and looked away from him, so he put his other hand on her elbow and tugged gently. "Come on, Gwen, it's never too late. Look at me. Please…. I have something to tell you and I can't keep it in any longer. I love you… No, don't look away. Please. I love you and I had to tell you. I loved you the first minute I saw you."

"I thought you were Steve's friend?"

"I am, but if it comes down to my friendship for him and my love for you—my love for you wins out every time. I can't help it."

"What can I say? You're making me uncomfortable. I'm not—"

"Don't say anything, just hear me out. Let me come by your motel tonight. We'll go for a moonlight drive and just talk. No pressure, nothing more. Just let me talk to you. Give me a chance.

"I'm going back to my seat."

"I'll pick you up at eleven tonight. I'll take you wherever you want to go, and we'll just talk."

"You're not picking me up," she said sternly, twisting her arm free from his grasp. "I hear what you say but I'm sorry. I love Steve. We're getting married. And that's that. I'm sorry, Luis."

She turned to walk away so he pounced. (*The Move* wasn't working so it was time to swing wildly for the fences.) He took her in his arms and pulled her close. "You don't have to save yourself for me. You can have me now. None of this waiting crap. If you were my fiancé there'd be no waiting. You're too beautiful a woman. Don't you want to feel a man inside you?

Don't you want to feel me inside you? Come on, grab a handful and let's get it on!"

"Help!" she cried.

Startled, he let her go and stepped back.

"You're disgusting," she said. "Stay away from me or I'll scream. Steve's going to hear about this. Just wait and see. I'm going to tell him everything."

"I'm so glad you said that," he replied earnestly, feigning great relief. "*Thank, God*. That's exactly what I wanted to hear. And I win the bet. Thank you, thank you, Gwen."

She had spun away but now stopped in her tracks and looked back at him. "What do you mean bet?" she asked. "What bet?"

"Well, it's kind of a long story, but one of the guys in our prayer group—I won't tell you his name—claimed you were a fake. He said the whole virgin thing was a fake and that you were out of Steve's league and played around on him. I called him a liar and almost got in a fight with him. I told him that in your case—and I knew you—that your virtue matched your beauty. But he kept dissing you so we made a bet. A hundred bucks. I bet him I would make a move on you and you'd turn me down flat. I have a reputation as a ladies man—"

"I've heard that."

"So he took the bet and here we are. I won and more importantly Steve won. He's marrying a true-blue woman… But you don't need to tell Steve all about this. I mean, my part he'd probably laugh at but you'd have to tell him about the guy in his prayer group who was putting you down. Then Steve would demand to know who it was and I'd have to tell him and then there'd be trouble. In the clubhouse, on the team. Trouble. So I'd appreciate it if we just keep this to ourselves… I'll give you half my winnings," he added with a joking smile, hoping for the best.

"Okay, Luis," she said smiling back. "I won't say anything. Not that I believe a word you say, but I wouldn't want to be the cause of a fight in the clubhouse. For now anyhow."

"Fair enough."

"I got to get back."

"Me, too," said Luis as he walked next to her. He glanced down at her necklace. The prize. To his amazed disappointment, he realized he wasn't going to get his hands on that by bedding her. He'd have to figure out another way.

In the top of the sixth the Yankees took the lead 5-3. It wasn't so much they were getting to Basset as it was Clinton the home plate ump. When Basset was on the mound, the strike zone was a postage stamp, but when the Yankees took the mound it grew to the size of Arizona. As a result of getting squeezed by Clinton (which, Shake was sure of, was intentional), Basset had to throw more pitches, which meant he got behind in more counts and had to groove more pitches that the Yankee hitters could take advantage of. Shake was close to fed up with it.

"He's at ninety pitches and we're only in the sixth," said Benedict.

"Let him finish this inning," replied Shake. "Get Tito up. He'll go in in the seventh."

"Right."

Basset got out of the inning but gave up three runs. As he walked off the mound, he glared at the home plate ump. Shake waited for his young ace to sit down and went over to him. "You're done for the day," he said putting his hand on Steve's shoulder.

"I got more."

"No, not with this dipshit behind the plate. Call it a day. Sometimes it's just the luck of the draw. Sometimes you get Paul Runge behind the plate and sometimes you get Mr. Magoo."

Steve nodded with a grateful smile and went to go look for his jacket. Lousy deal, thought Shake. Stuff like that could mess with a kid's confidence, but Basset was tough-minded and major league material. He was sure the kid would get over it. But not Shake.

The first hitter Hamilton, fearing anything close would be called a strike, swung at an 0-2 pitch and popped it up to second. As the Yankee second baseman back-peddled, he tripped on the cut of the grass and went down. The ball fell for a hit. Finally, thought Shake, a little luck. But Goff struck out on a called third strike at the letters. One out. The fans were on Clinton big time and the Kingsmen bench had been chirping at him all day. It was a steady rain of insults. He had gone into hunker-down mode, ignoring everyone, while effectively wreaking his revenge. The Kingsmen had been told by their coaches to go up there looking for a pitch to hit.

Burks followed orders and hit the first good pitch he saw through the hole into left field. Dane took second. That brought up Estrella. The muscle-bound catcher dug in and got ready to hit. The first pitch was high and away and called a ball, but Estrella fouled the next two pitches off to make it 1-2. The next pitch was over the plate but at his ankles and he laid off. Clinton turned and emphatically pulled the cord on his imaginary Black & Decker chainsaw, yelling "You're outta there!" The crowd screamed their outrage. The Kingsmen bench was merciless. Estrella looked at Clinton and shook his head in disbelief. Clinton ignored him and instead took off his mask and stared intently into it as though the meaning of life was written inside of it. Estrella shook his head one more time and then walked off, dragging his bat behind him.

Matt Horn strode to the plate like a man going to the guillotine. But he had a plan and that plan was to swing at the first pitch. The Yankee pitcher was no dummy; he knew he didn't have to throw a strike to get a strike. His first pitch was at the letters but Horn, geared for it, muscled it into right field for a hit. Dane took off from second and got the windmill from Kalecki. The right fielder charged the ball and made a nice scoop and throw. It was going to be a close play at home. The crowd stood. Everyone in the Kingsmen dugout came up to the railing.

It was a close play as the Yankees catcher put down the tag just as Dane slid into home. Clinton lifted his leg, did a pirouette, and gleefully called him out. Shake knew it was close—that Hamilton might have been out—but at this point he didn't care. He'd had enough.

Shake flew out of the dugout like a heat-seeking missile and Rick followed him fearing the worst. But Shake had no intention of banging the ump. Even enraged he knew where the line was. All he planned to do was get in Clinton's grill and let it rip, scream bloody murder and unburden himself of a day's worth of piled-up garbage. What followed was an entertaining show that included face to face bellowing laced with Elizabethan profanity topped off by Clinton swirling his finger in a high arc signaling Shake's ejection from the game. Shake took off his cap and threw it into the stands where it was gobbled up by adoring fans.

Shake started to walk back to the dugout, thought better of it, and spun around for further comment. Rick was between him and the ump so Shake had to spit out his parting words over Rick's shoulder: *"Past hope, past cure, past help!"* The crowd roared their approval.

He walked through his dugout, past the looks of admiration on his player's faces, and disappeared into the tunnel. The belief that an ejected manager was banned from the field and therefore banned from managing the rest of the game was the biggest fairy tale in baseball. Some went into the clubhouse and set up a relay system with their interim manager (in this case Rick Burton). Others lurked in the tunnel, out of sight of the umps, and dispatched instructions from there. Shake was a little bolder than that. He donned a hooded jacket, snuck into the bullpen, and called in his orders over the phone while his pitchers shielded him from view by milling around in front of him.

From the bullpen, Shake watched his team tie it up with an exciting rally in the bottom of the ninth. It was highlighted by an inside-the-park homerun by Prince. Shake called in his sometime fifth starter and long reliever "Kid" Curry to take them into extra innings. The game went fifteen innings, their longest game of the year, and Curry pitched well until the top of the fifteenth when he gave up a homer to the Yankees lead-off hitter to make it 6-5. The Kingsmen rally in the bottom of fifteenth fell short and their eight-game winning streak game to an end.

Shake followed his pitchers across right field and back to the clubhouse. He wore his hood up and strolled across the field with his hands in his jacket. The stands were quickly emptying. Someone had won a nice snow-blower, he thought, but for those who stuck it out (which was most of them) they were leaving disappointed. And to make matters worse, the beer batter hadn't struck out once all game.

Shake sat in his office and fielded questions from the local press. The hot topic was umpiring but he was careful not to openly disparage the umpiring crew, or to call out any one umpire in particular. That would lead to a league fine. Instead he mentioned in passing a questionable strike zone that may have influenced the game. The press could read between the lines. Balt the journalism student was missing but Shake chalked it up to summer vacation. After the interview, Orson stuck his head in and said hi. He appeared to Shake to be moping around about something—probably Rex—so he refrained from asking him anything about the old man.

Shake took a long time to complete his post-game report. He wanted to get it right. The line on Basset was misleading and he wanted to make it clear the kid was their indisputable ace. Even with this anomaly, Basset still carried the lowest ERA in the Eastern League. Shake put Sinatra on the cassette player and carefully worked on his report, treating it almost like a damn deposition instead of just a game summary, and when he thought he had it right he faxed it over. (The big club loved his post-game reports. They found them part news story, part literature, and always entertaining.) Besides the fax, Shake would call both the Director of Player Personnel and the Director of Player Development tomorrow to make things crystal clear.

With that done, Shake changed clothes and walked out through the empty clubhouse and into the parking lot. He half expected to run into Rex and for Rex to act like this morning had never happened. But Shake was not in a forgiving mood at the moment. Out of curiosity he glanced over at Rex's parking spot and saw his car still here, and when he looked closer he could see Rex sitting in the driver's seat. He hesitated a moment and looked at Rex. The old man just sat there like a statue. Screw him, thought Shake as he started for his car, but he stopped, said "Shit!" under his breath, and walked over to Rex's car where he rapped on the window.

Rex rolled down his window and quickly asked, "Where am I?" as though he had stopped a passing pedestrian.

"Beehive Stadium," answered Shake without missing a beat.

"Where do I live?"

"I think you're at the Marriot in Farmington."

"How do I get there?"

Shake took his cap off (Speed had given him a new one), scratched his head, and looked into Rex's eyes. It was legit. There was no light of recognition. "Well, first off, you go out this gate—" He proceeded to give Rex directions to the Marriot, which Rex listened to intently and nodded understanding. When he was done, Rex thanked him and rolled up his window and drove out of the parking lot.

Three to one he'd get lost, figured Shake, but he wasn't about to follow him home. Not his caretaker, he told himself but knowing, as he thought it, that it was easier said than done. His refined humanity wouldn't allow it, or perhaps it was his innate sympathy for the human predicament that would never allow him to condemn a man without first trying to get in his shoes. The old man had built up a wall of self-justification, and Shake feared that only some great earthquake would tear it down. Rex needed Corey back in his life. Everybody needed something. What he needed was a cold beer and the Mermaid was only minutes away.

On the drive over, Shake turned down the radio and let his mind wander. He needed to relax. It had been a long grueling day and the day still wasn't over. He thought about Lucy—her and her Fire Festival of Lithia—and inevitably began to compare her to Mimi.

When to the sessions of sweet silent thought
I summon up remembrance of things past

Twenty-five years later and he still compared women to Mimi. He did this with all the women he had dated over the years and all of them, including Lucy, came up short. Besides her sublime beauty, Mimi had possessed a quiet intelligence that glowed like a halo around her. She loved Shakespeare and baseball, and not because he did but because she possessed an artist's soul. He had loved her dearly, and wherever she was, there was the world. Lucy wasn't the world

Then what was Lucy, he wondered. She was like his favorite candy—affordable, savory but, in the end, not very filling. There was a thing missing. Yes, he had to admit to a hunger within him that, over the years and into middle age, had grown rather than subsided. It was a restlessness that wouldn't leave him alone. The real question was: what was he looking for when he knocked on Lucy's door at night? He fumbled through the bat rack of his thoughts looking for the answer but the best he could come up with was one word. "Cathedral." He was looking for a Cathedral. It was funny way to say it but it got closest to the truth. Was he getting religious after all these years? He wouldn't say he wasn't religious. He was brought up a Catholic, for crying out loud, but he didn't attend church much. So what was it? But suddenly he found himself too tired to run this thought down, so he fell back into his comfort zone. Baseball was his religion, he concluded. What was it Durocher said? "Baseball is like church. Many attend, few understand." Exactly.

The wheel of his thoughts came back around and there was Mimi again. Yes, she had been his world—until he called her a whore and destroyed it all. "But enough of that," Shake told himself as he pulled into The Mermaid Tavern. "Enough of that. *'I'll see what physic the tavern affords.'*"

Kalecki and Benedict where there but Burton and Larkin, both married men, were home this Saturday evening with their families. He realized he was starving so he ordered a French Dip with fries and sat down with his two coaches to drink beer, eat, and talk baseball. When their pitcher of beer emptied Bernie, just starting her shift, came over to take their order for a fresh one. This shifted Shake's attention. He had carried out his part of the conspiracy and told Larry about overhearing Bernie tell Lucy she still loved him. Lucy had done her part with Bernie, and now Shake was curious to see the fruits of their labor.

She came up next to Larry. "Another pitcher?" she asked.

Shake and Bob waited for Larry to jump in and start the verbal brouhaha, but he was silent, so Bob said, "Sure. Make it a Miller this time."

"I'll get you a new glass," she said as she leaned over Larry, resting her breasts on his shoulder while grabbing his glass. She paused there for a moment before straightening up.

"You're a sweetheart," replied Larry, looking up and winking at her. She walked off with one empty pitcher and one empty beer glass.

"What the hell was that?" demanded Bob sounding like a man who had just been robbed of this evening's entertainment. "*'Sweetheart'*... What the hell do you mean by '*Sweetheart?*'"

"Nothing," said Larry with a shrug. "She's a sweet kid. We made a pact not to argue anymore."

"A pact?"

"Yeah, and I'm taking here out to dinner tomorrow night."

"Dinner, huh?" commented Shake. "Well... will wonders never cease."

"She's a sweet kid."

"If you say so," said Bob still reeling from the one-eighty. "I think you're just going soft."

Shake chuckled and changed the subject back to baseball. Larry looked grateful. Bernie returned with a full pitcher for all and a frosted mug for Larry. She poured them all a fresh beer starting with Larry, said "Enjoy," and left them alone. Bob shook his head in mock disgust and drank his fresh beer.

Their brain trust broke up about ten o-clock and Shake found Lucy sitting at the bar. He could ask her about the festival or he could not. He could tell her how nice she looked or he could not. Maybe they would end up having sex tonight and maybe they wouldn't. He didn't really care—he was still carrying the game around with him like a golden sombrero. That and everything else today had put him in a bit of a funk. It was the same kind of funk you got as a player when you struck out four times in a game.

"Heard you got ejected today," she said matter-of-factly.

"Yeah. Same jerk who ejected me last year."

"Currents of spiritual energy were working against you."

"Something was. The whole day's been off... Off center, if you know what I mean."

"I do."

"Got a spell to counter that?"

"No, but I did get you something." She fished into a black bag on the bar and pulled out a chain. "It's a rune necklace—for men." She spread it apart and slipped it over his head. "It brings prosperity and well-being to the wearer."

Shake was surprised—he'd never known Lucy to be a gift-giver—and he looked at the silver chain with its strange markings and said, "Thanks, Luce." She smiled warmly at him. "I'm not really a big jewelry guy," he added as an afterthought. "But I'll keep it with me." He noticed her warm smile fade away.

"It needs to be around your neck to get its full power."

"Okay," he replied as he slipped the chain over his neck and then leaned over to kiss her on the cheek. Her warm smile returned.

He tucked the chain inside his shirt as Lucy brought up the topic of Bernie and Benedict. She was pleased that their little ruse had worked, at least to the point where the two had stopped arguing and were now going out on a date. She wondered out loud where it all might lead to.

"We'll see if they survive their date first," commented Shake.

Lucy laughed and stepped away to take care of some business in the back. Shake took off his new cap to check what it was that kept bugging him and found a paper label. He tore it out and leaned over the bar to throw it away. As he did, the chain around his neck fell out and caught his beer bottle on the way back nearly spilling it. He took the chain off and stuck it in his pants pocket. Lucy returned and leaned into his ear.

"Meet me upstairs in twenty minutes," she whispered. She leaned back and suddenly frowned. "Where's the rune necklace?"

"What? Oh, it got in the way. Almost spilled my beer so I put it in my pocket."

"It's got to be around your neck."

"I know. You told me."

"Then why'd you take it off?"

"Cause it got in the way. I already told you I'm not a jewelry guy. See?" he said as he spread out his ten ring-less fingers.

"If you were married you'd wear a ring."

"Maybe. But I'm not married and don't plan on getting married." He said it bluntly and saw again that change of hue in her face. He'd seen that only once before when he turned down her invitation to go to the festival. It was like a shadow passing over her face.

"You need to give a little, Shake," she said with thickness in her voice.

"Give a little? What do you mean? Give what?"

"Never mind. Let me have it. Give me the necklace back."

"Suit yourself." He took the chain out of his pocket and handed it to her. She took it back angrily, balled it up, and suddenly threw it. The chain ball opened up in mid-flight and landed heavily on a table full of people, upsetting their prosperity and well-being.

"Shit!" she said under her breath and hurried off to apologize to her customers.

Another precedent broken, thought Shake sizing up the situation. Anger, expectations, hurt feelings. She was suddenly acting more like a wife than his laissez-faire lover. More like Doris Day than Brigitte Bardot. What was bringing all this on? Menopause? Iron poor blood? Lack of fiber in her diet? Whatever it was he didn't like it. He also didn't relish the idea of talking to her anymore in this state.

> *A woman moved is like a fountain troubled,*
> *Muddy, ill-seeming, thick, bereft of beauty,*
> *And while it is so, none so dry or thirsty*
> *Will deign to sip or touch one drop of it.*

He left the bartender a generous tip and beat a hasty retreat.

(Here concludes the longest chapter of our story. In it we witnessed not only the longest game of the season on the longest day of the year, but also all the mustard and pepper that flavor our main course. But before we close this over-lengthy chapter, we'll leave you with our customary couplet: The sun today woke early and stayed late, lighting the paths of their impending fate.)

14
CHAPTER

I don't care how long you've been around, you'll never see it all.
Bob Lemon

It was the weekend before the All-Star break. Since the Fire Festival of Lithia, the Kingsmen had played .500 ball. Leading up to today, Sunday the 6th, they had played fourteen straight games and gone seven and seven with six losses on the road. It wasn't really a tailspin (they were still two games up in first) but it was a bit of a funk. Shake knew that every good team had one and it was how a team handled it that mattered. Hitters were in mini-slumps, pitchers weren't hitting their spots, and two of their top players—Burks and Horn—were on the DL with injuries. But slumps and injuries were part of the game. A team knows when it was good—they just knew—and Shake could still see that confidence in the clubhouse. He wasn't too worried.

Shake had shuffled his rotation around a bit and had Chuck Davis going against the Nashua Pirates today. That gave enough rest for his big three—Basset, Santiago, and Ellsworth—to pitch in the All-Star Game Wednesday. Svoboda took Burks' spot in left field and Rosecrans, a utility infielder, was starting for

Horn at first. Rosecrans had shown some pop lately in pinch-hit appearances and the big cub wanted to see him get some regular at bats.

It was Dairy Day and there was a cow-milking contest before the game. Guida's Dairy, Deerfield Farm and others had stands set up selling half-off ice cream. The temperature was pushing ninety and they did a brisk business throughout the day. The game was also brisk and entertaining. The Kingsmen won 4-0 and Davis pitched a three hit shut-out. In the fourth, Rosecrans broke his bat but hit one out for a homerun. Shake had never seen that before and, like most managers who'd been in baseball nearly all their life, he'd seen just about everything.

After the game, most of the players scattered to the four winds to enjoy the extended All-Star break, some to catch up with their families, some to go fishing, and others just to chill out and mend their aches and pains. Shake and Rick, along with six Kingsmen, didn't have that luxury. They had an All-Star Game to play.

Shake finished up his paperwork and took a shower and changed into some nice clothes. He was taking Lucy to the theatre to see *The Taming of the Shrew*. First he planned to take her to dinner and then they'd walk over to The Repertory Theatre to see the play at 8:00. Their relationship had been a little strained lately and this was his way of making it up to her.

The theatre was rather small and the performance was sold out but he had tickets in the third row, dead center. Shake and Lucy sat down in their seats and read the program. His brother Gilbert had told him about this production. It was set in the Wild West, in a Texas saloon, with Petruchio as a cowboy and Kate as a Calamity Jane-type character. Gil said it was fresh and clever and Shake was looking forward to it.

The house was full and everyone waited for the lights to go down. A man appeared on stage with a microphone and walked towards them. At first Shake thought that the show, for some reason, was going to be delayed or cancelled, and he was sure of it when the man introduced himself as the director. But unexpectedly, the director sat down on the edge of the stage, smiled at the audience, and took up his microphone.

"Thank you all for coming," he said. He had the demeanor of a cool college professor, the one who finds it important to relate to all his students. "We'll get things started in just a moment, but I wanted to take a few minutes to talk about *The Taming of the Shrew* and our good friend Will Shakespeare... Shakespeare was a product of his time. This play—*The Taming of the Shrew*—is a product of that time. It was a time when women were worse than second class citizens. If they were a daughter, their father ruled them with an iron hand. If a wife, their husband was their lord and master and they were no better than slaves. Today, in our enlightened twentieth century, we find such a state of affairs to be contemptible, even barbarous. But even a great playwright like Shakespeare was still a product of his time and you will find things in this play that may offend you. We've taken some liberties with the play and set it in the Wild West to give it a more American feel, yet, with all due apologies, it's still burdened by the patriarchal tyranny of sixteenth century England. Some critics have pointed out that Shakespeare, in all his genius, should never have allowed—"

"Hold it there!" cried Shake as he rose from his seat. "Where the hell do you get off apologizing for Shakespeare?"

The startled director lowered his microphone and looked at Shake. There was a smattering of applause at his outburst and someone in the back said, "Here, here." A woman in front of him turned around and told him to sit down but Shake remained standing.

"Let me finish," said the director, trying to regain his composure.

"Let me speak," countered Shake loudly. The same woman told him to sit down again, and she was joined by her partner who told him not only to sit down but to shut up as well. Shake looked down at the two of them and said,

> *My tongue will tell the anger of my heart,*
> *Or else my heart concealing it will break.*

Many in the audience recognized that as a line from the play and laughed. The two women turned back around and looked at the stage.

"No, go on,' replied the director in a way to show the audience he was open to all opinions. "What is it you have to say?"

"It's rather pretentious, don't you think, to come out here and apologize for Shakespeare? He's been doing quite well up to now. Let him speak for himself. Let his play speak for itself. We don't need you to explain things to us like we're school children, who need to be coddled and protected. Give us a little credit for being grown-ups and get out of the way of genius."

The smattering of applause increased as the audience rallied behind this unexpected rebel. They welcomed his message; *they were* grown-ups and *they didn't* need to be coddled. Seeing all this, the director stood up and politely bowed to the audience. "Fair enough," he said curtly. "On with the play."

Shake sat back down next to Lucy and glanced at her to check her reaction. She looked amused, and she bumped shoulders with him and said, "You're a bad boy."

The play ran its course and at the end Shake joined whole-heartedly in the two standing ovations. Gil had been right—it was fresh and clever—and he was glad he saw it. In the lobby he waited for Lucy to go to the restroom. A few folks came up to him and patted him on the back or shook his hand. One tall fellow yelled over the crowd, "Hey, Shake. Still arguing with umpires I see."

Lucy came out and as they went to leave they ran into Dane and Delia.

"Hey, Coach," said Dane. "This is my friend Delia."

Shake introduced Lucy and shook hands with the two of them. Dane no longer looked like a monk. Sporting a v-neck sweater with a shirt and tie, his hair parted on the side, he looked quite the Ivy League gentleman. His girlfriend smiled coolly at his side. She had long blonde hair and the most beautiful, sad blue eyes. She wore a corsage as though they were on a prom date.

"I loved your speech there," said Dane. "I don't think he was expecting anyone to interrupt his spiel."

"Couldn't help myself.

"I totally agree with you. I'm just glad someone had the guts to get up and say so."

"My dad was an English Lit professor. Specialized in Shakespeare. He would have rolled over in his grave if I hadn't stood up... But what would you have done?" (To Lucy.) "Don't know if I mentioned it but Dane here knows his Shakespeare. We've gone 'round a few times." (Back to Dane.) "If I hadn't made a fool out of myself first, what would you have done?"

"Hmm, let me think about that," replied Dane while rubbing his chin in thought. "I probably would have let it go, but sat there all steamed-up inside for the rest of the night."

"You said your last name is Hamilton?" interrupted Lucy. "You live around here?"

"During the season, but I grew up in Ithaca, New York."

"Went to Cornel," added Shake.

"Is that where your family is?" asked Lucy.

"Yes, well just my mom. My dad passed away when I was ten."

"Oh, sorry to bring up sad memories."

"That's okay."

There was a moment of awkward silence that Shake quickly filled: "Lucy owns The Mermaid Tavern and we're going over there now. If the two of you aren't doing anything, come by."

Shake noticed Delia with the beautiful, sad blue eyes tug gently at Dane's coat.

"No, we got to go," said Dane with a self-conscious smile.

They said their goodbyes and Shake and Lucy walked out into the night air. It was still warm outside. They walked together the two blocks back to the car. Lucy was quiet most of the way.

"Is he a nephew of yours?" she asked.

"A what? Nephew? No," he answered with a surprised chuckle. "Why?"

"No reason. Just curious."

Shake found the question odd, but as he walked a little further he got the connection. "He's a second baseman. So was I," he said. "We all look alike."

Luis Santiago pulled the necklace out of his pocket and admired it. It was worth a hundred dollars he was going to get from Phil for it—but it was worth even more than that. It kept his rep as the team's Casanova intact, and that was worth more to Luis than the hundred bucks. And it hadn't been easy getting his hands on it. All it took was the seduction of a hotel house maid (a cute Latina and probably an illegal), then stealing her master card-key, pulling the fire-alarm, and slipping quickly into Gwen's room as she rushed out. Luck played its part: he figured she took her necklace off when she slept and he was right. He found it on the nightstand next to the bed, pocketed it, and got out of there fast. All in all, he had to admire his own ingenuity.

Luis knocked on the door to Phil Cappadona's apartment. Phil let him in where he found Chuck Davis on the couch watching TV. Luis and Phil were scheduled to leave the next morning for the All-Star Game.

"He's here to pay up," said Phil cheerfully.

"Or collect," said Chuck.

Luis didn't answer and walked into the living room like a matador walking into the bullring. He eased gracefully down into a chair, ignoring the two of them.

"Well?" asked Phil. "Time's up. Did you get it?... Well, did you?"

"Don't tell us you got it," said Chuck hopefully.

Luis regarded them aloofly and then looked away at something more important.

"He's not going to tell us," added Chuck.

"That's cause he didn't get it," claimed Phil with smirk. "He didn't nail her. Despite all his plots and schemes, he struck out. He's here to pay up. Am I right or am I wrong? Tell me I'm wrong?"

There was a large wooden spool that once held telephone cable that acted as Phil's coffee table. Now Luis stood up and held his closed fist over the table. He let slip the necklace but caught it in time so it dangled enticingly over the table before he let it drop.

"Holy shit!" exclaimed Phil as he grabbed up the prize. "You did it!"

"Why would you doubt me?" replied Luis returning Phil's earlier smirk.

"Dammit, Tiago," said Chuck. "I was hoping you wouldn't do it—but you did. Not good... It's not good. Basset will find out about this?"

"She's not going to tell him."

"Wait," said Phil. "How do I know this is her necklace and you didn't just go out and buy one just like it?"

"Open it up and read the inscription."

Phil opened the locket and read the inscription out loud: "To my beloved Gwen. Corinthians 13: 4-8." He looked at Luis with renewed awe. "Holy shit. You did it!" he repeated.

"How do you know she's not going to tell him?" asked Chuck. "They were engaged and now what? Is she going with you now? In that case she'll have to break it off and tell him."

"She won't say a thing. Trust me. It was a one night stand and I told her that. She's not going to break off her engagement."

"You better hope not," said Chuck. "And how is she going to explain the missing locket?"

"She lost it. Someone stole it. That's her problem."

"You're a cold-hearted bastard, bro," replied Chuck shaking his head sadly. "I could never do that to a woman."

"No doubt, Davis. You gotta be willing to do whatever it takes, which is why me and Cap are going to the All-Star Game and you're staying home."

"Eat my shorts."

"Time to pay up," Luis said to Phil. "I'll take fives and tens, or twenties if you have 'em."

Phil got up and went into his room and came back with a wad of cash. He counted out five twenties and handed them to Luis.

"And the necklace," said Luis.

"Wha—no way," protested Phil. "I paid good money for that. It's mine now."

"Hand it over," replied Luis, suddenly stone-faced.

"No way, bro. It's mine now."

"What do you want it for? Give it back… Look, I took it off the nightstand when she was in the bathroom and I'd like to give it back to her."

"How you gonna do that?"

"Slip it in her coat pocket or in her purse when she's not looking. It's the right thing to do."

"'*The right thing to do*,'" repeated Phil with a sarcastic laugh. "If you cared about the right thing you wouldn't have screwed your buddy's fiancé and stolen her necklace. I know you. You're just going to pawn it."

"Give it back, asshole."

"Fuck you. It's mine now."

In the dominion of young male egos, where rightful possession is at stake, one thing inexorably leads to another. In no time, Luis and Phil were standing face to face yelling obscenities at each other. In a second it would come to blows.

"Stop it!" yelled Chuck as he stepped forcibly in-between them. "Back off! Both of you!" They stepped back but glared at one another. "There," added Chuck. "I told you this thing would lead to trouble. Now give me the locket." (To Phil.) "Goddam it, Cap, give it to me. What do you need it for? Nothing. Now give it to me... Okay." (To Luis) "And you're not getting it either. I'll make sure she gets it back. Just like you said—I'll find a way to slip it in her purse. But I'll take care of it... Okay? Are we good?"

"We're good."

"Yeah, we're good."

Everybody sat back down and Chuck grabbed the TV remote and switched on Major League Baseball highlights.

"The least you could do," said Phil half-jokingly, "is buy us dinner with your winnings."

"Can't," replied Luis standing up. He brushed off his pants. "Got a date. See you later." And with that he left.

After the door closed, Phil looked at Chuck. "What a jerk," he said.

Chuck didn't disagree.

Mike Faust, trainer for the Kingsmen, sat in his apartment watching *MacGyver* on TV. He really wasn't paying much attention to the story as his thoughts dwelled on more pressing matters—his divorce, his financial problems, and his side business. His empty stare at the television masked a busy mind, and the internal dialogue went something like this:

"Goddam bitch wants everything. And her lawyer can do it, too. If I had a better lawyer this wouldn't be happening. But I can't afford one. The whole system is rigged in favor of the woman. Men get screwed every time. She won't even talk to me. If I could talk to her, we could work it out without these blood-sucking lawyers. But she won't talk to me so I'm fucked. Screw her.

"Ten grand for a lawyer. Maybe more if we go to Divorce Court. I can't borrow any more from my parents, or my brother. I can turn off my cable service—that would save a few bucks. What else? Eat fast food? I already eat too much goddam fast food. Sell some stuff? My stereo system? My car? No, I need my car, but I could still sell it and buy a cheaper one… I don't know. My side business is making me some money but I need to expand it. How though? I'm selling Deca to three players, whites to a few more, but it's not enough. I need more.

"How though? It's a balancing act and I have to be careful. The guys on Deca are showing results—just look at Estrella, for Christ's sake—but how do you get the word out? What's it, eighth-thirty? Rosecrans will be here at nine. I know Greg's been talking to some of the other players, but so far no bites. I know some of the other Dominicans would go for it but they think it's needles and they don't like needles. Dumbshits. I could put them on an oral treatment. Takes a little longer but still works. Estrella needs to help me. He owes me. He needs to pass the word onto his buddies that they can get the same results without needles.

"But too many people can't know. *Be careful.* What would the organization do it they found out I was selling steroids? Whites?—that's one thing—they'd probably slap my wrists. But steroids—that's another thing. What would Shake do if he found out I was selling Deca to his players? Tell the big club. But what would they do? Fire me? It's not a banned substance. It's not cocaine, for crying out loud.

"In a just world they'd thank me and give me a raise. I'm performing a service. I'm creating better, stronger ball-players and that all translates to more W's on the scoreboard. It's win-win. The player turns his career around, gets called up to the majors, and signs a fat contract. Who's to say that's wrong? Look at Estrella. The guy's probably got family living in poverty in the D.R.. I turn him on to Deca, he gets called up and makes the big money and pulls his family out of poverty. How's that make me a bad guy? I turn out faster, stronger ball-players. Word gets out that I have a system that gets results, and that's all they care about—results.

"Yeah, that's it. That's what it comes down to—results. Let's not kid ourselves that there's anything noble going on. Whatever gets results. That's the bottom line. If I can get a rep as a trainer who gets results then they'll bump me up to Triple-A. Maybe the Show. That means more money and getting out of this hole I'm in. Wouldn't that be sweet? And they won't care how I get the results, just that I get the results. Who are we kidding? They don't care. They know it's the wave of the future. They'll look the other way. Guaranteed."

Mike's reverie was broken by the sound of the doorbell and he got up and let Greg Rosecrans in. That was another thing, he thought, as he gave Greg his bi-monthly dosage and took payment for it: what would they do without him? Get it off the streets? Without guidance, they'd over-dose, under-dose, or maybe end up with hepatitis or even AIDS. He instructed them on the right cycle, proper dosages, and the need to take testosterone supplements. He made it safe.

Greg left and Mike sat back down in front of his TV feeling a little better about himself. He switched to baseball highlights and played a game with himself where he tried to guess which players hitting homeruns were juiced or not juiced.

Let Will Shakespeare speak for himself, said Shake; Luis got his keepsake; Faust his piece of cake.

15
CHAPTER

It was mid-day in the alley behind Quick's Cocktail Lounge. Hank and Busta finished off a jay and entered Quick's through the back door where they found Papi sitting with a woman in the back room. The woman was in her mid-forties with exceedingly large breasts and a tooth missing that only showed when she smiled big. She and Papi had spent the night together and Papi, with a King Cobra in one hand and the woman in the other, was in fine spirits. He was singing loudly when Hank appeared.

Papi
Hey, Sweetness, wat up, playa?

(Sings)
'Rebecca, Lolita, Veshawn and DOLL,
Every time you do the Double Dutch you really turn it on'.

Doll
Glad u-could include me in there.

Papi
Always, Doll, always.
(Pulls her on to his lap and sings.)

'Come on get on my Double Dutch Bus.'

Hank
Got anythin' 'round here ta eat?

Papi
Ur-stoned, Sweetness.

Hank
And ur-fat.

Papi
I am phat. Phat an' funky. No doubt 'bout it. I'm phat round the world. Jus' ask Doll.

Doll
He's fat an' phat.

Papi
Cause I'm a double dutch bus. Now, chill out, Sweetness. Be a Prince an' hav-a cold one. We'll git sumthin ta eat later on.

Busta
Anyone hear from Fo-Five?

Papi
Nah, still in the clink. Unless one-a you-two wants to go bail him out, that's where he's gonna stay.

Busta
I still doin get-it. Who called the jakes?

Hank

Doin ask him. He was out cold. When the fight started, Off-cer Warwick jumped inta break it up. Only he was off duty. Ya-know, the Eric Dickerson-lookin' dude who sits at the end-a the bar. Wid glasses. Works security at Beehive.

Busta

Oh, yeah.

Hank

First name's Clarence or Clay, I fo-get.

Papi

It's Off-cer Clarence Warwick, nick-named Clay like Cassius Clay. He's a persnal friend a' mine.

Hank

Sho' he is. So's the mayor. Anyhow, he jumps in an' pulls Fo-Five off an' Fo-Five's piece falls on the floor. Boom- busted. Fo-Five takes a swing at him and Dickerson puts him in-a choke hold and drags his ass out the door.

Busta

I saw that part.

Hank

Next thing he's han-cuff'd in back of-a pa-trol car lookin' like sum sorry ass nigga who's jus been bust'd fo' jay-walkin'. An' that's the straight dope.

Busta

Mutha-fuckin' sheet.

Hank

An' Chief here was playin' possum the whole time. Weren't you, Blubba? One punch and ur-down and out like Liston, all curl'd up and smilin' like sum big, fat kitty cat. But-I know betta—you was playin' possum. Admit it. It took ten of us to carry-ya inta the back room, an' u-was smilin' the whole time.

Papi

I admit nuttin. I got hit from behind. That's all I know. Next thing I wake up in the arms of Doll and it was like wakin' up in heaven. But I tell ya one thin, Sweetness, an' u-can take this ta school. Sum-times discretion's the betta part of valor. Sum-times it's betta to stay down, stay low, an' wait fo' the ruckus ta pass ov'r head.

Busta

But you start'd the fight.

Papi

That's a-matta' of opinion. It wassa question of honor.

Hank

Honor? Wat-u know 'bout honor? You took a dive.

Papi

I said it wassa question of honor—which I answer'd. Honor's fo' sucka's, dawg. Honor's jus-a word. Thin as air. Honor's fo' the dead. U-gotta know when to give it up an' stay alive. Lisen-ta me, Sweetness. I'm tryin' to school u-here.

Hank

School me? Only thin I learn'd from you is the name of ev'ry bartender in town.

Papi

And yo richer fo' it—say, doin u-have a game today?

Hank
Yeah.

Papi

Ur-gonna be late again, foo. U-can't be hangin' out here when you's got's a game. Aren't you scared Glover's gonna put-u back in the dawg-house?

Hank

Nah. I always talk my way outta it.

Papi

Fo' real? I know's u-can lay down sum serious smack when u-wanna, but u-been benched, cuzz, an' fined. That don't sound like ur-talkin' ur-way outta anythin'. Come on, u-betta practice on me. I'll be Glover. Dis is my office. Pretend like I jus' called u-in.

Doll

This sounds like fun.

Papi

Come on, Sweetness. Let's see wat kind'a rap u-got. I'll be Glover.

Hank

Sho-nuf? Okay, homie. Busta, give-em yo Kingsmen hat... There now. That's betta. If'n ur-gonna act the part, u-gotta look the part.

Papi

Back like this, right? There... '*To be or not to be.*'

Doll

What's that mean?

Papi

That's Shakespeare, as in Shake Glover. Git on board, Doll... Now, where was we? I call'd u-inta my office, Sweetness. Wat u-gonna say?

Hank
You have-ta start.

Papi
Awright... U-late again, Sweetness... er, Prince. Take a seat. You amaze me, son. We got's rules an' you don't wanna follow them. Yo wastin' your potential, your god-given talents, an' it hurts me to see it. Yo cavitatin'—

Busta
'Cavitatin'?

Papi
When a ship's propella's goin' 'round but it ain't movin'—jus' stayin' in one spot. Cavitatin'. Doin interrupt... Yo cavitatin, son. An' people are startin' to point fingers at you. Here you are, heir-apparent to the centerfielder job and all u-wanna do is get high and run 'round town. If you ass-me, it's the company you keep. You heard'a muck, right? Well, they're the muck and mire of society, an' if'n you keep hangin' out with them your gonna get that muck and mire on yo-self. You need betta company. There is one man I've seen you with—a big, stately man. I've heard he's gotta heart of gold. Wat's his name?

Hank
Wat's he look like, sir?

Papi
Stout, maybe a little fat, butta cheerful sort. He's handsome, noble-lookin', maybe in his fifties though he looks younger. I 'member now. His name's Stallworth. I see goodness in him. If he's not good then there's no good left in the world. Stay with him an' he'll steer you on the right course. Now, tell me, son, where you been? Why you late again?

Hank

Nah, nah, nah. That's not how he talks. Gimme the hat. I'll be Glover an' you be me.

Papi

Fired awready? Well, give it yo best shot, Sweetness, but it won't be as good as me.

Hank

Now, Hank, where you been?

Papi

Charity work, sir.

Hank

I've been getting' serious complaints 'bout you. Serious complaints.

Papi

Those are mutha-fuckin' lies, sir.

Hank

Don't you use that kinda language with me—an' sit up. Now I'm gonna tell you wat's wrong with you. You got a devil after you and that devil looks jus' like a fat old man. An' the question is—why do you associate with a tub of lard like that? Wat's he good for other than to lead you into temptation? He's a stuffed chicken, a gob a' fat, an old pus-gut. Line up all the fat people in town and he'd be three of them. All's he's good for is eatin', drinkin' and gettin' high. That's all that's ever on his mind—other than screwin' and findin' ways to take your money. He's a bad influence. Get rid of him.

Papi

I'm not followin' you, sir. Who you talkin' 'bout?

Hank
Stallworth—the drug dealer. Papi Stallworth. You know him.

Papi
I do, but yo sellin' him short, sir. I know him to be fine, upstandin' gentleman. Yes, he's old—but wise, like one-a dem three wise men that found our Lord an' Savior Jesus Christ in the manger. Yes, he's fat—but jolly like Saint Nick. If fat's a crime, whadda we gonna do, lock up John Candy? Put Aretha Franklin in jail? An' yes he eats and drinks and gets high, but if all that stuff's a crime then we're all goin' to hell. So, no, sir, doin get rid of Stallworth. Get rid of Busta or Fo-Five but doin get rid of old Papi. If'n you get rid a' him, you get rid of the whole world.

Hank
But I will.

Just then La-Ron entered and told them that the cops were there and looking for Papi. "Wat fo?" Papi wanted to know but La-Ron didn't know. All he knew was that they were on their way. The fat man jumped up with surprising quickness and looked around the room for a hiding place. He turned to Hank. "Sheet! Sweetness—Hank, help yo friend out here," he pleaded.

Hank told him to go hide in the stock room and they would all cover for him. Papi nodded, grabbed his King Cobra, and shuffled nimbly into the back store room. In another moment, Officer Warwick and another officer entered.

"We're lookin' for Stallworth," Officer Warwick said loudly. "Is he back here?" He noticed Hank and did a double-take. Warwick worked security at Beehive Stadium and knew all the ball-players. "Hank, what you doing here? Don't you have a game?"

"Yes, sir," replied

"Then what you doing here?"

Hank was calm and polite: "Jus' droppin' a friend off. I'm on my way now. But I haven't seen Stallworth all day." The others around Hank nodded in agreement.

Officer Warwick ignored Hank's excuse. He was skeptical that none of them had seen Papi all day. He looked past Hank's shoulder and glanced around the room suspiciously. As he made a step for the back room, Hank swore that Stallworth wasn't around—that if he was here he couldn't have missed him since Papi took up a lot of space. Officer Warwick stopped in his tracks, snorted a laugh, and agreed that was true.

"His Harley's parked out back," said the other officer.

Busta jumped in and claimed he'd seen Papi drive off last night in a black caddy. That's the last anyone had seen of him. The other officer considered this for a moment, then quickly asked, "Did it have chrome rims?" Busta was sure it did and everyone agreed. The officer turned to Warwick and said, "I think I saw it over on East Main."

"All right," replied Warwick. "We'll go check it out." He turned his attention back to Hank and looked him up and down in a paternal manner. Warwick was a tall man and looked formidable in his blue uniform. "You need to get over to Beehive. Now," he said to Hank. "And one piece of advice: stay outta this place."

"Yes, sir."

Satisfied at this answer, Officer Warwick and his partner left. Hank and his homies breathed a sigh of relief, and he and Busta went back to the stock room to let Papi know the coast was clear. They found him curled up like a fat cat and snoring loudly.

Busta
Sum-bitch. Look at 'em. He's sleepin'.

Hank
Shh! Doin wake him. Let's see wat he's got on-'em.

(They go through his pockets and Hank finds his wallet.)

Got it. Shh, let's go. When he wakes up he'll figure he's been ganked and scream bloody murder. I'd love to be here. I'll come by afta' the game and give it back to 'em.

Busta
Sho-nuff. He'll 'cuse everyone here of rippin' him off.

Hank
Awright. Later, bro. Here's yo hat, I gotta run and play ball, if'n I'm late it'll be my downfall.

16
CHAPTER

Baseball is the belly-button of our society. Straighten out
baseball, and you straighten out the rest of the world.

Bill Lee

It was after the All-Star break and the Kingsmen were at home
against the Reds for a short series before taking off to New York
for seven games against the Tigers and Yankees. Dane sat at his
locker listening to his transistor radio. His latest concern for the
world was Mad Cow Disease but at the moment his thoughts
were on other things. He was thinking about the upcoming road
trip. At their stop in Albany he planned to visit his father's grave.

It was time, thought Dane. His father died sixteen years
ago and he had not visited his grave site once. He remembered
the funeral like it was yesterday—the open casket (jarring to a
youth of ten who loved his dad) and the pictures of his dad set up
around the room, many of them taken when he was young and
happy. But most of all he remembered the cold shoulders and
looks of recrimination from his dad's side of the family towards
his mom. They blamed her for his death. His mom took him
home early and she drove the three hours back to Ithaca listening

to the Yankees game and crying. She never took him back to visit the cemetery and he never had an urge to go himself.

But over the last year the urge had grown, and lately it had grown particularly strong. He couldn't intellectualize it or explain it; he just needed to visit his father's grave. He knew it was part of the process. For most of his teenage life he had been mad at his dad—mad at him for killing himself and leaving his wife and son alone in the world, mad at him for not saying goodbye, mad at him for not even leaving a note of explanation. As he got older and understood better the machinations of men and women, he wondered why his father—if he was so damned unhappy—didn't just divorce his mom or cheat on her or get psychiatric help. Of all the options available to him he chose to off himself and that made Dane even angrier. But over the last year, and especially now for some inexplicable reason, the anger had receded, leaving him with a desire to make peace with the past.

On the other side of the locker room from Dane, Luis Santiago was slowly getting undressed. Steve Basset walked up to his locker, which sat next to Luis', and placed his bible on the top shelf.

"You quit our prayer group," he said to Luis without reproach and simply as a statement of fact.

"Huh? Oh, yeah," he replied quickly. "I'm in another prayer group with my girlfriend. It's kind of serious."

"*You're serious about a girl?*" said Steve with a slight smile. "That's nice to hear."

"Yeah, well, we'll see," answered Luis playing the string out on his small lie. Steve nodded at him, accepting the lie like some innocent child, and quietly went about rummaging through his locker. Luis couldn't help but notice Steve's subdued manner. Usually after his prayer meeting, Steve was ebullient and talkative but now he was seriously intent on finding something in his locker. Luis was slightly curious to know why.

"What you looking for?"

"Gwen's locket," he responded, not pulling his head out of his locker.

"The one you bought her that she wears all the time?"

"Yeah," he said as he pulled his head out and looked at Luis. "That one. She said she lost it."

"Why would it be in your locker?"

"Who knows… Maybe… I don't know. Just covering all the bases. We had a fight last night about it."

"You two? Nothing serious, I hope."

"No, but I don't get how she could lose it. Really. She never went anywhere without it, then all of sudden she loses it. How does that happen? It's careless.

"Ahh, don't worry about it. I'm sure it'll turn up.

"I hope so."

"But you're welcome to look in my locker—just clean it up while you're at it."

Steve smiled at the joke and said, "No need, my friend."

Luis walked out onto the field and found Chuck Davis and told him about the conversation concerning the locket. Why hadn't Chuck found a way to get it back to her, he asked.

"I'm not buddies with them like you are," answered Chuck. "I haven't seen her or had a chance to slip it in her purse. I was thinking about sticking it somewhere in his locker but now that's out. I was also thinking about paying off one of the ushers to say he found it under her seat in the stands—but that would make another person who's in on this mess. But I'll figure it out. Don't worry about it."

"Not worried," said Luis aloofly as he walked away to go shag flies in the outfield.

Shake welcomed Ron Deer into office and had him sit down. Ron had been in professional baseball going on fourteen years. Early in his career he had bounced between Triple-A and the big leagues but now, older and slower, he was still hanging in there in Single-A baseball. The Kingsmen needed a back-up infielder and a reliable pinch-hitter, and Shake had made a few calls and brought Ron out from Fresno to fill the need.

"How was the trip?" asked Shake.

"Fine," replied Ron. "Had to change planes in Chicago but made it."

"Well, you know the deal here. Horn's still hurt and I need another first baseman and a good bat, so I thought of you. I made a few calls and here you are."

"Appreciate that."

"You're not gonna start. Right now we got this kid Rosecrans filling in at first and he's lookin' pretty good, but you'll get some starts here and there. Double-headers. Four game series, night to day games. You know the drill."

"Sure."

"But I brought you up here for your bat. Someone I can rely on late in games to give us a solid at bat. You fill that bill to a 'T'."

"Understood. Glad to be back in Double-A. It smells better all ready," he said with a laugh. Shake laughed as well because he knew it was true (Double-A did smell better than Single-A).

"Just as long as I get some at bats, I'll be happy," added Ron.

"Two things I never promise—wins and the weather. But I can promise you at-bats."

"Cool."

"How's Tim doing?" asked Shake, referring to the Fresno manager. Shake already knew the answer to that question since he had talked to Tim at length the other day, but Ron's lengthy reply gave him a chance to thoughtfully regard the veteran.

In his prime, Ron Deer was a 4A player—someone who habitually tore up Triple-A pitching but could never make it in the big leagues. As the years went by he lost his legs and went from outfielder, where he could truly run like a deer, to first base where dead legs went to rest. In time the call-ups ceased and Ron slowly but surely began to sink down through the layers of minor league baseball until he ended up as a thirty-five year old first baseman in Single-A. Now he was back in Double-A looking bright and chipper. *Is it not strange that desire should so many years outlive performance*, thought Shake. But one thing the guy could always do was hit. Shake had both played with him and managed him and he knew that to be a fact—that the guy could hit—as well as he knew that the sun would come up in the morning. Deer was like one of those veteran basketball-players who could no longer drive or post up but still had that deadly jump shot from twenty feet out. And you could take that to the bank.

When Ron finished talking, Shake told him to track down Speed and get set up with everything he would need.

"That guy still around?" chuckled Ron. "Wasn't he in Bristol?"

"Yep. Every year I cut him off at the roots, but he keeps growing back like a thorn bush."

"I'll find him," said Ron as he got up from his chair. He extended his hand to Shake. "I really appreciate this, Shake," he added with a hint of emotion in his voice. "You don't know what it means to me."

"I think I do," replied Shake as he pressed back against Ron's strong handshake before letting him go. Shake knew what he was thinking because it was the same thing he would have been thinking. It was the same thing every fading star thought about who was holding on, looking for one last hurrah: "this is my second chance and anything can happen." In a minor league player's mind, call-ups are just a phone call or an injury away. And once it comes, old legs become new again and anything is possible. *True hope is swift, and flies with swallow's wings.*

A tap at the door brought in Mike Faust. His trainer looked worried.

"What's up, Mike?"

"You're gonna have to scratch Rosecrans."

"Why's that? Here—have a seat." Shake waited for his trainer to take a seat. "What's wrong with him?"

"He's got an infection with a fever. He needs to go on antibiotics."

Shake waited for more but didn't get it. Shit, here we go again, he thought. Next he'll clear his throat and look away. "Why?"

Faust cleared his throat and looked away. "He got an injection in his hip," he said finally. "Somehow it got infected and now he can't run without pain."

"Injection for what?"

"He says he went to the doctor to get a B-12 shot and a couple days later the site got infected. We'll start him on antibiotics today and he should be feeling better in a few days."

"So he's out for the series?"

"Yes. But he should be good to go for Glens Falls."

"All right," said Shake more to himself than to Faust. He needed to go tell Ron Deer he would be starting today. He would also talk to Rosecrans himself. Get the straight scoop. He knew some players took B-12 shots but he had never heard of anyone getting an infection from it. He suspected that there was more to the story than Faust was giving him, which was becoming a habit with this guy, and it irritated him. The players swore by him, so maybe he just needed to make things clear. "Anything else," he asked Faust.

"No," Faust replied as he got up to leave.

"One more thing. It would help me a lot if you would give me a full report on a player without all the questions. Give it to me straight, from top to bottom, and don't leave anything out." Shake paused for a split second as a quote from the Bard occurred to him. Maybe it didn't fit the situation (as Dane had accused him of)—after all, he was talking about thoroughness and not honesty—but he went ahead and said it anyway: *No legacy is as rich as honesty.*

Faust cleared his throat before answering: "Will do. Sorry. My mind's pre-occupied with a lot of crap and this infection thing came out of the blue. But I hear you."

"Fair enough," said Shake. He got up and followed his trainer out the door and went looking for Ron Deer. Before he found him he ran into Rex Lyon. As predicted, all past craziness was forgotten and the old man was pretty much back to normal. Shake found him more subdued lately, and he had also lost about ten pounds which gave him a gaunt look in the face.

"First team to wear numbers on their backs," said Shake, starting the game.

"The Yankees," replied Rex with a wane smile. "Too easy, Glover. Why was Ruth's number three?"

"Numbers went by batting order. Ruth batted third."

"Right. Weren't you a second baseman?"

"That I was."

"So was John Dillinger."

Shake laughed at that. He could see that the old man was trying to make a joke, which was encouraging. "What's your point?" he kidded back and then added, "Where's our boy Orson?"

"Not here. He's off on 'personal business'."

"'*Personal business,*'" repeated Shake sarcastically. "There's no personal business on game day. What's with that? You need to train that boy better."

"Yeah, I've been too easy on him."

"I doubt that," said Shake with a chuckle as he put his hand on Rex's shoulder. With that he continued his search for Deer. He found him setting up his new locker and told him the news that he'd be starting and batting sixth. Deer smiled a big smile and hurried out to batting practice.

Some miles away in the small town of Newington, Orson parked in front of a nice house and got out of his car. This was the address Rose Porter gave him. Rose Porter—Balt's twin sister. Orson knew that Balt had a sister but it was only after talking to her on the phone that he learned she was his twin. That conversation had taken place two days ago, and it had been over a month since The Kiss in the parking lot of the golf club. He had left message after message for Balt but never got a response until two days ago when Rose called him back.

In their phone conversation, he learned that Balt was in L.A. for the summer and wouldn't be back home until late August. Rose was very apologetic about the whole thing and wondered if she and Orson could get together to "talk about her brother." Orson happily agreed. Anything to get him closer to Balt made him happy. Her first spot of free time was on game day but Orson didn't care and set the date. They agreed to have him pick her up at her house (the same one Balt lived in) and then go for a bite to eat.

He walked up the steps but the door opened before he got to it and Rose stepped out to greet him. "Hi, Orson," she said cheerfully. "Right on time."

"Hi, Rose." They shook hands. Orson was struck by how much she looked like her brother. "A pleasure."

"The café is two blocks down and around the corner. We can walk from here."

"Sounds good."

They walked shoulder to shoulder along the white sidewalk, past manicured lawns, making small talk until they reached the café where they sat down at a table across from one another. Orson studied her face and found much to his liking. She had the same brown eyes as her brother, the same nose and mouth, and her neck line was remarkably the same. But there were differences. She was not near-sighted and didn't wear black-rimmed glasses. In addition, she wore a touch of make-up including lip rouge that made her lips look velvety. Her thick brown hair was long, past her shoulders, and she wore it parted on the same side as her brother's hair. He smiled at that. Her fingernails were also long and painted with a dark pink nail polish. All in all, Orson found her quite lovely.

They talked easily over dinner, and this is what Orson learned about Balt: he was in L.A. to pursue his career and working hard to break down barriers in sports journalism. Orson wasn't sure what those barriers were since Balt was neither black or a woman or anything else other than a white male but Rose didn't expound on it. If the boundary was the fact he was gay, she didn't mention it and Orson didn't dare bring it up at this point—though he secretly suspected that was it. She said Balt had spoken to her numerous times about him, and she knew about his position with the Kingsmen and his golf game. The mention of golf gave Orson momentary hope that the conversation would lead to that day in the parking lot—that her twin brother had confessed The Kiss to her—and she was here to act as a love broker. But she didn't pursue it any farther.

Instead, something else was occurring. He was sure of it. She was coming on to him. It was the tilt of her head, the tender touch of his hand as she emphasized a point, the lilting laugh at one of his jokes. It was all there and he was quickly becoming dead sure of it. At first he doubted it, then came disbelief followed by a growing fear as he recognized the inevitable trap. He had done nothing to lead her on or encourage it but it didn't matter. She seemed determined, and with her determination his fear grew. He didn't dare shut her down. That might risk making an enemy and losing Balt in the process. He couldn't flirt back for obvious reasons. He was in love with Balt, not his sister. The whole thing was another one of his conundrums and it gave him a stomach ache to think about it.

During desert she made an effusive point about how much she was enjoying his company. Maybe they could do it again, she said. Orson couldn't hide his confusion and looked very much like a little leaguer who'd just seen his first curveball. His befuddlement brought a look of disappointment on her face.

"Yes, I'd like that," he said, recovering his composure.

"When?"

"Well, uh, let me get back to you. I have to check my schedule," he said lamely, and as he said it he knew it was lame and that she'd push back and that he would agree to a date.

"Are you traveling with the team after Sunday's game. No? Good. Let's meet for dinner after the game.

"Sounds good."

Orson could see that she was pleased, and they finished their desert in relative quiet. She was certainly forceful and liked to have her own way, he thought. He had to admit he found that attractive. This admission troubled him and he quickly turned that line of thought off like a light switch. It just caused him confusion. Thankfully the bill came and he paid it.

It was a beautiful summer night in Connecticut and they walked leisurely back to Rose's house. She set the pace, which was more a stroll than a walk, and talked about baseball. She was a big Kingsmen fan. When they reached her door, Orson stuck his hand out for a handshake and she took it, pulled him close, and kissed him on the cheek. He caught a hint of her lovely-smelling perfume and guessed it was "Beautiful" by Estee Lauder

"See you Sunday," she said happily.

"Sunday," repeated Orson. "Looking forward to it." And he turned around and walked back to his car, slowly confronting the truth that, yes, goddammit, he was looking forward to it. How strange, he thought, to be one of two minds, like a child's toy that winds and unwinds.

17
CHAPTER

Touching this vision here,
It is an honest ghost, that let me tell you.

Hamlet

The Kingsmen took two out of three against the Glens Falls Tigers and moved down to Albany-Colonie to take on the Yankees in a four game series. Dane waited until after the Saturday day game to take a cab out to Our Lady of Angels Cemetery.

First he had dinner with his roommate Greg Rosecrans. Greg was frustrated and wanted to talk about the game. They had lost a close one 2-1 and Manager Glover had taken Greg out after his second at bat and put in Deer. He wasn't so much frustrated at Deer (the guy could hit), or for Deer at getting thrown out at second in the ninth (on a play he could have made standing up), no, he was frustrated at Glover for taking him out. Yeah, he admitted, he wasn't hitting as good since he came back from his hip infection, but a hitter needed time to get his swing back—his timing back—and Glover wasn't giving him that time. He kept pulling him and putting in Deer.

Dane listened to Greg rave on. He liked Greg or, more accurately, he liked to hear Greg scheme and rationalize and complain. Strangely it made him feel better about himself in the same way, he imagined, a plain-looking girl felt better about herself by hanging out with her fat and ugly best friend. He laughed at that analogy and Greg asked him what he was laughing at and he quickly replied, "Nothing. Thinking about something else."

Greg was also frustrated with their trainer Mike Faust, and he decided to open up this can of beans and give Dane the straight scoop (confirming what Dane already suspected). His hip infection had come from a steroid shot, and whether it was a mistake or just plain negligence Greg wasn't sure, but he was sure he didn't trust Faust anymore. If he couldn't trust Faust anymore where was he going to get "juiced-up" and get his edge back?

"Certs me," said Dane while thoroughly enjoying his perfectly roasted pork loin.

Greg continued to talk and vent his frustrations through dinner. Dane thought about asking Greg to accompany him to the cemetery as a form of diversion but then thought better of it. Greg was already depressed and a visit to a cemetery would probably just make him more depressed. They said their goodbyes and Greg went back to the motel room.

Dane called a cab from the restaurant and got to the cemetery at dusk. On the way he picked up a bottle of Crown Royal—his father's favorite—and kept it wrapped in a brown paper bag. He found his father's tombstone on a long sloping hill next to other like-sized tombstones and sat down Indian-style in front of it. He twisted off the cap on the Crown Royal and took a long drink. The whiskey was warming and smooth with a hint of caramel at the end of it.

How to start, he wondered? He was skeptical of the afterlife and had never put much store in communing with the dead. Yet he knew people—sober, intelligent people—who believed in angels and spirits and swore by their existence. There were a lot of things in this world that couldn't be, and never would be, explained by science. It came down to Pascal's Wager, he figured. Since nothing could be proved one way of the other, he chose to take the gain that came with believing in an afterlife, at least for now. But there was another thought that occurred to him that he liked even better: maybe by talking to his dead father he was really just talking to that part of himself that was his father. Even at a minimum, that was better than nothing.

"Well, dad," he said in a low whisper, "here I am. Didn't think I'd make it, or maybe you did… I brought you some Crown Royal, you're favorite. Crown Royal on the rocks—that was your drink, right? We kept a bottle in the house after—for years—and I used to sneak drinks from it as a teenager until mom caught on and poured it out… I'm guessing you know I'm playing professional baseball. Second base. Got a good contract and hope to make it to the bigs next year. We'll see… Remember when we used to play catch? I used to hound you to hit me grounders. You weren't very good at it but you did it anyway. Thanks for that. It helped. And at least you got to see me play little league… I went back to get my Masters in Philosophy. That should make you happy. Maybe someday I'll teach like you. At the moment it doesn't quite fit in with my chosen profession. There's not much need for Kant in the batter's box. Though I got a coach who's kind'a philosophical. He's big on Shakespeare. Quotes him all the time. You'd probably get a kick out of him. I know mom would…

"Kierkegaard was your guy, right. I read one of your papers on him that I found in your stuff a few years back. Did you really buy into that 'knight of faith' crap? I guess you didn't. In the end you didn't or else you wouldn't have offed yourself. When you closed the garage door and started the car, where was Kierkegaard then? You should'a gone with Socrates or Robeck. That would have made more sense… So why'd you do it? I haven't been able to figure it out, so give me a clue. Just one clue, that's all I ask. If you couldn't stand being married to mom then why not get a divorce? I don't remember lots of fighting. Just silence between you. But mom doesn't talk about it... Did you love her? Did you love her and she didn't love you back? Maybe that's it. You loved a woman who didn't love you back but you couldn't stop loving her so you lived in misery until you couldn't take it anymore. How terrible...

"No, I don't think that's it. Too romantic and not your style. I think it comes down to something else, something deeper and darker... It was a philosophical question you answered. And what was the question? You knew it better than most. You knew the fundamental question—why or why not commit suicide? That is really the one and only philosophical problem to solve. Suicide. Is it worth living life or not? That was the fundamental question of philosophy you answered by closing the garage door. It wasn't worth living. Finito. Done. It was an aesthetic choice. A philosophical choice. Any maybe there's nobility in that...

But I forgive you... It took me a long time to get here but I forgive you. Whatever your fucking reason was I forgive you... I love you, dad... I know you loved me. You told me lots of times and I won't doubt it... Remember when we went to the Yankees game with mom and we left her to go look around. We found the monument to Lou Gehrig and you stared at it for a long time. I looked up and saw tears on your face, so I started crying too and you kneeled down and wiped my face and told me it was all right... Well, it's all right..."

Dane put his head down and sobbed quietly. His speech had been punctuated by long pauses, and in those pauses he had drank from the bottle of Crown Royal. He was drunk now. He stopped crying and lifted his head up, wiped his eyes with his shirt sleeves, and laid back on the grass using the half empty bottle as a pillow. His mind was clear and calm and in a minute he was asleep.

"Wha?!" he cried, coming up on his elbows.

"Dane."

"Who's that?"

"Dane."

Dane frantically looked around him. Behind his father's tombstone, in the starlit darkness, he saw the vague outline of a man. The shadow was just standing there. "Who's that?"

"Your father."

"Wha?!"

"I'm your father."

Dane tried to get up but his legs wouldn't work. He peered intensely into the darkness and the shadowy features began to coalesce. It was a man wearing a sweater vest. The kind of sweater vest his dad used to wear. "My father?"

"Dane."

"Yes."

"Listen to me."

Dane was sure it was a dream. Calm down, he told himself. It's a dream and you're talking to your dead father. Go with the flow. "I'm listening," he said loudly.

"It's not right to call myself that," said the shadow in a voice he remembered as his father's. *"I'm not your father."*

"Yes, you are," he answered quickly. His father's ghost was expressing guilt but he would make it better. "I forgive you. It's all right. Believe me."

"Listen to me. I'm not your father."

'Yes you are. It's okay."

"No, Champ, listen to me. I'm not your father. I'm your step-father."

"My what?!" exclaimed Dane. His head was spinning off its axis. He was sure a dream couldn't tell you anything you didn't already know but here was a dream doing just that. "What do you mean you're my step-father?"

"Simple. I did not father you. I embraced you as my son. Raised you as my son. But I did not father you."

"Holy shit!" gasped Dane. Dream and reality ducked behind each other like a fly ball lost in the darkness and then in the lights. "But how? When?"

"*Your mother can tell you.*"

"But why are you telling me this—now?"

"*Because it's the truth and it's time.*" The shadow seemed to step back and raise its hand in a farewell.

"Wait! Wait!" Dane stammered. "Don't go. Talk to me some more."

"*I must go. My time is up.*" His father's ghost took another step back.

"No, no. Wait! Just tell me one more thing. Why'd you kill yourself?

"*You know the answer to that.*"

"No I don't. Tell me. Does mom know why? Can she tell me?"

"*Leave her alone. Her pain is great enough. Leave her alone,*" said his father's ghost in a sad, fading voice. The apparition stepped farther back and began to disappear. "*Find your real father,*" it said, nearly gone.

"Where? Where is he?"

"*Close... He is close.*"

And with that the shadow disappeared and Dane jumped to his feet. He leapt behind the tombstone and in a frenzy looked about, throwing his arm out into the darkness to try and touch whatever it was. But it was gone and he bent over at the waist with his hands on his knees. He straightened up and took deep breathes in an attempt to clear the confusion and Crown Royal from his head. As his head began to clear he realized it was late and looked at his watch. It was 2:30 in the morning. Way past curfew. He swore to himself and took off running.

The motel was over two miles away but he set his mind on running the whole way back. Dressed in dark clothes, he sprinted along the empty streets. A patrol car pulled him over after three blocks and he had to show ID and tell the cop who he was. The cop believed him without blinking an eye and told Dane to get into the passenger's seat.

A half a block from the motel, the cop pulled over to let him out. "It's probably past your curfew," he said with a knowing grin. "You can sneak in from here. Good luck."

Dane thanked him and snuck back into his motel room.

Once in his room he picked up the phone and dialed up his mom. He glanced over at Rosecrans who was asleep. The guy was a heavy sleeper and was currently snoring and Dane ignored him. It rang three times before the receiver came off hook, and he heard fumbling and banging of things on the nightstand.

"Yes, huh. Hello?" answered his mom in a sleepy voice.

"Mom. It's Dane."

"Dane? What's wrong? Are you okay?"

"I'm fine. I'm good... Who's my father?"

There was a pause at the other end, and Dane could hear his mom moving in bed. She was probably sitting up. "Your father?" she asked. "What do you mean? You know who your father is. Why are you calling me at this ungodly hour to ask me that? Are you drunk? You sound drunk.

"No... Well, yes, I was. But I'm pretty sober now."

"You don't sound it. What's wrong?"

In the darkness of the motel room, Dane sat on the floor with his back against the bed. Greg was snoring in the background. "I went to visit dad's grave."

"Okay... I'm glad." Her voice was sincere with no hint of sarcasm. "Is that why you're so wound up?"

"Yeah, it is. I was standing out there thinking about the past, thinking about everything, and it hit me. My dad—Brian, your husband—was my step-father. Wasn't he? Tell me I'm wrong."

"Don't you have a game tomorrow?" she replied in a motherly tone. "Shouldn't you be sleeping? ... I can tell you're all wound up about something. You know how you get. Go get some sleep now and we can talk tomorrow."

"No!" he cried then lowered his voice to a fierce whisper. "No. Tell me now, mom. Tell me the truth. He's my step-father." There was a long pause at the other end of the phone and the longer it lasted the surer he was of the answer.

"Who have you been talking to?"

"No one. It just came to me like a revelation. So just tell me the truth. I need to know. Just tell me, Mom... Are your there? Mom?"

"Yes, I'm here," she replied in a weary voice. "Okay... He's your step-father."

"I knew it! Goddammit, I knew it!" He caught himself and looked up to see if he'd awakened Greg but his roommate snored on peacefully.

"But I'm not going to talk to you about it now," his mom said sternly. "Not over the phone and not at this ungodly hour. I'm not. I'm going to come out to New Britain on your next home stand and we can talk in person.

"Drive over to Albany and we can talk tomorrow."

"No, honey, I'm not driving three hours to Albany. I'd rather take the bus to New Britain. Next weekend on your home stand, I'll be there. Is that okay? Can you do that for me? Please, honey? Just wait a little longer and I'll explain everything to you in person. Please."

He knew he wasn't going to change his mother's mind, and her combination of resolve and affection had its usual effect on him. "Okay, Mom."

"And keep in mind one thing for me," she said, her voice cracking for the first time. "Just one thing, that's all I ask. There are reasons for everything. Don't pass judgement until you hear the reasons."

"I won't. I promise."

"I love you. More than anything."

"Love you, too."

"Now get some sleep. Your head needs to be in the game tomorrow."

"Okay, mom," he said, sniffing a short laugh and thinking that she sounded like his coach. He hung up and quietly undressed and slipped into bed. Greg was still snoring. He tossed and turned in restless wonder, at the ghost he'd seen and fate's loud thunder.

18
CHAPTER

Pitchers, like poets, are born not made.
Cy Young

The Bullpen, Part 1

Before the first pitch, Burton leaned over Shake's shoulder and looked out at the bullpen. "It must be Ten-cent Hot Dog Nite," he said with a chuckle.

Shake looked out towards the bullpen and saw that almost every one of his pitchers was holding a hot dog. Well, afterall, he thought, *it was* Ten-cent Hot Dog Nite and *they were* pitchers. Pitchers were like the high school band of baseball. Each was a little off center, and they stuck together in their little whacky fraternity. And the bullpen was a good place for them. They had the choice of sitting in the dugout during the game or hanging out in the bullpen where there was no coach or chaperone to watch over them. If he were a pitcher that's where he'd hang out.

"If the 'beer batter' strikes out, keep your eye on them," quipped Shake, and he and Burton laughed.

The bullpen consisted of a high chain-link fence that closed off an alcove in the right field bleachers. There was a phone, a wooden bench, two mounds, and an array of gray metal chairs that the pitchers sat on during the game. Most were already sitting down eating their hot dog.

Fan 1
Hey, no eating on the job!

Fan 2
Where's the beer! Can't eat a dog without beer.

Phil
Get me one, dude! But put it in a thermos and lower it down.

Fan 2
You got it, dude!
(exits)

Andy
Think he'll do it?

Phil
No. He'd need a thermos and a rope. Too many things to remember.

Chuck
Christ! Who cut the cheese? Not even through the first and someone's cutting the cheese.

Scott
Not me. What's it smell like?

Chuck
Like rancid refried beans.

Andy
Must be Tito.

Tito
Fuck ju guys. I don't cut cheese. Pendejos.

Phil
Oh, I got it now. That's putrid, man. Gotta be Tiago.

Scott
He's not talking to us. Anyhow, he holds them in so it can't be him.

Andy
That's not good for you—gives you bad breath.

Chuck
That's an old wives' tale.

Phil
Hey, keep Tito's wife out of this

Tito
Fuck ju guys. Pendejos

Between the top and bottom of the third there was a jousting match along the first base line. The jousting match consisted of two willing participants from the stands who dressed up in suits of armor made of foam. The foam was thick and bulky and made them look like ripe squashes. Each one held a broomstick-style lance that had a large nerf ball stuck at the end. The object was to run full tilt at one another and try to knock the other down using the lance. There was the Green Knight and the Black Knight. Once a knight went down, they bounced over and around on the grass to the delight of the crowd and needed attendants to get them back up.

Phil
Five bucks on the Green Knight.

Chuck
You're on.

Andy
I'll take some of that.

Luis
You're both idiots. The Green Knight always wins.

Andy
Bullshit he does. We counted it last year and the Black Knight was forty-four and thirty-four.

Luis
Better winning percentage than you.

Scott
The girl always wins. The Green Knight's a girl. That's why Phil's betting on her.

Chuck
No way. What makes a girl better at this than a guy?

Scott
They're better at handling the lance.

Luis
I'm sure they are.

Chuck
Ope, here they go…

(They watch as the Green Knight quickly vanquishes the Black Knight.)

Phil
Ha! I told you. That'll be five bucks—from each of you.

Andy
Unbelievable. You're right, though. She was good with the lance.

Scott
I told you. They grab it and know right where to put it.

Luis
I'm sure they do.

In the top of the seventh, the Kingsmen starting pitcher Ken 'Kid' Curry started to labor and the pitchers in the bullpen, especially the relief pitchers, began to take a keener interest in the game. But that didn't stop their game of movie trivia.

Scott
'Two men enter, one man leave.'

Andy
Mad Max, Beyond Thunderdome. I just saw it.

Chuck
'That ain't a knife, this is a knife.'

Tito
Cocodrilo Dundee!

Chuck
What he say?

Phil
Cocodrilo Dundee. Are you deaf?

Chuck
Lucky guess.

Scott
Curry's leakin' oil. We're gonna get the call. A right-hander, probably Tito. I got one for you: 'I have a need, a need for speed!'

Luis
Davis talking about his fastball.

Chuck
Funny guy. That'd be *Top Gun*.

(The bullpen phone rings.)

Scott
Told ya. Who they want? Tito? Knew it. Here comes Manning with his catcher's gear.

Phil
'Leave the gun. Take the cannoli.'

Andy
The Godfather. Why is it whenever we play this game you always quote *The Godfather*? Don't you know any other movies? Just one time I'd like to hear you quote another movie.

Phil
Okay… 'He was stupid. I was lucky. I will visit him soon.'

Andy
That's the same movie, dude!

Phil
No it's not. That's *Godfather Part II*.

Just then they heard the whack of a bat on the ball followed by the groan of the crowd. A long fly ball was heading their way. The pitchers stepped out of its path and watched it land in the bullpen for a homerun. The ball rolled to a corner and Phil walked over and picked it up with his fingers like it was a rotten apple. He looked up and tossed it to a fan.

Fan 2
Thanks, dude!

Phil
Hey, where's my beer?

Fan 2
Oh, sorry, dude, I drank it.

Phil
(to Andy)
See, told ya'. Too many things to think about.

The Bullpen, Part 2

It was a Saturday game on a hot broiling day. In the stifling bullpen there was little to no breeze and the pitchers moved their chairs against the arc of the sun to stay in the shade. Their path was littered with spent sunflower seeds, Styrofoam cups (for spitting dip), and chewing gum wrappers. It was the fifth inning and the Kingsmen were winning 4-0. Ellsworth was on the mound and looking strong—painting the corners and consistently spotting his nasty splitter. The Kingsmen were up to bat and Prince had just walked to bring Hamilton to the plate. The pitchers were hot and bored.

Chuck
Listen. The math is easy. The runner's got to go in less than 3.2 seconds. It takes 1.4 seconds for the pitcher to deliver the pitch—unless you're Tiago, then it takes over two seconds—and it takes the catcher 1.8 seconds to throw down to second. That's 1.4 plus 1.8 equals 3.2 seconds. But that's if everything goes right. If it goes right you're gonna get him 'cause most guys can't go in less than 3.2 seconds, except for Prince. So you got to get rid of the ball out of the stretch in 1.4 seconds. Don't you ever listen to Benedict?

Steve
Sure, but it also depends on his lead. You got to keep him close.

Chuck
But it doesn't change the math. It's still 3.2 seconds whether he's close or got a big lead... Wait, here goes Prince... Now... Safe! ... Bet you that was less than 3.2 seconds. Anyone got a stopwatch?

Ken
How 'bout a sundial?

Scott
Hey, stop hogging my shade.

Ken
Am not. It's almost time to move.

Steve
They shouldn't have Bring Your Dog Day when it's hot like this. Look at 'em. They're dying out there in those metal stands. It's animal cruelty.

Scott
Remember when they had the Cowboy Monkey Rodeo?

Chuck
It was fricken' hilarious. PETA made 'em stop it.

Phil
Party poopers.

Luis
Walked Hamilton and he's about to walk Goff. There he goes.
How about a donation to this walk-a-thon?
(*The stadium speakers start playing 'Walk of Life' by Dire
Straits. The pitchers laugh.*)
Where's he get that stuff?

Phil
Anybody ever meet the P.A. Announcer? Chuck, you?

Chuck
Never.

Phil
Don't you find that odd, that no one's ever seen him?

Chuck
Not really. He's like that guy in Magnum P.I. Robin Masters.
You never see him—only hear his voice.

Scott
Burks is going to drive one here.

Sure enough, Burks hit a sinking liner to right field which
got past the right fielder and rolled to the screen in front of
the bullpen. When the right fielder got to the ball he kicked it,
picked it up and dropped it, and finally got hold of it and threw
it back into the infield. As all this occurred, the bullpen had
their fun.

Luis
Stick a fork in it!

Phil
Hey, Cinderella! Get to the ball!

Scott
Make that glove in metal shop!?

Ken
Hey, two-six, you're gonna have to wait the full five years to get into the hall. Hey, two-six, you hear me? I think he's ignoring me.

Chuck
You hurt his feelings.

Scott
Ohp. They're pulling Heller. Told you—the guy's strictly five and dive.

They watched as the opposing team changed pitchers. After warming up, the new pitcher got Estrella and Rosecrans out but walked Hoffman. That brought the pitcher Ellsworth to the plate and got the full attention of the bullpen.

Phil
What's your pool at?

Chuck
Three hundred and twenty bucks. Basset's in the lead at .236 but Andy can pass him here with a hit.

Phil
What you at?

Luis
Chuck couldn't hit an elephant's ass with an ironing board.

Chuck
At least I'm on the interstate. A certain person here who I won't mention, but who's name rhymes with 'blurry' as in Kid Curry, is O for ten.

Scott
He needs a slump buster.

Tito
Sloomp booster? Que es eso?

Scott
Tito, stop, you're killing me. Not 'sloomp booster'. It's sll-ump buss-ter. Slump buster. A slump buster is a fat ugly girl you pick up and screw to break out of your slump. Even Basset knows what a slump buster is.

Steve
Keep me out of this.

Tito
Ju-mean, puta grasa. Ahh, haha, sll-oomp boos-ter.

Luis
Close enough.

Chuck
Ahh, grounded out. Basset's still got the lead.

Phil
Hey, check it out! The Dallas cheerleader is back.

"No way! Awesome!" came the replies as the pitchers moved as one out of the shade and over to the edge of the bleachers. Some brought their chairs to stand on. They gathered at the low point where the chain link fence met the stands and craned their necks and stood on tiptoes or chairs to see over into the crowd. The object of their interest was a beautiful blond in short-shorts and a halter top. She noticed them ogling her and waved back with a smile, causing them to collectively fall backwards as though staggered by a mighty punch.

Scott
Man, I'd love to get her on a slow boat to Bedford.

Phil
Come off it, dude. You couldn't get to second base with her.

Scott
Sure I could.

Phil
No way.

Chuck
How are we defining 'second base' here? First base is a kiss but second base is what?"

Ken
Second base is copping a feel—under the bra, down the pants—copping a feel. That's definitely second base.

Scott
Then what's a blow job.

Phil
A homerun.

Chuck

No way. A homerun is penetration

Scott

No, no, a blow job is a homerun.

Ken

Quiet and listen to me. You might learn something. It's simple: First base is a kiss. Second base is copping a feel. Third base is oral sex and a homerun is screwing. Third base can also be a hand job.

Phil

You just said copping a feel is second base, so a hand job is, by definition, second base.

Ken

No, copping a feel and getting a hand job are two distinctly different things. One is just a feel while the other one takes concentrated effort. It's like warm-up pitchers versus the real thing.

Chuck

I don't know. I think I agree with Cap. 'Copping' means they got their hand on it. They're handling it. So handling can be the same as a hand job.

Ken

You're not appreciating the legal nuances here. It's a matter of duration and intent.

Phil

Okay, Matlock. Just admit you're wrong.

Scott

They're both right. I think a hand job is somewhere between

copping a feel and a blowjob. That puts you like between second and third caught in a pickle.

Ken
Yeah, she caught your pickle all right. Listen, don't ask me, ask Santiago. He's the expert here. If anyone knows what third base is, he does. Tiago, tell them. What's a hand job?

Luis
Third base. And that means Phil gets to third base with himself every night.

Phil
And you can go hit a homerun on yourself.

Tito
I find one! I find one!

Scott
What? What did you find?

Tito
A sloomp booster.

Chuck
No shit? Let's see.

Scott
Me first.

Phil
Out of my way

　　Our boys stood on chairs and craned their necks, to confirm his find for slump-busting sex.

19
CHAPTER

As the season moved into late July, the Kingsmen sat atop the Eastern League by seven games. Shake would have preferred a ten game lead but he'd take seven because he knew, barring a collapse, the New Haven Admirals in second place had little chance of catching them. He was just being objective—unflappably objective—like one of those great generals of the past who could step outside themselves and coolly assess their strengths and weaknesses against their enemies. Their pitching was too good. It was as simple as that. Nobody in the Eastern League had their pitching. So, short of a catastrophe, like Basset and Ellsworth and Santiago all getting hurt at the same time (and he knocked on wood when he thought this), their chances were excellent on finishing first and being the top seed in the play-offs.

And what did the top-seed in the play-offs buy you? Not much, he knew. You got home field advantage and were matched up in the first round with the fourth place team. At that point, anybody could get hot and win a five game series. Theoretically, you could finish the regular season up by twenty games and get knocked out in the first round of the play-offs. He'd seen it happen. They were sure to lose Basset to a September call-up, maybe even another pitcher, but everyone was in the same boat. His job and his coaching staff's job, at this point in the season, was to keep their players sharp, in a groove, and minimize the risks of injury. If they got to September in good shape, he felt confident about their chances of repeating as champions.

Repeating as champions was not a thing Shake dwelled on. He would never tempt fate like that. That would have been hubris—pride before the fall—and as an English Lit major and a seasoned baseball manager he knew the dangers of hubris as well as a deep sea fisherman knew the signs of an approaching squall. If there was one thing he kept better than most it was perspective. And when it came to winning and championships, it was his hero the Bard that kept him grounded:

> *The painful warrior famoused for fight,*
> *After a thousand victories once foil'd,*
> *Is from the book of honour razed quite,*
> *And all the rest forgot for which he toil'd*

After their New York road trip, the Kingsmen faced the Pittsfield Cubs for a three game series starting on Tuesday. They won Tuesday and Wednesday and were going for the sweep on Thursday but drew their old nemesis Todd Clinton as home plate umpire.

Luis Santiago was pitching and looked sharp, but with Clinton behind the plate he was going deeper into counts and throwing more pitches. Shake and his pitching coach Larry Benedict watched Santiago closely. He was known to throw tantrums on occasion when things didn't go his way. In the seventh, with a 3-1 lead, Santiago walked a batter who then stole second on him. He went 3-2 on the next batter and threw a beautiful slider that painted the outside corner for strike three.

Only Clinton called it ball four and Santiago kicked the mound and screamed up at the sky.

"Go calm him down," Shake said to Benedict.

Shake watched as Benedict jogged out to the mound to talk to Santiago. Benedict waved the other infielders off—he wanted to talk to Santiago alone—and only let Estrella listen in. Santiago nodded at Benedict's words, glared over Estrella's shoulder at Clinton, then nodded some more at what his pitching coach was telling him. When the visit ended, Shake could tell by Santiago's body language that he was still angry.

"Come on, Luis!" yelled Shake. "Bear down! Let's get two here!"

The first pitch was close for ball one. Santiago called his catcher out and they huddled together, talking with their heads down. Hamilton jogged over to join them but they brushed him off. "Careless Whisper" by Wham started playing over the speakers. Finally Estrella walked back to home plate and got back down in his squat. He gave Santiago the sign and waited for the pitch.

It was a high fastball that Estrella short-armed, and it ticked off the edge of his glove and hit Clinton squarely in the mask. The sound of a ninety-three mile an hour fastball hitting metal shot through the stadium, and it was followed by a groan from the crowd. Clinton's mask flew off from the force of the blow and he stepped backwards, stunned, then sat heavily down as though he'd just received bad news from the doctor. The other umpires hurried towards home plate.

"Shit," exhaled Burton. "Down goes Frasier."

Shake glanced at his pitching coach and they locked eyes. They were thinking the same thing. Back out on the field, the other umpires were bending over Clinton. Shake looked for his trainer and saw him talking with Rosecrans at the end of the bench. "Hey, Mike!" he yelled at him. "Get out there."

Faust ran out to home plate and kneeled next to Clinton. At one point smelling salts were administered, and after ten minutes

Clinton was helped to his feet and stood up shakily. He looked punch drunk and the crew chief ordered him to follow Faust into the clubhouse to get first aid. It took another ten minutes for the crew chief to don his gear and get behind home plate. They would go short-handed but the game would continue.

"If they did that on purpose, I'll string 'em both up by their short hairs," Shake said to Benedict.

Larry nodded in agreement but then shrugged his shoulders. "If they fess up," he replied. "I doubt they will."

With a new umpire behind the plate, Santiago got out of the inning without giving up a run. He returned to the dugout with a smirk on his face. Benedict walked over to Estrella to find out what had happened then came back to give Shake the story. According to Estrella, he got crossed up. He called for a curve and got a fastball and wasn't expecting it. He blinked and it got past him.

"*Right,*" said Burton sarcastically. "So not the twinkie defense but the blinkie defense?"

Shake couldn't help but laugh at that, which probably gave both Santiago and Estrella the wrong idea since they were watching him out of the corner of their eyes. "I'll deal with them after the game," he said simply and turned his attention back to the game.

They won 4-2 and back in the clubhouse he called Santiago and Estrella into his office. They still had their uniforms on and Santiago, with his jersey off, had an ice pack taped to his shoulder. Shake closed the door and cross-examined them at length but they stuck to their story. "How did you get your signs crossed?" he asked. Because we changed them, claimed Santiago. "Why?" Because we thought the runner on second was stealing signs, testified Estrella. That was the reason for the meeting on the mound, but the change mixed him up. His mistake, not Santiago's. Shake listened patiently then delivered his summation. If he thought they were lying, he'd bench them. If he knew they were lying, he'd suspend them. A baseball traveling at ninety-three miles per hour could severely injure a man, ruin his career, or even kill him. They had no right to put a man's life or career at stake. None. No matter who he was. And if they ever did anything like that again, mistake or not, he would run them out of professional baseball. Did they understand?

They nodded their heads somberly while still holding onto the look of innocent bystanders. He dismissed them and followed them out the door where he heard cheerful greetings and the kind of the commotion that usually surrounded a celebrity. It was Chili Leonard. The celebrated center fielder came up with a smile and shook his hand.

"How's it shakin', Shake," he said.

"Can't complain," replied Shake, smiling back. "Come on in."

Chili came into his office but could not help noticing the somber looks on the faces of Santiago and Estrella as he passed them by. "What's that all about?" he asked cheerfully. "Thought you guys just won?"

"Nothing. Got a couple idiots playing assassin... Sit down, man. How's it going? How's the knee?"

Chili Leonard was the starting centerfielder for the big club, an eleven year veteran, and two time All-Star. He was in New Britain for rehab starts. His knee was far enough along that the big club wanted him to get some playing time in the minors to test its strength and get his timing back. The Kingsmen were chosen because the big club had an East Coast swing coming up, starting with the Mets, in little over a week. They were hoping that Chili's stint with the Kingsmen would get him ready for the Mets and Shake hoped so, too. The players loved it when a big-timer came through on a rehab assignment but it never ceased to give Shake yet another thing to worry about. He loved Chili, but high profile rehab assignments were a two-edged sword. First, you got his talent but it disrupted the line-up. Second, if he was successful he went back to the big club ready to contribute, but if he got hurt again it was bad news all around and usually viewed as the minor league manager's fault.

Chili said that his knee was feeling much better and he was ready for action. They talked a little more before Shake asked him whether he wanted to play centerfield or not. As baseball royalty, he had his choice.

"You got Prince in center, right? Let him be for now. Give me right. Maybe give me center for my last start. How's that sound?"

"You got it," said Shake as a thought suddenly struck him. "How well do you know Prince?"

"A little. He played the one season for us but I didn't get to know him that well. Found him a bit immature."

"Right. So you know the scoop on him. Five-tool player. Could be the next Chili Leonard. I've seen it—the speed, the bat control, how he closes on a ball. It's all there except for the fire that burns. Know what I'm saying? He'd rather hang out with his buddies and get stoned than put in the extra work it takes to be great. I've tried to motivate him. I've fined him and benched him, but nothing seems to sink in. But maybe if it comes from a player like you—a veteran—it might make a difference. I'd consider it a great favor."

"No problem, Skip. I'll talk to him."

"Appreciate that. Now, where you staying? At the Marriot?" He and Chili talked awhile about accommodations and a little about the upcoming series with the Waterbury Indians before they were interrupted by a knock on the door. It was Dane Hamilton. Introductions were made and Chili pardoned himself so the two could talk.

"You wanted to see me?" said Dane.

"Yeah, real quick. Got a question for you." Shake didn't expect to get a straight answer here. There was a code at work—a code he was very familiar with—and it was unlikely Dane would break it. "What were Santiago and Estrella talking about when you walked up to them in the seventh?"

"I didn't catch it. Luis told me to get lost."

"All right."

"Whatever it was, they didn't want me to hear."

Well, thought Shake to himself, that was a little more than I expected. Hamilton was a smart cookie. He gave me the answer without breaking the code. "Okay. That's all, thanks."

"My mom will be here for the weekend. I'll bring her by to meet you."

"The Shakespeare buff. Love to meet her."

When Shake walked into The Mermaid Tavern he noticed Todd Clinton and two other umpires sitting at a table eating burgers and drinking beer. He went up to Clinton and put his hand on his shoulder and asked him how he was feeling. Better, replied Clinton, and Shake said he was very glad to hear that. When he chose to, Shake could put on the charm as well as any talented diplomat, and he did so now. He addressed each man by his first name, asked about their families, and laughed heartily at their jokes. Through his ingratiating small talk, the table of umpires turned warm and convivial. Before parting, he got serious for a moment, put his hand back on Clinton's shoulder, and explained the cross-up in signs that led to Clinton's beaning. He assured them all it was not intentional and that he would never ever tolerate a thing like that. He was so relieved to see Todd was feeling better since the league could not afford to lose a professional and talented umpire like him.

Clinton looked up at him, genuinely moved by Shake's words, and said thank you. Shake patted Todd on the shoulder and asked them what they were all drinking ("Bud"), and told them the next round was on him. "*Come, gentlemen,*" he quoted. "*I hope we shall drink down all unkindness.*" And with that he left them in good cheer.

At their round table he found all his coaches. Bernie was there standing behind Benedict rubbing his shoulders. Larry had his head down, clearly enjoying the massage. Rick wanted to know all about the confab at the umpire's table and Shake filled them in. This led to a discussion about targeting—intentional beanballs, spiking and collisions—that each of them had performed or witnessed over their careers. Bob had once seen a center fielder take out his right fielder, whom he hated and owed a substantial gambling debt to, by streaking after a fly ball to right and putting his head down at the moment of impact, breaking the right fielder's ribs in the process. This topic grew into a larger discussion as to what sport had the worst targeting. Hockey won hands down.

Dark Lucy stopped by and stood next to Shake. She said hi and asked about the game while putting her arm around him and playing with his ear. This mildly surprised him given they had not talked in a while. He brought his arm down off the table and slipped it around her hips. When she was done listening to the game report, she tugged Shake's ear lobe—the signal—and went upstairs.

Shortly thereafter, Rick and Teddy went home to their wives. Bob met up with his live-in girlfriend and Larry wandered off somewhere with Bernie. Shake sat alone at the round table and thought about what awaited him at the top of the stairs. Mostly trouble, he thought. There was intent and determination in her manner, and what she wanted was nothing less than to have his heart on her pewter platter. The smart move would be to go home, he told himself. But he knew himself better than that... *Such is the simplicity of man to hearken after the flesh.*

After the grand ritual of the knock, the drink, the impassioned quotes and the rambunctious sex, he found himself in a familiar position—that of lying on his side in bed watching her roll a joint. She was naked and sat cross-legged and reverently performed each step in her fixings as a priest does the Eucharist. She licked the paper and sealed the joint, then lit it and took a deep drag before handing it to him.

"Do you love me?" she asked as she breathed out her smoke.

Shake was in the middle of his toke, stopped, choked, and started coughing. "Huh? What?" he replied as he handed her the joint back.

"Do you love me? ... No Shakespeare quotes... Just a simple answer... Yes or no."

"No."

She took another big hit and held it in. When she exhaled, she looked down at him and the combination of swirling smoke, disheveled hair and dark piercing eyes, made her look like the malevolent witch Morgan le Fay. He found the image both chilling and, well, bewitching.

"Do you love... someone else?"

Shake declined the joint she offered back to him. He needed to keep his head clear and speak straight and true. The moment wasn't a surprise to him—he'd seen it coming for some weeks. He'd hoped they could go on indefinitely, like Marshall Dillon and Miss Kitty, but it wasn't meant to be. And it wasn't the first time it had happened to him—where the woman he was casually dating and screwing suddenly demanded more from him. He had learned from those earlier experiences that, at this precise moment, *honesty is the best policy.*

"No," he said. "I did a long time ago. Maybe I never stopped."

"Where is she now?"

"Dead."

She was quiet for a moment and abruptly waved her hand around her head to disperse the lingering smoke. "I'm not dead," she said softly. "What about us? ... We have something good... Don't we?"

"We have lust. Or I have lust. You're fun to be around. A kick. But I don't love you."

"Lust can turn into love... Sometimes you can't tell the difference."

"Yes, you can," he answered firmly, and with that he disobeyed her request to keep Shakespeare out of this:

> *Love surfeits not, Lust like a glutton dies;*
> *Love is all truth, Lust full of forged lies.*

"I hate Shakespeare," she said with a sigh.

Shake detected resignation in her voice. It was almost a kind of stoned-out, let-it-be surrender and he jumped in after it. "No you don't," he replied cheerfully. "Come on, tell me, what's your favorite Shakespeare play?"

'I don't know," she sighed again. "Let me think." She focused her attention on attaching a roach clip to her joint. "I haven't seen them all."

"Of the ones you've seen then," he encouraged. Shake was of the firm belief that you could tell a lot about a person by their favorite Shakespeare play. *Romeo and Juliet* meant you were a tragic romantic at heart; *Henry V* signaled you had a martial spirit; *Hamlet* indicated you were a thinker and probably a reader of books; and if your play of choice was *Titus Andronicus* it was a sure sign you had deep-seated problems.

"*Macbeth*," she said finally.

"Hmm." That surprised him a bit—but then again maybe it didn't. *Macbeth* had witches in it and the scheming and relentless Lady Macbeth. Not the best role model but a strong female character nonetheless. He had a quick image of himself married to Lucy Macbeth and murdering his way to a manager's job in the big leagues while she cheered him on. Funny. Then for no reason at all he remembered Mimi's favorite play—*A Midsummer Night's Dream*. A lovely choice.

"Good pick. A little dark for me but good pick."

She ignored his rather back-handed compliment as she snuffed out the remains of her joint and started putting things away.

"If a good production comes around," he said brightly, "maybe we'll go see it together."

"Maybe."

With that "maybe" he felt the final tear, from his Wiccan and their wooly affair.

20
CHAPTER

As there comes light from heaven and words from breath,
As there is sense in truth and truth in virtue

Measure for Measure

Saturday was a glorious day. It was warm but not too hot, the blue sky dotted with cumulus clouds, and a breeze from the east brought with it the smell of the sea. Shake was in a buoyant mood and he walked around the infield like a king over his realm. Ball-players in uniform were playing catch. The stands were nearly full. He waved at the umpires huddled behind home plate and they waved back. As he walked between the first base line and his dugout, he noticed a group of fans calling his name and trying to get his attention. It was four attractive young women and Shake walked over to them.

"What have we here?" he asked with a smile.

"Can we get your autograph?" asked the brunette in front. Each one, in their late teens, fresh-faced and pretty, stuck out a program and a pen at him.

"My pleasure," he said stepping in close to them. "How you gals doing today?" They happily chirped their answers. He took the first program thrust at him (the brunette's) and readied the pen. "What's your name?" he asked her.

"Janet. Sign it to Janet from Shake."

He followed her instructions and handed the finished product back to her. He asked each one their name in turn before signing their program. The last one, a short redhead with freckles on her nose, said her name was "Mimi."

The name startled him and he asked her to repeat it and she did. "Mimi." He looked closely at her face but saw no resemblance to his old flame.

"I knew a girl named Mimi once," he said as he signed her program. "What's your mom's name?"

"Connie."

"Hmm. Here you go. Who's your favorite player?"

The brunette answered first: "Luis Santiago."

"You're partial to pitchers then?"

"Not really. But he's gorgeous." Her other three friends laughed at this and heartily agreed.

"Well, at least you're honest. '*For honesty coupled to beauty is to have honey a sauce to sugar.*'"

"Is that Shakespeare? It is, isn't it? Do some more."

"You like the Bard?" They all nodded energetically. "What's your favorite play?" Two of them immediately blurted out "*Romeo and Juliet*" and the rest chimed in the same. "Why am I not surprised?" replied Shake with a smile and, pausing momentarily, added:

> *For never was a story of more woe*
> *Than this of Juliet and her Romeo.*

They giggled in delight. Shake doffed his cap and turned to walk away but they pleaded for more. He turned back and looked straight at the brunette. She was the ringleader, he had no doubt, and if he was eighteen she'd be the one for him. He took her hand in a courtly gesture and quoted Suffolk from *Henry the Sixth:*

> *She's beautiful, and therefore to be wooed;*
> *She is a woman, therefore to be won.*

And with that he kissed her hand, raised it, and let go of it with a flourish. The brunette held her hand triumphantly in the air as she led her cheering friends back to their seats. Shake followed her raised hand but suddenly caught an image of something higher up in the stands and stepped aside to see better. An unlocked memory spilled out into his consciousness and he strained his eyes to find the floppy sun hat he'd seen a moment before. Mimi's floppy sun hat. He tried to block the sun with his hand as he scrutinized the spot where he'd seen the hat. But it was gone.

Shake caught himself and lowered his hand. The whole thing suddenly reminded him of that movie *The Natural* where Roy Hobbs looks up in the stands to find his true love. He laughed at himself and walked back to his dugout. He tried to dismiss the illusion as a thing triggered by a girl's name, but when he got to the dugout steps he looked back up in the stands to make sure. It wasn't there.

He stepped down and found Speed sitting on the bench. It was the clubbie's spot where he sat for most of the game. From that vantage point he could comment on the game, throw one-liners at Shake and his coaches, or run off if need be to refill tubs of sunflower seeds or Bazooka gum.

Speed
What you looking for? Tell me and maybe I can find it for you.

Shake
I doubt it.

Speed

What do you doubt? The thing you're looking for or that I can find it?

Shake

Both

Speed

That makes you a double-doubter, which may not be as bad as double-trouble but is definitely not as good as double-chocolate chip. Double-chocolate chip cookies with vanilla ice cream. Mmm, my favorite. But doesn't Doubt have a twin brother? I read that somewhere, maybe on a bathroom wall. It said Faith is Doubt's twin brother.

Shake

Profound.

Speed

Thank you. But not identical twins. More like fraternal twins, and Doubt is the uglier of the two.

Shake

Which is why we say, 'When in doubt, lights out'. Nobody wants to look at that ugly mug.

Speed

Exactamundo... And I have a riddle for you today.

Shake

'If you be not mad, be gone, if you have reason, be brief'... So, let's hear it.

Speed

He sold his soul to the devil, and now he's set on amending your constitution.

Shake

Is that it? Okay, got it... Now I got a game to manage so sit there and be quiet.

Speed

As a church mouse.

After the game, Chili Leonard and Hank Prince sat at a table in an upscale Chinese restaurant off Main St. in downtown New Britain. By sheer coincidence, Dane Hamilton and his mom sat at another table while Orson Kent and Rose Porter shared yet another table. The three couples were each aware of the other, had nodded and said hi, and didn't find the coincidence odd. It was a popular restaurant.

"Ever had Chinese food?" Chili asked Hank.

"Nah."

"Let me order. We'll try a few different things. Broaden your horizons." The waiter came and Chili gave him their order, then he poured himself some tea. "What was it growing up? Fried foods, right? Maybe some ham hocks and Hoppin' John."

"Yo, fo' real. My mom wassa badass cook. Flatback. Chickin' fried steak wid gravy. Sweet potato pie, my fave."

"Got brothers and sisters?"

"A full crib, bro. Fo sistas and three bruthas. In Houston. Sunnyside was-my hood. Mom raised us. My dad was loke an' neva-round."

"Do me a favor?"

"Wass-that?"

"Cut the ghetto brogue."

"The wha?"

"The ghetto-talk. It's a dead give-away." Chili suddenly put his collar up and turned his head sideways. "Hey, nigga. I can talk-it-too. From East Saint Louie. East Boogie, where-dey do drive-byes on Sat-day and gang-bang yo sista on Sunday. I tapp'd the streets an' sole sherms and piff. But-I got out cause I could play ball. U-hear me? I got out. Now I'ma baller chillin in my crib getting hella pussy, twenty-fo seven. So keep it trill, playa and cut that nigga-talk."

"Wha, u-wan-me to talk cracker-talk?

"No, just like a man of means. A professional. Not like some baby G-n."

Hank didn't respond and instead took a drink of his beer. It was some Chinese beer. Tsingtao. It was pretty good.

"Want endorsements someday? Do a beer commercial or sell your own tennis shoes? Then stop talkin' like you're standin' on-a corner in Sunnyside."

"Okay." Hank took another sip of his Chinese beer and looked across at Chili and nodded. He was the man, he admitted to himself. He knew how to dress, how to talk and act. He had style and money and success. He even did car commercials and played in celebrity golf tournaments. He was no poser or wannabe. Hank was surprised and grateful at his dinner invitation. So he'd listen because the man had style and was worth listening to.

Platters of food soon arrived and Chili explained each one. One was Mongolian Beef, another pot stickers, and another Moo Shu Pork. Chili showed him how to take the thin pancake and fill it with Moo Shu Pork, add a little plum sauce, then roll it up like a burrito. Hank copied him and raised the rolled, stuffed pancake to his mouth and took a big bite.

"Mmm, that's good," he said as he gulped it down. He quickly finished it off and started making another one.

"How's your season going?" asked Chili.

Hank told him. There were ups and downs. He led the league in steals but was only batting .302, which they both knew was low for the Eastern League. He was honest about his fines and benching but was adamant he had a great June and should have been an All-Star.

"Why do you think that is?"

"I don't know."

"Yeah, you do. You'd rather get high and hang out with your homies than put in the extra work it takes to be great. And don't con me that ain't it. What would your mama say if she knew you were smokin' weed and runnin' round with gangbangers instead of workin' hard?

"She'd whup me."

"Damn right she would. So would my mama. You got to stop disrespecting the game, bro. Take it serious. It's your job and you get paid a lot to do it. You got skills. No doubt about it. But everyone's got skills in the pros. It's hard work that sets you apart. I mean, where do you want to be in five years? In the show playing on TV before millions of people, married to a model, living in a mansion in Bel-Air—yeah, right, you hear me now—or do you want to end up back at your mama's house washing cars or delivering mail for a living? Easy answer, right? But I'm not feelin' it. You look to me like you're going the wrong direction. You slid out of the bigs, slid out of Triple-A, and now you're sliding your way out of Double-A. Next you'll be out of baseball, and when the money runs out cause it always runs out, it's back to Sunnyside for you."

Hank listened to Chili's words and saw the two pictures clear as day. No one had ever put it this way before. He wanted the first picture. With all his heart and soul he wanted the first picture. Not the second one. Back in Sunnyside. Getting high and trying to stay out of trouble. Hell no.

"I hear you," said Hank sincerely.

"Good... Now try one of these pot stickers—but dip it in hot oil first like this."

Orson didn't know what to make of it all. Officially, this was their third date, and Rose had already set another date for them to play golf next week. He looked across the table at her and watched her efficiently pick apart a plate of Kung Pao Chicken with her chopsticks. She was very attractive. No doubt about it, he thought, but was that because she looked like her twin brother Balt or because he found her attractive on her own merits? He wasn't sure. But one thing he was sure of—he was sure what *she wanted* out of this relationship. That had become clear on their last date when he walked her to her door. Standing there in awkward silence, she had suddenly grabbed his shirt and kissed him. A hard, long kiss with tongue and all. And to his undying shame, he had kissed her back.

"How's the chicken?" he asked her.

"Mmm, good. They spice it just right. Chili and garlic. I love it."

Rose was certainly a woman who knew what she liked, thought Orson. She had made the date and picked the restaurant, and when she ordered off the menu she knew exactly what she wanted without hemming or hawing or asking advice from the waiter. He admired that about her. She was also aggressive, especially when it came to moving their relationship along. He found himself being led but, for some odd reason, he had no compunction to fight against it. And it struck him as funny that two of the traits he admired most about her were traits that most women would admire in a man.

"Here," she said sticking out her chopsticks towards him with morsels attached. "Try some of this Kung Pao Chicken... Come on, try it. Don't be a sissy. There. How is it?"

Orson swallowed down the spicy morsels. "Mmm, good," he lied.

"Told you."

"Heard from Balt lately?"

"Who?"

"Balt, your brother.

"Oh, yes. Just the other day. He's doing well. He asked about you."

"Really. What he say?"

"Just asked how you were doing... What do you want to do after dinner?

"I don't know. What do you want to do? … What did you tell him when he asked how I was doing?"

She hummed, "I don't know" while chewing her food, swallowed, then said, "Told him you were great and that we were dating."

"Dating? You told him we were dating? What'd he say to that?"

"Sure. Why not? He was happy to hear it. He thought we would get along really well, and I said we do. We do get along really well. Don't you think?"

Orson put his head down and thought about Balt's words. It was his greatest fear coming true—that this little tryst with his sister would cause him to lose Balt. But breaking it off with her now would be even worse.

"Don't you think," she repeated.

"Think about what?"

"Don't you think we get along really well?" She hunched down and lowered her head to catch his gaze, caught it, then brought his head up with hers as she locked eyes with him.

He looked into her brown eyes, at her velvety lips, at her long brown hair and exquisite neck line and said, "Yeah, I like you… A lot."

"I like you, too… A lot," said Rose with a light laugh. She brought her chopsticks up to her lips and tapped them thoughtfully. "You're funny sometimes," she crooned, her eyes playing over his face. "I've decided what I want to do after dinner."

An anxious premonition came over Orson. "What?"

"Don't you live close by here?"

"I do."

"Let's go there. I've never seen your apartment."

"There's not much too it. Kind'a boring."

"Does it have a bed?"

"Yes."

"Good, and we can have leftover Kung Pao Chicken for breakfast."

Dane's mother was still a beautiful woman. At age forty-eight, her honey blonde hair looked the same as it did when she was in her twenties. She did not color it or touch it up and wore it shoulder length with a natural wave and curl to it. Her striking blue-green eyes were wide-set, and together with her arched eyebrows gave her a slightly sultry look. Lauren Bacall came to mind when you first saw her and like the famous actress she wore her clothes in a style fashion designers would call "studied carelessness." She was graceful in her manner and had grown comfortable with her good looks (which meant she didn't mind men looking at her), but she rarely smiled and projected an aura of guardedness as though she wore an invisible shield.

"Decided yet?" asked her son as they sat looking at their menus.

"Nearly."

Dane was anxious to order and get their food so they could get down to business—the business of talking about his two fathers—but he knew his mom well and knew that no serious talk would begin until she was composed and settled in.

She set her menu down and on cue the waiter appeared and took their order. When he left, she took a sip of her white wine and regarded her son.

"How's Delia doing," she asked him.

"Fine."

"You two still dating?"

"I guess."

"What do you mean, 'you guess'? Either you are or you aren't... Really, Dane. You need to treat her better. She's a wonderful girl, but if you don't think so then you must break it off and stop stringing her along. You can't wonder if she's your girlfriend while you keep having sex with her. I mean, really."

Dane shrugged his shoulders. His mom had a way of succinctly putting things, and the fact that she talked about his sex life didn't surprise him. They were forthright and at times blunt with each other, and bringing up his sex life was as normal to him as if she had brought up his height and weight. Theirs was a close relationship.

"I don't want to talk about Delia," he said flatly.

She nodded once and looked around the restaurant. "Chili Leonard. Who would have thought?" she said almost to herself. "It was great to meet him. He seems like a great guy. Not stuck up like some professional athletes. And Hank Prince. He seems like a nice kid. But I'm a little worried about him. Do you hang out with him at all? I'm not sure he takes the game seriously. Like you do. He seems to be going in the wrong direction. Maybe Chili will talk some sense into him."

"Maybe," he said quickly after she paused between sentences. She was meandering, he thought to himself. It's what she did when she didn't want to talk about something unpleasant to her.

"I was very proud when you got named to the All-Star team."

"Thanks, Mom."

"But you deserve it. You work hard and take the game serious. Of course, you take everything serious."

The waiter brought their appetizer—a plate of spring rolls with sweet and sour dipping sauce—and Dane watched her pick up a roll and dip it. They'd been sitting here long enough, he told himself, and now it was time.

"Who's my real father?"

She chewed her bite of spring roll and set the other half down on her plate. After she swallowed, she took a deep breath and closed her eyes. "I will start at the beginning," she said calmly, opening her eyes. "And listen to me without interrupting or judging me. Let me tell it all before judging me." And here she quoted Paulina from *Winter's Tale*:

It is an heretic that makes the fire,
Not she which burns in't.

Dane did not answer her and simply sat back and waited.

"I met your real father in college and fell deeply in love with him. We were going to get married and we talked about getting married and having a family almost every day. I was so sure—so sure that we were going to get married that I got careless with my birth control. But I'm getting ahead of myself... We were in love as deeply as two people can be in love. At least I thought so, and I still think so. He was—is—the love of my life. I was ready to give up my Masters Program, get married and follow him on the road into the minors. He just got drafted. You see? Your real dad was a professional baseball player. Isn't that funny? And when I tell you his name you'll..."

"A baseball player?"

"Yes, and I was all set to move to Fresno or Springfield or Timbuktu, it didn't matter. Just as long as we were together. But it was all a dream, *'Too flattering sweet to be substantial'*. He had a friend, his best buddy, who used to hang out with us all the time and I thought the right thing to do was to do the same— treat him like my best buddy. So I did. I held hands with him and joked with him and treated him just like a close friend, but it back-fired. It went terribly wrong. Your dad thought we were cheating on him and he went crazy. Crazy with jealousy. He said horrible things to me, called me a whore, and broke it off..."

She stopped abruptly and waited as more dishes were set down on the table. After the waiter left she got ready to resume but Dane interrupted her.

"He must have found out the truth sooner or later. Didn't he try to apologize?"

"No... I don't know. It was too late by then. He said things you can't take back—at least I thought so then. I moved back home with my parents and transferred my Master's Program to Cornell and moved to Ithaca. That's where I met Brian."

"But you were pregnant by then."

"When I moved home I was but I didn't know it yet. When I got to Cornell I knew it but I wasn't going to turn around. Call it what you will—anger, stubbornness—I wasn't going to turn around. Then I met Brian and he didn't care that I was pregnant with another man's child. He wanted to marry me and raise you as his own. Just remember this was the early sixties. A woman didn't just have a child out of wedlock and not pay for it in some way—with her parents, with her career. So Brian was a godsend and the whole thing became easy…"

His mom paused here and fingered the small golden crucifix that hung around her neck. She always did that when she felt sad or guilty about something and it reminded him once again how much religion played a part in her life. They were not particularly religious when he was growing up, and certainly not church-goers, but a few years after his father's suicide she rediscovered her Catholic upbringing and embraced the Church. She asked him early on in her re-awakening (as he called it) whether he wanted to go to church with her. He was fifteen and said no and she never asked him again but now, at this instance, he was reminded once more how much her faith colored her picture of the world.

"Maybe not the right thing," she added sadly, "but the easy thing."

"But you didn't love him."

"I did… In my own way," she replied in a way that bared her soul to him. "It was just not the way he wanted me to love him."

He was going to ask her "Is that why he killed himself?" but he didn't. He already knew the answer to that and to make her say it would only be cruel. There was really only one thing more he wanted to know.

"So who's my real father? The pro ball-player? He's retired by now, right?

"No."

"He's still playing? How can that be?"

"He's a manager."

"What's his name?"

With a breath she revealed her lover, and sighed the name of Shakespeare Glover.

21
CHAPTER

Blow, winds, and crack your cheeks! rage! blow!
You cataracts and hurricanoes

King Lear

Sunday was a double-header to make up for an earlier rain-out against the Indians. It was a single ticket double-header, which meant two-seven inning games, and the Kingsmen had Kid Curry going in the first game and Basset in the second. Shake planned to start Leonard in the first game but sit him out in the second. The double-header gave him a chance to play his reserves—guys itching to get some at bats—and he'd give both Ortiz and Svoboda starts in the outfield in the second game and give Leonard and Burks a rest. Manning would catch the second game and Deer would go to first. A core of players—Prince, Hamilton, Goff and Hoffman—would start both games.

The Kingsmen lost the first game 5-2. Leonard hit a homerun and went three for four and Prince stole two bases but it wasn't enough to overcome fourteen hits by the Indians and two key errors by Hamilton. His first error in the third was on a tailor-made double play ball that went through his legs. As Shake looked out in disbelief, Burton said wryly that "He played every bounce right except for the last one." In the top of the ninth, with the score still close at 3-2, he misplayed another grounder that cost them two runs.

Over a long season, everybody had a bad game or two. Mental fatigue, bad luck, even just the law of averages eventually caught up with you to throw you off your game. Normally Shake wouldn't be too concerned with errors by his star second baseman, but given the fact Hamilton went O for three at the plate and seemed to be acting a bit "out-of-it" caused his concern meter to tick up a bit. More than once he'd caught the young man staring at him. Knowing his history, Shake wondered if Hamilton was once again stewing over world events but he couldn't think of anything out of the ordinary. There was apartheid in South Africa, violence in Northern Ireland, trouble in the Middle East—the same ol' same—and Shake couldn't imagine what it could be. Whatever it was, he expected a better effort out of him in the second game.

During the break between games, Shake went looking for Rex Lyon. He was curious to know why his oldest daughter was lurking about. Before the game he noticed Rae and Ed Cornwall, along with a couple suits, taking a tour of the ballpark. Potential buyers, he wondered. As a shareholder in New Britain Professional Baseball Incorporated he had a right to know. He couldn't find Rex so he asked Orson who told him the old man was up in the press box. Shake figured he'd see him later so let it go.

In the second game Basset was lights out. He carved up the strike zone and had a no-hitter going into the eighth that was ruined by a duck snort to short left field. He finished with a one-hit shutout and the Kingsmen won 6-0. It was a quick game, barely two hours, which was a good thing since a surprise summer storm complete with thunder and lightning was closing fast.

Besides the win, Shake was pleased by two things. First, despite a throwing error in the first, Hamilton shook it off, beared down, and played better including the key hit in the fifth that broke the game open. And second, Prince went four for four, stole three bases, and flashed the leather by making a spectacular running catch in the gap. In the dugout he sat next to Chili Leonard and listened intently as the veteran talked to him about game situation, tendencies and the art of base-stealing. It warmed Shake's heart to see it.

After the game, Shake managed by walking around and touching bases with all his players. He congratulated Basset on his one-hitter and told him within earshot of all his teammates that he thought he was "ticketed for a September call-up." He acted awed by Prince's running catch and told him that he was sure Hank would "shatter the league's stolen base record." Manning "called a helluva game," Deer was his "human hitting machine," and Goff played "the hot corner like he was born there." He stopped next to Hamilton, who was slowly undressing, and put his hand on Dane's shoulder.

"A rough start but a strong finish," said Shake with a smile. The young man looked up at him and stared intensely into his face as though he was confronting a ghost. Shake found it a bit unsettling.

"Thanks," he replied, and Shake thought for a moment that the young man wanted to say something more, but he didn't and instead bent over to unlace his cleats. Shake took that as a cue to move on but he suddenly remembered something.

"Weren't you going to bring your mom by to meet me?" he asked.

"Huh? Oh… yeah," he said straightening up. "She couldn't. Maybe another time."

"Love to meet her. Let her know."

Dane nodded and rubbed his chin while Shake moved on to his next player.

Shake was in his office finishing up his paperwork when he heard the first distant roll of thunder. By the time he was done the thunder was nearly on top of the stadium. It cracked loudly and the roaring thunder shook the walls of his office. Just then Orson burst into his office wet with rain.

"Shake!" he cried. "I need your help! It's Rex!"

Shake shot out from behind his desk and followed Orson down the hallway and out the door into the parking lot. It was blowing rain and the air felt electric. As they raced across the empty parking lot, the dark violet sky erupted in a flash of white followed immediately by a deep booming thunder. Shit, thought Shake, we're going to get electrocuted, but he didn't stop chasing after Orson. They went out a gate into a field that sat between the stadium and the woods. Orson slowed his pace and Shake could see they were approaching two figures—one kneeling and another bending over the other. It was Rex and Speed.

A lightning bolt struck into the woods and Shake lowered into a crouch as though he were under fire. When he got to Rex he could see that the old man was drenched with rain. Speed was calmly talking in his ear while trying to get him to stand up. Rex was having none of it. He had a maniacal look on his face, and as the thunder roared he roared back at it.

Rex

Have at it! Come get me! I'm right here! Don't waste your bolts on trees, hit me here—right here in the head!

Speed

Come one, sir. Please. Rant and rave inside where it's nice and dry. Where's there's no lightning to kill you. Whoa! See? Lightning bolts don't care who they hit. They'll fry rich and poor alike.

Rex

Let it fry me! Come on, right here! I won't fault you, do your job! Strike me dead and end the life of a sick and hated old man!

Shake
We need to get him out of here.

Speed
He won't get up.

Shake
Then we'll all carry him.

Rex
Who's that there!?

Speed
A rich man and a poor man.

Rex
Who's that?!

Speed
Shakespeare and Kent.

Rex
Shakespeare? Fuck Shakespeare! It's all his fault! ... No, let me go! Let me go!

Shake
He's getting away. Grab his leg!

Orson
I can't. Ouch! He's got old man strength.

Shake
Speed! Goddammit! Hold his arm.

Speed
His arm is like the army. It fights back!

Orson

We need to get him inside before we all get hit by lightning.
(A lightning flash))
Holy Shit!

Rex

Show it all! Let me see my enemies. Rae! My own daughter.
You've killed me! Murderer! You've killed me. My own daughter!
Rae! You can't hide from the light! God can see you! ... Corey!
Where's my Corey... Corey, Corey, Corey!

Shake

You got him? Okay. To my car! Hear me? My car!

*(The three of them carry Rex across the field and place him in
the backseat of Shake's car where they attend to him.)*

Rex
(To Speed)
Speed. My boy. I think I'm losing my mind. You're all wet. Aren't
you cold?

Speed

Yes, sir. I'm wet and cold, cold and wet. Can't have one without
the other. Like power and corruption. Can't have one without
the other.

Rex
(weakly)
Ha...True...

Orson

He's shivering all over. He doesn't look good. Should we get
him inside?

Shake

No. Speed, go run and get some towels and blankets.
(To Orson)
Here—start my car and crank the heater up.
(Speed exits)
Rex? Rex? Do you hear me? Let's get you warmed up.

Rex

Where's my Corey? Have you seen her?

Shake

I'll call her. I'll get her here. I promise.

Rex

Who... are you? Oh, Glover... My friend... You'll find Corey?
Bring her here?

Shake

I will.

Rex

Thank you... Shake... Which President threw out the... the
first... *(he passes out)*

Shake

(To Orson)
We need to get to a hospital. You drive. Conn Central, on
Grand. You know it?

Orson

Got it.

Shake

(Cradles Rex in his arms)
Taft... It was William Howard Taft.

At the hospital, the ER Doctor came out to look at Rex as they were lifting him up onto the gurney. He felt his pulse, looked into his eyes, and barked at the orderlies to take Rex straight to ICU. Shake and Orson walked into the waiting lobby and Shake found a pay phone. From there he called Corey and told her what happened—told her, too, that her father was calling for her—and he heard the phone drop as she rushed out the door. He also called his coaches and told them to stand by for news. Rick Burton said he was coming down to the hospital. Shake thought about calling the Cornwalls but didn't.

Corey showed up ten minutes later and had a million questions that Shake couldn't answer. She was naturally high-energy, and with the news that her father was in ICU it was like trying to contain a small tornado. She badgered the receptionist, quickly way-laid any nurse that walked through the lobby, and generally rattled everyone's cage. Shake got her to sit down and tried to calm her. Burton came in, saw them and disappeared, bringing back coffee a few minutes later.

"Decaf," he said as he handed her a cup.

She took it and managed a short laugh.

"What do we know?" he asked Shake.

Before Shake could answer "Not much" the large doors of the emergency room opened and a nurse appeared. "Corey Lyon," she called out.

"Here!" cried Corey, almost spilling her coffee.

"Your father wants to see you."

She handed her coffee back to Rick and followed the nurse through the doors, peppering her with questions as the big doors slid shut behind them.

In ICU, Corey tiptoed towards her father's bed. He was hooked up to an IV, a heart monitor, and wore a nasal cannula that fed him oxygen. He appeared to be sleeping peacefully. She sat down next to him and laid her check against his arm. The touch of her cheek brought him back to consciousness.

"Daddy."

He blinked his eyes and beheld his daughter. "Are you an angel?" he asked in his confusion.

"It's me. Corey."

"Corey... My little girl," he said weakly.

"Shh, it's okay. I'm here now."

"Where am I? What time is it?" he asked. She told him where he was and why he was there and he listened quietly. Tears formed in his eyes and he took her hand in his. "Corey," he said again, this time with a frail smile. "My little girl."

"I love you, Daddy."

"I love you too, baby... Can you forgive an old man? I'm a fool... A senile old fool."

"Shh, it's okay. Everything's okay. There's nothing to forgive. I know you love me and always loved me. There's nothing to forgive. It's all right, Daddy. Everything's all right. I'm here now."

"I bless your marriage."

At these words, she lifted their clasped hands to her face and started crying. She struggled to gather herself. "You're coming home with me," she finally said in a voice fierce with emotion. "You'll stay with us and I'll take care of you. Don't worry about anything, Daddy. I'll take care of you."

"I'm happy... I'm..." But his eyes closed and he fell back asleep before he could finish. Corey laid his arm back down on the bed and rested her cheek against it again. A nurse came in and checked his vitals and left. After a while, Corey felt his arm move and she looked up to see his eyes opening again.

"It wasn't a dream," he said looking at her. "Rocket." ("Rocket" was his pet name for her.)

"Daddy-O."

"Where's the doctor?"

"He'll be here. They need to run some more tests, so just relax for now. We'll get you out of here. And you're coming home with me so I can take care of you."

He nodded his understanding and looked at her warmly. "I need a hug."

She leaned over awkwardly but was able to get her arms around his shoulders while she rested her head against his chest. She squeezed gently and he managed to raise both arms and hug her back.

"Better," he said as she sat back down. He glanced over at the heart monitor. "How'd I get her?" he asked.

"Shake brought you in his car. He also called me."

"Glover. Good man... Where is he?"

"They're all in the lobby."

"Ask him to come in here... I want to tell him something."

"They only let family in here. You need to rest right now. You can see him later."

"No... I need to see him now. Please, Rocket."

"Okay, Daddy. I'll get him"

Speed had figured things out and come to the hospital, and he and Shake and Rick and Orson sat without talking in the waiting lobby. The big doors slid open and Corey appeared. Immediately they all stood up.

"He's stabilized and resting," she told them. "They have some more tests to run before they let him go." The four men were relieved to hear the news. "He wants to see you, Shake," she added.

"Me? Is it okay?"

"Yeah, come on."

"All right—hey, you guys should go home. No sense in sticking around here. If anything changes I'll let you know, but it sounds like he's doing better."

Rick and Orson agreed that was a good idea and got ready to leave. Speed stayed put. Shake followed Corey to the big doors but they did not budge when she pushed on them. She knocked loudly and a receptionist leaned out her window to see who it was then leaned back. The doors opened but a no-nonsense-looking nurse met them on the other side. She looked sternly at both Corey and Shake.

"Is he family?" she asked Corey.

"Yes."

The no-nonsense nurse doubted the answer but let them pass. When they came into ICU Rex was sleeping, so they both stood and waited next to his bed. "He said he had something to tell you," she said. Shake nodded his understanding. Corey touched her father's arm, rubbed it gently, and the old man's eyes opened. "Shake's here," she told him.

"Glover," he said, barely audible. He said something else that Shake couldn't hear so Shake came in closer and bent over him. "I have my little girl back," said Rex weakly.

"I see that. It makes me happy."

"I had something... I wanted to tell you. Come closer." Shake bent down lower and turned his head to better hear. Rex spoke, his voice feeble but clear:

> *For God's sake let us sit upon the ground*
> *And tell sad stories of the death of Kings.*

Shake pulled back and looked into Rex's sorrowful eyes. He gently squeezed the old man's shoulder and was about to say, "No, it's not time yet" when he heard loud noises outside in the hall. It was the voice of Rex's oldest daughter Rae. When he looked back at Rex his eyes were closed. Shake followed Corey out to the hallway where they met Rae and Ed Cornwall.

"What's he doing here?" demanded Rae. "Only family is allowed in here."

"Daddy wanted to talk to him," said Corey

"I don't care. Where's the head nurse?"

"Rae, dear, please," said Ed in a conciliatory tone, glancing first at Corey and then at Shake. "We just got the call and rushed here as fast as we could, so we're a little flustered as you can imagine. What's the doctor say? How's he doing?"

"I just talked to the doctor," said Rae curtly. "They have more tests to run. Due to his heart problems."

"Oh, yes, his heart problems," replied Ed nodding. "Of course."

"What heart problems?" shot back Corey. "No one ever told me daddy had heart problems."

Rae cut off her husband before he could answer. "Why's that you think?" she retorted. "You're never around. He has early Alzheimer's and heart problems, but how would you know?"

"You know why that is," said Corey briskly.

"Yeah, he disowned you. But what? Now you're reconciled? Did he forgive you?"

"There was no need. Daddy loves me and he's going to come live with me."

"How sweet. Now you're finally going to help me with him? It's a little late."

"Excuse me a moment," said Shake interrupting, his voice rising in anger. "But when we found Rex out in the storm, he was damning you and calling you a murderer. Why would a father say such a thing?"

"Because he's out of his mind—but what business is that of yours," she snapped angrily. "This is family business and you don't belong here. Where's the head nurse?"

"Rae, dear, please."

"Daddy asked for him," said Corey. "He wanted to say—"

But before she could finish an alarm sounded from Rex's room and a nurse rushed in to see. She left immediately and returned with a doctor wheeling a crash cart. Corey was on their heels but the nurse turned and gently pushed her back and closed the curtain behind them to block the view. His angel Corey, weeping and afraid, bowed her head and hoped and prayed.

22
CHAPTER

*It is not the honor that you take with you,
but the heritage you leave behind.*

Branch Rickey

Rex Oliver Lyon II died that night in the hospital of heart failure. Ed Cornwall was quick to get the story to the papers and even the New York Times and Boston Globe carried small articles on Rex's passing. He was born on November 11, 1903 and died at the age of eighty-two, and most newspapers gave a short summary of his life that included his founding of the Lyon Bolt Manufactory in 1929 at the age of twenty-five along with his ownership of the New Britain Kingsmen, a Double-A affiliate in the Eastern League. Local papers carried more extensive obituaries, noting that Lyon Bolt Manufactory, in its hey-day, had factories in four states, employed five thousand people, and was awarded the Army-Navy "E" Award for excellence in war production during WWII. Other papers mentioned his more notable charitable endeavors.

Shake spent a long night at the hospital comforting Corey, and when he boarded the bus the next day for New Haven he appeared somber and bleary-eyed. The team already knew about

Rex's passing so he didn't need to make an announcement and instead plopped down in his seat next to Burton. Rick handed him the morning paper with Rex's obituary and Shake read it as the bus started up. When he was done he sorted through the box of VHS tapes. There was a TV and VCR player on the bus and most of the tapes were either WrestleMania or comedies. Shake found a Steve Martin movie and stuck it in the VCR. He needed cheering up.

In New Haven, they settled into their hotel rooms and then got ready for their four-game series against the Admirals. Shake had given Corey his hotel information and told her to call him if she needed to talk. She called him Tuesday morning and in a shaky voice let him know that funeral services would be next Saturday. Yes, she knew the team had a series in Waterbury that weekend but was sick and tired of arguing with her sister about it who refused to postpone it so the whole team could attend. Could Shake come to the service anyway, she asked. Say something on behalf of the team? Of course, he said, he'd be there no matter what. She made him promise.

Shake wanted to ask her about ownership but he didn't. She had enough things on her mind. He hoped to get the straight scoop from someone at the funeral, though he had a bad feeling what that scoop would be. Rae Cornwall wanted to sell the team and in the interim they'd probably have to deal with her husband Ed. He didn't look forward to that.

The Kingsmen split the series against the Admirals and headed on over to Waterbury. Shake managed the Kingsmen to a win on Friday and handed over the reins to Rick Burton for Saturday's game. It was all arranged with the big club and Rick wished he could go with Shake, but he understood the situation and asked Shake to pass on his condolences to Corey.

Services were at 1:00 at St. Mary Church and Shake got home in plenty of time so he could dress in the appropriate attire. At 12:15 he left and picked up Speed and Orson. Rex's employees at Beehive Stadium—the ground's crew, ticket-takers, concessionaires and parking lot attendants—would all be there.

A Nigerian-born priest spoke sparingly about Rex's life and quoted scripture. He had a thick accent, which Shake found difficult to understand, and Shake suspected that the thirty-something priest had never met Rex personally. Ed Cornwall gave a dry eulogy that focused primarily on Rex's empire-building and charitable works and never once mentioned Rex's passion in life—baseball and his beloved Kingsmen. Corey read a long poem she wrote about her father. It was eloquent and touching, comparing their father-daughter relationship to a great lion and his cub, and Shake was left like many with a lump in his throat.

When Corey finished she looked out at Shake. "I've asked Shake Glover to come up and say a few words on behalf of Daddy's ball club, The Kingsmen, which he loved very much. Shake and my dad were good friends... Shake."

Shake stood up. He noticed that Rae Cornwall glared at her half-sister from the front row. Shake was not listed on the printed program as a speaker but Corey, to her ever-loving credit, had outplayed her sister and invited Shake to come up and speak. Shake smiled to himself at that, pulled out the folded speech from his inside pocket, and strode to the podium.

Shake

Thank you Corey. On behalf of myself, my coaching staff, the players, and all the employees who worked for Rex at Beehive Stadium—many who are here today—we would like to pass on our heartfelt condolences to the Lyon family for their great loss. Rex was a good man and we'll miss him dearly.

Those of you who know me know that I'm a great lover of William Shakespeare. I call him the Bard and quote him frequently, sometimes to the great man's detriment. But I have found that when something needs to be said, something stirring and profound—like at the passing of a good man—then I find the Bard is my go-to guy and can be counted on to hit a homer. Rex, for all I know, was never much of a Shakespeare fan. We never played the quote game. Our game was baseball trivia—arcane baseball trivia, like how many stitches are there on a baseball—and we played it whenever we found a chance. We did our best to stump the other. For the record, Corey, I never once stumped your dad.

But there's another reason I have for relying on the Bard today to help me say what I want to say about Rex, and it has to do with his last words. They were spoken to me on his deathbed and was the one and only time he ever quoted Shakespeare to me. You've read his last words in the newspapers, the quote about sitting on the ground and telling sad stories of the death of kings, and I've thought long and hard about why he picked that quote. It's from *Richard the Third*, which is the story of a deposed king, and maybe that's what drew him to the quote. I don't know. But there is another quote from the play spoken by Richard himself—and this is after he's been forced to give up his crown—that I think very much captures the mood of the day.

> *Let's talk of graves, of worms, and epitaphs;*
> *Make dust our paper and with rainy eyes*
> *Write sorrow on the bosom of the earth,*
> *Let's choose executors and talk of wills:*
> *And yet not so, for what can we bequeath*
> *Save our deposed bodies to the ground?*
> *And I will lean on him heavily herein out.*

We've heard much today about Rex Lyon the businessman, the empire-builder, and what can one say other than

> *His deeds exceed all speech:*
> *He never lift up his hand but conquered.*

But over-shadowed somewhat are all his charitable works—his philanthropy and good will towards men. He was no Scrooge. Far from it. The newspapers have listed many of his gifts to the community—The Lyon Children's Hospital, AmeriCorps, Big Brother and Sisters. The list goes on and the evidence of a life well-lived is right there. Here is someone to admire, a man guided by the belief that people owe something back to the community they live in. There is not a person in this Church today, certainly no one associated with the Kingsmen, who have not been touched at some point by his generosity. Who then will fill this void? Who will pick up Rex's mantle? A man of great deeds has left us and it feels like

> *The breaking of so great a thing should make*
> *A greater crack: the round world*
> *Should have shook lions into civil streets,*
> *And citizens to their dens*

But I'm not here to canonize Rex as a saint. He wasn't a saint. He was a man—a man with good and bad in him just like the rest of us. If each of us has been touched by his generosity, then we have also been touched at some point by his wrath. He was a complicated man whose *'taints and honours waged equal with him.'* He was not what people today would call 'politically correct', and he could be sunny one minute and a raging storm the next and say things that he was sorry for later. But he spoke his mind and

> *He would not flatter Neptune of his trident,*
> *Or Jove's power to thunder. His heart's his mouth.*

So, yes, he had his faults. As do we all. His just seemed bigger at times because he himself was bigger than life. But I can't imagine Rex any other way, or would I want him any other way. When

I think of him in this way, I am reminded of one of my favorite quotes from *Measure for Measure* since it fits Rex to a tee:

> They say, best men are moulded out of faults;
> And, for the most, become much more the better
> For being a little bad

I believe a man is defined by what he does. We have the business empire Rex built and his many wonderful charitable works—all these things help us to define Rex, but there is one thing missing, one key ingredient missing from our picture of Rex. Without it we miss one of the very things that gave him joy. And that thing is *baseball*. His love of baseball also helps us define him. He understood that baseball is a game of perfect distances and beautiful numbers, with its own sages and poets. He heard wisdom when Yogi spoke and genuflected at the altar of Durocher. Willie Mays was his favorite player and he surely agreed with the person who once said 'There have been only two geniuses in the world, Willie Mays and Willie Shakespeare'.

If you were to ask me what a perfect day would be to Rex, I would tell you this: a day game at Beehive stadium. The sun is out, the stands are full, and Corey walks by his side. He talks to his concessionaires, making sure the hot dogs are hot and the cold beer is cold, probably barks at one of you to refill the cup dispenser, then climbs the stairs into the stands where he visits all the season-ticket holders, calling them by name and asking about their kids, before he parks himself in his box with a beer and bag of peanuts to watch the game. And the Kingsmen win, maybe on a dramatic homer in the ninth, and Rex shouts for joy and hugs Corey then leaves the box to close up shop. And once the stadium is empty of fans and the players have scattered to the four winds, Rex taps a kegger and calls on his employees to join him for a beer in the settling dusk underneath the stands. And there he toasts the team and the victory, sure in that moment that all is right with the world

Branch Rickey, the great owner and greater man, once said, 'It is not the honor that you take with you, but the heritage you leave behind.' Based on that true and simple formula, we can say goodbye to Rex confident in the knowledge that he left a rich heritage behind him. And so, now, I have only my last goodbye to say to Rex and I will let the Bard say it for me:

> *Now cracks a noble heart. Good night sweet prince:*
> *And flights of angels sing thee to thy rest!*

Shake and Speed were pall bearers and they helped lay Rex to rest in the St. Mary Cemetery. Mourners were invited to the Lyon Estate for a brunch in memoriam. Only Shake and Orson attended from the Kingsmen. Speed and the other employees left for their homes after the burial with no intention of visiting the castle of the Wicked Witch of the East. All of them, to one degree or another, blamed Rae Cornwall for Rex's death and feared what was coming in terms or ownership.

Shake had been there for about an hour, had a couple beers and some food from the buffet table, when Rae came up to him. She held a glass with a mixed drink in it, scotch by the looks of it, and it wasn't her first one, he figured. Her naturally frowning brow was somewhat softened.

"Shake," she said affably.

"Mrs. Cornwall."

"Call me Rae." She took a sip of her drink and studied him for a moment as though he were an odd-looking fish in an aquarium. "Youuu don't like me much, do you? Doesn't matter... That was quite a eulogy you gave. Very poetic. But I don't know who you were talking about."

"Your father."

"That's not the father I remember. And just for the record, all those 'charitable works' you mentioned were done for one reason and one reason alone—tax write-offs. There was no 'good will towards men' about it."

"Why does any of that matter," replied Shake coolly, "It's the act of giving that matters. The reason is irrelevant." As she said, he didn't like her and he was certain she didn't like him so he was curious where all this was going. Why was she talking to him, he wondered.

"I suppose you could look at it that way," she said doubtfully. "But the man I grew up with was something different all together." She paused here and Shake thought that was it—she's made her point and would move on—but instead a strange look of earnestness came over her face as though what she'd come over to really say to him she was going to say now. "People have their opinion of me but they don't know. They've got no clue what I've been through with my father. He was not a good man. He divorced my mom and used his high-priced legal team to prove she was an unfit mother. It destroyed her and she ended up in a mental institution. He never gave me much love—not like Corey—but I stuck by him and pulled him out of his money problems and took care of him when he started forgetting things and drinking too much.

"You have no idea what it's been like in this house over the last year. He had poker parties here with his drunken buddies, and we would find him the next morning wandering around the house in boxers not knowing where he was. When I tried to help him he would yell and scream terrible things. It was abusive. And I couldn't get him to see a doctor. He refused and screamed at me that I was trying to commit him. So I had to take a stand. For his own good, I had to take a stand. And now that he's gone, what's left? Memories of abuse. That's pretty much his heritage to me. He owed a debt to my mother and he owed a debt to me but he never paid it."

She seemed to finish, swirled her drink and took a sip, then added, "Well, anyway" and turned away.

"Rae," said Shake, and she stopped and glanced back at him. *"He that dies pays all debts."*

In the downstairs den of the Lyon House that same evening, two lawyers sat behind a large mahogany desk and peered lawyer-like out at their clients Ed and Rae Cornwall. Corey sat in a big leather chair.

Rae
I thought we were here to talk about Corey. When my father disowned her he removed her from the trust and we'd like to discuss her options. Is there something from the trust we can give her? Isn't that what we're here for?

First Lawyer
In part. We can certainly talk about those options as well.

Second Lawyer
We're here to talk about the baseball team. The New Britain Kingsmen.

Rae
We plan to sell the team. We already have buyers lined up.

First Lawyer
Well, that will be up to Corey Danzig.

Ed
What do you mean?

First Lawyer
It means that sole ownership of the baseball team passes to Ms. Danzig. It's clearly stated in his will and was never amended

otherwise. She inherits the New Britain Kingsmen lock, stock and barrel.

Ed

But—how can that be? All titles and ownerships were transferred into my wife's name, including the ball club.

Second Lawyer

No, it wasn't. The baseball team was not included in the transfer. Your father-in-law was adamant about that. He should have told you. He said he would. We assumed all this time you were aware of this provision in his will, since you never asked about it or questioned it.

Rae

YOU never asked about it? How stupid is that, Ed?

Ed

Well, I assumed it was all a part of the terms of receivership. No one told me any different. Rex never mentioned it and I'm not in the habit of reading hundred page legal documents. I rely on my lawyers to do that.

Rae

Perfect. Just like him. One last insult from his grave... So what are our options?

First Lawyer

Options? As I've said, that will be up to Ms. Danzig. She can sell or not. The team makes a sustainable profit every year but I'm sure she can make a larger profit if she chooses to sell.

Rae

(to Corey)

We have buyers lined up. One million dollars they're willing to pay. One million, Corey—for a baseball team… Let's work something out here, dear. We've done all the leg work for you. Once you sell it we can split the profits and you'll have more than enough to live on for years to come, especially after we kick in some money from the trust. You can't run a baseball team. You don't want that kind of headache, dear. Grab this opportunity and let us help you sell the club.

All four—the two lawyers and Ed and Rae Cornwall—looked expectantly at Corey awaiting her answer. She rose from her leather chair, and with hands on hips eyed her sister and brother-in-law. She raised her head and laughed—a strong hearty laugh—and looked back down at them with a triumphant smile on her face. "I'm not selling," she said and left the room.

Rex Lyon is buried, long live the king; it's Corey the Rocket, his loving offspring.

23
CHAPTER

Thou art sad; get thee a wife, get thee a wife!
Much Ado About Nothing

August 1ˢᵗ came and went and with it the trade deadline. No one on the Kingsmen was optioned, traded or designated as a player to be named later. Everyone breathed a little easier and it showed. August brought the heat but it was always a lot less hot when you were winning. By the end of the first week in August, the Kingsmen were ten games up and headed for the top seed which gave them home field advantage throughout the playoffs.

Shake kept writing glowing progress reports about Hank Prince. The kid was a revelation, spraying base hits to every field, stealing bases at will, tracking down everything in the outfield, hitting the cut-off man, not missing signs, showing up early and working hard at his craft. He even dressed better. Gone were the high-top sneakers and baggy pants. Instead, Hank came in to the clubhouse nowadays wearing slacks and a sports coat, looking sharp and snazzy like a young Billy Dee Williams. It appeared Mr. Hyde was under wraps and Dr. Jekyll was here to stay. Whatever elixir Chili Leonard served Hank, it worked, and Shake wanted the rights to bottle it.

Saturday the ninth was a day game and had been re-named from Papa Dodge Day (where a car was given away) to Rex Lyon Day. A car was still going to be raffled off by Papa Dodge of New Britain, and there would be plenty of media coverage to please the local car dealership, but the real focus for the day was a tribute to Rex Lyon. A nice-looking plaque with his image on it, his years of ownership, and the words "Vivat Rex" (Long Live the King) engraved upon it was presented to Corey before the game. She thanked the loyal fans and gave a short speech. Shake also spoke at the ceremony as did a number of dignitaries. A good friend of Rex's—President Reagan—sent a thoughtful telegram and it was read by the P.A. Announcer.

Corey quickly and firmly established herself as the new owner of the New Britain Kingsmen. Like the rookie Barry Bonds—the prodigy well-schooled by his old man—she walked the clubhouse hallways with an easy confidence. The first day Shake saw her on the job as the new owner, she was talking to the groundskeepers but pulled up and yelled out at him, "Toni Stone!"

Shake stopped and smiled. Game on. "First woman to play pro ball," he responded. "What team?"

"The Negro League."

"No, no, no. You don't get off that easy, Danzig. What team?"

"The… San Francisco Sea Lions. Right?"

"Right," he said with a laugh. He saluted her and she saluted back. Shake suddenly felt a wave of pride and happiness—almost as if she were his own daughter—and he spun around and went back to his office before anyone could see the tears welling up in his eyes.

The drawing for the car was in the sixth inning and a woman won. She leapt from her seat, hugged her equally excited husband and two kids, and bounded down the steps, almost tripping in her rush, and claimed the keys to her new Dodge Omni. The game itself was another win for the Kingsmen, 4-0, with

Santiago pitching a shutout over the Vermont Reds. After the game there was a free concert put on by Corey's husband's band "Bone Dry."

Shake hurried up his postgame paperwork, skipped the concert (which wasn't his cup of tea), and drove over to the Burtons for their barbecue. Linda Burton met him at the door with a cold beer and he took it, said "Merci beaucoup," kissed her on the cheek and walked out into the backyard where he found Rick barbecuing and the rest of his coaches sitting around a patio table. A chair was waiting for him and he sat down.

The Burton kids immediately ran up to him to say hi. They were dripping wet from swimming in the Doughboy pool. The boys, Ricky and Gordy, were eleven and ten while the youngest, their daughter Sophie, was eight years old. The boys tussled playfully with him and demanded he play catch with them later. He promised he would and they ran off satisfied, leaving Sophie behind. Her nickname was "Pooh" or "Pooh Bear" because Winnie the Pooh was her favorite thing in the whole wide world. "Pooh Bear" was also Shake's favorite human being in the whole wide world.

"Hey, Pooh Bear," he said happily. "Where's my hug?"

The little girl jumped into him and gave him a big hug, leaving a wet imprint on his clothes. Shake didn't mind.

"Where's your witch friend?" she asked innocently.

"Huh?"

"Your witch friend. Mommy says you have a witch friend."

The adults sitting around laughed at this and Shake looked over at the sliding glass doors but Linda had ducked back inside. "Yeah, where's your witch friend?" added Benedict with a grin. Shake gave him a mock frown and looked back at Pooh Bear.

"She got on her broomstick and flew away," he said convincingly.

"Really? Where to?" she wanted to know.

"Ahh, the Emerald City, but she said she might fly by later, so keep an eye out."

Pooh Bear looked up at the sky, scanning north and south. "Really?"

"Really, so keep a look out. If you see her let me know right away."

"I will," she promised, but the adult laughter caused her to look half-suspiciously at Uncle Shake. He changed the subject to her dancing and she happily gave him a progress report. The other kids started calling her name from the pool and the enticement was too great. She struggled to remain standing there.

"Go swim," encouraged Shake. "Go. If I see her fly by I'll let you know."

She was happy with that answer and skipped back to the pool, glancing up in the sky as she went. She wanted to see a flying witch, for sure, but she wanted to swim with her friends even more. When Pooh Bear was out of earshot, Shake called out for Linda.

"Hey, I know you're hiding back there!" he yelled trying to suppress a laugh. "I'm gonna get you for that. 'My witch friend'. I'll give you 'my witch friend'. Bang, zoom, to the moon, Alice!"

Everyone was getting a good laugh out of it. Teddy was there with his wife and kids, Bob brought along his live-in girlfriend, and Larry was there with Bernie (who were now a serious couple). Orson Kent was there and introduced Shake to his date. She looked a lot like Balt Porter and turned out to be his twin sister. Also at the barbecue was Mike Faust who brought his date—an attractive, chiseled gal that looked like a body-builder—but Shake never learned her name and they left early. There were a few other friends and family of the Burtons, all couples, and Shake quickly figured out he was the only one there stag. Speed was absent (because he drove Rick crazy) and there were no ball-players.

Rick cooked up his famous barbecued spare ribs, Linda made her delicious potato salad, and the beer and wine was plentiful. The first time Shake finished off his beer, Linda appeared and handed him a new one and whispered, "Has she flown by yet?", and Shake tried to swat her butt but she got away in time. By the time he finished off the ribs and potato salad and other good things, Shake had had a few more beers and the shade had grown longer in the backyard. The conversation was light and witty and Shake was on his game, cracking jokes, telling tales, and offering witty observations on just about any subject. Despite being the only one there without a main squeeze, he felt comfortable and relaxed as he always did at the Burtons.

When Shake sat back down at the patio table after playing catch with the boys, Larry stood up with Bernie. She wore a beaming smile. Larry clinked his beer bottle.

Larry
Hey folks! Listen up. We've got something to tell you... Bernie and I are engaged.

Bernie
(showing off her engagement ring)
We're getting married!

All
Whoa! Yeah! Congratulations, you too. Wonderful news!

Bob
I liked it better when you two used to fight all the time.

Larry
I know you did, Bob. But I like it better this way.
(kisses Bernie)

Bob
Another one bites the dust. That only leaves Shake.

Linda
When's the happy date?

Larry and Bernie
(simultaneously)
Next summer—Next spring.

Bob
So when is it? Next summer or next spring?

Bernie
(whispering)
I thought we agreed on next spring.

Larry
(whispering back)
No, you agreed to next spring. I agreed to next summer.

Bernie
I said 'spring' and you said 'okay'. As usual you weren't listening. Why did God waste ears on men if they're not going to use them?

Larry
Well, they're working now and I wish they weren't.

Bernie
Hey, folks, if we get married it will be next spring—not summer.

Larry
'If we get married'? IF… If's a big word, almost as big as your—But I won't go there. If we knew what we knew, there'd be no ifs—only dreams that come true. We'd all be coaching in the big leagues. Kalecki would have all his teeth. The Red Sox would win the World Series. Babies would change their own diapers.

And women—wives, girlfriends or fiancées—would have our backs and only wear nighties to bed.

Bob
Here, here.

Bernie
And husbands, boyfriends or fiancées would pick up after themselves and go all night.

Bob's Girlfriend
Here, here.

Larry
There you go. That makes us even and the only thing left to do is get married. In the spring. Next century.

Bernie
You won't live that long. You drink too much.

Larry
I have good reason to.

Bernie
Excuse us, folks.
(she pulls Larry away)
We'll be back in a few. After I sober him up.

Larry and Bernie, arm in arm, walked back into the house still arguing with one other under their breath. "Now that's more like it," said Bob. *"Bob!"* chastised his girlfriend but everyone laughed quietly.

"*Hanging and wiving goes by destiny,*" quoted Shake.

"Don't be so cynical," replied Linda. "Some people spend fifty years of married life happily arguing with one another. It spices things up. It's their music, like one of those Johnny and June Carter Cash duets."

"All right, so be it," said Shake with a glint in his eye. "*If music be the food of love play on.*"

It got later into the evening and Larry and Bernie only reappeared to say their goodbyes. The kids went inside to dry off and watch TV. Couples and families soon drifted away leaving Shake, Rick and Linda sitting out on the deck. It was a pleasant warm evening and the patio lights gave off enough of a glow to see each other's face. The bug zapper was working overtime.

"So, Shakearoni, where's your witch friend?" asked Linda with a laugh. "Why didn't you bring Lucy?"

Shake expected this. Whenever he visited the Burtons, it usually ended up with a heart to heart with Linda. Rick would listen in, contributing a word or two, but would eventually wander off to see after the kids. She was intelligent and refreshingly blunt like his mom and could get him to fess up things he wouldn't otherwise. He pretended to dislike these talks but the truth was he really enjoyed them.

"It's kaput," replied Shake matter-of-factly.

"Sorry to hear that... I think"

"We dated for three years. It was a good run."

"It wasn't a Broadway show, bub. So what happened? Wait, don't tell me. Your screw-buddy suddenly got serious and wanted to get married, so you broke it off?"

"'*Screw buddy*'. Jeez, where'd you get that? Rick, you need to limit her late night television... So, yeah, smartass. That's pretty much it."

"Shake shakes another one."

"At midfield and on in for the touchdown."

"Only you don't go in for the touchdown. You go home to an empty bed. But don't get me wrong. She wasn't right for you. I'm sure you found that whole witch thing campy and cool but you don't marry a woman like that. She'd turn you into a toad."

"Good thing I didn't marry her then. I don't want to be a toad."

"But you need to marry someone. But I shouldn't say it that way. You need to fall in love with someone."

"Got anyone in mind or can I choose for myself?"

"Quiet and listen. I used to think you had something against marriage, maybe even women, but I figured it out. You're against love. I even told Rick that. You have something against love. You got burned once and now you're all against love. Such a tragic figure. So tell me coach, when you struck out the first time why didn't you quit baseball."

"I love baseball."

"My point exactly. It's time for you to get back in the batter's box there, sweetie, and fall in love. Get married, have kids."

"I'm too old to have kids."

"Never say never… Did I just quote Yogi Berra? No, he's the one who said, 'It ain't over till it's over'. Right? Anyhow, never say never. Who knows what life has in store for you."

Shake chuckled at this. He could see she was enjoying herself. She was a little drunk and having her fun. He thought maybe he could turn the tables a bit to get the heat off.

"So, you two," he said affably. "What's the secret to a successful marriage? Like yours. What's the secret?"

"Love," said Rick.

"That's no secret," she said. "He wants to know *the secret*. So let me ask you this… what's the secret to a successful manager—to the marriage between a manager and his team. Like what you have?"

"I knew you'd find a way to turn this back around… Okay, I'll tell you. Tommy Lasorda said it the best. He said, 'Managing is like holding a dove in your hand. Squeeze too hard and you kill it; not hard enough and it flies away.'"

"There you go," she cried with delight. "That's the secret of a happy marriage. Couldn't have said it better myself. Who says baseball managers are all knuckle-draggers."

"Yea, who says?"

Across town in a motel room, Dane and Delia were lying in bed together. Dane was spent and wanted to sleep but Delia felt like talking. For Dane, the same cycle had repeated itself yet again. The ancient Greek punishment. The evening had started with dinner and small talk, then a fight, followed by quiet small talk again, desert and sex. What was one to do? It was cruel fate.

"Dane."

"Hmm."

"You were going to tell me something. Something important. What was it?" She nestled her head deeper into the crevice of his shoulder.

Dane roused himself out of sleepiness. He knew what "something" meant to her. She hoped to hear him say he loved her or wanted to marry her or some such nonsense.

"It was about my father," he said.

"Your father?"

"My father isn't really my father. He's my step-father... My mom finally told me who my real father is."

"What?" she said coming up on an elbow. "What do you mean your father isn't your father? Who's your real father? What did your mom say?"

"Shake Glover."

"What! Your manager? Why didn't you tell me this before?"

"I just found out myself." And with that he proceeded, sleepily, to give her the entire back story, even the part about the ghost in the cemetery. Her big, sad blue eyes danced over his face as he talked.

"Does he know?" she asked. "Have you told him?"

"Not yet. It's complicated... One minute he's my manager and the next he's my father. Plus my mom's not sure she's ready to see him again. She's afraid. They were lovers in college... and she still loves him, I think, but she's afraid of his reaction when

he learns he's had a son all this time and she never told him…
It's complicated."

She was on top of him now looking straight down into his
eyes. "It's not that complicated," she said. "Tell him. Tell him
tomorrow. It's not that complicated."

"We'll see."

She kissed each side of his forehead and said, "You think
too much" and then nestled her head back into the crevice of his
shoulder. They laid there awhile in silence.

"Dane."

"Hmm."

"Are you happy he's your father?"

"I don't know yet. I suppose."

"Dane."

"Hmm."

"Are we getting married?"

"Yeah," he sighed, resigning himself to cruel fate. "I suppose
we'll have to at some point."

Love and marriage, sings the blue-eyed crooner, is better
later rather than sooner.

24
CHAPTER

Baseball is a ballet without music. Drama without words.
Ernie Harwell

It was mid-August and Hank's torrid play had not let up. In the three game series against the Pirates in Nashua, Hank went eight for ten with four walks, swiping eight bases including a steal of home in the first game. In Shake's favorite moment of all, Hank had three legs of a cycle in game three—a homer, triple and double—and on his final at bat he hit another double. His teammates yelled at him to stop at first but he ignored them and hustled into second to set up another run in a tight game. He was now batting .328 with an OPS of .855. Shake in his time had seen great players get on hot streaks—Willie Mays, Dick Allen, Joe Morgan—and it was always a wonder to behold. Hank's hot streak was no less wondrous and Shake believed that Hank had a damn good chance of being included in the September call-ups.

Nashua was part of a lengthy road trip that started on August 11 and ended on the 21st. During the road trip, the Kingsmen clinched first place in league and home field advantage for the play-offs. There was no champagne celebration in the clubhouse. Shake came into the locker room with his coaching staff and formally congratulated the team, reminding them that they still had twelve games left in the season with the play-offs to follow. That night Shake treated his coaches to a steak dinner.

It was past midnight when the team bus rolled into New Britain on Friday the 22nd. They had a game that night and Shake cancelled batting and infield practice and told everyone to get a good night's sleep. It was a sleepy but cheery bunch that got off the bus and headed home.

As Shake walked to his car in the dark parking lot, Dane walked up next to him. He had his bag slung over his shoulder. "Yo, coach," said Dane. "I'd like to talk to you."

"Sure thing. Now?"

"No, after the game tomorrow."

"You got it. By the way, great road trip. Hitting, fielding, all of it. You look like a ballet dancer around second, and you're a smart player—probably be a manager one day, God forbid. One more double play and you tie the league record held by some knucklehead named Shake Glover... Who taught you to play second? Your dad? He did a helluva job. You can say so from me."

Dane nodded with a weird look on his face and veered off to his car. Odd duck, thought Shake with a chuckle to himself. Wonder what he wants to talk about? Probably the volcanic eruption in Cameroon or Reagan's policy on the Sandinistas.

When Shake got into his office the next day he got on a conference call with coaches and directors from the big club to talk about potential call-ups come September 1st. On that date, major league teams were able to expand their roster from twenty-five to forty players. Most call-ups came out of Triple-A but Shake could always count on a handful of his players, especially pitchers, getting the nod. The big club was entrenched in third place and actually having a good year, but they had no shot at catching the Astros in first and wanted to finish strong and hopefully overtake the Reds in second place. Pitching was at a

premium and the Kingsmen's top three starters and ace reliever—
Basset, Santiago, Ellsworth, and Cappadona—were the topic of
lively discussion. There were also three position players the big
club was looking at—Prince, Estrella and Hamilton.

Call-ups were a balancing act. The big club, everybody in
fact, wanted to give deserving minor leaguers a shot at the
big time. But big league teams, depending on their situation
(in first place versus last place or fighting for a play-off spot),
all had different ideas as to what they needed to finish out the
regular season. Whatever the need, it had to be filled without
decimating their minor league teams who, like the Kingsmen,
were headed to the play-offs. Triple-A and Double-A teams were
always left short-handed come the play-offs in early September.
It was normal and expected, but the drive to win a league
championship never wavered. So, it was a balancing act as to
who went and who stayed. Shake would have been genuinely
happy to see all seven of his players get called up.

The brass really wanted to know about Hank Prince, and
Shake told them. He repeated the numbers, especially over the
last month (which they knew) and talked about his work ethic.
The kid was a serious ball-player and a major league talent.
Gone were the missed signs, the missed curfews, the missed
opportunities. But he couldn't take credit for the turn-around,
Shake told them. It was their own man Chili Leonard. It was
really Chili who set the kid straight.

When the call wrapped up, the players were beginning to
wander into the clubhouse. The Pittsfield Cubs were in town for
a three game set. Friday night was Scout Night and the stands
would be filled with Boy Scouts, Cub Scouts, Girl Scouts and
Brownies, all in uniform showing off their achievement badges.
After the game they'd get to run the bases.

In the top of the fifth inning in a tight game, with a man
on first, Hoffman fielded a grass-cutter while Dane waited at
second for the throw. The double play would tie the league
record. The throw came just as the runner barreled into second

with his spikes up and Dane danced out of the way to avoid serious injury. There was no throw to first. Shake watched the next ten seconds closely. The runner at second was out and he got up to dust himself off. Dane said something to him and the Cubs runner glanced at him, began to jog off, then said something back at Dane over his shoulder. Shake was pretty sure the exchange went something like this:

Dane: "Come in like that again and I'll take your head off."

Cubs Player: "Screw you. That's how I play."

Shake had never seen Dane lose his temper on the ball field but he could see his second baseman was seething about that slide when he came into the dugout. He didn't blame him—he'd have felt the same. The offending Cubs player also happened to be their second baseman. That made it even worse, thought Shake. That was like a cop giving another cop a speeding ticket. It simply wasn't done. It was an unwritten rule.

Dane was due up second. With one out and no one on he pulled a pitch through the hole on the left side for a hit. It was a single but Shake, watching from his spot in the dugout, had a feeling and that feeling became certain when Dane cut the bag at first and charged for second. Yep, he thought, here we go. The left fielder came in to field the grounder and got ready to throw to his cut-off man when he suddenly realized that Dane was trying for second. He turned and reloaded and fired to second. The throw was high and the second baseman leaped for the throw. Dane, sliding hard, caught the second baseman's foot with his raised knee, causing him to summersault and land flat on his back. The impact knocked the wind out of the Cubs player. The ball rolled out of his glove and the second baseman lay there gasping for air. Dane stood on top of second with his hands on his hips and watched as the Cubs coach and trainer ran out to assist their player.

"Wish I had a video of that," snorted Larry.

"Looks like you standing out there," Rick commented to Shake.

Shake rubbed his chin in thought and smiled. That's the way to do it, he said to himself. Wait for the moment, seize it and deliver payback. No one is really hurt but the message is delivered. Bravo, kid.

The Cubs got their own payback by winning the game 5-2.

The pitchers were done running foul poles and Luis Santiago sat at his locker getting dressed. Chuck Davis was also getting dressed on his left. Steve Basset's locker was on his right but Basset was still in the shower. So was Cappadona.

"I heard they had a big call today about September call-ups," said Chuck.

"Oh, yeah? What you hear?"

"Just rumors. From Speed. They're looking at pitchers. I'm sure you're on the list along with Basset, Cap, and probably Ellsworth. If I had to guess I'd say they'll probably go with two—Basset and Cap."

"Why Basset? I got as many shut-outs as he does. My record's the same."

"Get real, bro. He leads the league in ERA, plus he's on a fast track… And Cap leads the league in saves. So those two make the most sense. But they might go with three."

"Hmm," replied Luis thoughtfully. He went on with the mechanics of dressing as he brooded on this possibility—the possibility that he would get passed over once again for a call-up to the big leagues. And as he brooded, a poison herb of a plan sprouted in his mind and he manured it with his ambition. He looked around to make sure Basset wasn't approaching.

"You still have that locket?" he asked Chuck.

"Shit yeah. I never found a chance to slip it back to her. Why?"

"Let me have it. Cap won't know. You missed your chance to get it back to her and you've got no more use for it. So what's the big deal? I'd like to have it."

"What for? Another war trophy?

"I'd just like to have something to remember her by. They'll get married and raise a family and I'll never see her again. Kind of corny, I know, but I'd appreciate it."

"It's yours. I don't want it," said Chuck as he reached into his locker. "I never liked having it in the first place." He pulled out a small box from the back of his locker and opened it to take out the chain. He looked around first before giving it to Luis. "Don't let Cap know," he said.

"I won't. Promise."

Both Basset and Cappadona came back from their shower and the talk was all about September call-ups. Chuck finished dressing and left, but Luis sat half-dressed at his locker and chewed the fat with Steve and Phil and some of the other pitchers, speculating about which of them would get a call-up. Everyone agreed that Steve would go for sure. After a while it was just Luis and Phil. A couple of position players like Dane Hamilton lingered by their lockers across the room. Finally Phil took his brush and comb and went into the shower room to finish his grooming.

In a kind of silent film pantomime, Luis pretended to lose the handle on a roll of athletic tap and it rolled over to Phil's locker. He scooted along the bench to retrieve it. Now in front of Phil's locker, he stood up and pretended to stretch. Phil had an extra pair of cleats he kept on the top shelf of his locker and Luis quickly lifted one and slid the locket into the toe. He walked back to his locker and finished dressing, immensely pleased with himself.

Shake was in his office working on his postgame report when there was a knock on the door. Most of the players were gone so Shake was a little surprised to see Dane pop his head in until he remembered that Dane wanted to talk to him.

"Oh, yeah," he said. "Come on in, have a seat. What's up?"

"Thanks," replied Dane as he sat down and rubbed his chin in thought. Shake waited for him to speak. "Remember the other day when you mentioned my dad? He died when I was ten. Just thought I'd tell you."

"Crap, sorry about that."

"No biggee. How were you to know?"

Shake nodded at that and waited. It was obvious this talk wasn't going to be about baseball. That didn't bother him. It was part of the job. In his office over the years he'd talked players off the proverbial edge, administered intense psychoanalysis, and even held crying men in his arms. Nothing fazed him.

"What was it you wanted to talk about?"

Dane took a deep breath before answering. "You said you wanted to meet my mom—the Shakespeare fan?"

"Is she out there? Bring her in."

"No, no, she's not here. She's in town but she's not here… I was wondering if you could meet her tomorrow? She really wants to meet you."

"You bet. Bring her in the clubhouse before the game."

"Well, I can't. She's not staying for the game. I was wondering—and I know this is kind'a weird—but I was wondering if you could meet her earlier in the day. Our game isn't until 6:00. So it'd be earlier in the day. Downtown."

"Downtown?"

"Yeah… At The New Britain Museum of American Art. Ever been there?

"Sure."

"We'll be there around noon."

Shake thought quickly. He didn't normally socialize with players outside the ballpark and meeting a guy's mom in a museum was kind of odd. Was Dane trying to set them up, he wondered, and that thought triggered another one—Linda's advice to find someone and fall in love. Who was this woman then? She was a widow who liked baseball and Shakespeare. Well there you go. And the chances of her being good-looking were probably pretty high since Dane was a good-looing kid. The whole thing piqued his curiosity.

"Okay. Where do you want to meet? In the lobby?"

"Yeah, in the lobby at noon. That'd be great."

Shake folded back a yellow post-it that had Speed's riddle written on it and wrote down the time and place for himself. He pealed off Speed's riddle and read it again.

"Any good at riddles?" he asked Dane who stood at the door.

"Riddles? I don't know. Maybe."

"Well, Speed gives me these riddles every so often that I have to unravel. It's irritating—he can't just tell me—but the riddles, believe it or not, usually have something important to say. The guy knows everything that goes on around here. Anyhow, here's the latest one: 'He sold his soul to the devil, and now he's set on amending your constitution.' Now the first part might refer to Mike Faust. Faust sold his soul to the devil. But I'm stuck on the 'amending your constitution part'."

A sly grin came over Dane's face. "Constitution can also mean body or physique, right?" he said. "So amending your constitution could mean 'changing your body'."

"Hmm, never thought of it that way but you're right. It could mean body. But whose body? As a trainer he fixes bodies, which isn't quite the same as amending or changing bodies. So whose body is he amending?" Shake rubbed his chin in thought. He read the riddle again.

"Look to Estrella," said Dane quickly.

Shake looked up but Dane had ducked out the door and was gone.

Shake pulled into the parking lot of the museum and walked into the lobby exactly at noon. Dane was waiting for him. "She's inside," explained Dane, so Shake paid for admission and followed his second baseman into the museum

The museum specialized in Colonial and Federal-era portraits along with landscapes and some impressionist works. There were also sculptures by artists such as Borglum and Rogers. Shake noticed they were headed into the area that displayed a variety of plaster, bronze and stone statues ranging in size from miniature works to life-size. Once in the room, Dane looked around for his mother.

"I thought she was in here," he said absent-mindedly and wandered off.

Shake didn't follow and instead looked around the room. There were only a few other people—a young couple and an older man—and Shake shifted his attention to the sculptures themselves. There appeared to be a couple new pieces since his visit last year and he meandered in their direction, reviewing some of the older pieces as he went along. He reached the first new piece and looked carefully at it. It was a sculpture of a woman in a white dress sitting on a small marble bench, head down, holding a floppy sun hat.

Shake felt a chill across his neck as he stared at the statue more closely. It was remarkably life-like. It wasn't bronze or stone, he concluded. Maybe plaster, but the flesh tones and long honey blonde hair were too real-looking to be sculpted. The thought struck him that it might be a wax figure, like something from Madame Tussauds, and the more he studied the figure the more he was sure that had to be it. But there was something else, something too ethereal to put into words, that fluttered suddenly from his unlocked heart and caused him to stare dumbfounded at the statue. He sensed someone standing behind him but did not turn around.

He had the sensation of running and running for a foul ball, of diving for it and thinking he missed it, of rolling over and being amazed at seeing the ball in his glove. *They say miracles are past,* he thought to himself and, as he thought it, he pulled back in dream-like fear and told himself it was just a coincidence that the statue looked like Mimi. His beloved Mimi. Just a coincidence. He went down on a knee and leaned over to look at her face. As he did he touched one of her hands. It felt warm to the touch and the discovery startled him. He peered in closer and saw that the eyes were shut. It was Mimi's face. Older but still beautiful. Mimi's face. And he whispered aloud:

> *Such tricks hath strong imagination,*
> *That if it would but apprehend some joy,*
> *It comprehends some bringer of that joy*

At these words the woman's eyes opened and she looked up at him with those blue-green eyes. *"What angel wakes me from my flowery bed?"* she said.

"My God!... Mimi!"

"Shakespeare... Louis... Glover," she replied with a smile.

"Good God! It can't be... How can it be?" He took her two hands and raised them both to their feet. He stared ravenously at her face, devouring her eyes, her lips, her cheeks and chin. She did the same. He barely heard the words spoken from the person behind him.

> *Jack shall have Jill;*
> *Nought shall go ill;*
> *The man shall have his mare again, and all shall*
> *be well.*

Holding his hands, she slowly turned the two of them around until they were facing Dane. Her eyes left his face and she looked at her son. Shake followed her eyes and regarded Dane for a moment. He thought he understood and asked simply, "Your son?"

"Our son," she said with all the world behind it. "He's our son."

Shake knocked and the cathedral opened, finding the fix for what had been broken.

25
CHAPTER

*I have had a dream, past the wit of man
to say what dream it was.*

A Midsummer Night's Dream

Shake was in a daze during Saturday night's game. His coaches noticed it and even Rick asked him what was wrong. He ignored the question and resumed his happy sleep-walking. Whenever the Kingsmen were in the field, he stood in his spot in the dugout and watched Dane, his son. Between innings he looked up in the stands and found Mimi, his beloved. She was still there, and each time he looked up at her she waved at him and smiled. He was like some lucky bum who's just won the lottery and keeps glancing down in disbelief at his winning ticket, but at the same time can't help but fill his head with all the ways he plans on spending his good fortune.

The Kingsmen won and Shake was still in somewhat of a pleasant daze when he met with the local press. They asked questions and he answered them without much thought behind it. He did notice that Balt Porter was home from summer vacation and back on the job. After they left, Dane poked his head in.

"Mom said she'd meet you back at the motel," he said.

"Oh, okay... Come in for a second. Sit down," urged Shake gently. Dane complied and stepped into his office. He was in his baseball socks with a t-shirt and uniform pants. Shake studied him carefully as the young man sat in the chair and settled himself. He had an overwhelming urge to talk to Dane and keep on talking to him until he found out everything there was to find out about his new-found son. They'd talked a little already and agreed to keep their relationship quiet until after the play-offs. But Shake frankly struggled against the urge to go out into the clubhouse and cry out the news. Now was not the time, he knew, and he also knew that their long talk could not happen today, so he was contented with studying Dane's face and mannerisms and seeing the resemblances that had always been there.

"I thought maybe we could get together, maybe on our off-day Monday, and have a long talk?"

"I'd love to," replied Dane.

Rick Burton rapped on the door and came in. "Hey, what's with you today, pal," he said to Shake. "You left your clip board in the dugout." He handed the clipboard to Shake and made a move to exit.

"Rick, hold on a second," said Shake. "Close the door." He watched as Rick closed the door and turned back to him with a quizzical look on his face. Shake possessed a big, beautiful secret and he could not keep it from his best friend. He indicated Dane with a glance and said calmly, "I'd like you to meet my son."

"Your what?!"

"My son."

Rick paused, taking it in, and quickly composed himself. He looked from Dane to Shake and back to Dane again. "Well," he said simply. "That explains a few things."

"It's a secret for now," explained Shake. "Just you know, so we'd appreciate it if you'd keep it to yourself for a short while."

"Sure. Of course. How long have you known?

"A day. Dane's known for a few weeks but he wanted to find the right time to tell me."

"No shit. Will wonders never cease… You don't mind if I tell Linda."

"Of course not… We just think that this late in the season, with call-ups coming and play-offs and everything, we don't want to lose focus."

"Yeah, the kid'll get a good razzing."

They all laughed at this and Dane got up to leave. "I gotta get dressed and tell mom. See you later," he said. But before he could leave, Rick grabbed his shoulders in both hands and looked him up and down.

"Rubbing the chin should'a given it away," he said to father and son. They all laughed again and Rick let Dane go to finish dressing. "What he mean by 'mom'?" he asked Shake.

Shake gave him the quick lowdown: Mimi, his college sweetheart ("Yes, that one.") was pregnant when they broke up. She married and her husband—Hamilton—raised Dane as his own. The husband died years ago, Dane became a professional baseball player, and of all the gin joints in all the towns in all the world, he got drafted and assigned to the Kingsmen. "Fate, my friend," concluded Shake, but then added the couplet:

> O God, *that one might read the book of fate*
> *And see the revolution of the times.*

Rick left Shake's office in his own sort of daze. He couldn't wait to get home and tell Linda all about this.

It was Speed's turn to poke his head into Shake's office.

Speed
There's a whole lott'a shakin' goin' on, Shake.

Shake
What you mean? And no more riddles.

Speed

Trouble. More trouble than you can shake a spear at. So you might want to shake your booty. Shake, shake, shake.

Shake

Trouble where? In the clubhouse?

Speed

It's about to shake, rattle and roll. Shake your world. Shake your foundation. Shaken not stirred. So you better shake a leg, Shake, before we get all shook up.

(There is loud shouting and banging heard from the locker room)

Oops, too late. The salt's outta the shaker.

Shake hurried out the door into the locker room and found a fight going on. Basset was swinging wildly at Cappadona, and Chuck Davis was trying to hold Basset back while others jumped in to separate the two. Shake had never seen Basset this way and it startled him. His affable, Christian ace pitcher was red-faced and wild-eyed.

"What the hell!" shouted Rick coming on the scene at the same time as Shake.

"Stop! Now!" yelled Shake. As he made his way into the heart of the melee, he saw Basset break free and run out of the clubhouse half-dressed. "Steve!" he hollered after him, but it was too late. He was gone.

Everyone stood down and Shake looked first at Cappadona, who stood licking his bleeding lip, then over at Chuck who seemed to be in the know. "What's going on here?" he asked Chuck.

"Just a misunderstanding," he replied between hard breaths.

"I can see that. What started it?"

"Can we talk in your office?"

"Yeah, in my office—you and Phil. Someone see if they can find Steve. Rick, join us." Shake led the march to his office.

"We'll need Tiago," said Chuck.

"Santiago! In my office!" yelled Shake without stopping. The four of them filed into his office. Phil and Chuck both sat down and Shake handed Phil a Kleenex for his lip. Luis appeared and looked confused. "Why me?" he asked but Shake ignored the question and told him to shut the door.

"Now tell me what the hell's going on?" he asked as he glanced at each player. He rested his eyes on Chuck who looked ready and willing to spill the beans. "Chuck? You're the veteran here. What happened?"

And Chuck told him, mixing facts with sound deduction to paint a full and ugly picture. It all started back before the All-Star break when Luis bet Cap a hundred dollars that he could screw Basset's fiancé. The bet was made and proof had to be provided in the form of her gold chain and locket. When Luis produced the locket, Cap paid up but there was an argument over who'd get to keep the locket. He settled the argument by taking the locket himself and promising to find a way to secretly get it back to her. He was never able to that, but just the other day Luis asked him about it. Luis wanted it as a memento and promised not to tell Cap, so he gave it to him. What happened next, he could only guess but he was pretty sure of—Luis slipped the locket into Cap's locker and told Basset it was there. Steve found it and the fight started.

As the story was told, Shake noticed Phil nodding in agreement while Luis stood quietly without an expression. When Chuck was done, both Shake and Rick looked at one another in shared astonishment.

"So let me get this straight," said Rick, glancing at Phil and then Luis. "You made a bet that you could screw your own teammate's fiancé. Why would you do a stupid thing like that?"

"I warned them," said Chuck.

Phil had his head down so Rick focused his attention on Santiago. "Why in god's name would you screw your teammate's fiancé? Why would you do a thing like that?"

"I didn't," replied Luis coolly.

"You didn't?"

"I didn't. I bribed a hotel maid for her room key and I went in there and stole it. I never went to bed with her."

"Son of a bitch!" growled Phil as he started out of his seat.

"Shut up and sit down!" commanded Shake, and Phil sat back down muttering to himself. Shake turned his full attention to Luis. "So you're the architect of this whole mess. What did you tell Steve that triggered this fight?"

And Luis told them, without emotion or drama, like a man relating "*a twice-told tale, vexing the dull ear of a drowsy man.*" He put it in Steve's ear, as his friend who was looking out for his best interests, that he had seen his fiancé in a car with another player. He wouldn't say who but the two of them were awful affectionate. Steve begged him to tell who it was. He said no but Steve insisted, so he finally told him. It was Cap, he lied, and after that lie he told him ("for his own good") that he'd seen her lost locket in Cap's locker. In the toe of his spare cleats. The rest took care of itself and he was a little surprised at how easily Steve was willing to believe him.

Rick rubbed his hand over his face in frustrated anger. "Un-fucking-believable," he sighed in disgust. "You're a total piece of shit, kid."

"But why?" asked Shake, trying to wrap his brain around this betrayal or callousness or cruelty or whatever the hell it was. "Why do a thing like that?" But Luis merely shrugged and remained silent. Shake felt a strong wave of disgust at Santiago and he tried to check it, but in doing so he was left with its residue—a kind of oil-stained sadness.

How oft the sight of means to do ill deeds
Make ill deeds done!

He thought about Mimi and it had a cleansing effect. "I don't want to hear anymore. I want you all out of my sight. The coaching staff will talk this over and I'll let you know what happens tomorrow. I want you all in my office at 10:00 am. Got it? Meanwhile… Luis, you owe Cap a hundred dollars and, Cap, stay away from Luis. And all of you stay away from Steve until I can talk to him and calm him down. Now, get out of here."

In a moment they were gone. The two veteran coaches— Shake and Rick—shook their heads at one another in a way that said "I-thought-I'd-seen-it-all-but-I-guess-I-haven't."

"Suspend the bastard," said Rick.

"Yeah," replied Shake engrossed in his thoughts. "I'll have to call the front office… He's on their list of potential call-ups."

"Fuck him."

Teddy Larkin appeared and told them that they had found Steve Basset. He was sitting in his car in the parking lot and refused to come back into the clubhouse. Shake said he'd take it from here and asked Rick to fill Teddy and the others coaches in on what was going on. He threw his jacket on over his uniform and left.

Shake found Steve sitting in the driver's seat of his Nissan. His forearms rested on the steering wheel and his head was buried between the vise of his arms. He looked like he was praying. Shake rapped on the window and Steve's head came up. His cheeks were streaked with tears.

"Unlock the door," said Shake. "Let's talk." He walked around to the passenger's side and heard the doors unlock. He got in and closed the door. Steve was hunched up, almost in a fetal position.

"Oh, Jesus, Jesus… Help me," he moaned to himself.

"Steve, listen to me," said Shake firmly. "Steve! Listen up!" he repeated, and Steve raised his head and looked at him. The young man's eyes were a mix of confusion and sorrow. "It's going to be okay," Shake assured him. "I got the truth out of Santiago and you've been lied to."

"Huh? What?"

"He lied to you. You've been duped." And with that Shake launched into the story. When he finished, Steve stared at him in disbelief with hints of anger growing around the edges of his face.

"But why?" he asked. "Why would a person do such a thing? It's the work of the devil."

"I don't know," sighed Shake. "I really don't. Some people just like to tear things down."

Steve shook his head woefully and then began to roll it in an exaggerated motion from side to side. "Holy Mary, Mother of God!" he cried out and began beating his head with his fists.

"Steve! Stop! Calm down—just calm down. Tell me what's wrong?"

He stopped beating his head and stared out into the night as he spoke: "It's too late...I ran out here and found Gwen—my fiancé. She was waiting in her car... I screamed at her and called her a whore and told her it was over... Oh, God, Jesus, what have I done?"

"Not again?"

"What?"

"Where is she now?"

"She probably went home—to Hartford."

"Let's go find her," said Shake as though speaking from the Mount. "Right this minute. Are you good to drive?"

"Yeah," replied Steve, hope blossoming on his face. He wiped his cheeks dry with the flat of his hand and started the car. "I can drive."

"All right. Swing by the Ramada first. I have to leave a message with someone."

The Nissan sped out of the parking lot and pulled into the Ramada Inn five minutes later. Shake got out and knocked on one of the doors and Mimi answered.

"Shake?" she said, surprised to see him. "Why you still in your uniform?"

Their hands came together. Since reuniting, they were unable to keep their hands off the other as though, by touching, they kept this sweet dream alive. They had spent an all too brief hour alone together in this very motel room lying in bed, fully clothed, talking.

Shake explained the situation, and as he spoke and she listened, an ancient bell echoed in their psyches. They knew this story, knew it all too well, and when Shake finished Mimi simply said, "You must go."

They kissed and Shake jumped back in the car and it peeled out. The driver was in a hurry and on a mission from God. It was only a fifteen minute drive to Hartford and Shake spent it thinking and not talking. He thought about the miracle of Mimi, about whether they'd find Gwen (they had to!), and about the fragility of love. Why do lovers always believe the worst, he wondered. But he knew the answer to that: it was a weakness in man to lose faith so easily.

They found Gwen at home. They could hear her sobbing through her apartment door. She refused to respond to Steve's voice so Shake took over. "It's Shake Glover. Steve's manager. Open up, sweetheart. We need to talk." The sobbing quieted and they could hear her gathering herself up. The door opened tentatively and she looked out at them. Her face was puffy but beautiful, her eyes filled with hurt. "Let us in, sweetheart," said Shake in a fatherly tone. "You'll want to hear this."

They sat down and Shake told his tale. Steve sat at the edge of his chair, penitent, hopeful, closely watching Gwen's face. She sat with her hands in her lap, her attention fully on Shake, and listened with a thin reluctance. To Shake she was a locked safe, but as he spoke and explained and revealed the awful truth, he could see the tumblers fall one by one. When the safe opened, Shake could see by her face that she understood completely—they were victims, they'd been played—and she saw it clearly as an act of evil. She looked over now at Steve. He held her chain and locket out in his open hand. They came together like the wind and the rain, blustering their apologies, pouring out their love, swearing their allegiance and thanking God.

In an earlier time of his life Shake would have found this scene maudlin, almost cornball, but now, at this moment, it touched him deeply. A sense of joy and of a mission accomplished welled up inside him and it inspired him to say to the both of them *"The course of true love never did run smooth."* They both looked up at him, wrapped in each other's arms, and laughed happily.

"Now, who's going to give me a ride back to the park?"

The next morning in his office, Shake and Rick spent a minute talking before the three players were due in. The coaching staff, Rick included, wanted Luis Santiago suspended for the rest of the season and the playoffs. They'd all been ball-players and appreciated better than any the elements that went into the living organism that is a team. There was common cause, camaraderie, and a thing they would have called "got your back," and they held these things as sacred. Teammates didn't need to like each other, but when the shit went down they'd better have your back, and if they didn't then that "teammate" was no better than a cancerous virus. In an earlier age, they would have voted to put Santiago to the rack.

Shake knew all that, too, and felt all that, too, but as usual his Negative Capability got in the way. He'd talked to the front office, giving only enough detail to make his point, and they trusted his judgement and left the punishment up to his discretion. The jury in his head was still out.

Chuck came in and sat down. "Where's the other two?" asked Rick.

"I have a favor to ask," said Chuck. "Let us take care of this. Let the team take care of this in our own way."

"How?" asked Shake.

"Kangaroo court."

"That's played out for fun," said Rick.

"This won't be."

Shake considered this for a moment while studying Chuck from behind his desk. He trusted his veteran. He was a good teammate and usually always had the best interests of the team at heart.

"This'll be done right. I promise," insisted Chuck. "Everyone knows what happened and they're sick and tired of Santiago. Just let us handle it."

Rick was about to object but Shake cut him off. "All right," he said. "We'll let the team take care of this. But it needs to be done quickly, understood. It can't fester."

"It won't. I promise."

"All right. Go on then."

Chuck got up, said "Thanks, Skip", and headed out the door.

Rick called out after him, "Make sure to clean up the blood when you're done." He glanced over at his buddy Shake for a reaction but his buddy merely rubbed his chin in thought. But how was Rick to know: from lies had come pain, from evil heartbreak, but harmony prevailed thanks to Shake.

26
CHAPTER

No game in the world is as tidy and dramatically neat as baseball, with cause and effect, crime and punishment, motive and result, so cleanly defined.

Paul Gallico

During Sunday's game Orson made his way up to the owner's box and sat down next to Corey to watch the game. A five foot partition separated them from the press box where Balt Porter sat with two other reporters. Orson ignored him. He'd been avoiding Balt ever since he showed up at the stadium last Friday night. Orson knew he would have to talk to him eventually—confront the truth about The Kiss and tell him the newer truth about his feelings for his sister—but he was in no hurry to do so.

He was also afraid of something else and this something else plagued him like an itch that wouldn't go away. Yes, he and Rose were an item. They were more than that—they were lovers. They'd had sex, more than once, and gone was the letdown and that old feeling of coming up short. Sex had turned into love-making and it was hardy and intense and lasting. And, yes, he loved her and told her so. She said she loved him and had plans for their future, and he didn't argue with that. But what if...

what if he confronted Balt and the old feelings returned. What would he do then? His head just spun to think about it.

In the third inning, Orson got up to use the restroom. There was a small unisex bathroom that served the owner, the press box, as well as the P.A. Announcer, and it locked from the inside. Orson found it unlocked and went in. Suddenly he felt a body push in from behind. It was Balt, and he locked the door behind him and stood in front of Orson.

"You've been avoiding me," he said to Orson in a playful tone.

"What? No... Just been busy. It's great to see you. How was L.A.?"

"You're fibbing," said Balt with a glint in his eye. He stepped closer to Orson and Orson backed up. "You've been avoiding me. Admit it." He stepped closer, backing Orson against the wall, and placed his hands on Orson's shoulders. "Didn't you miss me? I missed you. Admit it."

Balt's face was right in Orson's and he could smell Balt's aftershave—"English Leather"—and feel his hands gently squeeze his shoulders. He put his hand against Balt's chest to push him back but there was no strength in it. Balt's face came even closer.

"You missed me, didn't you? Say you missed me."

Orson closed his eyes and surrendered. "Yes, I missed you," he whispered heavily.

In the next moment Balt's lips were on his and they were passionately making out and tearing at each other's clothes. Balt's hand slipped down and grabbed Orson's crotch. He already had a hard-on. At the same time, Orson unbuckled Balt's belt, unzipped his fly, and hungrily stuck his hand down and found—

Nothing.

"What the hell!" cried Orson in shock, pulling his hand out as though stung by a bee. Balt still had his hand on Orson's crotch so he pushed Balt back. "You're a... woman!" accused Orson. "A woman!"

"Of course, silly," she said in a voice that was now Rose's. She laughed and took her black-rimmed glasses off and pealed one of her sideburns off. "I thought you knew."

"Rose?"

"Who else?"

"But... I thought... you were..."

"You thought I was my make-believe brother? Now that's funny." She put both hands in her hair and shook it all loose, revealing Rose in full flower. "I'm Balt. I'm Rose. I'm both. You okay with that?"

"Sure," he said without thinking. The shock was wearing off and he was finding, quickly, and to his delight, that he was okay with it. He felt like he'd just found a secret room in his house, one that made it bigger and more complete. "But... why the deception?"

'Now that's a long story," she said as she put the toilet seat down and sat upon it. "But I'll make it short." And with that she quickly and succinctly explained everything to him like a good reporter should: she was breaking down barriers in sports reporting. In a scheme concocted with her college editor, she dressed up as a male reporter to cover the Kingsmen, getting access to the players and coaches that she would never get as a woman. Next year, as a senior, she planned to appear on the job as herself and, by comparison, reveal the hypocrisy and sexism rampant in the male-dominated world of sports journalism. She already had a book deal with Simon and Schuster for her expose once she completed it.

The only hitch in her whole plot, she confessed, was Orson. Once on the Kingsmen beat, she ran into him all the time and couldn't help but find him attractive. She soon realized she was falling in love with him, so she amended her plan, got rid of Balt for a while, and introduced his twin sister Rose. She wasn't sorry about it—all was fair in love and war—and she hoped this didn't make a difference.

"Still love me?" she asked with a leering grin (because she knew the answer).

"Of course I do."

"Still confused?"

"No."

"Good… Now where were we?"

After the game the players convened a private meeting in the locker room. No one but players were allowed in, not even the coaches, and Mike Goff was tasked with checking all the doors to make sure they were locked and no one could listen in. The kangaroo court was in session. Luis Santiago was on trial for crimes against the state, a serious offense. Phil Cappadona also stood trial on a lesser charge of stupidity. Normally, Chuck Davis presided over kangaroo courts in the Kingsmen clubhouse, but given he was a key witness for the prosecution he had to recuse himself. The fourteen year veteran Ron Deer took up the gavel in his stead.

Many wanted to be the prosecuting attorney but the job fell by consensus to the "professor" Dane Hamilton. Given his education and cynicism, it was decided he had the best tools for the job. Matt Horn, currently on injured reserve, was assigned to defend Cappadona and he prepared diligently for the case by talking at length to all the key parties. No one wanted to defend Santiago so the unpleasant task was finally assigned to Kid Curry, a fellow pitcher, despite his objections. The muscle-bound Jose Estrella was the bailiff and stood behind the sitting Santiago throughout the trial to make sure he didn't try to flee.

Court was gaveled into session and Judge Deer read the charge against Cappadona: "That on a night back in April, at the Lyon's picnic, Mr. Cappadona did knowingly and willingly enter into a wager with Luis Santiago. Said wager being—that Mr. Santiago, known womanizer and Lothario, could not bed the fiancé of fellow teammate Mr. Basset before the All-Star break. The bet was for one hundred dollars to be paid either way depending on Mr. Santiago's ability to produce or not produce a gold locket worn around the neck of said fiancé. The charge is terminal stupidity. How does the defendant plead?"

Matt Horn rose gingerly (he had a bad hamstring) and said, "The defendant pleads guilty—with special circumstances."

"What special circumstances?" asked the judge.

"My client has a serious gambling addiction. It's a well-known fact that he'll bet on anything—that new coke tastes better than old coke, that Adrian Adonis is going to beat Junkyard dog." He waited for the jeers to die down before finishing: "He bets on the jousting match in the third inning. And if that's not bad enough, he even bet once that Tito's drool, while he was sleeping on the bus, would drip on his shirt before we hit Glens Falls. It's a disease, your honor."

"Fuck ju guys. Pendejos," said Tito.

"I object, your honor," said Dane. "Where's the diagnosis from a qualified psychiatrist? None has been introduced into evidence. This is just hearsay."

"Good point," agreed Judge Deer. "Objection sustained. The defendant is found guilty. Before we move into the punishment phase, is there anything the defendant would like to say to the court?"

"I just want to point out one thing," said Phil, rising to his feet. "I bet against him. I bet that he *wouldn't* do this thing. That should count for something."

"It counts for very little," replied Judge Deer sternly. He pointed his finger at a couple of veterans standing nearby—Burks and Svoboda—and they huddled around him for consultation. They adjourned in apparent agreement and the judge looked over at the defendant. "Mr. Cappadona, you have been found guilty of terminal stupidity. In punishment for your crime you will be required to carry the bags of Misters Burks, Svoboda and myself to and from the bus throughout the duration of the play-offs. You will also be at our beckon call for coffee, beer or late-night snacks. Failure to abide by this punishment will be met with swift reprisal. Do you understand everything I have just said?"

"Yes, your honor. And I thank the court for their leniency."

Next was the case against Luis and the mood in the mock courtroom changed dramatically. Gone was the light-heartedness and playfulness from before and in its place rose an angry quiet. Some players stared daggers into Luis's back while others avoided looking at him as one might avoid looking at a pariah. Many of them wanted their pound of flesh and would have preferred to dispense with the kangaroo court and just beat the shit out of him.

Judge Deer somberly read the charges that included "back-stabbing a teammate" and "sowing team dissension" and worst of all "casting dispersions on a young woman who happened to be a fine, upstanding Christian." The judge asked Dane if he had missed anything and Dane replied, "That about covers it." All eyes turned to Steve Basset who sat alongside two fellow pitchers. The two were there as guards in case Steve went after Santiago, but the likelihood of that was minimal. Steve was struggling with Christian forgiveness but he'd given Shake his word not to go after Luis and he was a man of his word. He looked up at the judge and said he had nothing to add to the charges.

"How does the defendant plead?"

Kid Curry got up, shrugged, and looked over at his client for help. "What do you want to plead?" he asked him.

"Nothing," said Luis. "You know what you know. Don't ask me anymore questions."

Kid Curry threw his hands up and sat down. "In that case," said Judge Deer, "the court will enter a plea of 'not guilty' on your behalf. Prosecutor, you can call your first witness."

"I have only one witness, your honor," replied Dane. "I call the one person who knows the entire story—Chuck Davis.

Chuck, you're to tell the whole truth and nothing but the truth so help you, God. The floor is yours."

Chuck told the story from beginning to end—from the bet at the Lyon's Picnic to the dénouement in Manager Glover's office—and did not gloss over his own knowledge of the bet. He ended his story by relaying Santiago's own confession in Glover's office. There were angry murmurs around the room at this confession. Dane waited for things to quiet down before asking his only question of Chuck.

"What was his motive? If you had to conjecture an opinion, what would it be? Why would a player purposely lie and cheat to cause a fight between two fellow teammates?"

"Other than the fact he's a fucking jerk? … I'm sure he planted the locket right after we talked about potential call-ups. I offered the opinion that if any pitchers got called up it would probably be Basset and Cap. He disagreed. So you see—he hoped the fight would get them both suspended and get him to the big leagues."

Nobody disagreed with this conjecture and the angry murmurs got louder. The judge quieted the courtroom. Dane gave a stirring summation. At his turn to speak, Kid Curry threw his hands up in surrender and merely said, "We throw ourselves on the mercy of the court." Judge Deer conferred with Burks and Svoboda and both verdict and punishment were agreed upon quickly.

"The verdict is guilty," said Deer loudly. "And since the defendant has waived his right to speak I won't ask him if he has anything to say before we hand down punishment… There will be no mercy today. The punishment is the 'Circle of Shame' which, as I understand it, has never been administered in Kingsmen history. And in case the defendant is under any delusion that this is all for show—that the 'Circle of Shame' carries no weight behind it—let me set him straight. Mr. Santiago, don't ever again expect one of your teammates to bust his ass for you. You need a diving catch to save a shutout? You need one of us to take an extra base or lay down a perfect bunt or go the extra yard to get you a run? Know now it ain't going to happen. You've set yourself apart and there you'll stay... Gentlemen, let's line up."

Every player got up and formed a circle around Luis. One by one, starting with Ron Deer, each player turned away until all twenty-four of his teammates stood with their backs to him. They held it a moment for affect and then calmly dispersed to get undressed and hit the showers. Luis Santiago sat where he was for a while before slowly getting up and going over to his locker.

The end of August brought the end of the regular season. On the Friday before the final home stand, Shake got official word on September call-ups and he summoned each player into his office to let them know the good news. Basset and Cappadona were going along with Hank Prince and Jose Estrella. Despite his lobbying, Dane didn't get the nod but there was one delightful surprise—Ron Deer. When Shake told Ron he was called up, the veteran at first stared at him in disbelief, quickly came unglued, then cried for joy and repeatedly hugged Shake, thanking him profusely. They both knew it was a "good guy promotion" and that Ron would probably be a hitting instructor somewhere in the system next year but it didn't matter. He was off to the bigs and walking on air. Shake got a kick out of it.

Shake had put the pieces together regarding Faust and Estrella and steroids. He and Rick confronted Faust about it and at first got denials and then excuses. Yeah, okay, Faust said, he was helping a few players improve strength and stamina but it was ultimately their decision to make—not his—and he merely made it safer for them. What was the big deal anyhow? It wasn't a banned substance and it was very likely the wave of the future. Shake found the man's rationalizations to be *a tale told by an idiot, full of sound and fury, signifying nothing.* No more, Shake told him in no uncertain terms, and made it clear that his tenure as team trainer was over at the end of the season. He passed on everything he knew to the front office, even the scoop on Estrella, and the GM thanked him and said they would "address it in the off-season." Rick scoffed at that but he tended to be more cynical about the business of baseball than Shake was.

Shake and Dane had their long talk and began the process of settling in as father and son. They knew it wouldn't feel genuine until their families, the team, and the whole world knew they were father and son, but in the meantime they could share a look or share a nod and know it was more than just between a player and his coach. Mimi was in town for the home stand and she and Shake were looking around for a house to buy. (How swiftly love re-united transforms its once lonesome shack into a cottage built for two.) There was no going back for them or any hesitation at a future together. It was like finding a precious thing thought lost long ago and picking it up right where you left it, only with the knowledge that you're a little older and wiser for the wait. It inspired Shake to his core, so much so that he found himself carrying out the vow of Don Armado in *Love's Labor's Lost:*

> *Be still, drum, for your manager is in love: yea,*
> *he loveth. Assist me,*
> *Some extemporal god of rhyme, for I am sure I*
> *shall turn sonnet.*

Sunday was a busy day. It was Fan Appreciation Day and lots of cool gifts would be given away. It was also the day for call-ups to catch their flight from Harford to the West Coast. Steve, Phil, Hank, Jose and Ron all met up at the airport with packed bags and grins of excitement. Back at Beehive Stadium, the Kingsmen won their last game of the season 4-1. Mimi sat in the stands wearing her floppy sun hat and kept score.

Papi Stallworth, Busta, and La-Ron sat in a corner booth at Denny's eating a late breakfast. Spread out before them were plates of bacon and eggs, stacks of pancakes, and glasses of orange juice which they spiked with a bottle of cheap vodka.

Papi
A toast ta Busta. To the man wid the scrillah. Health an' long life, brotha'.

Busta
Whatever ya wants. Enjoy. It's on me.

(Enter Fo-Five)

La-Ron
Yo, there's Fo-Five. How's he know we here?

Papi
Fo-Five, my man. Wat up. Nigga? Wat wind blew u-in? Take a seat an' have'a gran slam on us. Have'a drink. We're oil'n the O.J.

Fo-Five
Yo, wat up Chief? Where's Sweetness?

Papi
U-tell me. I haven't seen 'em in weeks. I'm kinda worried 'bout 'em. Busta went by his crib only he wouldn't let-em in. Sumthins up. Maybe gotta wifey.

Fo-Five
Nah, that ain't it. I got the straight dope. Ur-Sweetness bin promoted. Ur-Prince issa king. He got call'd up—goin to the big leagues. He's flyin'outta Hartford ta-day.

Papi
No shit? Fo' reel?

Fo-Five
Legit. Yo'a big man now.

Papi
I's always been a big man, case u-didn notice... But that's wat I'm talkin' 'bout. We gonna be rich, my homies. Rich. I gots fam-ly in Oak Town. We'll set up shop there. I'll be pers-nal trainer ta Sweetness. And, Busta, you'll be my assistent.

La-Ron
How 'bout me?

Papi
Assistent to the assistent. We'll have free runna the clubhouse, come and go like royal-tee. We'll only deal to the super bloods and make a forchun... Come on, we gotta-git to the airport ta see 'em off. Hurry up. Chow down and let's git-goin.

At Bradley International airport, Papi and Busta and La-Ron (minus Fo-Five who said he had better things to do with his time) sat in the terminal waiting on Hank to appear. A group of young men approached carrying their bags, surrounded by a retinue of wives and girlfriends, as well as fans who had recognized them as Kingsmen on their way to the big leagues. Hank Prince walked next to Ron Deer as they made their way to their gate.

Busta
There he is! Wat-ju gonna say?

Papi
Stan next ta-me. La-Ron, git behind me. Jus' watch his face when he sees me.

Busta
Here he comes.

Papi
Yo, Sweetness! Hank! Yo, my boy! Prince!

Ron
(to Hank)
You know that dude?

Hank
Him? … No.

Papi
Wat the dilly, yo! Hank, wassup? It's Papi!

Ron
(to Papi)
Back off, friend. We're trying to catch our flight.

Hank
(to Papi)
I don't know you, old man. Let us through.

(The players and their retinue pass by, leaving Papi and his two friends alone.)

La-Ron
Wat he say? That he didn' know you?

Busta
That's wat he said. I heard 'em.

Papi
Ahh, he hadda say that. He can't have no big reunun out here in front'a ev'rybody. He's too smart fo'that. He'll call me late'a

and git it all set up. Jus-u wait an' see. He'll call me late'a and make it up. He'll make it reel. Jus wait an' see.

(They exit)

Orson, Tiago, Papi, one and all—each got their due from the God of Baseball.

27
CHAPTER

So foul and fair a day I have not seen.
Macbeth

Playoffs started on Saturday, September 6th and the Kingsmen steam-rolled over the Vermont Reds three games to none to take their divisional series. The New Haven Admirals finished off the Glens Falls Tigers three games to one to take their divisional series. That set up the championship rematch between the two archrivals in a five-game series starting in New Britain on Friday night.

With the loss of his ace Basset as well as Cappadona, Shake and his pitching coach Larry Benedict went with a four-man rotation—Ellsworth-Santiago-Davis-Curry—and would rely primarily on Scott Stewart and Tito Romero out of the bullpen to bail them out of trouble or nail down a win. Burks shifted to center and Svoboda slotted into left field in place of Prince, and back-up catcher Curt Manning ably replaced Estrella behind the plate. Matt Horn was back at first from his hamstring injury and brought his big, beautiful left-handed swing with him.

Across the diamond, Bennie Jonson would be playing with a stacked deck. There had been no call-ups from the Phillies

Double-A affiliate, and rumor had it that Bennie was the reason for it. Rick Burton had it "on good authority" that Bennie stymied any call-ups, thus leaving his roster intact for the playoffs. This included his top two pitchers and one of the best center fielders in the league in Hank Percy. Shake knew that Rick was a conspiracy nut but he half-believed the rumor to be true. There was no doubt in his mind that Bennie wanted to dethrone him in the worst way. The Phillies were also twenty games out of first place, so it was very possible that their front office was more interested in the prestige of an Eastern League Championship than in calling up their Double-A players to pitch a few innings or get a couple at bats.

Conspiracy theories aside, Shake and his coaching staff had a job to do and the Kingsmen had a championship to win for their New Britain fans. Andy Ellsworth took the mound in the first game against the Admirals and pounded the strike zone all night, completing a 2-0 shutout and putting the Kingsmen up one game to none. Shake sent Luis Santiago to the mound for game two. He hoped that the one-two punch of Ellsworth-Santiago would get them up two games to none but it didn't work out that way. Santiago gave up three runs in the first, and though he settled down nicely, the Admirals ace hand-cuffed the Kingsmen all night long and they ended up losing 3-1.

Game three was in New Haven and Chuck Davis pitched a gutsy game. He left in the bottom of the seventh with the score tied 2-2 and Romero got the Kingsmen out of a bases-loaded jam to take them into the eighth still tied. In the top of the ninth, with the score still knotted-up at 2-2, Matt Horn (who was on fire and hitting .625 in the play-offs) hit a three run jack to put the Kingsmen up 5-2 and Stewart came in to shut the door in the bottom of the ninth for the win. The Kingsmen went up two games to one.

Game four in New Haven was a tragedy all its own. Kid Curry's curveball was dropping off the table until the fourth inning when it stopped dropping off the table and flattened out.

In the science of cause and effect, a curveball that stops curving means only one thing—base hits—and the Admirals knocked out seven of them in the fourth to go up 4-2. Shake took Curry out to limit the damage and from there on in it was a bullpen game for the Kingsmen. But in the top of the fifth Matt Horn went yard again with another three run homer, putting the Kingsmen up 5-4.

A certain stress had been building throughout the series. Part of it was natural—two talented and highly competitive teams going at it with good old-fashioned hard-nosed baseball—but there was an undercurrent of nastiness that festered and was due to pop. These two teams didn't like each other and the managers were old adversaries. Their history was one of brush-backs, beanballs and bench-clearing brawls. In the fourth game the nastiness began to seep out and reveal itself in the bench chatter. Usually biting and sarcastic to begin with, the chatter took on a ruthless tone as players denigrated their opponent's play and threw out catcalls and horse laughs at every strike-out or error. Even the umpires felt something coming on and kept a wary eye out for it.

In the bottom of the fifth, an Admirals player grounded to short for what looked like a routine out. As Matt Horn stretched for the throw, the runner came across the bag and stepped on Matt's heel with his cleats. It was Enos Slaughter spiking Jackie Robinson all over again, only the Admiral runner wasn't white and Horn wasn't black. Horn yelled out in pain and immediately fell to the ground grabbing his ankle. The runner was out, and as he made his fish-hook turn to go back to the dugout, Dane came up into his face and yelled at him. They pushed one another. The umpire quickly got between them and the two teams came up onto their dugout steps. But the Kingsmen stayed put. Their focus was their first baseman who sat next to the bag rocking back and forth and holding his bleeding ankle.

Shake ran out to Horn along with Rick Burton and their trainer Mike Faust. He kneeled down next to Matt and saw that his sock was soaked in blood. The back of his heel and part of his Achilles tendon (they learned later) was sliced open. The fielders collected around Matt, throwing out words of encouragement, and watched as the trainer examined Horn's ankle. As this was going on, Shake glanced over at the Admirals dugout and witnessed Bennie shake the hand of his paid assassin. The trainer tied a towel around Matt's ankle to stem the flow of blood, and Shake and Rick helped him off the field. Two bench players took it from there and helped him into the clubhouse. Shake signaled for Rosecrans to go in for Horn.

Every Kingsmen out in the field or in dugout or out in the bullpen—coaches and players alike—knew the spiking was intentional. They didn't need Don Vito Corleone to tell them it had been a hit job. Rick and Bob yelled accusations across the diamond at Bennie. Mike Goff at third pointed angrily into the Admirals dugout and told the third base coach they were "a bunch of chickenshits!" The bench chatter became blood-thirsty. Shake stood in his spot next to the bat rack and stared across at Bennie. The son-of-a-bitch smiled at him. Shake knew it was intentional—he'd seen the handshake—and he was hot, but his natural equilibrium overrode his emotion and told him to wait. Now was not the time, he knew. Not when they were hot with anger. But the time would come, maybe in the later innings of this game or maybe the next game, but it would come. Afterall, revenge was a dish best served cold (which sounds like a quote from the Bard but isn't).

The loss of Horn turned the tide. Twice Rosecrans came up in Horn's spot with runners on base and struck out. Twice Rosecrans failed to dig out a low throw to first and each time it led to a run. Even at that, the two teams were tied 7-7 going into the bottom of the ninth. It was then, in the ninth, that Hank Percy (who was playing like a man possessed) hit a walk-off homer to the delight of the home crowd. Percy flipped his bat in triumph, stood and watched the ball sail into the bleachers, then took a leisurely stroll around the bases with one flap down to rub it in. He was mobbed by his teammates at home plate.

The loss made Shake sick to his stomach and he didn't feel any better when he learned that Horn was out for game five. He was stuck with Rosecrans (whose play had fallen off since his hip infection), but they had Ellsworth and his splitter going for them in game five. The championship game would be in New Britain and the stands would be packed. Manager Glover and his team filed onto the bus for the ride home grim-faced and determined.

It was Friday night and the Kingsmen were on the field taking batting practice. Shake stood next to his coaches and watched his hitters take their swings. Shake could feel it—the mood. It was one of somber anticipation, like before a heavyweight bout. He scanned the stands and saw that they were filling up quickly. A sight caught his eye. Dark Lucy was standing at the rail next to the Admirals dugout talking with Bennie. The sight was just too odd to ignore and Shake walked towards them.

As he approached, Lucy noticed him and handed Bennie something that he took from her and placed around his neck. It was a chain. She turned her back and walked up the stands in her purple, medieval dress as though she was ascending the steps of an ancient tower. Bennie waited for Shake to walk up.

"You and Lucy an item now?" Shake asked him with an amused smile.

"An item? Nah," he replied. "She was just giving me a good luck charm."

"You think you need one?"

"Can't hurt, right?"

"Either can wearing a red nose or big floppy shoes."

"You've always been a witty fool, Shake."

"Better a witty fool than a foolish wit."

"Well said, but then you say a lot of things that were said by other people."

"Ah, you're right, I do. So then I'll leave you with one more, and from an old relative of yours: 'Ambition, like a torrent, never looks back'. Never look back, Bennie."

"I don't plan to... Good luck, Shake."

"Good luck, Bennie."

Shake walked away and headed towards his own dugout. He fingered the small gold crucifix that rested around his own neck. A present from Mimi. He looked up to her seat but she wasn't there yet. Someone yelled "Heads up!" and Shake turned in time to see a foul ball heading his way. He fielded it with his bare-hand and tossed it to a young boy in the stands.

"Nice play, Shakespeare," said the P.A. Announcer over the speakers. Shake saluted up to him and the song "The Best Is Yet To Come" by Frank Sinatra started to play in the stadium. That was Shake's favorite Sinatra song. It used to be "Summer Wind" but now it was "The Best Is Yet To Come" but he had no idea how the P.A. Announcer knew these things.

Batting practice wrapped up and the Kingsmen returned to their clubhouse. Shake passed the umpires in the tunnel, exchanged greetings, and he heard one of them say to himself, "It's a nice night for a prize fight." It caught Shake's ear and he repeated it—"It's a nice night for a prize fight"—and found that it tripped nicely off the tongue. He would say it to Rick and get a laugh, and the melodious line would roll around in his head for most of the night.

He ran into a very busy Corey and they briefly played baseball trivia together—then she bounced off like a pinball to get her stadium ready for a standing-room-only championship game. It would be a lot of hot dogs and beer. The groundskeepers Doug and Barry let him know that the field was "Pimped and proper" and he listened to them drop a few more malapropisms before thanking them for their diligence and returning to his office. At the door to his office he happened to glance down the hallway that led to the parking lot and saw Balt Porter, the journalism student, kiss Orson Kent on the cheek. They parted and Orson walked towards Shake with a big smile on his face and wished him the best of luck as he passed by. Shake rubbed his chin in thought then shrugged and went into his office.

Shake didn't give many pep talks but he was going to give one tonight. The situation called for one. He picked up the Sports section of the New Haven Register, found the plastic bag he was looking for, and waited until his players were dressed and ready to go. When he walked into the locker room, Rick saw him and on cue yelled, "Listen up!"

"I have a few things I want to share with you men before tonight's game," said Shake in a loud and commanding voice. "So lend me your ears." He came up next to Matt Horn, who sat with a cast on his foot, and placed his hand on Matt's shoulder. "We all saw what happened to Matty. And we all know why it happened. In the New Haven paper I have here, Manager Jonson was asked about the play and says, quote, 'It was just one of those things'. He claims it wasn't intentional and that he 'plays fair and coaches his team to do the same'. He also goes on to say that 'Horn leaves his foot on the bag and it was bound to happen at some point'. In other words, their spiking of Matty was, according to him, Matty's own fault. Never mind that Matty has never been spiked before—it wasn't their fault. And who am I to argue with Bennie since he is a fair man.

"We miss Basset and Cap, Prince and Estrella. We'll miss Deer's bat. And now we'll be without Matty. Who do Bennie and the Admirals miss? Nobody. Rumor has it that he talked the big club out of calling up players so they could come at us with a full deck. That's how bad they want to beat us. So some of their better players over there like Percy, hard-working, deserving players, are denied the chance to go to the show because Bennie wants a trophy. But he denies this rumor, and who am I to argue with him since we all know he's a fair man.

"And here sits Matty. Out for the game he worked so hard to get back to. But I guess it was his own fault. I guess this—" (Here Shake pulled out Horn's bloody sock from a plastic bag and waved it in front of his players.)—"is his own fault. Matty's blood? Not their fault. Beanballs and dirty play? Not their fault. And who are we to argue with them since Bennie is a fair man. But take a look at Matty here, at his foot and these crutches, *at this sock*, and ask yourself, 'Whose fault is it?' Do you think it was fair play—or foul?" (His team cried "Foul!") "Look at Matty and look at this sock and tell me it was fair play." (His team yelled "No!") "Right! I don't have the words or the wit any longer to stir your blood. I only speak from the heart and tell you what you already know. The rest is up to you."

At that the Kingsmen erupted into a growling cheer and began to chant "Matty." Pumped with adrenaline and ready for battle, they barged out of the locker room, through the tunnel, and into the dugout pounding and slapping each other in readiness. Shake walked next to Rick as they followed their team through the tunnel.

"What was that?" asked Rick with a knowing grin. *"Henry the Fifth*, right?"

"No, *Julius Caesar*."

Starting line-ups were announced and "The Star-spangled Banner" played. Shake saw Mimi in the stands and waved at her. Linda and the kids were on one side of her and Delia, Dane's fiancé, was on the other. Mimi had a scorebook opened in her lap and was ready for the game. So was Shake. He let Kalecki take the line-up card to home plate while he took his spot along the dugout rail. "O Fortuna" started up and the Kingsmen ran out onto the field to loud cheers.

It was a scoreless, well-pitched game through five. The defense was sparkling on both sides. In the top of the sixth with two outs, the Admirals hitter got on with a swinging bunt. That brought the pitcher up. On a 1-2 count, Ellsworth, who was maybe impatient for a strikeout, grooved a fastball instead of his nasty splitter and the pitcher hit a long fly ball to left. Shake leaned out and watched the trajectory of the ball, quite sure it was going foul, as it sailed high over the foul pole. The third base umpire ran towards the foul pole, stopped, and incredibly twirled his finger to signal homerun. Shake saw three things in succession:

1. The fans in left field jumping up and pointing that the ball was foul.
2. His left fielder Svoboda gesticulating at the third base umpire that it was foul.
3. And his catcher Manning turning around and screaming at the home plate umpire Rob Goodfellow that it was foul.

Shake shot out of the dugout and sprinted towards the third base umpire Todd Clinton. When he arrived, Clinton turned his back and Shake had to keep dancing in a circle to stay in eye contact with him. "Ask for help," pleaded Shake. "Just ask for help." Clinton refused.

Shake turned away in frustration and took his case to the head umpire Goodfellow. Despite looking sympathetic, Goodfellow wouldn't overturn the call. Shake pulled out the stops in his effort to sway the jury, pointing out the thousand umpires in the left field bleachers who had a better look than any of them. Manning saw it was foul. Svoboda saw it was foul. The fact that Clinton blew that call was just further proof he didn't belong in the Eastern League let alone on a playoff crew. Goodfellow patiently waited for Shake to finish and replied:

> If you have any pity, grace, or manners,
> You would not make me such an argument

The lines from *A Midsummer Night's Dream* caught Shake off-guard. Clever guy, he thought, figuring Goodfellow had probably memorized those lines just for this game and couldn't wait for a chance to use them. Shake took off his cap and scratched his head. He'd been checkmated. He started to walk out to the pitcher's mound but couldn't help but leave Goodfellow with this: *"Here's my journey's end and here's my butt."* He might have been checkmated but he wasn't going to be out-Barded.

He called his infield together at the mound and calmed everyone down. It was now two-zip but they had plenty of time to get those runs back. Shake knew that Hank Percy was up next and he laid out his plan. It was payback time.

They pitched Percy high and tight—ball four was under his chin—and he went to first base livid with anger. The kid was a hothead and they had stoked the fire. Shake knew Percy was itching to steal second and he called three pick-off throws in a row. Each time Rosecrans slapped his glove down hard on Percy's helmet. Nothing would stop him from going now and Shake signaled his catcher for a pitch-out. It came and Percy went and Manning threw a perfect seed down to second.

Percy was out on a close play and immediately jumped up and got in the umpire's face. All his pent-up anger came spewing out like a lit lava cone on the fourth of July, and within fifteen seconds—even before Bennie could run out there to pull him away—Percy was tossed from the game. The P.A. Announcer played "Brain Damage" by Pink Floyd as Bennie dragged Percy off the field.

"That worked like a charm," said Rick with a grin.

"Yep," agreed Shake. "Now we need to string some hits together."

But hits were not forthcoming in the bottom of the sixth or the seventh and the Kingsmen went into their half of the eighth still trailing 2-0. Hoffman led off the inning. On a brush back pitch, the ball nicked his jersey and he was awarded first base. That brought up Rosecrans, who was 0 for 3, but to everyone's surprise he stroked a single up the middle.

"O brave new world!" shouted Speed gleefully. Shake looked over at him and laughed. Speed liked to think he knew the Bard but whenever he quoted him he usually mangled it. But this time

he got it right and it delighted Shake to no end (both the quote and the hit).

Shake thought about pinch-hitting for Ellsworth but instead let him be announced and waited to see if Bennie would change pitchers. He didn't. Shake gave the bunt sign and Ellsworth put a beauty down to move both runners up. It was one out with runners at second and third and the Kingsmen finally had something going. The crowd could feel the momentum shifting. That brought Bennie out of the dugout, and he called in his ace reliever.

Travis Burks strode to the plate and Dane, now in the on-deck circle, carefully watched the at-bat. Dane knew the book on this guy: a big right-hander with two pitches—a ninety-six mile-per-hour fast ball and a circle-change—and when he was on he was tough to hit. Burks struck out swinging on a 1-2 change-up and he slammed his bat to the ground in anger. That brought Dane up with two outs and runners in scoring position. He stepped into the batter's box and got prepared to grind out an at-bat.

In a beautiful at bat, Dane worked the count full and fouled off pitch after pitch. On the twelfth pitch of the at-bat he popped another one foul behind home plate. The catcher threw his mask off and took a bead on it. The ball headed towards the stands, by the rail next to the Admirals dugout, and the catcher raced over and leaned against the rail next to three fans. In everyone's attempt to claim the prize, the ball hit the catcher's glove and popped loose and fell to the ground.

Bennie charged out of the dugout and argued for fan interference but Goodfellow would have none of it. After a five-minute interval of argument during which the P.A. Announcer played "Who's Zoomin' Who," Dane looped the next pitch over the second baseman's head for a hit. Hoffman and Rosecrans scored to tie the game and Dane, on a heads-up play, saw the throw-in sail over the cut-off-man's head and took second base. That put the go-ahead run on second with two outs.

Mike Goff dug into the batter's box. With a base open, Shake didn't think Goff would get anything good to hit but on a 2-0 count (a hitter's count), Goff (badly fooled on a change-up) managed to reach out and hit a shallow fly ball to center. Shake saw it all unfold in his mind before it happened on the field. Hank Percy, with his great speed, would have burst in and snagged the shallow fly at his shins, but the new centerfielder got a bad jump and in his panic dove headfirst to make the catch. The ball bounced off his glove. Dane, off on contact, cut the bag hard at third as Kalecki wind-milled him home to score the go-ahead run. The fans roared and the stands shook in celebration.

Dane was welcomed back in the dugout with high-fives and slaps on the back. In between the mob of bodies, Shake caught Dane's eye and said, "Nice job, Son." Dane smiled and replied "Thanks, Dad." In the general clamor, the meaning of those words were lost on everyone but the two of them.

The moment was short-lived as the next batter Manny Ortiz was hit in the helmet on the first pitch. But we'll let the play-by-play announcer and color commentator for WDRC AM 1360 take it from here:

Jim
Oh, that hit him.

Don
On the helmet. It sounded like the helmet.

Jim
And here we go. Here come the Kingsmen out of the dugout. Now here come the Admirals led by their red-faced manager Jonson. We knew this was coming. It's been brewing all series and it was just a matter of time. Once Horn went down on a cheap shot—can I call it a cheap shot, Don—we knew this was going to happen.

Don

You can call it a cheap-shot, Jim—cause it was.

Jim

The umpires are in the middle of it but they're like kites in a storm. These two teams want a piece of each other and no one is going to get in their way. Oh my, and here comes Percy charging out like a bull. He was ejected in the sixth for bumping the umpire.

Don

I guess they didn't lock the clubhouse door.

Jim

I guess not, and it's taking three coaches to keep Percy from attacking someone. Good luck with that... There's a lot of pushing and shoving going on right now...

Don

Well, it's quickly turning into your typical baseball fight—what I call the big waltz. Everyone's grabbing each other and waltzing around.

Jim

Oh wait. Look at that! Managers Glover and Jonson are now going at it. They're rolling around on the ground. Burton's in the middle of it trying to break it up—or he's helping Glover. I can't tell which. Now Goodfellow's in the middle of it. Maybe it's a tag-team.

Don

This is better than WrestleMania.

Shake and Bennie rolled around in the dirt. How they got there, Shake wasn't sure. They had come face to face and he said to Bennie, "It's a nice night for a prize fight" and the next thing he knew they were on the ground locked up tight like earthworms in heat. He could hear "Disco Inferno" playing over the loud speakers. "I'm too old for this," he said in Bennie's ear, and to his surprise Bennie replied back, "So am I." At that they got up, assisted by Burton and Goodfellow, and dusted each other off with a grin and a handshake. The air went out of the fight when the players saw their managers shaking hands and the donnybrook ended. Order was quickly restored and miraculously no one was kicked out of the game, but a warning was issued to both benches. Ortiz, who was unhurt, took first base and play resumed.

The next hitter Joe Svoboda almost took the lid off the house by hitting a ball deep to left but it was caught at the wall for the third out. *"Once more unto the breach!"* cried Shake and the Kingsmen bounded out onto the field needing only three outs for a championship. Shake and Benedict talked and decided to leave Ellsworth in for the ninth. Pitch count was not an issue and he was still getting ground balls with his splitter. Both Romero and Stewart warmed-up in the bullpen.

Ellsworth induced a ground ball against the first batter but it found a hole on the left side for a hit. With the eighth place hitter due up, Shake was betting on a bunt. Sure enough, the batter squared around to bunt and fouled it off—then proceeded to foul off the next two pitches for strike three.

"I wonder what Bennie has to say about that?" Rick wondered aloud.

"A bunt, a bunt. My kingdom for a bunt!" yelled Speed. Everyone in the dugout laughed at that. So did Rick, who usually found Speed annoying. Even he had to admit that Speed was on a roll today.

The pitcher's spot was due up for the Admirals and Bennie went with a pinch-hitter. Shake knew the guy had power, and since it was a righty-lefty match-up, he went out to the mound and brought in Tito Romero. For Shake, it had turned into a game of percentages and match-ups; they'd be out-matched in an extra inning game so he spun his limited options out in his head.

> *My brain more busy than the laboring spider,*
> *Weaves tedious snares to trap mine enemy*

Romero paid off by getting a ground ball to first, but Rosecrans didn't trust his arm to try for the double play and instead took the sure out at first. It was two out and the tying run on second.

Shake waited for the Admirals batter to be announced then went out to the mound and brought in Scott Stewart. The lead-off hitter was Percy's replacement and Shake thought it unlikely that Bennie would pinch-hit for him. He was right, and now he had the final match-up he wanted. As he walked back to the dugout, Mimi nodded with approval at his strategy. He smiled back at her.

Stewart was amped up and his first pitch sailed over Manning's head. The runner on second easily took third and now was a wild pitch, a pass-ball, or a slow-roller away from tying the game. Manning went out to settle down his pitcher. The next pitch was a get-it-in fastball that the Admirals hitter sliced down the third baseline. Shake dug his hand into Burton's shoulder and looked out to see the ball land a foot foul. Clinton called it right and it was now one and one. Stewart went into his stretch as the runner danced off third. Unseen by everyone but Shake, Dane moved two steps over to his left against the right-handed hitter and Shake knew why. Because he was smart.

The next pitch was a cutter that would have painted the outside corner for a strike, but the batter hit it hard towards the hole between first and second. Dane broke to his left on the crack of the bat, laid out on the grass, speared the ball in his glove, and came up on his knees to throw the runner out at first by a step. Game over.

A dog pile ensued on the infield. Fans jumped up and down and high-fived each other. Shake and his coaches hugged and slapped each other on the back then walked towards the dog pile. He glanced over at Bennie who stood ashen-faced next to his dugout. Bennie saluted him and he saluted back. Queen sang "We are the Champions" over the loudspeakers. There would be a trophy presentation, an MVP award, then beer and celebration in the clubhouse—but before all that happened, Shake spun around and walked back to his dugout.

Mimi awaited him at the rail. He opened the small, swinging gate and let her down onto the field. They came into each other's arms and kissed. "I love you," he said.

"I love you."

"Our son did good."

"I know. So did you... I'm so happy... Is it just a dream?"

"If it be thus to dream, still let me sleep."

They kissed again, hard, to make sure it wasn't a dream, and Dane came up to them. He pulled on Shake's sleeve. "What is it?" asked Shake, smiling at his son.

"Come on, Dad," he said. "You're missing all the fun."

EPILOGUE

Say farewell to Shakespeare Glover, to Mimi, Orson and the others. The bright lights in Beehive have now gone down, and our stage is empty as a ghost town. Each player had their entrances and displayed their finer arts; each player had their exits and played their many parts. These actors, these spirits, have melted into air, and the time has come to end this pleasant affair. The Ol' Bard and Baseball have had their run, and the game's been played and fairly won.

The actors in this novel-drama are mere shadows, the stuff of dreams, and will not be found in the *Register League Encyclopedia* or in the annals of *Baseball America*. Shake Glover never stood in his spot, next to the bat rack, in Beehive Stadium and his beloved Mimi never wore a floppy sun hat or kept score in the stands. Rex did not build an empire nor live and die, and his clown Speed never uttered a pun for anyone to hear. But we're keenly aware that audiences must have closure. We view life as a narrative unity. It is human nature to desire a fitting end, to know that the heroes lived happily ever after and that the villains got their just deserts.

As the character Papi might have said, "I feel you, dawg." What work of fiction, what film, can truly leave us satisfied unless we know how our main characters, even the minor ones, fared in the end? Afterall, they fretted and strutted their hour upon the stage and we invested interest in their well-being. So we'll call forth the wine-bearer and fill your cups. What became of Shake and Mimi, of Dane and Delia or Orson and Rose? Did Faust find happiness in the Steroid Era or did Santiago break one heart too many? If we are to give them life beyond this three-penny opera, it might look something like this:

Rick Burton remained best friends with Shake and he and Linda raised their three children within the friendly confines of Connecticut. Poo Bear never saw her witch but she played one, many years later, in a London production of *The Wiz*.

Larkin and Kalecki, along with Bennie Jonson, coached in minor league baseball for many years to come. They mended troubled swings, sent home thousands of runners, drank too much, told tall tales, and applied their trade for a fair wage. Bennie never overcame his jealousy of Shake but he finally won a championship with the Zanesville Greys in the Frontier League in 1993.

As for the players—Goff, Hoffman, Horn and Cap, Davis, Ellsworth and all the rest—they went on to varying degrees of success. Some like Estrella peaked and plummeted while others like Burks got their moment in the sun and took advantage of it. A few like Rosecrans, having lost their edge, quickly faded from the scene and found nine to five jobs outside baseball. And some like Ron Deer toiled many years in the minors before hanging them up and going into coaching.

Steve Basset and Gwen Cymbel, the Posthumus and Imogen of our drama, remained chaste until the night of their marriage, then made up for it with a vengeance by producing seven children and buying a bigger house every other year. Steve pitched successfully in the bigs for five years until elbow problems and surgeries took him out of the game, but a big payday and wise investments made the transition a soft one. He and Gwen run a popular retreat for Christian couples in the mountains of Western North Carolina.

Iachimo or Iago, Don John or Proteus– taken as a whole, our villain Luis Santiago was fated for a fall. It happened the next year when he got a dose of the clap and learned, rather quickly, that he was allergic to penicillin. He nearly died from anaphylactic shock, and his subsequent convalescence and loss of strength led to an ERA of 7.05 and a record of three and ten. He was traded to the Padres, had some small success, and married a Mexican beauty who beats him over the head whenever he looks twice at another woman.

As Shake promised, Mike Faust was let go as the Kingsmen's trainer. He hooked up with a Double-A team in the Texas League and found takers for his alchemy. Baseball banned steroids in 1991 but that didn't deter Faust. By the mid-nineties, he was employed as a trainer for a Triple-A team and riding high, but a combination of failed drug tests and follow-up investigations finally led to his downfall. He resurfaced sometime later as a "personal trainer" to a big homerun hitter in the National League and is now serving time for obstruction of justice.

To round out our villains, Ed and Rae Cornwall remained married and childless for another four years until Ed found love and offspring in the arms of a kinder, gentler woman (his Administrative Assistant at Lyon Bolt Manufactory). What followed was a nasty and protracted divorce. Today Rae lives alone with her servants in the Lyon castle and the local boys (who will be boys) occasionally, on a dare, throw rocks at her door and run away.

Corey Lyon-Danzig—the Cordelia to Rex's King Lear— eventually dropped the name Danzig (and the drug-addicted musician who went with it) and married a Rock Concert Promoter. It shouldn't be a surprise to learn that her husband is hot-blooded and prone to mood swings and that only Corey, in her magic, knows how to manage him. She enjoyed many years of success as the owner and GM of the New Britain Kingsmen and introduced a number of popular promotions such as Murder Mystery Night, Revenge of the Nerds Night, and Fred Flintstone Night. She is regarded as a pioneer for women owners and an icon in the Eastern League.

Corey also kept Speed on. Our favorite clown and wise fool became the oldest serving clubhouse manager in the minor leagues. He still sleeps on a cot, does the team's laundry, inventories sunflower seeds, and makes sure each player has their favorite beverage waiting for them after the game. The young players tip him generously and listen politely to his puns and riddles. His rapier wit is lost on most of them but occasionally one will get the point.

Rick Benedict and his bride Bernie have their spats but it is always *much ado about nothing*. To paraphrase the Bard, they were too wise to woo (or wed) peaceably. They raised a flock of sharp-tongued daughters who are all excellent softball pitchers.

There's not much to say about Dark Lucy, only that she finally found a man to dance with her at the Fire Festival of Lithia. And it wasn't Bennie.

Papi Stallworth enjoyed *a gallimaufry of gambols*. His Prince Hal never returned his phone calls so—as the Bard might have said—he resettled in a town full of *cozenage* (cheating), followed after *flirt-gills* (loose women), visited *the stews* (brothels), and continued to *hic and hack* (drink and whore) his way through life until he died of a heart attack in bed with a bosomy *doxy* (prostitute). To his *bully rooks* (friends) he was a *spruce companion*, even if he was a bit of a *popinjay,* who could *outswear* and outdrink any man in Christendom. Setting the attractions of his good parts aside, he had no other charms and was a fellow past saving.

His Sweetness—Hank Prince—fared much better than this *creature of bombast*. After his call-up in '86, he never looked back and played sixteen years in the big leagues. A five-time All-Star, Hank did commercials for shaving cream, breakfast cereal, and became a spokesman for inner city sports programs. He got his mom and siblings out of Sunnyside and bought them a big house in Atherton, California where they live today. Like his mentor Chili Leonard, he took a number of young players under his wing and taught them the ropes, including how to order and properly eat Chinese food.

Orson Kent married Rose Porter or, maybe we should say, like Rosalind in *As You Like It*, she married him. Certainly the date, the venue, the guest list and honeymoon destination were all fixed by her. Not that he objected. Orson worked himself up through the ranks—Director of Player Development, Manager of Baseball Operations, etc.—and eventually took over principle ownership of the big club from his father. Rose is a published author, mainly sports biographies, and is a frequent guest on *Oprah*. Together Orson and Rose make a fashionable couple, and if the gender lines appear blurred at times, they don't seem to mind and who are we to judge?

Dane Hamilton, our erstwhile Hamlet (only with better parents), found that he'd *rather bear those ills we have than to fly to others that we know not of*. With a hint of reluctance he wed Delia and, with somewhat less reluctance, sired two sons even though he knew he was probably adding to the list of thieves and murderers in the world. Mankind still troubles him and Delia patiently listens to him rant, but he has baseball, an *enterprise of great pitch and moment*. Like his father before him—first as a player in the big leagues and now as a manager in the minors—he finds solace in the poetry of baseball and agrees with the poet Sharon Olds who once said, "Baseball is reassuring. It makes me feel as if the world is not going to blow up."

Which brings us finally to Shakespeare Louis Glover and his beloved Mimi. If Shake plays many roles—baseball manager, the Bard, Henry the Fourth, Leontes in *The Winter's Tale* and a bit of Prospero from *The Tempest*—then Mimi plays but one role. She plays his other half. Together they built a winning roster of loved ones that features Emmanuel on the mound, the Bard catching, and friends and family in the field. Their love for one another fills the stands. But before we strain this metaphor any further, let us visit Shake and Mimi in their retirement. It's in a big house on "Top of the Hill" in Daly City, big enough to hold grandsons over the summer and entertain the many guests (baseball stars, old coaches, and alumni) who come by to visit them. On occasion, Shake walks over to Jefferson High School to watch a baseball game. Mimi enjoys working on her quilts while listening to the Giants game. In-between they are inseparable and can be said to be happy (if happiness is more than mirth and laughter) and together share a love that is both large and small in its expression. *If this be error and upon me proved, I never writ, nor no man ever loved.*

If by our fictions we have offended, remember but this and all is mended: When sweet spring awakens, baseball is near, the season for cheer, crackerjack and beer. Green grass and ground balls, blossoms and base knocks; it all returns once we spin up the clocks. So close the cover and pick up a mitt, the time is nigh to work up a spit. Take it up the middle, around the horn, a lazy fly ball and a can of corn. Give it a ride, get off the schneid, ducks on the pond and Roger Kahn. Pick it clean and look dead red, a little chin music and all is said.

Printed in the United States
By Bookmasters